Prelude to a Scream

Prelude to a Scream

Jim Nisbet

Carroll & Graf Publishers, Inc.
New York

First Carroll & Graf edition 1997

Carroll & Graf Publishers, Inc.
19 West 21st St., Suite 601
New York, NY 10010-6805

Nisbet, Jim.
    Prelude to a scream / Jim Nisbet. -- 1st Carroll & Graf ed.
    p. cm.
    ISBN 0-7867-0408-X (cloth)
    I. Title.
PS3564.I7P74 1997
813' .53--dc21   97-6787
                                                                      CIP

Manufactured in the United States of America

Thanks to the inimitable Dennis Jakob for the Gottfried Benn poem; to Drs. Andrea Hanaway and Brian Grossman for stimulating medical advice; to Dr. Arthur Baker for a tale of cannulation; to Adam Osborne for *fusion viper*; to George Malone for his Tom Collins recipe; to my father, JD, who has always believed; and to my brother, Jack, who has always listened.

Thanks also to Tom Raworth for thinking it up in the first place and, in the second, for permission to quote from *in think*, which originally appeared in *Ace*, Copyright 1974, 1977.

♦ ♦ ♦

This one is for Robin Cook
1931 - 1994

On the tomb of a student, named Novillo, there was
an inscription half effaced by the passage of time,
"God has interrupted his studies to teach him the truth."

Curzio Malaparte, *Kaputt*

Prelude
to a
Scream

Bon
Weekend

Chapter 1

Drive-by fellatio was Stanley Ahearn's favorite. Always had been, always would be.

In matters drive-by the Tenderloin has always been a place to deal. Day or night, war or peace, plague or maternal remonstrance, its sidewalks serve.

On this particular night, weather had briefly made a difference. An hour after dusk a violent storm scoured the streets. The creatures washed up under awnings, in doorways and bars. For another hour sheets of rain, wind-blown until they shredded, gave the district the feel of a ruined armada, as if, its rigging in tatters, its crews cowering, the entire enterprise might founder into the black asphalt. For an hour nature asserted herself in an inconvenient, unmarketable form. Yet, in the subsequent drizzle, like a field of storm-nourished poppies, the trades blossomed again.

Tires hissed and horns honked and all light redoubled in the liquid spangle. Girls and pseudogirls scanned the beaded fields of lacquered steel for the eyes they could pick out through mottling safety glass, eyes that might reflect a groin's signal to a work boot or tasseled loafer, its command to lift off the accelerator, to cause the machine to coast and slow, to redden a brakelit face caught behind a wet windshield.

Friday night was Stanley's night for sex, and drive-by fellatio was his choice. Not the missionary position, not sodomy, not the grunting of athletic endeavor, not theatrical groans, not sweat bucking off the tip of his nose, not a damp sheen in the little dimples at the base of a spine, not a circular mauve davenport with pale yellow *fleur-de-lys* and a brass-framed smoked mirror on the scarlet ceiling, not champagne and caviar and a lot of adenoidal commentary concerning Debussy's evocation of the fountains that sob with ecstasy in Verlaine's poem, not candle wax dripped on nipples, nor violent trysts naked under raincoats in piss-etched phone booths: none of these things interested him. For Stanley Ahearn, drive-by fellatio would do fine, sordid and simple, with maybe a hissed obscenity for imprimatur like the wax seal on a papal bull. He'd thought about these things. Outside the cab of a pickup truck the idea of sex attenuated. Something there was about the smells of transmission fluid and the mildew between the floormat and the rug, of defroster-baked invoices on the dashboard, of the whole miniclimate overwhelmed by a really cheap perfume.

If someone brought up the subject of sex while Stanley was absorbing radiation from the television, he'd agree with anything said, just so long as no thoughty chat came between him and the screen. But when his head was clear, when someone raised the subject of sex with Stanley Ahearn, in between, say, the second and third whiskey, or during halftime, he wouldn't say a word but think to himself with the utmost clarity, give me drive-by fellatio with a complete stranger and, insofar as we have control over these things, preferably with a woman, and, all other things being equal, give me the rest of my life to be alone. In a pickup truck at night in the rain, somewhere in the Tenderloin or, if you can get the girl to trust you that far, at speed on the freeway while she's performing it—it was more than a tolerable experience; it made for a decent Friday night. After work and before food, with a couple of whiskies in between, at speed on the dark freeway with Percy Sledge on the radio singing *When a Man Loves a Woman*, the left arm crooked out the open window and angling back to the pint, the whiskey in its bottle animated by the vibrations of the steering wheel, and one of those precisely vulcanized Japanese condoms of infinite ductility, of sanguine impermeability, and the edge of an infinite loneliness afterwards like a front of weather over Wyoming—the *optimum embodiment*, as they say down at the patent office, of sex without responsibility.

A pint of Bushmills for her to gargle. Make her feel wanted and warm and all Prozacky inside. Anything more—conversation, the name of a home state, some encouragement for the Forty-niners or the

Giants, even so much as a banality about the weather—and a relation-ship had begun. If the idea of marriage loomed over all Stanley's habi-tude like the specter of an avalanche over a sleepy alpine village, he spent all his time antipodally, sufficiently distant from the threat of the paired recliner chairs, the microwaved food, the dwindling gallon of *Andrei Rublev* vodka, the surprisingly heated argument over the sex appeal of a newscaster erupting through the murderous lassitude devolved of a marriage made for the sake of halving the rent.

If a reactionary cliché of marriage was enough to rob any evening of its magic, the mandate of prophylaxis had been a terrible thing. At first, he'd had to use his imagination when girls brought up the subject. Get her to put it on for you, sure. Get her to work it over with her hand first, too. But, in the end, a quick study, he'd learned to provender the glove compartment with the thin Japanese ones, the tip of each embossed with the kanji for *raincoat*. The girls won't spend the money necessary to get the superior—which means *sensitive*—ones. The girls carry the prophylactic equivalent of an inner tube for a bicycle tire—much cheaper. Twisted like a licorice whip by the twin strands of his sensitivity and paranoia, what a guy wants is the strong, lubricated, space-age thin, flavored ones, that taste exactly like a mint daiquiri made with Rebel Yell and toothpaste, for the maxima in sensation and distance. A twelve-pack of the really good ones can run to forty dollars. "Cheaper than a kid," he would invariably say to the sales clerk, who would invariably be not amused. Can't be natural membrane, either, has to be synthetic. The human immunodeficiency virus penetrates sheep intestine like a bullet penetrates silk. It's not a joke, prophylaxis. But neither is looking at the world through a sheet of glass.

A girl liked to see them, actually. They put a certain distance between a girl and her work.

These mint-daiquiri jobs were the ones he'd started out with. He still kept a few of them in the glove compartment. But he had long since augmented them with a jalapeño flavor certain hookers liked. True, it kept them warm on those particularly brutal nights, when the cold and the damp were enough to give a girl pneumonia, let alone spiritual tor-por and goose-flesh (a turn-on, to a certain kind of fella) or even chilblains, standing on a street corner in a bun-hugging mini with her blouse tied just under her boobs and heels high enough to park her blisters along with her sinuses in the jet stream. But the truth is, jalapeño fumes clear a coked-up sinus. A girl likes to breathe when she's giving head. Jalapeño's the one on the right. No, don't turn on the light. Darkness is for people who couldn't care less about what they make it with, as much as it is for people in love. Darkness suits people with illusions no less than it suits people with goals.

In a doorway at Taylor and Turk two plainclothes cops, in pineapple shirts and pastel windbreakers cornered a miniskirted thing with a white rat stole and heels like two sequined banana clips while a third cop radioed for the paddy wagon. Double-parked not twenty yards upstream was a Cadillac with a too-tall black thing leaning into the driver's window. Her gold lamé mini looked like it was wrapping two anisette lollipops, the skinny twin stalks depilated for payday, so tall she had to turn her wig sideways to get it in through the car window. Neither the gold mini thing nor the one with the two cops was female—not that the cops cared either way; this was San Francisco, after all. There was too much of everything in this neighborhood: plenty of work to go around, and plenty to let go.

The light at the top of the block was red. As Stanley waited, a bleached blonde he'd never seen before stepped off the curb and rapped at his passenger window. He leaned over to roll it down.

"Wanna date, honey?"

"Just a little head."

She gave him and the interior the once-over. No obvious handcuffs, chains, knives, footlockers, oversized syringes, nets or guns in view, she said, "Twenty bucks." By the light of the hotel marquee behind her and the taillights of the airport shuttle bus in front of them she wasn't bad looking, with no visible Adam's apple. Stanley unlocked the passenger door.

A rouged face miraculously un-fissured by the rainwater, which rolled over her complexion like tequila over travertine, contemplated Stanley—the pause before the abyss; or better, another tiny pause before another tiny leap. The rain abruptly slacked off to intermittent ticks on the thin sheet metal over their heads, it could have been the audio track for the apostrophes spilling over the brim of a neon martini glass above a bar named the OVERFLO', across the street.

"Okay."

A cloud of cheap perfume wicked through the humid air like acetone through a cotton diaper, a Southwestern accent escaped the red lips. "Honey," the accent said, "I'd lip-twist a cutie like you for $19.95, and I got the nickel to prove it."

Her tone, her demeanor, the cast of her eyes, they all added up to one thing, honey, Stanley thought: a girl in over her head, too young to be talking tough like that.

Sugar, she honestly might have replied, you got twenty years on me, but I'm getting older faster than you are.

Put a Southwestern way, he silently insisted, you're all hat and no cattle.

Look, she didn't say: you want a blowjob or not?

"Let's go."

She slammed the door.

Stanley drove through the intersection.

"Brrr," she said. "Myself, I wouldn't mind a little heat."

He pushed the defroster to high, which placed enough demand on the truck's electricals to dim the headlamps slightly.

"Thanks." Her voice shivered. After a block she said, "I had a disk drive on my first computer, where I worked after high school? Sounded just like that heater."

Stanley handed her a Dixie cup and the whiskey. "Fill the cup and give me the bottle."

She did so.

He gestured with the bottle. "It's okay stuff." He fit its neck to his lips and tipped it.

She watched him carefully, noting the level of fluid in the flask before and after he drank.

"You don't have to worry." He puckered his lips, appreciating the whiskey's sting on a cold sore inside his cheek. It might have been perspicacity, that narrowed her eyes. "That so? Have another."

"Thanks."

"You're welcome."

When he lowered the pint a quarter of it was gone.

She threw back the Dixie shot.

"Yup," she said, coughing once. "Listened to that disk drive all day long for six-fifty an hour. Drier in that office than in here, though," she reflected. "Warmer, too."

Day job, thought Stanley. High school, marriage, kids — day jobs.

"Whew!" she said. "My goodness! That's good whiskey, mister."

He handed her the bottle. "Have another."

She took it, poured. "No," she said, but threw back her second cup anyway. "Sometimes whiskey on these steroids makes me a little giddy."

Stanley kept his face straight ahead, but his eyes slid over to the right. "Steroids, huh?"

"Yeah. Hipnogynazones, or something. Thing in Polk Gulch gave 'em to me, said they would make my tits grow. I'm a little shrill, though."

He heard the unmistakable click of pills trapped in a film canister. Here's a girl, thought Stanley, naive enough to buck Ahearn's First Assumption for Self-Preservation, which is, Never break more than one law at a time.

"They sound just like a rattle," she giggled. "Nuff to make a baby laugh and a bachelor man jump." She shook her fist. "Genetic craps. Ya wanna play?"

"Where you from?"

"Colby, Colorado."

"Daddy a cowboy, was he?"

"Ain't seen him to ask."

"Lived here long?"

"Three months." She rattled the fist.

"Finish the drink."

"Oh," she said in a little voice. "All business. Hombre de negocios. Well, it's gone."

"Help yourself."

She refilled the cup. "Eagle flies on Friday, huh mister?"

He watched her turn it up. Her throat was smooth and straight. No whiskers. Pretty, almost. Young, for certain.

Her mouth sagged visibly. "Sheeee..." she said, almost to herself. "Gotta get straight..."

The roots of the hair behind the ears were dark and curly, the lobes shapely, the eyes small and cute though narrowed defensively, the nose a little peyote button.

She watched him watching her. After awhile, her eyelids slowly descended to half-mast.

"What else you on?"

Her eyes sprang open, her voice, a little girl's, whispered, "On...?" She turned as if to watch the wet city unfold over the windshield. Her hand covered his thigh as she did so.

"Yeah," he said softly, turning north on Polk, driving slowly. "On."

"Oh," she said, gently kneading his thigh. "Steroids, hormones, whiskey, coke, vitamin C, stress B, Valium, hypothermia... whatever...."

"A balanced diet."

"You know," she said, "I grew up in Colorado. Spent three-quarters of my life asshole deep in snow. But I never heard of hypothermia till I came to San Francisco. Hey," she brightened, "that rhymes."

"No smoke?"

"I wish you could smoke hypothermia," she said evasively. "I'd be a stoned little girl."

The light at O'Farrell stopped them. From the right a man with one foot wrapped in rags carried a pair of crutches through the crosswalk. A man in a raccoon coat passed the other way, followed by two identically dressed young men arm in arm. These latter customers wore peaked visored caps, zippered jackets, chaps, and combat boots, all of it black leather. Exposed by the cut of the chaps, their naked buttocks jiggled like so much carnivorous mutton. These passed an eastbound dwarf in a motorized wheelchair. After the wheelchair came a pneumatically muscular young man with a quarter-inch of blonde hair on the top of his head, the back and sides shaved away. He also affected a square moustache, tight pink short-shorts and a black gym bag no bigger than a twenty-four ounce can of lager. The back of his pink tank top advertised NOBODY KNOWS I'M GAY in silver sequins. The front of the tank top had ragged circular cut-outs to display how each end of the dog chain draped over his broad chest was clevised to zircon annulets that pierced his nipples.

The wipers clicked across the windshield and stopped.

Her hand arrived at his groin and covered the handle on his Friday Night. "Please, Officer," she whispered.

"Please," he repeated, "—Officer?"

"Don't bust me," she pleaded, barely audible.

He wanted to let it pass, figuring that, if he thought about it, he'd have a difficult time getting aroused by someone dumb enough to take him for a cop.

But then another angle occurred to him, and he said, "How'd you make me?"

She worked the hand.

Steam rose from the hood. The guy with the crutches carried them back the other way, putting plenty of weight on the bandaged foot.

"I'm nobody. Really," she said, using the hand.

"I know it," Stanley said, as if world-weary. "There's real criminals out there to think about."

"Truly, Officer."

"Motherfuckers."

She worked the hand.

"I'm not busting you." He looked at her. "Just do a good job."

She looked at him. "I got smoke, too."

"Anything else?"

"That's all."

"That's all?"

She shrugged. "Ludes," she said. "Dude don't want no ludes, on duty and all." She unbuttoned his fly. "Does he?"

The cross-street's light turned yellow. Next to Stanley's truck a faded Plymouth suddenly jumped the still-red signal. A Mercedes pushing the downtown light slid at an angle into the intersection and stalled a foot short of broadsiding the Plymouth, the distinctively unpleasant Mercedes klaxon piercing the night.

The Plymouth continued north up Polk Street, as unperturbed as a fish drifting over a sunken wreck.

The light turned green. The driver of an old Datsun, facing south on Polk, blocked by the Mercedes, stood on his horn.

Behind Stanley, a car horn sounded insistently.

Stanley turned right onto O'Farrell.

A double-parked tour bus, two stories high, was disgorging Japanese tourists, all men, in front of the Mitchell Brothers Theater, beneath a marquee that invited them to come in and shower with live nude girls. Attendants held umbrellas over the file of customers.

Stanley piloted the pickup around the idling bus and continued east, back into the Tenderloin. By the time they got to Stockton Street, he'd know whether or not to head for the freeway.

The girl lifted the bottle with her free hand and had a swallow.

"What about that smoke," he said.

"Got it right here," she said. "Sense. Twenty bucks a gram. Free to you, of course," she added quickly. "But first things first."

He fished the folded twenty out of his shirt pocket, slid it down the front of her blouse, and put Andy Jackson's side-whiskers to sanding a nipple.

"You don't have to pay me," she said sweetly. "Bail's a hundred."

"I know it."

"I come out eighty bucks ahead."

"Maybe I'll take that nickel change," he said.

She smiled that distant smile, and let Andy do his thing.

"Aw," she said, in a voice even more remote than the smile, sliding closer to him, filling both hands now. "Ain'tcha gonna tip me?"

He showed her the folded twenty, turning it in the uncertain light, before replacing the bill into his shirt pocket. "No," he said.

"Oh, Officer," she said. "I'm so grateful for my freedom…"

She filled her mouth with whiskey and went down on him.

Chapter 2

Five blocks away and two hours later, Stanley was three drinks into his evening at Saturnia, an empty Bar and Grille.

He was appreciating the fact that the first twenty dollars worth of tonight's fun was going to be compliments of a hooker dumb enough to have taken him for a cop, when a woman took the stool to his right.

He thought it must have been a woman, but he didn't look at her to confirm it. A scent came with her, and the whisper of textiles—accoutrements, to his mind, of femininity. A certain skepticism is incumbent, however, in Saturnia as in life, upon him to whose engine gender makes a difference.

She placed a green butane lighter stamped with the brass logo of a South Tahoe casino atop a pack of brown 120 mm cigarettes, slid the stack into the easement between her and Stanley's elbows, and ordered a Tom Collins.

"Oh," said the bartender, not moving, "bust my balls."

"Anytime, sugar," the woman said.

"I got no limes, too."

She plucked a lime from a pocket of her jacket and showed it to him. "Now what's the problem?" she said.

He stared at the lime.

"Five bucks," said the woman, in an aside to Stanley, "he blinks first."

Stanley said nothing.

The bartender blinked.

"Aha," said the woman. "The day I meet a man who can stare down a lime, that's the day I get married again."

With a sigh he took the lime, dropped his foot off the sink, and began opening and closing doors behind the bar.

"Hey," Stanley said to his drink. "Where'd you get that lime?"

She shot him a glance. "Off the family tree. What's your excuse?"

"Oh..." Stanley said, not looking up. But he didn't finish the thought.

"That's what I like," she said, looking away. "A lightning bolt for a mind."

Except for the bartender, who was whistling because he had something to do, the bar went silent again.

After another while the woman said, "I know that tune."

The bartender stopped whistling.

What tune, Stanley thought to himself. That was a tune?

"What the hell's taking so long?" she snapped.

"We got a highball glass around here somewhere," the bartender said deliberately. "I saw it just last week."

"Bars these days," the woman groused.

The bartender retrieved a spoon from a coffee cup and inspected it by the red light of the Coors sign. He wiped the spoon on his vest and inspected it again.

"You want a mixed drink," the woman continued, "better get the parts and take them home and mix it yourself. Bars these days, they want you to swill the straight sauce or go for the exotic homebrews with names like *Devil's Quench* or *Crepuscular Bollard*. One or the other or you're shit out of luck. There's no in-between."

"We're of the former persuasion," the bartender said.

She ignored him. "I remember Christmas, last year, when some idiot with a hydrometer and a copper tank put out his annual *Rinse of Christfest*. The gimmick, see, is every year the *Rinse of Christfest* tastes different than last year. Since the customer is into the *shock of the new*, he waits for the *Rinse of Christfest* like the wise men waited for the star." She flicked Stanley's arm with the back of her hand. "You see the title for the sermon last week on the board in front of Saint Paul's on Gough? Says, 'There is a Light, and it's not a beer'? Ahhh, ha, ha, ha..."

Nobody laughed with her.

"Goddamn atheists," she said. "So last December, here comes the

Rinse of Christfest. I'm a game girl. I love a change, if not a shock. So I spring for a bottle."

Nobody spoke.

"So, somebody might ask, What's it taste like?" she finally said. "It seems like the next logical question."

She turned to Stanley.

Stanley watched his drink.

She looked at the bartender.

The bartender cut the lime.

She turned around on her stool.

"Eggnog," she said loudly to the empty bar. "The goddamn *Rinse of Christfest* tasted like goddamn eggnog."

"You're telling us this was deliberate?" asked the bartender, dealing half the lime off his knife.

She turned back to face him. "What the hell do you mean, deliberate? I told you it was for Christmas, didn't I? You want to drink beer at Christmas, it's got to taste like eggnog. Where have you been, darling?"

"With — what's that stuff? — nutmeg?"

"Nutmeg? What about the cloves?"

The bartender made a face.

"Yep, they had the works. It was a beer, it had bubbles, it tasted like eggnog. One sip and you were ready for spring."

The bartender considered this. "I knew a guy, once," he said thoughtfully, as he squeezed the juice of a quarter lime into the glass. "He lived in the country and had piles of old tires in the weeds around his place. Every Christmas Eve, he'd go out and dip the rainwater out of a tire casing into a fruit jar. Said a thimbleful of that tire-water made the best eggnog. Said it was aged just right. He showed me the thimble."

"A thimble," said the woman.

"Just one."

"Just the one thimble."

"For flavor."

"Flavor."

"Said the hard part was to be sure to get at least one or two mosquito larva in each thimbleful."

"Mosquito larva."

"Said they were wholesome."

"As opposed to nutritious?"

"Oh, he was a dedicated man, so far as his guests went. Nothing was too good for them."

"Sounds to me like everything was too good for them." The woman turned suddenly on Stanley and barked, "What are you, an anthropologist?"

Stanley closed his eyes and said nothing.

The bartender looked over his shoulder. "Care for a cherry?"

"Only if it's glistening with Red Dye Number Two."

"Eggnog beer, huh?" said the bartender, dropping a bright red cherry into the glass. "A lot of malt, too, I'd guess."

"I guess," the woman sighed.

"I was in detox last Christmas," the bartender said matter-of-factly. He poured gin until his jigger overflowed, dumped it into the glass, and did it again. "In any case, I missed the eggnog beer."

"You didn't miss a damn thing," the woman said.

Stanley had been keeping his eye on the family of wet benzene rings engendered by the arrivals and takeoffs of the bottom of his whiskey glass as it periodically made the round-trip from the bartop to his mouth. "Now," he said, almost to himself, "What's in a Tom Collins?"

The woman cast a glance at him, looked to see what it was that he might be studying in the bartop, glanced again at him, and finally looked away. "Nothing you'd notice."

"Maybe you should drink something stronger," Stanley suggested to the hexagons. "So I'd notice."

Over the years, Stanley had learned better than to posit drinking benzene to a woman he hardly knew, not only because it might put her off, but also because, if it didn't put her off, she might take him up on it.

But now, inexplicably, with an unaccustomed temerity he would never, in retrospect, comprehend, he had uttered the deliberately provocative, "So I'd notice."

She turned to look at him. "I hardly ever notice the company I keep. Although," she added thoughtfully, "I do sometimes notice its money."

Stanley now looked at her for the first time. He was surprised how attractive she was.

She beamed him the smile that said *Buy a girl a drink*; expertly enough to tag its interrogative with the equally silent appositive, *sucker*, slyly enough to leave its determination ambivalent. The smile hung in the air between them like a banner strung carelessly from opposing windows of the Boredom and Quickfuck buildings, facing each other over an alley called The Straits of Messina. *Buy a girl a drink? Now, this moment, the future is in Stanley's hands. But, until just Now, a future was something Stanley wanted nothing to do with. Up until Now Stanley was just fine, with the one future he's had for a long time, his future as a relic of his own past, which always neutralized his present. Now, right now, here before him perched an alternative: opening this door instead of heading for that other door that's ever-ready for Stanley, the door to his past, the one he always walks through this time of night. Let him try this other door. It might go somewhere. Who knows? The price of a drink might make a sucker out of him, or, though it seems incredible, it might make a winner out of him. After all, that these barroom situations almost never work out only makes it more probable that, sooner or later, one of them almost has to work out satisfactorily. The price of a drink seems little enough to risk. This perfect smile, the product of a moment, promises nothing while it promises everything. Where, oh where, would a girl learn such a smile? When, oh when, would a man learn to mind his own business...?*

She had black hair and lots of it, waved below the shoulder and cut in bangs that fringed bright green eyes. Stanley had been about to glance away, reflexively, as he always did when a woman looked him in the eye and dared him to bore her. But he didn't look away. He couldn't. Instead, he stared at her. She returned the stare. He'd never seen such eyes. Behind the black bangs they looked like caged radium.

The bartender came up to clear the glassware and pass his rag over the bartop, obliterating the damp geometry in front of Stanley. He deposited a napkin in front of the woman and centered on it a tall, slender glass, into whose cloudy fluid disappeared the shank of a fine, red straw.

"We ain't got no umbrellas," he said sadly.

Stanley fished the twenty out of his jeans and handed it over the bar. "So give us a discount. I'll cover hers and have another myself. You never make mine that big," he added ruefully.

The barkeeper snatched the twenty. "I'm watching out for your diabetes. The same?"

"As before."

The bartender moved down the bar.

Raven-tress thanked him, and helped herself to a demure straw-sip. Interesting lips. A mouth of considerable pulchritude.

Stanley returned to a self-conscious tracing of the memory of a benzene ring on the bartop in front of him, acutely aware of the three whiskies he'd nursed over the past hour. While not enough alcohol to allow him to blurt suggestions of questionable taste, as it were, concerning the drinking of benzene or the comeliness of a stranger's lips, it was, however, enough to make him question his wit, as it were, dulling it in any case, since drinking benzene was the only thought, funny or otherwise, lingering in his mind since he'd noticed those green eyes. On the one hand he resented this, because he'd always been of the opinion that to pursue one's wit, wherever it led, was to step effortlessly from one bleak pinnacle of inanity to another, as Shelley once, almost, put it. But to check the suggestions of one's wit is to stifle the impulse altogether. Wit is a chain reaction, or, as in Stanley's case, and he's not alone, a chain of blurts. Having stifled one impertinent remark, suppressing a blurt from a paucity of blurts, Stanley could not reasonably expect another immediately to surface—not so soon as to salvage the present conversation, at least.

Also he was always shy in the presence of an attractive woman, unless he was paying her to be there, in which case he could screw up the courage to make demands of her. Commerce rules, and that's a verb. Even the grocery wholesaler's logo on the door of his pickup truck gave him a place to hide, socially speaking.

These thoughts, confronting her lips and eyes, caused his face to burn with shyness.

"Ahem," said Green-Eyes, after a protracted silence.

Another moment spasmed and died. She shrugged, turned away, and lit a cigarette without so much as bothering to wait for Stanley to finish evaluating his impulse to light it for her. Leaving him to flounder in and finally resent his own excruciation, she exhaled a column of smoke toward the Olympia waterfall twinkling over the bottles behind the bar, and observed, "I think it was Cocteau who mentioned the Angel of Silence, who passes over a gathering of three or more every fifteen minutes. Wasn't it?" Silence. She waved the smoke away from her face and muttered, as if to herself, "The little s.o.b. must have crashed and burned in this dump."

Stanley blushed crimson as the bartender returned with a whiskey on ice. Before the glass had settled onto its coaster Stanley snatched it up and threw back half the drink.

"I'm sorry I stared at you," Stanley stammered, as he carefully set the glass back on the bar.

"I'm used to it," the bartender said.

Stanley's eyes flashed up to the bartender, then quickly to the woman. They were both laughing. Stanley was mortified. When they saw the appalled expression on his face their laughter redoubled. Stanley looked back down at the bar, in rage and amazement. How could they possibly know he wasn't the kind of guy who'd go out to his car and return to shotgun the whole place for such an insult? Or, if he could break the rim of his glass just so, he could gouge the four eyes out of the two of them... But that would waste what remained of the whiskey. Better to finish it first. Revenge is best tasted cold. He set about sending an impulse to his hands, instructing them to quit shaking and raise the glass to his mouth.

A hand with finely boned fingers and unlacquered, long, neatly trimmed nails covered the two of his hands and the glass quivering between them. Stanley twitched like he'd received a kiss from an electric eel.

"Hey, Jack..." she said. "Take it easy."

"Yeah," began the bartender. "Relax, buddy."

"I'll handle this," she said firmly.

"Sure." The bartender went away.

"The, the n-name ..." His throat constricted his voice. He inhaled and exhaled before he managed to say, "The name is Stanley." Even to him, his voice sounded as if it were coming through a wall.

"Stanley," she said gently. Her touch suffused his entire being, depriving it of a quantum of tension as neatly and accurately as if his soul were a guitar string suddenly, with great precision, by her sure hand detuned an entire octave and stroked there, satisfyingly on pitch. He might have explained it, if he'd cared to, by admitting that this was the first time he'd heard a woman utter his Christian name in perhaps a year, or been touched for free in even longer a time. But he didn't care to. He hadn't wanted to explain anything for a long time.

The ring on her middle finger looked fake. It had a small, faceted stone, translucent green set with four tiny diamonds in yellow wire, very fine, very discreet. Still, after a half minute of looking at the finely boned ring finger and its mates, with the two sets of his own blunt digits beneath it, he found in himself the courage to look up and into the eyes of its owner.

Caged radium. A dappled pair of sunlit leaves beneath a darkening canopy. Tracers of uncorrupt light. "Stanley," she said again.

The sound of his name calcified his rage into a single, tight-lipped, "What."

"Lighten up, Stanley."

"Yeah," said the bartender, from down the bar.

Stanley shot him a glance.

The woman released his hand and pulled a twenty out of her jacket pocket. She showed it to the bartender. "Bring the man another drink."

"On the house," said the bartender, reaching for the quart of Bushmills. "It's about time I had a laugh in this morgue."

She pushed the twenty across the plank. "I'll get the one after that, then. Won't you join us?"

"That's the nicest thing anybody's said to me all day." The bartender upended a shotglass on the rubber-toothed mat in the gutter beyond the twenty and topped it.

"Here's to jokes at other people's expense," he said, raising his shot.

"And all other mitigating traumas," the woman added. She removed the straw from her drink and dropped it on the napkin.

The bartender hesitated, his glass halfway to his mouth. "A big vocabulary makes me paranoid," he said.

"Let me rephrase." She raised her Tom Collins.

The bartender waited. Stanley raised his glass, too.

"Whiskey river, take me down," the woman said.

"And sure but a neater corrective was never issued by the State Department," the bartender said. He threw back his shot.

Stanley did likewise.

Green Eyes had a healthy swallow of Tom Collins, and pushed the twenty a little further over the bar.

The bartender covered Stanley's ice with whiskey.

"Yours, too, if you like," she said.

"I like," said the bartender, who topped his own glass again and raised it. "Yours," he indicated to Stanley.

His temerity, if not his eloquence, awakened by the whiskey, Stanley turned to Green Eyes and said, raising his glass, "May I remember your name tomorrow morning."

"Frank," said the bartender.

Stanley grimaced.

"Vivienne." She smiled and touched her glass to his. "May you remember it five minutes from now."

"No problem," said the bartender, throwing back his shot.

"Any second name?" Stanley asked, emboldened by quip and the knowledge that the bartender's mouth was full.

"Carneval."

"As in the Brazilian segue from fast to carnality?"

"Sí."

"Or is it the other way around?"

She smiled. "Take your pick."

"Spanish?"

"Portuguese and Swedish."

Stanley was staring again. "Why does that turn me on?"

She stared back. "Which way is on?"

They drank.

The bartender was staring, too. "You can make another Tom Collins, now," Stanley suggested.

The bartender blinked, as if saddened. "Yeah," he said. "I guess my chestnuts is burning."

"Christmas again already," Stanley said. "Maybe this year they'll do a chestnut beer."

"You could leave the bottle," Vivienne suggested. "As a present."

"You could pay for it," the bartender replied, "as a matter of fact."

"I did pay for it," confirmed Ms. Carneval, indicating the twenty.

"What about the Tom Collins?"

"I'd rather switch than go into shock."

"Hey," said the bartender suspiciously. "Something wrong with it?"

"Nope," she said. "Perfectly good drink for a fairy."

"You ordered it."

"I wasn't sure what kind of joint this was."

"What kind of joint is it?"

"A regular joint. It reflects its clientele."

"You got something against fairies?"

"Not so long as they buy me drinks."

"Hey," said Stanley.

"What about those chestnuts," she said.

"What, you want some?" the bartender said. He moved down the bar without waiting for an answer.

Vivienne pushed the Tom Collins aside. "And bring me a glass. With ice."

The bartender returned with the setup and went away with the remains of the Tom Collins and the twenty-dollar bill, leaving behind the half-empty quart of whiskey.

Stanley poured her a drink.

"What are you doing in this joint?" he asked, setting aside the bottle.

"Same as you, I'd guess. Having a drink where they don't know me." She picked up her glass, touched it to his on the bar, and had a dainty sip.

Stanley suddenly became shy again. He'd neglected to realize that the bartender's contribution to the social equation had made things easier for him.

"They don't know me any place."

"Yeah? So start fresh. What's your name?"

"Stanley. I told you."

"No. Your last name."

"Ahearn. Stanley Clarke Ahearn."

"Why, that's the gentlest, most solid name I ever heard," she said earnestly. "It sounds like a building standing all alone against a record number of snowflakes falling on Minneapolis at two o'clock in the morning a week after New Year's Eve."

Stanley was so amazed by this remark that the smile it elicited from him hung between a grimace and a smirk.

"Plus or minus a little pollution," he managed to mumble.

"They'll get it cleaned up," she said. "They have to. Ever read Jonathan Schell's *Fate of the Earth*?"

"Oh, Christ," said Stanley. "She's going to do the eco-dozens on me. Let's get this over with: No, I haven't read it. And I'm not going to read it. For the last three years I've done little beyond watch *Star Trek* reruns and drink this particular brand of whiskey and drive a delivery truck for a grocery wholesaler in Chinatown. I live alone and I like it that way. I have no friends. My only ecological requirement is that there always be a large bottle of aspirin in the glove compartment."

"So demanding," she said. "So forward-thinking."

"Yeah," he said.

"I can't talk about *Star Trek*," she said. "I get vertigo in space, televised or not."

"Maybe it's morning sickness."

She shot him a fierce glance. "Mind your own fucking business."

Stanley's jaw dropped a little.

"Sorry."

She took a sip of whiskey larger than her previous one.

"Don't mention it."

He sipped his whiskey, racking his brain for the conversational tag immediately preceding the subject of *morning sickness*.

Suddenly compliant, his mind sent *televised space* scrolling across the foreground of his perception, like the sign above Times Square, big enough to read without glasses.

"I probably would get it, too," Stanley ventured charily. "Vertigo in televised space, I mean. I've seen them all, every episode, and I can't remember a single damned one of them. Except for one time they have to go to Altair, see, and —."

"So let's change the subject."

"Well," he began again. "I hear they're translating the King James Bible into Klingon."

She straightened up, looked toward the back bar, then at him, then away again.

He smiled wanly. "So let's change the subject."

In fact he remembered dozens of *Star Trek* episodes. The enormity of the lie squatted on the bar between them like a ruptured Tribble, enforcing an additional silence. Vivienne toyed with her drink without tasting it.

Stanley became uneasy. "So much for our first date," he said at last.

"Hey, no pressure from me," Vivienne said. "You want to look at your little round face in that little round pool of whiskey all night, help yourself."

"The trouble is, it's a habit," Stanley admitted morosely. "Habits are hard to break."

"Especially for a lousy reason," she added acidly.

Stanley nodded. "Especially for a lousy reason."

She smiled, just a little.

"Is this becoming self-flagellant?"

"Pan-flagellant," she said. Her tone hinted that she already knew all she needed to know about such habits.

"Married?" Stanley said abruptly.

"Not so's you'd notice."

"Divorced?"

"That too. You?"

"Never married."

"Really? How old are you?"

"Forty-seven."

"How'd you miss the banana boat to bliss?"

"It left without me."

"Either you're whining, or you're better off."

He looked at her.

She looked at him.

Caged radium. He hadn't shaved. "Yeah?" he said. Turning away he tipped a little whiskey over his lower lip, staring over the glass held by both his hands.

"Yes," she said. She ran a fingernail around the rim of her own glass. "It's an institution designed to eat you alive, husband, house, kids and all. It turns your mind into a La Brea tar baby. It turns your heart into a suppurating retaining wall. It turns your soul into a firefly in a jar. It turns... It turns..." Her voice stopped. After a moment she added, "I guess you could call me biased."

Stanley shrugged. "First off, I wouldn't have to live with a husband. I'd have to live with a wife."

"That's a good point. We girls got that strike against us. Right out of the box. As it were."

"Second... I never took the chance."

"Stop whining. You're better off."

"Or maybe I should say..."

She finished it for him. "The chance never took you."

He shook his head. "I never took the chance."

"Like I said—."

"I'm better off?"

To Stanley, who thought he must by now be somewhat drunk, the repartee sounded like the same old ping-pong. *Pock:* Husband this. *Pock-pock...* What wife? *Pock...* Had your chance. *Pock-pock...* You call that a chance? *Pock...* Anything beats waiting on tables. *Pock-pock-pock:* Except getting beat yourself. *Pock...* That's the truth. *Pock-pock-pock...* I was lucky to get out with all my teeth. *Pock...* That rough? *Pock-pock...* All I ever did was darn his socks and wait for him to decide he had time to fuck me. What? You heard what I said. The guy must have been crazy. Drunk, mostly. He ignored you? Like an empty mailbox on a dirt road to nowhere. How existential. Nothing to shoot at, even. He never, ahm, he never made love to you. No, and he never fucked me, either. I find that very hard to believe—. So fuck me. Fucked you? Fuck me.

Fuck you? Me. Here? Why not? What, in the toilet? That's right: why not? Can't I finish my drink first? You see? Fuck me, stupid. Why? Why not? I'm shy. So am I. Shy but desperate. Besides, I-I don't have a condom. What about—you don't even know me. I feel like I know you. A thousand years, right? That time on the Nile you poured wine into the pasta instead of olive oil? We were oxen together, with a common yoke. I don't know you, either. What's to know? *Pock....*

"So she had red hair, huh?"

Stanley abruptly looked up. Had he been maudlin out loud? What had he said? He looked at his glass. Had he blacked out? He looked at the bottle, at her glass. They all had some whiskey in them, though less than before.

More to the point, what had she heard him say?

"Ahm, look," he began. "If I've been rude..."

"That red hair's a known killer," she said. She came a little closer. "That's only if you're particular, of course."

Caged radium.

Had he blacked out and mentioned the red hair?

They would look good with red hair, those green eyes.

They looked damn good with black hair.

He turned away from the green eyes to refill his glass and to cling to it, along with his clichés about barroom conversations. *Pock...* Boring, metronomic, concentric, claustrophobic, taking no chances, revealing little. *Pock pock...* All the same after ten o'clock. *Pock...* Maudlin blurts. *Pock...* Based on country-western songs. *Pock-pock...* Premature ejaculation, that would sting. *Pock...* Nothing so *existential* as trying to impress a woman who doesn't love you anymore... *Pock...* Backfire of all backfires... *Pock-pock...* But its subject unrepressed a strange feeling in Stanley and, he eventually realized, staring at his drink, that this red-haired feeling in his breast, unexpectedly freed by this green-eyed presence, but more likely by the alcohol, although probably by the combination of both, had managed to fill his eyes with moisture.

He curled his lip and breathed heavily. The air around him turned ochre. Let not one tear fall, he thought, not a single one, lest I destroy this bar completely. Everything in it. Between his two hands the drink trembled a little. Through the moisture in his eyes he could see the viral filaments conspicuous to strong alcohol adrift in his whiskey, like malaria in a bloodstream. And somewhere, similarly adrift in his neural sea, a voice, long-unheard, unexpectedly called his name.

He almost answered it aloud. But something arose in him, dignity perhaps, for lack of a better concept, which forced him to say something—anything—else.

"I've always suspected," he croaked, "that a life lived within an uninterrupted field of television, alcohol, and a dumb job would leave a man right where he started, emotionally speaking."

"I'd suspect," she said, "it'd leave him with even less."

"I'm beginning to believe it."

The back of her ringed finger almost managed to brush the tear off the cheek below his right eye before he jerked his head back, like a startled horse.

He looked away and wiped his cheek himself.

"I'm drunk," he said, turning back to her after a moment.

She smiled boozily. "The chemistry is mutual."

He cleared his throat. "It's like a time machine. You get in with a certain set of problems and it seems like maybe five minutes have passed while the lights on the dashboard go on and off and maybe there's a little vibration in the chassis while you're watching the news. And then something clicks and you open the door and stick out your head to look around and it's a week or three months or a year later. It doesn't seem so long to you, though. But you get out and stretch anyway because if that much time has passed you better get a little exercise.

"The days are longer or shorter than you think they ought to be because the season has changed; all the kids tell you they're seniors in college but look too young to be in high school, which you attended with their parents; the cars have changed subtly, they've gotten smaller and more alike; there are many, many more places where you can't smoke; and the corner grocery doesn't sell anything made with meat anymore either: they've even changed the President.

"But you? You've got the same set of problems you got into the machine with, when those kids maybe weren't even born yet, when the guy those kids elected President was two classes behind you in high school, and you realize that it's true, that television puts you into a dream state very like the real thing with this important difference, that when you're dreaming you're metabolizing, and when you're watching television you're not. In psychic metabolism real-time experiences are broken down into energy-yielding substances for use in vital emotional

processes. Other constructs, necessary for mental health, are synthe-
sized by dreaming. Under the influence of sleep and work and play
and, uh, sex, psychic metabolism gets to do its beneficial thing. But
under the influence of television it doesn't. Under the influence of television your experience just sits there, letting all that fake, pre-masticat-
ed pseudo-experience television serves up to you, that nutritionless *pap*,
pile up on top of whatever slender, *bona fide*, unresolved experiences you
might have managed to accrue under your skullcap, right up until the
time you picked up the wand."

"The wand?"

He held thumb above forefinger in front of him and made the clicking motion.

"Zap," he said softly. "Zap, zap."

"The remote control," she concluded.

"The wand of non-awareness," he confirmed, as if to himself.

She nodded, ever so slightly.

Stanley sighed heavily. "You're up on the latest football scores. You
know what they're doing to each other in Rwanda. But you're way, way
behind on vital matters of psychic metabolism. And it's so scary or dis-
heartening or whatever that non-emotion is that you close the access
port and fire up the television if it was ever fired down and crack the
cap on another quart and hope that urban development doesn't
deprive you of cheap rent and they don't raise the price on this Irish
whiskey because you came down a notch or two for economy's sake
already just last year and maybe that rickety little operation you're
working for can hold on until the day your social security kicks in, if
that new President whatshisname knee-high to the wand of non-
awareness doesn't spend it all first, and they don't..."

"Stanley." She put her hand on his arm.

"...blow the whole goddamn place to kingdom-come unless of
course it's the day before you're in a bus on the way to the discount
liquor store and you see *her*, walking through the crowd on the sidewalk
in Chinatown, a full red head taller than everybody around her, just
before the bus roars into the Stockton Tunnel—."

"Stanley," she said again. "You mentioned sex."

"Too soon would be right on ti— I did?"

"Yes," she whispered.

"I—. No, I didn't. You did."

"No, no. It was you. You mentioned it."

"No, it can't be. I can't bear to think about it. You, it was you. You mentioned sex."

"You mentioned it first."

"No, it was you who brought it up. *Then* I mentioned it. I would never—."

"Okay," she said, "I mentioned it first. Then you mentioned it."

"Don't you want another lil—?"

"Mention it again."

"What? Me? Oh, I couldn't. Please excuse..."

When she smiled now she had four lips. Four beautiful, beautiful lips. "How'd you get so funny?" she said.

"Me?" he said. "You should see you."

Her laughter sounded like windchimes on nocturnal Kauai.

"There hasn't been a man to make me laugh in..." She looked puzzled, then sad.

"No wait," Stanley said. "Don't go there, I just came from there." He wagged a forefinger between their faces. "It's a nasty, sad, godforsaken, flickering place illuminated by nothing but televisions."

Vivienne, herself, seemed to be blinking back an untoward memory.

"Like my apartment," Stanley nodded, "if you could call it anything so domestic. Its walls reek of despair—a squalid place suffused by darkness and mildew, lit only by that noisy little window onto a thousand fake worlds—."

A tear rolled over her cheek, and headed for the corner of her mouth. But the smile, there swelling involuntarily, threw it off to the side, whence it fell onto her...Stanley tried to catch it, failed, his hand brushed her breast....

"Is that cashmere?" he stammered.

Her beautiful mouth quivered between laughter and despair.

"Oh no, oh no," Stanley said. "Please..."

"I-I can't...," she sniffled. "You won't..."

"No, please," begged Stanley, "don't cry. You're too beautiful to cry. Wait, here, I've got a handkerchief."

A large flowered bandana bloomed out of his hip pocket into his hand and he gestured ineffectually with it. Another tear rolled over the same cheek, and followed the path of its brother. Sister? Stanley adroitly dabbed beneath her eye with a corner of the kerchief.

They were very close now, head to head, and she said, almost inaudibly, "What's a girl...?"

"Don't cry," Stanley whispered.

"Say it," she whispered back. Her eyes were not eighteen inches from his.

"S-s..." Stanley began.

The eyes were big and filled with tears. "Say it," she repeated softly. "Please say it."

Stanley allowed a sibilant to escape his teeth.

"I can't hear you," her lips said, inaudibly.

Stanley managed to whisper it, just below the threshold of audibility.

"What?" she breathed.

Stanley pulled her gently to him. She did not resist, and rested her head on his shoulder. The smell of her suffused his senses, and with it he swept a handful of her hair to his face. She was warm. She smelled good. He could feel her breathing.

"Sex," he said softly, directly into her ear. It was the first time he'd ever used that word as a verb in the imperative[1], in the transitive[2], and as an affirmative[3], too.

1. imperative: 3. [Grammar.] Of, relating to, or constituting the mood that expresses a command or request.

2. transitive, 1. [Grammar.] Expressing an action that is carried from the subject to the object; requiring a direct object to complete meaning.

3. affirmative 1. Asserting that something is true or correct, as with the answer "yes"...

Chapter 3

There were shoes. White shoes with rusty dots on them. But the light was all wrong, as if a scarf were over the eyes. A drip. A drip into a metal pan...

"He's coming out of it." A high voice, strident.

"Take him back." A deep voice, with a strange accent.

"No way."

"He'll start screaming. Can't have him screaming. Take him back down, please."

"I can't yet."

"Do as I say."

"Look, Manny, I've got to stabilize him first. This guy's drunker than the usual customer. It's not easy, stabilizing a guy when he's tanked on booze and chloral hydrate. It's been four hours since he's had a drink. His sugar's kicking him awake, right through the sufenta. His sugar wants a drink."

This high voice sounds as if helium, or the toe of a boot, has been applied to the larynx.

"So give him a drink...."

"Right. Since he's flying first class we gently wake him, and ask if he'd prefer the Bordeaux or the Chardonnay. Then we can take him back down with Mezcal and curare. Doctor."

"This is insubordinate."

"Go eat the worm."

"Swine."

"Tourist."

First class? He'd never flown first class in his life. They say the seats are wider. They say the wine is free. Red, please, and keep it coming. He's never even met anyone who has flown first class. They say the first-class passengers are smarter than the ones in coach. And, please excuse him, but, while he's flying first class…

Where is he going?

"He's trying to say something."

That was a woman's voice.

"Take him back down!"

"I've got to stabilize him first…"

"Stabilize him?" Hysteria.

"Stabilize him?" Mockery.

"You mock me. ME…"

"Don't antagonize him," said the woman. *"He locks up when he's antagonized."*

"Oh. Brilliant's not enough. He's got to be sensitive, too."

"What the devil's that supposed to mean?"

"Nothing. Except that most brilliant people aren't sensitive at all. Whereas yourself… You're very sensitive. Doctor."

Jesus. The sound made by pinching the mouth of a balloon so the escaping gas makes a squeal.

"It's just that operating makes him…"

"It isn't operating that makes him… It's operating out of a textbook that makes him…And that isn't the only thing that makes him… Getting up in the morning makes him…."

"You're spitting on the fascia."

A whispered groan.

"You see? He's coming out of it. That moan…that's… that's a prelude. A prelude to a scream!"

"Hey. Prelude to a Scream, *that's a good one. Good name for a band. Better than* Tenesmus."

"No, no," came a chorus of voices. *"Stomach Punk is better…"*

"Wielding the guitar and playing air scalpel, instead of the other way around. We're definitely in the wrong racket," said the high voice. *"But we knew that. Didn't we? Doctor?"*

"I've seen this before. He's going to be screaming at any moment! I tell you, he'll bring the whole neighborhood down on us."

"Doctor, not to be so dramatic. Permit me to give him a local."

"A local?"

"Sure. Lidocaine the T-6."

A chuckle.

"That stuff's expensive."

"So? Let him scream, then."

Silence. The whisper of cutlery. A moan.

"Well?"

"He... He's almost up, isn't he?"

"You're the goddamn anesthesiologist. Is he almost up or is he not almost up?"

"No. I mean...not quite. He's...he's hovering just below consciousness. Like a hawk on the morning air. If he doesn't catch a thermal, he'll be okay."

"A thermal?" the woman asked breathlessly.

"Something emotional, some jet out of his subconscious, a nightmare, a memory. Some buried anguish, an inner heat can lift him right up..."

The woman laughed. *"Just don't mention red hair...."*

A louder moan. The room had a strange resonance to it... the acoustic reflection of hard, parallel surfaces...?

"Hey, he heard you. What's that about?"

"Man, that really works..."

"Whoa, sweetie. Hold on... A little less of sufenta, a taste of curare. Okay... He's stabilized. Okay... I can hold him..."

Blackness. That is to say, an absence of vision as received through the organs of sight. A dream of cute little rockets, playing tag with one another through thickets of stars...

"Who...," said the accent. *"Who'd come around this place at night anyway? Who's to hear? I mean, what's more disconcerting: knowing what goes on in here or not knowing what goes on in here—?"*

"I'm glad you asked that question. If knowledge is a tiny subset of the unknown, one would have a hard time containing one's curiosity. But if the unknown is the greater part of consciousness, why tamper with the status quo, otherwise known as God's plan?"

"Put a cork in it, Jaime."

Hard to put a name to this accent. A non-native speaker of English making radio theater, maybe... Coming on like the BBC... Authoritative, informed... The only voice available to missionaries in the jungle at the time of the uprisings... Hidden in the root cellar... Crushing the headphones to the ears so as not to let a phoneme escape, betray the tunnel to the rebels... Password *Crepuscular Bollard*... Where did that come from...?

Another moan.

"That was appropriate. He groans every time you make a decision."

"It's getting softer, though," said the woman hopefully. *"Isn't it?"*

Now the playful rockets come in loud and low. Too loud. Too low. Businesslike. Run for cover....

"Hold him...!"

The bluish stars against blackness became rusty splotches against whiteness, interlaced by textured contrails and metal-rimmed eyelets. Fly buzz. Motor on a V-2 rocket... It's when it cuts off that you've got something to worry — There! It cut off—!

"You going to wait until this guy can read the number on my license plate already? Gas the bastard!"

"You telling me my job, Doctor?"

"You're working for me, aren't you?"

"Yeah, but at this moment my higher allegiance is to the patient, who needs me more than you need—"

"Jeeze," said the woman's voice, *"he's strong—."*

"Get the duct tape."

"Gas him I tell you!"

The helium voice: *"Vital signs not yet stabilized. Can't do... substantial risk. Who knows what that cocktail is doing to him? Alcohol, chloral hydrate, sufenta— I don't know if he's on Mars or the subway. Do you, Doctor?"*

A tearing sound. Somebody's wrapping a package. That lousy job in the shipping department, summer of '67, everybody else following the song to San Francisco...."

"We can't have him all the way up! Don't you realize the risk?"

"The risk is to us, he sees."

"Yes, to us."

"That's right. Us. Fuck the patient."

"Critical. Okay. He's quieting down, now. Yes. Look. Nobody's going to hear him scream, for chrissakes. Besides, he doesn't have the strength."

"My Christ when God was handing out brains this entire outfit stood on line with a communal thimble! I'm not talking about screaming. Let him scream. It's his see-ing that I'm worried about."

"Practically the old Random Walk, this guy's metabolism..."

Silence.

"There's always the eye bank," the radio voice mused.

"Eye bank," said the second voice. *"Eye bank? There's no going back, once that's started. Besides, who knows from eyes?"*

"Can of worms, it's a fact."

"Precisely! A can of worms. The can is the unknown, see, and the worms are the known..."

"Aw, can it, Jaime."

Silence. Rather, a roar that equates to silence, like looking into the mouth of a blast furnace. Then a single, deafening drip.

"He's hysterical, look at him. The guy takes me seriously."

"You shouldn't antagonize him."

"Antagonize him? Me? I'm just passing the time, waiting to see if my patient is going to die or not. Antagonize him? He might as well be passing a kidney stone."

"That's it. Maybe the guy's got a kidney stone. Is that possible? Maybe that's what woke him up."

"Doctor, darling, get a grip. What woke him up is ten thumbs retracting his colon."

"You know, you're in this a little too deeply to be talking like that. Deprecating my skills. Why when I was your age..."

"When you were my age, you and your fellow students were jerking off to Elective Affinities..."

The woman stifled a laugh, then tried to sound serious. *"You shouldn't antago—"*

"A good anesthesiologist knows how to keep a patient down, and not let a simple thing like pain and chemical confusion get in his way. And as for Goethe," the second voice said, *"YOU LEAVE GOETHE OUT OF THIS!"*

A moan, no longer a whisper.

Silence.

"It's us who'll hear the screams," said the radio voice morosely, a mere disconcerted shadow of its formerly shouting self.

"Take it easy," said the high voice soothingly. *"We haven't lost one yet. Right?"*

Silence.

"Right?"

"A can of worms. One day we'll open one up and it'll be exactly that."

"Gross," said the woman. *"Is that possible? Is he serious?"*

"Like he said. It's like a corpse completely covered with flies. From a distance it looks like a mildewed velvet suit. Fuzzy. But close up: everything is moving."

"Oh my God..."

"...just perceptibly moving..."

"He's got something there, you know. I remember a guy we took out of the Mission, last year—"

"How many times do I have to tell you about smoking around this oxygen?"

"Aw go bottle Mezcal with your worms. You see that little tube there? That's where the oxygen is. It's in that little tube, and that cylinder, and underneath the mask. Watch. See?"

"Stop waving that lighter around!"

"Okay, okay. Don't make a federal case out of it."

"It's against the law to smoke in the workplace."

"You begin to piss me off...."

"You're completely loco."

"Loco?" A chuckle. *"Loco...."*

"Next thing you'll be flicking ashes into the retroperitoneal."

"If ashes in the retroperitoneal killed surgery patients, no patient would get out of surgery alive."

"This isn't a hospital," the woman reminded him.

"This guy shouldn't have come up like this."

"The man shouldn't have come up like this, he says. You couldn't gas a cat."

"No telling about guys like this. You can gas them and gas them and nothing happens, they're just barely under. Then—"

"Then?" It was the woman, the woman's voice. He found himself waiting to hear it. What was it about that voice?

Oh...

Oh, yeah.

That voice has green eyes...

We're still together.

Green eyes like the lights on the out-of-control panel for some fabulous vehicle designed to surf gravity. Some sleek little rocket chasing another sadder little rocket through thickets of stars and a rattle of glassware, in and out of the twinkling Olympia waterfall that sounds like perpetually pouring whiskey, into a wisteria-wreathed sylvan tunnel that turns head-on into the roaring BART train, headed the other way and it's not stopping here...

We're still together...

Rat. A big rat. Got on in Fremont, rode all the way to the Embarcadero... Hunching across the platform...

"I don't know. They wake up. So you give them an extra taste, just a little extra taste and — whhtt!"

"What?"

"They go out for keeps."

The woman gasped.

"Not even so much as a Goodnight, Irene."

"You mustn't allow —"

"Oh, god." She has a heart.

"God has little to do with it."

Silence.

"You could be quoting Goethe here, Manny."

Silence.

"How about, 'One is not a man until one has built a house, planted a tree, fathered a son'?"

Silence.

"You ever planted a tree, Manny?"

A hiss of escaping gas.

"Of course, at this end of the century, were Goethe to have a look—."

"He'd start a band called Tenesmus," put in a faraway voice.

"And in his song lyrics observe," the high voice continued, not missing a beat, *"that one is not a man until one has cut down the tree one's grandfather planted, built oneself a dome with its timber, hatched a son by one's sister, red-lined the credit cards, burned down the works with one's family inside, and, finally, run out of ammunition and fallen under a hail of tax collector's bullets."*

Silence.

"Bust out with a little air scalpel there, doc, and we'll hunker down for the atrocious bass solo."

Silence. A clatter of metal on tile.

"Sorry. Another blade, please."

Silence. A whisper of cutlery.

"He's right, though, you are kind of cute tonight, Sibyl. It strikes me your cuteness stems from an apparent attachment to the patient, here."

Patient? What patient?

"This? How could I be attached to... what's left of... this?"

"He's only temporarily disassembled."

"Yeah. Besides, consider the ghost in the machine."

"When he's all sewn together, he'll be that machine, again. He'll rejoin that superset, the unknown."

"Same ghostly personality, unfortunately."

"Even then."

"So you're not... attached?"

"He's just a guy is all he is. Just a lonely guy..."

"Do tell."

Silence.

"Hey Sibyl, I'm feeling hetero tonight: How far would you go to keep this lonely guy alive?"

"What?"

"A total stranger."

"*I— You—*"

"*After all, neither of us has ever seen him before. Nor shall we again.*"

The woman said nothing.

"*Just a slight counterclockwise twist of this spigot...*"

"*Wait!*"

"*Or perhaps a clockwise twist of this one...*"

"*Stop it!*"

"*He's nothing to you.*"

"*He's alive, for God's sake. He's a human being.*"

"*Would you go out to dinner with me?*"

"*I— With you...*"

"*Try to conceal your disgust. I'm feeling hetero tonight, baby...*"

"*Please! I... Are you...*"

"*Am I what, Sibyl?*"

"*Are you buying?*"

The accent chuckled.

"*I like you, Sibyl. You think I won't twist this valve the wrong way?*" The high voice turned into a hiss, like escaping gas. "*Think of this man's life as a flame—the flame of a welder's torch. When it's cutting fine, the flame is well-defined, a knife of bluish-white. Twist the acetylene too rich, the flame goes all orange and awry, it dances as if it has bad dengue fever. Smoke lifts off the edge of the flame in black filaments like layers of burnt skin off a wraith of death. Twist the oxygen valve too rich, and,*" a pair of fingers snapped, "*the flame snaps out. Just like that.*"

Snap, again, of fingers sheathed in latex.

Silence.

"*I tell you,*" the high voice brooded, "*this very moment, if it's functioning properly... See it? No, that's the gall bladder, yes, just there... Juicy Lucy! Though it seems a tad distended... But if this man's liver is functioning properly, it's generating enough acetylene out of that whiskey to distort his flame.*"

Silence.

"*I can't explain it any better.*"

Silence.

"*Jesus...,*" whispered the woman.

"*Yes,*" said the radio voice abruptly, in a level, bored tone. "*I'm sure you can't. Equally, I think you won't twist that valve the wrong way. There would be... consequences.*"

"*A man would die. Not the first.*"

"*The first.*"

"Not the first. I—"
"The first!"
Silence.
"The first. Yes, of course. The first."
Silence.
"Can't have that."
"You sound disappointed."
Silence.
"Well. Isn't... Sibyl... a shapely... morsel."
"Thanks, I'm sure."
"That crisp little uniform... The little white shoes, their little white laces... "
"It almost looks real."
Silence.
"Sure," said the woman.
"Sure what," said the high voice.
"Sure, I'll go out to dinner with you... "
"I'm not sure I still have my... appetite. But you should have seen me before,"—
they all said it at once—*"Prozac!"* Through the laughter he continued,
*"We'll have a couple of drinks first, maybe a little smoke. Discuss nitrous oxide and
Malaysian piercing techniques... "*
A long, lingering moan.
"You're on... "
Silence.
"And Goethe, of course."
"Of course."
"It's a date," the high voice whispered. It sounded like a distant squeal
in a subway tunnel. *"I'm taking him down."*
"Thank Christ," said the radio voice, clearing its throat. *"It's four o'clock
in the fucking morning.... "*
Gas hissed. Cutlery whispered.
The radio voice began to intone softly, happily, lovingly, as if into a
microphone it knew to be plugged directly into its listener's ear.

> *Ein ersoffener Bierfahrer wurde auf den Tish gestemmt.*
> *Irgendeiner hatte ihm eine dunkelhellila Aster*
> *zwischen die Zähne geklemmt...*

"You might mention to Christ while you're thanking him," muttered the high
voice, *"that Kraut's poem is going to be the death of us."*

...Als ich von der Brust aus
unter der Haut...

"Really," the woman shuddered.

...mit einem langen Messer...

Chapter 4

He was awake.

First thing, he would have to introduce himself to these talkative people he didn't know, who spent so much time so close to him, with whose voices he felt so intimate.

The second thing would be to have another look at Vivienne.

A mockingbird sang like a tortured stoolie.

He couldn't see anything. A play of light. His eyelids were stuck together. His lips were rubbery and crusty, like two severed bits of the gore-encrusted hose used to torture the stoolie, and they were stuck together, too. It was a chore to separate them, but once accomplished, there was the matter of his breath, which stank with a penetrating reek, like a solvent. He heard the bird, but it took time to know it as birdness. Consciousness cascaded through his brain in silent slow motion, like a submarine avalanche, a molten density all silted up. Hindered and malfunctional. These and other troubles, less defined, the more sinister for being the more ambiguous, blinked here and there on the dashboard computer. A total reset might help. A fresh start. This meant he had to get out of the vehicle, raise the hood, and blow the breathalizer tube attached to the little alcohol computer capable of shorting the ignition. A lot of trouble. That's why they put it there, to keep you from driving when you feel like this. So you just curl up on the front seat. Get fetal. Go to sleep again.

Somewhere a power saw ripped a bevel through in a long board. Someone else used a hammer to drive big spikes. Manic birds, frenzied, as if a snake had coiled among their eggs. The mockingbird again. Perhaps a radio. Automobiles. A two-stroke scooter. Closer, perhaps so close it was somewhere inside him, he heard a rattle of cutlery, and tasted rotten steam, as if someone were sorting large amounts of silverware out of a restaurant dishwasher. Far away, never too far away, there was a car alarm, of the type that oscillated through eight or nine samples of the audio concept of "alarm". A quartet of beeps, a quartet of whistles, a quartet of croaks, a quartet of buzzes. Why was it called an alarm? It should be called an annoy. It was far enough away that only three or four of its annoyances were really discernible. But they hung collectively in his mind like a bat from the lid of his coffin, about an inch from his nose, a permanent annoyance. It would be nice, he thought, if they invented a car-annoy that only car owners could hear, like a dog whistle.

Strange someone would be operating a power saw so late at night. Its chattering metallic scream cut through his hangover as efficiently as it must be cutting through the board until, finally, it had cut through both of them. The two halves of the board crashed to a plywood deck, the two halves of his hangover crashed into his skull, and he opened his eyes.

A breeze pushed through boughs hanging protectively, closely over him. Many strange little fruit, teal and wrinkled, hung from the boughs. Each fruit had an eye that may have been interested in watching him.

Paranoia is just heightened self-awareness, Don Quixote. Sí, Sancho. Ten thousand extra eyes could only help. Ojos de Díos — Eyes of God. Ojos del Diablo — Eyes of the Devil. Son igual — They are equal. Sí, Sancho.

He closed his own eyes and turned his head. He knew cypress when he smelled it. Or was it juniper? He didn't remember its fruit, just the gin they flavor with it. He smelled something else.

He opened his eyes. Fifteen or sixteen inches from his face stood a middling pile of excrement. Two-and-a-half units. Not dog.

He closed his eyes. Not his apartment. Not… her apartment?

So he hadn't been awake. Try it again.

Wait. No sense in going for the same effect twice. Roll away.

He was deprived, however, of his freedom of movement. Something restrained him. Claustrophobia suffused his senses, and he kicked. His foot traveled but an inch before it was arrested, and a very sharp pain shot through his lower back. The pain took his breath away, and yanked open his eyes. He saw the trunk of a tree, and a tatter of yellowed newspaper with dark glistening stains on it. He closed his eyes against the tears that filled them, rediscovered his voice, and screamed, "Where the fuck am I?"

"Pipe the Christ down over there, man," said a sleepy, gravelly voice. He moaned.

"That's better."

He opened his eyes. A tear spilled over his downside cheek. He was on his back now, and the pain in it, though somewhat subsided, throbbed insistently. His side felt like it was in a vise. He tried to imagine the pain as something distinct and separate from himself, something with which he might become but marginally acquainted. He failed.

The cypress limbs quivered gently above him. I'm hurt, he thought. It's time to admit it. "I'm hurt," he said aloud.

"Trust in the Lord," said the gravelly voice. "'Less you got in-shore-ance."

"No, really," he reiterated, in a horse whisper, "I'm hurt," as if accepting the truth of the matter. He was hurt. If this isn't hurt, there is no chrome in Indiana.

And he was outdoors. Under a tree in a sleeping bag, between the tree trunk and a heap of steaming feces. Insult added to injury. To hurt.

He'd never owned a royal purple sleeping bag.

A crow flew overhead, calling to inaudible friends.

In his time he had invoked a few hangovers, and knew from experience that the thing to do, when awaking in unfamiliar surroundings, was to remain calm and locate the aspirin. In due course, whether it was sufficiently degrading or not, the rest of the story would tell itself.

The present degradation seemed a bit extreme, however. Usually the pain in a hangover was in his head and not in his back. Had he been mugged? It seemed unlikely that a mugger would leave him in a sleeping bag afterwards. Besides, he'd had very little money when he... When he...

When he what? Goddammit...!

The twenty dollars. He'd conned the young hooker out of it. A proud moment. Instant karma? What goes around, comes around? What he stole, got stolen?

Con a hooker, wake up under a tree?

Well, hey. In Sanskrit, "karma" means "action."

Beggars can't be choosers.

A bum in the bag is worth two in the cardboard...

Be calm, be calm. In due course, the rest of the story will degrade you.

Royal purple, a color the gay boy-scout troop might deem standard issue, and there was a big wet spot underneath him, oh dear, not far from the pain in his lower back. Had he been dragooned into a troop of gay boy-scouts?

This hangover might stack up with the really big ones...

The bag was zipped to his chest, his arms were inside, and in fact it was quite cozy in there. Too cozy. Perhaps he was sweating. His eyes drooped to half-mast again... snapped open. There seemed to be quite a bit of sunlight filtering down through the thickly matted cypress. So maybe the breeze shaking the tree would be the leading edge of a fog bank... That is to say, it could be the edge of a bank of fog... if...

If he were still in San Francisco.

If he weren't in Indiana.

Land of deciduous consciousness.

The cypress was a good sign. San Francisco has lots of cypress.

If he was still in California, everything was still half-way okay — right? Doesn't that stubborn optimism go hand in hand with the New World experience?

From close by he heard the sound of a filling sprinkler head, alternately spitting air and water.

"Oh shit," said the disembodied gravelly voice. "Here it comes, amigo. Rise and shine."

From the other side of the cypress he heard the rasp of a zipper and whispers of nylon and the hollow thump-thumps of shoes being clapped together.

"Goddamn earwigs," grumbled the voice, somewhat cheerfully, if Stanley wasn't mistaken. "If it ain't the fleas it's the lice and if it ain't the lice it's the earwigs and if it ain't the earwigs it's the park service and if it ain't none a them it's election year."

"You'd think they'd let a man rest," Stanley heard himself saying. His voice sounded as if he had someone sitting on his chest.

"Not me," said the gravelly voice. "I'd think they'd kill us all and be done with it."

"They might yet," Stanley rasped.

"Man's got to stay on his toes if he ain't got nothin' but toes to stay on."

Now under full pressure, the sprinkler head began to ratchet rhythmically.

"You ain't gittin' up?" said the voice. "It's fixin' to git a mite damp in here. C'mon'n git up. We'll score us a couple transfers and make it down to St. Anthony's for breakfast."

So he was still in San Francisco. "I take some comfort, knowing we're only a bus-ride away from St. Anthony's," Stanley said weakly, not even attempting to move. "But on what bus line, exactly, do we find ourselves?"

"Oh the Seven, the Six, that Noriega line... There's four or five buses, run up there on Haight..."

Ten feet above Stanley's head a powerful stream of water played across the axis of the cypress tree. Spray ricocheted off the downsloping branches, and the jet passed on. Moments later a few drops of water and several cypress needles ticked down onto the sleeping bag and his face.

He blinked, then opened his mouth and broadened his tongue. But no water fell on it.

"I'm hurt," Stanley whispered. "Thirsty..."

"What's that?"

"Hurt!" His voice wasn't any louder.

"You're fixin' to be hurt and wet both," said the man. "There's a difference, I happen to know."

"I can't feel my legs." He struggled to free his arms from the sleeping bag. One of them, twisted beneath him, asleep, lay as heavy and unresponsive as a pig of lead. The other arm he managed to extricate.

He still wore the pineapple shirt. The arm was in its sleeve and seemed to work all right. As he waggled the fingers of its hand in front of his face to prove its motor skills he saw the fat piece of gauze taped over the inside of his elbow, and a large purpling bruise sprawled across the skin beneath it.

He stopped moving his tingling fingers. He stopped struggling to free himself from the unfamiliar sleeping bag. He stared at gauze and bruise for a long moment, motionless.

The jet of irrigation water cycled back across the tree in the opposite direction.

The bruise was a few shades darker than the purple sleeping bag, and yellowing around its edges. So maybe it was at least a day old.

Stanley's eyes began to move in his head, now darting this way, now that. He didn't remember giving blood. Though, come to think on it, he'd had an HIV test about three months before.

Que pasa?

"Hey. Neighbor."

The man beyond the cypress trunk was busy packing things up. "No," he said. "You can't borrow my power mower."

"Where is this?"

"Come again?"

"You mentioned the Haight. Where are we, exactly?"

"The fabulous Panhandle of the famous Golden Gate Park in beautiful San Francisco in the Promise-Me-Anything-Land, Californ-eye-ay, where joints and screenplays grow on trees and the dream never dies, yee-hah."

"Do I know you?"

"I dunno."

"I like your attitude."

"Maybe I'll run for office."

"Do you know me?"

A grizzled face thrust itself between the two lowest limbs of the cypress, about two feet away and above Stanley's head. The man was old, with a weathered face bronzed by the sun and empurpled by wine, with lips to match, a swollen nose long ago flattened by a fist and stippled by burst capillaries, ennobled by a closely trimmed white beard and short white hair beneath a navy watch cap. A damp pair of alert, rheumy blue eyes looked Stanley up and down.

"Nope," he said. "That bag looks familiar, though. You in the gay boy-scouts?"

"What's your name?" Stanley said.

"Jasper."

Stanley held out his good hand. "Stanley."

Jasper extended a hand beneath the limb below his head. "Pleased."

As Jasper shook Stanley's hand he turned it, exposing Stanley's forearm with its bruise and bandage.

"I know where you can give blood and they won't hurt you like that," he said. "Give twenny-five bucks, a cookie, and a glass of apple juice, too." He dropped the limp hand. "Unless —"

Stanley had been about to protest that he'd never knowingly given blood in his life, but he said, "Unless?"

"You positive?" Jasper squinted.

"About what?"

"Positive. Sick. You know. Got the HIV?"

Stanley allowed his mouth to fall open, then closed it. "Ahm, no, I— Of course not. I mean, I recently tested negative."

The sprinkler ratcheted overhead again, and a thin trickle of water sprinted down the length of the cypress trunk between them.

Jasper nodded toward Stanley's elbow. "Looks like they tested hell out of it." He scratched under the back of the watch cap. "You know fer sure?"

Stanley was at a loss to explain what the bandage and bruise were about, but, for sure, he knew they weren't artifacts of a three-month-old HIV test. He held up his arm and looked at the bruise. "I just... know it, that's all. A man doesn't shoot dope..."

"Yeah...," Jasper said suspiciously.

"A man doesn't have sex with just anybody..."

"Yeah...?" Jasper said incredulously.

"A man doesn't have sex with anybody at all?"

"Yeah," said Jasper confidently.

"Well?"

Jasper nodded sardonically. "I guess you get the juice and the cookie, don't ya?"

"Look," Stanley changed the subject. "I need more than juice and a cookie. I can't even get myself out of this sleeping bag."

"You got into it, didn't ya?"

The intermittent jet of water passed back overhead. A drop of water fell onto the rolled brim of Jasper's watch cap.

"I don't know, Jasper," Stanley said.

Jasper studied him for a minute. Then he disappeared.

Stanley dropped his head onto the bed of cypress needles, thinking, so much for the first human contact of the day. The effort of talking had exhausted him, and he was having trouble keeping his eyes open. The solution to that was easy, however. He closed them. A moment later, his mind fell off a cliff.

The scraping was loud at first, but after it woke him the sound diminished to its proper volume. He had no idea how long he'd been asleep. His body was bathed in sweat. The pain in his back was focused, strong, formidable. He opened his eyes. The cypress limbs were still above him. His arm was outside the sleeping bag, the bandage and the bruise were intact. His other arm was dead. A jet of irrigation water swept the upper part of the tree, scattering partial, momentary rainbows in the patchwork of sunlight. The sunlight hurt his eyes. More and more water trickled its way down to him.

"Goddamn, what the hell am I doing," said Jasper, "gittin' my ass wet first thing."

Stanley turned his head. Jasper had eased a flattened cardboard twelve-pack carton beneath a remnant of the pile of excrement, which he now flipped away. Thus the scraping sound. Stanley realized he must have been asleep for only a couple of minutes. Perhaps unconscious was a better term.

"How in the hell a man got in here to squat and didn't shit on your face is beyond me," Jasper growled, wrinkling his nose. "A contortionist. Goddamn genius." He scraped cypress needles and dirt in the direction of the feces and flipped the cardboard after it. "Okay, Stanley, pard. Jist act like a drowning man and float along with the flow of things. Don't grab me by the neck or I'll kill ya."

Jasper showed Stanley the fat blade of an open clasp knife, about four inches long with a little picture of it cutting through the shank of a steel bolt stamped on the handle.

Stanley said nothing. The knife disappeared.

Jasper reached between the ground and the low cypress limbs, grabbed a fistful of the sleeping bag at Stanley's shoulder, and began to back out from under the tree, pulling Stanley after him, bag and all.

Stanley gritted his teeth, and used his good arm in an attempt to keep the painful location in his lower back from bouncing over the ground, but the exposed knuckle of a cypress root gouged him pretty accurately. The pain seared his hangover as definitively as the contrail of a jet chalks a cloudless sky.

Beyond the protective limbs of the cypress tree the grass was wet, and a spray of water doused both Stanley and Jasper as the latter pulled the former into the sunlight. Jasper didn't stop dragging Stanley until he'd slid him over the wet grass and clear of the cyclic plume of irrigation water, thirty or forty yards beyond the tree, into a small grove of eucalyptus.

The pain was more than Stanley had experienced in a long time. He could hear Jasper yelling, cursing the water, but it seemed that he was very far away. Just before he passed out, he recognized the roof of the Department of Motor Vehicles building beyond Baker Street, scene of perennial ignominy. So they were in the easternmost tip of the Panhandle.

Then Jasper's face was very close, but his voice was very far away. He could hear Jasper calling his name, asking about blood on the sleeping bag, the first Stanley had heard about it. Stanley tried to localize the pain he was feeling, but waves of something else isolated him from it, each more diminished than the last as they flooded through his system. He found himself in a dwelling all too familiar to him, an apartment from another time, belonging to a woman he'd known. Its Victorian rooms featured high, coved ceilings, crown molding, plaster walls, chair-rail, wainscot, baseboards and hardwood floor. The source of his pain was throbbing secretly in that apartment. A wall stood between him and that pain, a kind of buffer absorbing energy from both himself and the source of the pain. There was a door in the wall but it kept shifting around. When he went to close it against the pain it would dematerialize in front of him and rematerialize behind him, still open, beaming the pain directly at that place in his back. Realizing this, he turned and caught a glimpse of something glowing powerfully beyond the door. To partially shield himself against the beam of pain, he grasped at the door's handle while he searched this familiar hallway for that other door, the exit that would allow him to escape. Or maybe, if he was really clever, maybe he could move on down this hall and find Her waiting there. Vivienne? He didn't know a Vivienne. But for some reason he knew the name. The light was a pale bluish-gray. But now, yet another door was opening behind him and hands were pointing at his back. He tried to twist around to confront them because, after all, this was his back disembodied voices were now discussing as if it were the scene of a crime that happened just last week on the sidewalk in front of the local grocery where you could still see the stains. But the scrutiny hurt. And even while holding eyeballs hands shouldn't hurt like that — well you know, the scrutinies of some eyes do hurt like that. So he turned back the other way and was blinded by very bright lights. He tried to shield his face from them and, strangely enough, a very minor but nonetheless real pain spoke from the inside of his elbow, briefly dimming all other considerations. A tiny door in his elbow. And he looked up in wonder only to discover the very beautiful and caring gray eyes of Mary, a woman he'd lived with for three years and whom he may have loved although of course he'd only supposed that possibility about six months after she'd given up trying to convince him it was so and left with a stockbroker who could afford to take her to restaurants where you could be calm and well-served and take the time to figure out how you felt about almost anything, let alone Mary, of the red hair and gray eyes. Even now, nearly six years later, Stanley's heart knew its way down that hallway, between the bedroom on one side, her studio on the other, in the apartment he and Mary had occupied at the peak of their conjunction, even as it began to change into something else, someplace else, and the vision of Mary herself with the most pleased, affectionate, expectant, welcoming, embracing expression in her eyes walked right through him and into the arms of a mist behind him, but he could not see that mist loosely defined in the Dream Computer as Her Other — her Not Stanley — and, to ice the dream's service to him, he heard her voice. Teasing, full of laughter, pitched high with the strain of living with such a loser as himself, saying, "Goodbye, Stanley," as in, "You blew it, Stanley," as in, "Ciao, Stanley," "Don't forget what we had, Stanley," and "Don't forget till it hurts you like it used to hurt me," and certainly "Don't forget till it hurts and until long after I've forgotten you almost completely except for the bitter conception I will eventually conceive that I wasted three years on you and your indecisiveness," not that she would ever think such things as "limbs like these will never be the same, with or without such as Vivienne, Stanley," or, "Stanley, I'm buried alive with my kids in a suburb where hope can't follow…"

A Short,
Expensive Stay
In The Hospital

Chapter 5

He was awake in a white room. There were a light on the ceiling, a window in one wall, a door in another. High up on a third wall facing the bed a television perched on an articulated arm and displayed a Roadrunner cartoon in color. All its action zipped left or right, mostly right, or up and down, mostly down, a Cartesian mayhem, mercifully soundless.

There was a man in white with the tubes of a stethoscope and a single gold pen sticking out of the breast pocket of a white smock. He examined a clipboard. From time to time he retrieved the gold pen, made it click, wrote something with it on the clipboard. Replacing the pen, he absentmindedly missed the pocket once, twice, thrice. Each time he missed the pocket he drew a blue line down the front of it, until, the repetitive loop attracting his attention, he got it right. A minute later, retrieving the pen, clicking it, he was annoyed to find it wouldn't write until he clicked it a second time. Having written something, he repeated the attempts to pocket the pen again. At first Stanley, whose eyes had been roving about the purlieus of his third environment in as many bouts of consciousness, thought the man must be performing this act for his, Stanley's, amusement.

Then he decided it was a phase problem. He watched in fascination as blue lines intermittently flared down the front of the white smock, until he passed out.

Later, revived, Stanley lay flat on his back. He was in a hospital bed. Tubes entered his body at his nose, his right wrist and elbow, his penis. It took him awhile to ascertain this by moving and experiencing not pain but disconcerting tugs at disconcerting parts of his disconcerted anatomy. His penis, for example, felt vague and far away, yet confident and sheltered, as if it were merely upended in an umbrella stand behind a door. The pains he'd been experiencing when awake under the cypress tree were still with him but seemed manageable, buffered as they were by morphine, or perhaps Demerol, the effects of which he recognized. The pain existed at a distance; his nerves flashed him irregular word of it, like a sharp bit of light caught by a rooftop mirror a couple of blocks away.

The door to the hallway opened and admitted a nurse in a crisp uniform. The little white hat atop the heap of her brunette hair looked to Stanley like a distant sail on a moonlit Indian Ocean. She had violet eyes, open and frank behind the Spanish combs of their lashes, and a pale, hothouse skin without visible blemish. The blue nameplate pinned to her breast reminded Stanley of a sign he had once seen above tree line on the pristine slope of an eastern approach to the Sierra Madre, nearly buried in a winter's good snowpack, which read, "Road Closed, September 15 to May 15." He couldn't see them, but he just knew it: little, white, practical shoes. Why did that remind him of something?

"Hi," he said joyfully.

She had been about to hand a large envelope to the guy with the clipboard, and he had been about to take it from her. They paused over this exchange to look at him.

"You're back," she said, with a smile that looked like she cared. The movement of her eyes reduced the rest of the world to chador.

"Yes," said Stanley, with reckless enthusiasm. "I'm back, and I'm glad. Before I leave again," he extended his hand, "Stanley's the name. I didn't catch yours?" Next to the bed a wheeled stainless steel rack bearing plastic inverted sacks of translucent fluids clattered and followed his eager gesture.

The man in white watched Stanley over the rims of his spectacles a moment, then removed the slim gold pen from the pocket of his frock and made it click.

"General feeling of well-being despite mitigating traumas indicates untoward affinity for morphine," he darkly muttered, re-clicking the pen to make a note on his clipboard. He silently reread what he'd written as he stabbed the pen down the front of his coat, a blue line following its tip.

Though his own glad-handing gestures surprised him as much as anyone else in the room, this remark about mitigating traumas puzzled Stanley. Where had he heard that before?

The beauty next to the bed laughed and said, "Iris. This is your surgeon, Doctor Sims." Her laugh reminded Stanley of the bells of a herd of sheep following their Basque shepherd home through a mesquite grove in August, high in the Ruby Mountains of eastern Nevada, just before twilight: precisely.

She handed the large envelope to Doctor Sims and sat on the edge of the bed, gently taking Stanley's hand into hers.

"I feel better already. Can I go home now?"

She laughed.

"Where am I? Why am I where am I?"

"Oh." Her expression changed to one of concern. "You don't know?"

"No. Should I?"

A mere few thin layers of cotton cloth separated his hip from hers. She nestled his palm on her knee and covered it with one of her hands while she stroked the back of his wrist with the other. Thoroughly enchanted by her consternation, Stanley almost didn't care what was wrong with him.

Dr. Sims pulled a sheaf of X-rays out of the large envelope.

"How does it feel?" nurse Iris asked softly, stroking Stanley's hand.

"Like my first date," Stanley said.

Her blush looked like alpenglow on a west-facing slope.

"I mean your lower back," she said. "How does your lower back feel?"

Stanley smiled and repeated stupidly, "My lower back? What about my lower back?"

Iris glanced beseechingly over her shoulder toward her superior. But this individual's back was turned. One by one, he studiously held X-rays up to the window.

Stanley, for his part, marveled at the way her dark hair metamorphosed to a fine, invisible down as it progressed from her temple to her cheek. Never before had such a lovely neck betrayed to him the delicate architectonics of vulnerability. It would develop, he was sure, that little bumps would arise all along the flesh of her forearm, were he merely to draw his forefinger, just its tip, along the well-defined tendon that stretched from the lobe of her lovely ear to the hollow of her throat.

When she abruptly turned back to him, a certain resolve had taken command of her features. But when she saw him staring at her, she blushed and squeezed his hand.

"Stanley," she said, "Would you do something for me?"

"Absolutely anything."

"Place the palm of your right hand flat against your lower back, to the right of your spine, just above your hip."

"Over my kidney, you mean?"

She opened her mouth, then closed it. Finally she said, "Yes, Stanley. Place your hand over your... kidney."

She watched him. He released her hand and gingerly worked his arm beneath the covers, sliding his hand down along his ribs. He hadn't realized until now that he wore one of those hospital nighties that covers the anterior of the patient but leaves the posterior exposed; but it made it easy for him to discover the rows of knotted sutures that curved like a narrow-gauge railroad across his back for several inches, through the valley below the escarpment of his hip, to an abrupt terminus just below his twelfth rib, pinching together as it went the puckered fold of a long, numb incision he hadn't known was there.

Iris saw his expression elide from morphined eroticism to curiosity to fascination to puzzlement to concern to confusion to befuddled inquiry, directed back at her, and, finally, horror. It was like watching time-lapsed film of a rotting apple.

"Somebody's done cut on me," Stanley surmised.

Iris suppressed an odd smile. "Yes. You're... scarred."

"Have I... been in an accident?"

Iris appeared uncertain of the answer to that one.

Nor did Stanley have enough morphine in his system to check the sudden, fearful interrogative, *Who's paying for this?*

The hall door opened a few inches. A man wrapped his neck around the door stile to look inside, saw Stanley, then Iris, then the man with the X-rays. He opened the door just enough to allow himself the slot necessary to slip quietly into the room. The man was tall, with a moustache under a big nose and a corona of badly combed sandy hair surrounding a bald spot. Dandruff sprinkled the shoulders of his brown jacket like powdered sugar on pigeon pie. He was chewing gum. He wore brown slacks that didn't match the jacket and thick-soled brogans and his jacket was buttoned once, as low down as possible, causing it to flare unreasonably over the gun on his left hip.

A cop. A cowardly panic momentarily swept Stanley's other cares aside. Had he been driving when his accident happened? Had he been drunk? Had he wrecked Hop Toy's truck? Had he killed somebody?

Say nothing, he immediately decided. Don't tell this guy a goddamn thing.

Iris ignored the movement behind her, perhaps she didn't even hear it, and chewed her lower lip. "In a manner of speaking, Stanley," she said, "Yes. You've had an accident."

"I don't remember any accident."

The cop watched him with clear pale eyes.

Iris nodded. "That's probably just as well."

The cop asked, "What do you remember?"

"Who are you?" Stanley innocently asked.

"Inspector Corrigan, SFPD." He flashed a badge that for all anybody saw of it might have been the lid from a can of asparagus.

Stanley didn't even think about his answer. "It's not fun, trying to remember the last thing I can't remember. I tried and found nothing. Although my mother's maiden name came to mind…"

"Let's have it."

"Smith." Corrigan probably knew that already. Stanley's fingerprints weren't exactly a secret. At this thought, he looked at his fingertips and turned them over. They hadn't been inked, but that's not the way it's done anymore. There's this scanner, now, plugged into a computer. You just lay your hand flat on a glass plate and relax while the computer memorizes the entire intimate thing.

"Smith. Okay."

"The birth was difficult. Flash forward forty-seven years, to a juniper in Golden Gate Park. Sounds of traffic. I heard a construction project, a crow calling. There was a gent by the name of Jasper sleeping nearby. He pulled me out from under the tree. It hurt like hell. I'd like to thank him anyway. I remember an irrigation sprinkler, too."

Annoyed, the cop sighed. "Nothing else? Say, three or four days before that?"

"Nothing. Let's see. I went to work on Friday. I goofed off all week.

Stayed home. Watch movies on TV. I—."

"What movies?"

"Several. All of the *Star Treks*."

"Of course," said Iris brightly.

"It was a festival thing. That's the last I remember. Have I had an accident or not?"

"You could say that."

"What's that supposed to mean? Wait a minute. You mean something corny, like an accident of fate?"

The cop frowned. No jokes for Corrigan.

Then again, Stanley bitterly noted, the joke wasn't on Corrigan.

Iris clasped his hand to her thigh and stared earnestly into his eyes.

The joke is on Ahearn, and it's not funny. But this is one firm thigh beneath this thin layer of cloth. No slip. A stocking, of a material distinct from that of the skirt. It has a certain mesh to it. Then smooth muscular flesh. She frequents a gymnasium; she climbs the Stairs to Nowhere three nights a week: less often than Stanley descends them... So, despite an Accident of Fate, Stanley is alive, this gymnastic thigh tells him so. To hell with Fate. Stanley is alive and receiving sentient messages via the umbrella stand in the corner.

He pressed the thigh gently.

Her lips slightly parted. But she did not resist.

She knows how to bring them back from the brink, this nurse. Yes, I'm alive, Stanley thought, and he felt something like an electric current course suddenly into him, straight into the palm of his hand, like a yo-yo snapping back after rocking the cradle.

He stared into her violet eyes. "Are we talking about a crime, here?"

Corrigan shrugged. "That depends. Received any large sums of money lately?"

Stanley frowned stupidly. How could this guy possibly know about the twenty dollars?

"Ah, Inspector Corrigan." Dr. Sims turned away from the film he'd been examining and favored Corrigan with a thin, condescending smile.

"What's the verdict?" said Corrigan. "Any further wrinkles?"

"I've only this minute received the films," said the doctor. "I haven't quite had time to review all of them."

"Hop to it," said Corrigan.

Sims raised an eyebrow.

"Go on," said Corrigan.

Sims clipped a large rectangle of film to a lightbox mounted on the wall.

Thickened by morphine, curiosity and lust, Stanley's voice projected little authority. "Am I the victim or the criminal, here? What's going on?"

"We're about to make it official," said Corrigan.

"Make what official?"

Iris released Stanley's hand and stood up from the bed. "Please Sean," she began, "I know you're upset..."

Along with her use of the cop's first name, Stanley took umbrage at the antecedent of her sympathy. The *cop* was upset?

"...But don't annoy the patient. He's had a lot of trauma."

"How much trauma is a lot of trauma?" Stanley wondered aloud.

"Oh he has, has he?" said Corrigan.

"Yes, he has," Iris said, standing up to him.

"Is that what you call chasing hookers on payday?"

Stanley tried to sit up, the better to project his indignation. But he only succeeded in thrashing feebly in his bedclothes, giving his sutures a good tug, rattling the IV pole, and yelling, "That's none of your goddamn business!"

"Please, Stanley," said Iris, stepping to the head of the bed and placing a gentle hand on Stanley's chest. "Try to relax."

"Yeah," said Corrigan. "Like with the girls."

"Fuck you," said Stanley.

"Inspector Corrigan," said Iris, reverting to the cop's official title, "this is a hospital, not a church. And you're hardly a priest," she added knowingly. And then she threw in, "Judge not, lest ye be judged."

"Not only that but people who live in that glass whorehouse called City Hall shouldn't throw rocks," Stanley croaked feebly through his embarrassment. "Get to the point. What the hell's wrong with me?"

"You'd think he'd never paid for it in his goddamn life," Corrigan said mockingly, pulling a little palm-top computer out of his inside coat pocket. He pushed a couple of buttons and watched the tiny screen. "It's all here." He raised an eyebrow and said, "Does the name Dalmatia Snood mean anything to you?"

Stanley stared stupidly at him. "Are you kidding me?"

"Southwestern accent?" said Corrigan mildly.

"I don't think I'd easily remember a name like that," Stanley said finally. "And if I were able to remember it, I'd never be able to forget it."

"In other words, no?"

"In other words, no."

Corrigan massaged a key, stopping when he found an interesting screen to read. "Stanley Clarke Ahearn," he began, "aged forty-six years."

"Forty-seven, gumshoe."

"Happy birthday."

Iris laid a soothing hand on Stanley's brow. "Please, Corrigan," she pleaded. "He's really in no condition to get this upset."

Indeed, the scene had begun to spin around Stanley like a zoetrope.

"Stanley Clarke Ahearn," repeated Corrigan, looming like a seedy gargoyle over the foot of the bed. "Why does that name sound familiar?"

"You're probably my long-lost mother," Stanley said weakly. He couldn't understand why such a brief outburst of caustic antipathy had left him so exhausted. He could barely hold his head up. Iris smelled of talcum powder. "It's just a name, is all," he mumbled. "Just a goddamn name…" He broke out in a sweat. His voice was failing him. He couldn't track all the sensations coursing through him. "I just want to go home. I never should have left my room in the first place… Just a goddamn name…"

"Okay okay," said Corrigan, as if he were bored. "Stanley Ahearn; age, forty…" He pressed several keys with his thumbs, frowning and biting his tongue. "…seven years. Address, 17 Brooklyn Place, San Francisco, 94108. That address work for you, Stanley?"

"I wouldn't know. Nobody writes me."

"Sounds familiar, though? You got an address but you got no phone number. You got no kids, no wife, no mother to look after you. No friends to bring you flowers."

"There's no ring," Iris said brightly.

"He was cruising for hookers," said Corrigan harshly. "Ahearn!"

"Hey, man," Stanley said, not entirely faking his weakness, not to mention his nausea. "I'm the *victim*, here." He looked around the room. The room looked back. "…Aren't I?"

"He's got a point," Iris said.

"Bingo," said Dr. Sims, tilting his head back. He had his finger on the film covering the lightbox.

Corrigan and Iris looked at him.

"Bingo?" Corrigan said.

Sims grasped the temple bar of his glasses between his thumb and forefinger, the rest of his fingers splayed straight up, and tilted the lenses slightly as he looked at the film and announced, "Nephrectomy."

Iris caught Stanley's hand between both of hers.

Corrigan rolled his eyes toward the ceiling. "Hell's bells, Sims. I could have told you that much."

Stanley rolled his eyes in an attempt to see the nurse's, but she wouldn't look at him. "What's that? You mean I gotta have one? What's a knee- knee-freck...?"

"Very little collateral damage, however," Sims continued. "Other organs intact. No peritoneal intrusion. A clean job."

"This is his way," Iris whispered earnestly. "He's too sensitive to come right out and—."

Stanley ignored her. "Put that in English."

Sims tapped the film with his forefinger. "Definitely a single nephrectomy. And that's the extent of it."

"I'll bet it was the right one," Corrigan observed acidly.

"They took the right one," Sims continued, as if he hadn't heard Corrigan.

"They took the right one, he tells us," Corrigan repeated under his breath. "Goddamn wonder boy. Apple of his mother's eye. A tourniquet on the blasted leg of society."

"They took the right one?" Stanley wailed.

Sims removed his glasses. "They took your right kidney, Mr. Ahearn."

"Oh, dear," Iris sighed, turning to watch Stanley's reaction.

Corrigan exhaled loudly through his teeth, as if cursing, and began to thumb the keys on his little computer.

Sims leaned forward from his waist to puff a speck of dust off his film.

Stanley passed out.

Chapter 6

When Stanley regained consciousness, the first two things he saw were the eyes of Iris. *This too, shall pass*, these eyes reassured him. *We shall help to make it go.*

Of course they may also have been thinking, *We quit at five.*

She was still sitting on the bed, however, holding a little brown jar of smelling salts. The room had gotten darker.

The memory jolted him. "They took my kidney?" he said abruptly, pushing the salts away.

A man's voice said, "Afraid so."

"Who is this 'they'?" he croaked.

"We were hoping you might tell us that."

"I don't feel so good."

Iris retrieved his hand to gently squeeze it.

Rarely had he felt so badly. His mind scanned its imagination of his lower back, looking for a cavity or hole. A kidney was big, wasn't it? A kidney had volume, a certain mass? About the size of an avocado? A fist? A peach? But more intrinsic? How does this effect nutrition? Will I still be able to metabolize whiskey? If not, can we settle on wine or beer?

Ever since Stanley had been a younger drunk, a certain "familiar", a disembodied voice, advised him in times of stress. The voice occupied the catbird seat in the bar of Stanley's mind, where it could be found, figuratively, every afternoon at about five, nursing a beer and a shot while watching the world come and go through Stanley's eyes. A figment of Stanley's imagination, of course, and an undependable one at that. But it comforted Stanley to consult this erratic little presence. Right or wrong, it's nice to know you're not alone.

Take it easy, kid. Don't panic. There's a spare kidney, right? Everybody has two.

But to remove the one would leave a hole, Stanley said to it. Wouldn't it? A hollow or a pit? An excavation?

He imagined the voice as a paternal old prospector—spiculated salt and pepper whiskers in a beard like a hawthorn bush, the eyes a rheumy blue yet clear and bright from years of enduring his hangovers outdoors, a sweat-stained Australian bush hat wadded over his liver-spotted forehead, its left brim pinned to the crown by an Adlai Stevenson campaign button, and his favorite drink scotch and buttermilk. *Beats me*, the old man muttered now, copping out completely, and he lowered his eyes as he raised to his grizzled lips the brimming frosty glass of his first beer of the day. The image made Stanley thirsty, even as it faded.

His mental scan encountered only the new pain in his lower back, underneath the blanket of morphine and a row of sutures that felt, but surely couldn't be, as big as barbs on a length of wire. To touch it was a matter of revulsion. But there was no tangible awareness of a *missing organ*, like it was Sunday morning and... Altogether now,

Christ the Lord is risen todaaaay,
Haaa-al-aaaa-laayyuuu-uu-ya...

— Hey. This doesn't sound right. Where's the organ? "They" have robbed the church, and *they've stolen the organ*. Ah, ha ha ha... I don't feel so good. Take it easy, big boy, and above all don't cry. Those people are watching, The Staring Choir, good name for a band. Since when do I care about names for bands? Witnesses witnessing... Must be fascinating for them, to watch a man wake up somewhat less than he used to be, less than whole, reduced, partially diminished, decrementally dwarfed by his subconscious memory of his corporeal self, a man of kidney... if splenetic.

"The proper thing was to go in and have a look," the Sims guy was saying to Corrigan, as he exchanged a new film for the previous one. "No telling what else those renal bandits left in there."

Renal bandits?

"If it's the same gang it's clean as a whistle," said Corrigan, and he projected a chirp through the gap between his front teeth.

"And so it is," said Sims. "Snug ligations, purple aster, and all."

"Mm...," said Corrigan.

"Mr...," Sims turned from the film. "Ahm..."

"The patient is called Mr. Ahearn, Dr. Sims," said Iris coolly. She took her celestial lamps off Stanley long enough to glance at her watch. She'd been taking his pulse for a half hour, now.

"Thank you, Iris." Sims cleared his throat. "Now, Mr. Ahearn. Do you have any sort of... medical insurance?"

In other words, thought Stanley, am I a happy man?

His mind crept around his skull like a cowed dog hoping to pass a shooting range unnoticed. Sweat prickled the surface of his scalp. His eyes watered. *Mewling* came to his mind, if not to his throat. Even Iris, ever attentive, suddenly seemed foreign and undesirable. *Say yes*, implored her violet eyes, *Yes, I have insurance*! He removed his hand from hers.

"Who's 'they'?"

"What's your blood type, Ahearn?" Corrigan asked abruptly.

"How the hell should I know?"

"Many people know their blood-types, Ahearn."

"Are cable cars going up in flames because I don't know my blood type?"

Sims showed the cop his clipboard.

"My, my," said Corrigan, without surprise. "Blood Group O-Negative. The donor in demand."

"That lends you a certain... marketability," Sims noted, apparently under the impression that he was giving Corrigan a hand in his investigation. "Or should I say viability?"

Corrigan cursed under his breath.

Sims blundered on. "Although how could they know his blood type ahead of time? Let alone, *schedule the operation*?"

"Yes," said Corrigan acidly. "Schedule the operation."

It took Stanley a tremendous effort to bring his attention to bear on what Sims and Corrigan were saying. Whole categories of questions occurred to him. A recurring theme among them was, how had it come to pass that he now felt dirty? Unworthy? Abject? Debased?

Sims charged ahead, like a waiter with a big party. "I've got a complete workup here, Mr. Ahearn. Blood, tissue, major histocompatibility complex... As soon as you or your co-signer fill out a few forms, even though your blood type is least common, we'll put a beeper on you and find you a replacement donor in no time."

While Corrigan watched Stanley, and Stanley watched Sims, Iris busied herself with the apparatus plugged into his arm.

"But, Dr. Sims," Stanley said finally, "I have no insurance."

Iris said, "Oh," very softly.

Sims pursed his lips. Then he closed Stanley's file. He clicked the pen and drew a couple of blue lines down the front of his shirt. Then he parked the clipboard between his hands behind his back, drew himself up and said, "Of course with careful attention to diet and nutrition thousands of people find it possible to live quite normal and even productive lives on a single healthy kidney. Studies have shown life expectancies of healthy donors to be—."

At the word *donor*, Corrigan raised an eyebrow.

Sims droned on, "—to be no different than that of those with two kidneys within the general population and get plenty of rest and we'll have you out of here within oh," he shot a cuff and checked his watch, "tomorrow at the latest."

Iris mopped Stanley's brow with a damp cloth.

Stanley had been expecting this passage. But before the floor could open up and drop him into the parking lot he asked again: "Who is 'they'?"

"Ah," Corrigan finally said. "'They' is the rub." Sims looked nonplused that anybody was even wasting talk on Stanley.

"*They*," repeated Corrigan, mulling the word. "*They*, indeed. Perhaps you can help us determine the answer to that most interesting question," Corrigan's unctuous tone implied that, while he might be willing to pursue this other tack for sport and perhaps out of charity toward Stanley's feelings, he could in the end accept nothing less than a full confession from Stanley as to his own complicity in the crime.

Stanley didn't understand this attitude. Why should he be considered complicit?

"I asked a logical question, didn't I? Just a minute ago you said that if it were 'they' who took my kidney, 'they' would have done a clean job of it."

"Actually," said Corrigan thoughtfully, looking at his watch, "that was yesterday."

Stanley was appalled. "Yesterday...?"

"For a while you were not of this earth, as it were. But yes. Just yesterday, I did say that."

Her back to Dr. Sims as she adjusted Stanley's pillow, Iris cast her eyes toward the ceiling and stopped the bed's ascent.

"Thank you," Stanley said coldly to her. "Now get out of my field of fire. As for you, Doctor Sims, the last time I spoke with a doctor, we were sharing a narrowly pukeless bit of floor space in the Marin County drunk tank."

Iris suppressed a smile.

"You, flatfoot," Stanley continued. "If I get your drift, you are all but accusing me of selling my own kidney for profit. Nuts. You also have made reference to my commerce with hookers. Double nuts — it's none of your goddamn business. Then there's talk of advanced knowledge of my blood type. Treble nuts — my knowledge of my own blood type goes along with my brand of medical insurance: Neither exists. A ghoulish *they* have been suggested, too, yet you coyly withhold what information you may have as to their identity. Let's try something. Let's pretend for a moment that I know absolutely nothing about kidneys, about the selling of kidneys, about hookers, about donor blood-type statistics or insurance scams — no more than I know about who *they* might be. Is it in your experience that this 'they' generally do a clean job of removing kidneys from people who have little or nothing to say about it? That is, they steal them and they're good at it? Can we look at it that way?"

Corrigan, unmoved and unmoving, now said coldly, "Describe to me your movements of five days ago. Then maybe we'll see about, let's say, your interest in hookers."

Stanley bristled as well as a man can bristle, who's taking the high road on morphine. Then something caught up with him and he paused, looking from Corrigan to Iris to Sims and to Corrigan again.

"How many days ago? Did you say?"

"Let's say four to six days ago," Corrigan growled. "Start with last Friday night. We're interested in the unusual—." He held out a forestalling hand. "Don't start up with me. Given that a hooker is normal for you — don't deny it, Ahearn. You want a parade up here? They all know you in the Tenderloin, all the girls. They even extend their sentiments to you. They chew gum, they align their bra straps, they twirl their keys, and they think it's awful, what's happened to you. They wink, they say get well soon, they wonder if it's going to affect your,"

Corrigan glanced modestly at Iris, "*driving ability*."

"Oh," chirped Iris blithely, "just give it a week after the catheter's out and you should—."

"The point is," said Corrigan "you have a certain reputation. You want to hear more?"

Stanley said nothing.

"They also say you're very concerned with being safe. Which is interesting. I presume you know that most johns will pay more to a girl if she'll do it unprotected?"

"Why," put in Sims, "that's suicide."

"It might be going a bit far to presume Mr. Ahearn thinks life is worth living," Corrigan continued, "but let's do so. Let's leave the girls out of it too, for the moment. What if we presume your innocence? Let's say you didn't sell your kidney outright for cash. And, I admit, we haven't found any evidence of recent large deposits into your pitiful bank account. At least not into the one that's in your name."

Stanley rolled his eyes. "The Swiss wouldn't grant you access, eh? Why do you think I use them?"

"Right. But your presumed innocence leaves us with a different set of questions. Did you encounter anybody unusual last weekend? Somebody you didn't know? Was there someone who took an inordinate interest in you, say to the extent of getting you drunk and testing your blood while you were passed out on their couch? Were you followed home from a bar? Did somebody buy you a lot of drinks? Did you become irresistible to a beautiful stranger who, in the course of a surprisingly and increasingly intimate conversation laced with alcohol, discovered she couldn't bear to sleep another night without you?"

Stanley blinked. "How long did you say I've been here?"

Sims looked at his clipboard, then checked his watch. "Eighty hours and fifteen minutes."

Stanley stared at him.

Sims shrugged. "We charge by the half day."

Stanley blinked. "Four days?"

"Going on four, yes."

Corrigan began to read from the screen of his little computer. "A homeless guy broke the glass out of a fire box at approximately eight o'clock last Sunday morning. Arriving on the scene, which was in the Panhandle close to Baker at Oak, SFFD found you passed out in a sleeping bag. There was a lot of blood."

Sims checked his chart. "Four units."

"If that guy hadn't found you," Corrigan stated, "you'd have bled to death."

"It was that close? I thought you said this outfit does good work."

"Usually they do. You may have thrashed around and loosened the sutures. In any case, you lucked out. A homeless guy cared."

"A little luck at last," Stanley muttered bitterly.

Everybody looked at him.

"He's just weak," Iris said. "Tired."

Corrigan drew a breath. "A paramedic unit had you over here by a quarter to nine. The blood was coming from sutures torn out of a very recent incision in your lower back. There's a name for the incision."

"Subcostal extraperitoneal approach," Sims agreed.

"But the interesting part is, we've seen this cut before."

"A classic," said Sims.

"We'll get to that. A cursory examination indicated what Doctor Sims here has just confirmed, that your right kidney had been surgically removed sometime within the last couple of days. Since it was such a mess to start with, Dr. Sims and the emergency team elected to remove the original sutures, reopen the incision, inspect the intrusion for sap— sap…"

"Sepsis," Sims said.

"He means dirt," Corrigan offered.

"We explored as well for incompetent or traumatized ligations, failed hemostasis, complications due to dehydration, pulmonary congestion, gastric distention or intestinal ileus. Serum creatinine and blood urea nitrogen looked surprisingly good…"

"We thought we might find some evidence, too," Corrigan interrupted. "As long as we were in there."

"We?"

"Hey," said Corrigan, holding both his hands aloft. "I scrub for crime. And Sims did indeed find some disturbed suture ligations, and internal bleeding as a result."

"But neither the peritoneal nor the pleural cavity was violated, thank God," said Sims.

"Sims got everything shipshape…"

"A nip here, a tuck there, some simple irrigation." Sims shrugged. "Nothing major."

"Thanks," said Stanley.

"And he sewed you back up. You've been sleeping like a baby ever since. They're generous with the morphine, here at Children's."

"Children's? I'm in Children's?"

Sims pursed his lips.

"Children's is the best hospital in the city."

Sims inclined his head in acknowledgement.

"Consider it a fluke in the ambulance rotation," Corrigan suggested.

"You mentioned evidence."

"Ah," said Corrigan.

"A clue," said Sims.

"In my back?"

"Sure, why not?" said Corrigan. "It's the scene of the crime, isn't it?"

"What clues could you possibly find in my back?"

"Singular ones. In fact, we found the one piece of evidence that circumstantially proves your lack of complicity in the crime."

"A bolt from the blue," said Stanley.

"Not so fast, Ahearn. You may have had it planted there for just that reason. Just to throw me off. Don't think I haven't thought of that."

"Oh, no, Corrigan," said Stanley. "I'm sure you've looked at this case from more angles than I'm ever going to consider. But tell me."

"Yes?"

"Do people really sell their kidneys?"

"All the time, particularly if they're a peasant in some place like Calcutta, or Rio, or Cairo."

"Show it to him," said Sims, his impatience tinged with pride.

Corrigan fished a small manila envelope out of his jacket pocket and considered it.

"Technically," he said, "I suppose it's your souvenir."

Stanley frowned. "*Souvenir?*"

"And I'll show it to you. But I'll need to retain it as evidence."

Stanley shrugged impatiently. The tubes on the stainless steel tree rattled.

Corrigan handed the envelope to Iris.

Iris carefully opened the flap and gently inverted the mouth of the envelope.

A purple flower slid onto the palm of her hand.

Iris stared at the flower a moment, fascinated. Indeed, its colors went well with her eyes and hair. With a nervous glance at Corrigan, she held it closer to Stanley.

Stanley looked at it. "What the hell is this?"

"It's a flower," Corrigan said mildly.

"I can see it's a goddamn flower," Stanley snapped. "What's it got to do with me?"

"It's a signature," Corrigan said. "One that we've... seen before."

"It's a what?"

"Whoever this 'they' are, borrowing kidneys from people—."

"Harvesting," Sims interrupted.

"Whoever these thieves are, when they get to the last layer of stitches as they're coming back out, they leave this calling card, this signature, as we call it."

"You mean they sewed this thing up inside me?"

"No, outside you," said Sims. "Just after they closed. The stem was woven among the final sutures."

"Pretty, isn't it?" Iris asked him.

Stanley stared at the flower. It was purple, with a yellow center.

"Do tell him the rest," Sims encouraged Corrigan.

Stanley looked up, dazed. "There's more?"

Corrigan nodded. "The flower's always the same species. A purple aster."

"*Aster alpigenus*," Sims pointed out.

They all looked at him.

"I've always adored it," Sims added defiantly, "the alpine aster. It's a dwarf perennial, indigenous to the high Sierra. It grows in the Rockies, too." Indeed, Sims couldn't have looked at the aster more lovingly if he'd designed it himself.

"So?" Stanley said finally. "*So?*"

Corrigan looked up from thumbing his little computer, a kindly expression on his face.

"So some hangover, eh?"

Chapter 7

Stanley studied the flower in the palm of Iris' hand. "It seems small compensation for a kidney," he observed gloomily.

Sims pursed his lips, as if maybe he weren't sure.

"Not to make value judgments," Iris added, as if apologizing to the aster.

Stanley looked at Iris. He was beginning to wonder about her intelligence.

Corrigan gestured toward the flower. "You through looking at that?"

Stanley waved it away.

Corrigan waggled his fingers. "Don't drop it."

Iris gingerly slid the aster back into its envelope and handed it over to Corrigan, who tucked it into the side pocket of his jacket.

"Evidence," he said, gently patting the pocket.

"Of what?"

Corrigan shrugged. "Depends on how you look at it."

Stanley lay back on his pillows and stared at the light fixture in the ceiling above Corrigan's head.

After a while he sighed loudly.

"So today's Thursday."

"Good, good," said Corrigan, retrieving the palm-top.

"So it happened when?"

"You tell us. Last weekend sometime."

"The incision was very fresh," put in Sims.

Stanley flicked an eye at Iris. "Friday nights I like to get drunk." She winked at him.

Thumbing a note to himself, his mouth slightly open, Corrigan looked like a giant kid playing a video game. "Wednesday: Got... drunk. Let's go to Thursday."

"Ditto Thursday."

Corrigan looked up. "Again?"

Stanley was back to staring at the ceiling. "Again. Not drunk, actually. Say toasted. Medium crispy."

Corrigan typed and moved his lips in silence.

"What's the difference?" Iris asked.

Stanley was thinking, *the Tenderloin. That's the difference.*

"Okay." Corrigan was writing. "Wednesday drunk. Thursday... toasted. Friday?"

"Ditto Friday."

"Say, Ahearn, don't you have any outside interests? Bowling, for example? Butterflies?"

"I never drink outside."

"So where is all this debauchery happening?"

"Mostly my place. But sometimes...different places."

"Like?"

"Anyplace. Who cares? This town's full of bars. I even got drunk in San Bruno, once."

"Busy boy," said Corrigan sourly.

"Yeah."

"And this DUI in Marin," Corrigan said, paging the palm-top.

"Oops," said Stanley.

"On January twenty-second, two years ago." Corrigan continued. "DMV matched your prints for us. Hmmm..." Corrigan thumbed a hotkey that brought up a calendar, turning the screen against the light to study it. "January twenty-second, two years ago... That was... A Saturday."

"Not much of a Saturday, either," said Stanley. "Though it was a long one. You ever been locked up with a doctor for four hours?"

Corrigan smiled grimly as he reopened Stanley's file and typed. "Just another Saturday, eh?"

"Not even," Stanley muttered.

"How do you pay for all these holidays, and, uh —" he held up the palm-top, "—driving lessons?"

"I drive a truck."

"When you're sober of course."

"I make a point of it."

"For who?"

"For Hop Toy Wholesale Produce."

"Chinese?"

"Chinese."

"You're kidding, right?"

"Wrong. I'm not kidding. Why?"

"In Chinatown?"

"It's between Grant and Stockton on Sacramento, a block from Brooklyn Place."

Corrigan frowned. "What are you telling me? They don't hire no white guy in Chinatown."

"They hire this white guy."

"What makes you so special?"

Stanley said nothing.

"If this was 1950, I'd whack you with this computer."

Stanley shifted his eyes. Corrigan continued to stare at him, frowning. After another moment of silence Corrigan began to gently nod his head. He puckered his unshaven face until his mouth looked like a mollusk on a sunken wreck.

"Bingo," he said softly. He snapped his fingers and nodded.

Sims looked startled. "Bingo? Ah." He removed his glasses and began to clean them with a corner of his white smock. "An insight."

"Stanley Clarke Ahearn," Corrigan said.

Stanley said nothing.

Corrigan pointed at him over the foot of the bed. "There's that big rock," he began, "just below the old Sutro Baths."

Stanley closed his eyes.

"True," said Sims, holding his glasses up to the light. "I jog out there."

"Not far away a little trickle of a stream comes down the hill, passes along the edge of the ruins of the Baths, and ends at the beach. A lot of watercress and miner's lettuce grow wild along this stream bed."

Sims waggled his eyebrows, then refitted the glasses onto his face.

"People," Corrigan continued, "mostly Asians, gather greens there. The price is right."

"Is that what they're doing?" piped Sims. "I often see one or two people with baskets hunched down there, along the stream, when I'm out jogging. Always wondered what they were doing. And I guess they're always Asians, though I never paid that much attention to their race." He turned to Stanley. "I bought a place on 39th Avenue — just off Fulton? — when I worked at the VA Hospital. I like to do three miles at dawn every—."

"Can it," Corrigan snapped.

Sims frowned.

"Could I have some water?" said Stanley.

Iris produced an Erlenmeyer flask with a doglegged glass straw sticking out of its top, and placed the tip of the straw between his lips. "Morphine's very dehydrating," she informed him solicitously.

"Not like the leach of a cop's mind," said Stanley, sipping feebly.

Iris smiled.

Corrigan continued, "One day three or four years ago this Caucasian guy is taking a walk out there below the Baths, along the beach. An Asian kid, a little girl, is playing on the big rock there, while her mother and a friend gather greens along the stream. The kid's young; nine or ten, maybe. The westerly is up, the moon is close to full, a big spring tide is coming in. The waves are gnarly."

"Look Corrigan…," Stanley began, a little water running down his chin. "Let it go."

Iris dabbed at the driblet with a corner of a sheet. Corrigan ignored him. "Just as this guy is thinking the little girl shouldn't be taking a chance climbing up there — boom!"

Sims jumped, visibly startled.

"Right before the guy's eyes, a huge wave blasts the rock."

"Oh, no," said Iris, dropping the corner of the sheet to turn and look at Corrigan.

"What the sailors call a sneaker wave. An anomaly, two or three or even ten times bigger than what's running. When the foam drains off the rock, the kid is gone."

"Stop it," said Iris, covering her mouth with her fingers.

"The women up the hill start screaming. Our guy runs down the beach between the surf and the rock and spots the kid, fifty yards out and heading West like she's on rails. There's just her little hand and the arm, showing above the brine."

Corrigan stopped. Sims and Iris watched Corrigan, horrified. Corrigan, however, was watching Stanley, who in turn was watching his own thumb and forefinger idly pinch at the material of the white skirt covering Iris' thigh, his face visibly burning.

Finally Iris said, "Well? What happened?"

"That's a good question, Iris. Only one guy really knows. But the next thing, this guy has shucked his clothes and is in the surf, pulling for the kid.

"It takes him a while to get to her. Nip and tuck. They start out forty or fifty yards apart. They're both sawing back and forth in this tremendous surge. Every swell begins by bringing them twenty yards toward the beach and ends by leaving them thirty yards further away from it. It was a lot of work. It took time. There was nothing for the mother to do but watch. But then the kid is in the guy's arms, and the undertow is hauling the two of them straight West, out past Seal Rock, they're heading for Japan."

Corrigan stopped again.

Stanley said nothing.

"Well, finish it!" Sims finally blurted.

"What happened?" demanded Iris.

"There's a crowd of tourists and shopkeepers watching this whole thing from the north terrace of the Cliff House. Somebody calls SFFD, and their surf squad is there in eight minutes. Ever seen them work? A bunch of guys show up with a quarter-mile of rope. One guy wades out with one end of the rope tied around him. He's the lead guy. He's wearing what they call a farmer-john wetsuit, looks like a neoprene union suit with the arms cut out, so they're free for swimming. This guy is built like a truck. After fifty yards of rope another guy goes out, fifty yards after that another, if necessary. The rest of the squad belays the swimmers from the beach. The ones in the farmer johns swim in the open ocean every day, they're all athletes, very fit. They generally go into the surf up-current from the victim, with the hope they can drift across him before he freezes and drowns. Most times of the year they have about fifteen minutes from the moment of immersion, thirty at most. And of course if the victim is under water they have no time at all. So in this case, they send out about three of these guys in wet suits, that's 150 yards of rope, and they manage to bring them both in, the non-Asian guy and the little girl. It's a close thing. CPR on the beach, oxygen, space blankets — the works. The guy and the kid are barely alive, the cold nearly got them both." Still Corrigan watched Stanley. "They're cold, but they're alive."

"Brr," shivered Sims. "That water never gets warmer than sixty degrees, no matter what time of year. The moment you're in it, your thermal core starts telling your head that it's all too beautiful."

"It's fast water, too," said Corrigan. "Even the surfers respect it — some of them, anyway." He was still watching Stanley. Another moment passed, and then Sims was watching Stanley, too.

Iris followed their gaze, turned back to Sims and Corrigan, then slowly turned back to Stanley.

"You're a hero," she concluded, her eyes shining. She was still holding the flask of water.

"That's what the papers called him," said Corrigan.

"Television, too, I bet," said Iris proudly.

"Ahm, look," said Stanley softly, unable to meet the eyes of anyone. "The fire department saved us both. I just almost got myself drowned along with the little girl, is all I did."

Corrigan looked to one side and rubbed his bald spot with one corner of the palm-top. "So," he said. "The women gathering greens see the whole thing. One of them is married to this grocer guy, Hop Toy, that's how I remembered the story, and the little girl is their only child. A few days later Hop Toy shows up at the guy's apartment to thank him, and discovers the guy is out of a job. Not only that but he's sold his car, all his goods are pawned, and he's twenty-two days into a thirty day eviction notice. We won't mention all the empty whiskey bottles under the sink. Hop Toy guy takes action."

Nobody spoke.

"The story was news for a couple of weeks. That was — what — three years ago?"

"Three and a half," said Stanley quietly.

"So Hop Toy gave you a job and a place to live. I guess you been living off him ever since."

"Sean!" said Iris.

"Ever since," Stanley confirmed evenly.

"Good for Hop Toy," said Iris defiantly.

"So," said Corrigan. "You're that Stanley Ahearn."

"Yes," said Stanley, even more quietly.

"That clears up something in the CHP report." Corrigan thumbed his computer. "Their DUI write-up said they had to tenderize you a little bit, when they arrested you that night."

"Tenderize," Stanley repeated, with a little smile.

Corrigan kept his face straight. "But they dropped the one count of resisting arrest." He looked up from the palm-top. "Can I conclude that, before they booked you, somebody at Civic Center recognized you as the Ahearn who saved the little girl?"

"Whatever."

"So they jailed you DUI but dropped the resisting. Nice of them."

"Yeah," said Stanley, without enthusiasm.

Corrigan closed the notebook. "Made the news, of course."

"Once you belong to the news you're theirs forever."

"Yeah. So." Corrigan held up the computer. "That was nice of the CHP. Troubled hero and all that. Since the DUI happened over two years ago, and since you still drive for a living, may we presume you learned your lesson, and keep your drinking down to weekend nights?"

"Just nights. Including weekends."

"Never in the daytime?"

"Never."

"Seems reasonable."

"On the contrary, it's yet another triumph of economy over passion."

"Let's back up and try it again. Where were you drinking last Wednesday night?"

"At home, in front of the TV."

"And Thursday?"

"At home. In front of the TV."

"Yeah? What was on?"

Stanley colored. "All seven *Star Trek* movies. Just like Wednesday."

"That's true," Iris piped up, turning to Corrigan. "I watched a few of them myself." She turned back to Stanley, her eyes glowing. "I never get tired of that one — is it *Star Trek Three*? — where they need a pregnant whale because there's no whales left in the future and they use the sun as a gravity slingshot to go back into the past only but if you're still in the past it's, like, us in the here and now? Remember?"

They all looked at her.

"Right?" She looked at Stanley.

"That's the fourth one," said Stanley.

"And," she continued brightly, "Captain Kirk tells Mr. Sulu to put her down there," Iris pointed a gleeful finger, "in Golden Gate Park—?"

"Right where they put you," Corrigan interrupted loudly.

"—And everybody in the San Francisco theater goes absolutely *nuts*—?"

"And on Friday night?" Corrigan continued, even more loudly.

Stanley pursed his lips. "No idea."

"Do you remember getting drunk?"

"I didn't say I was drunk. I said I can't remember where I was. I was probably drinking. I also can't remember what happened, or who I was with." Stanley thought for a moment. "It's a good bet I was drinking, though."

"Have you had these blackouts before?"

Stanley bristled as well as a man can bristle, while he's taking the high road on morphine. "I've never had a blackout."

"Hmm," said Corrigan. "All that booze, no hookers, and no blackouts, either."

Stanley said nothing.

"There's always a first time, Stanley, when you drink."

"Thanks, Corrigan." Stanley lay his head back on the pillow and closed his eyes. "I'll be looking out for it."

"It's possible," said Sims sympathetically, "that with time and the narcotics wearing off he might remember a great number of things he's unable to recall at present."

"Is that so," said Corrigan acidly.

"Yes," Sims said.

"Say, Dr. Sims," said Stanley. "What's life like with only one kidney?"

Sims shrugged. "Perfectly livable, so long as the lone kidney remains healthy."

Hiyo, Lone Kidney, quipped an inner voice, to the French horns of the William Tell Overture.

"Livable? You mean normal?" said Stanley, swiping a hand at the voice as if it were a fly. The IV pole rattled.

"Sure."

"I can eat? I can... drink?"

"Moderation is always a good idea," said Sims. "Even with two kidneys."

"I'm feeling crowded, here," said Stanley.

"You shouldn't, Mr. Ahearn. It's a private room."

"Moderation I tried, already."

"And...?"

"Something missing."

"Like what?"

"Excess."

Corrigan was lost in thought. Iris seemed perfectly comfortable sitting on the edge of the bed, remembering *Star Trek* movies. Sims looked newly uncomfortable.

Stanley was feeling annoyed. He opened his eyes and focused them on Iris. She interrupted her reverie to smile at him. That soothed him somewhat.

"How much does a previously owned kidney cost, Doctor Sims?"

Sims cocked his head. "With or without insurance, Mr. Ahearn?"

Stanley shrugged. "Just for the presumption, let's say without."

"Installed? Uninstalled?"

"You can get them uninstalled? Stand-alone?"

"They have to be very recently uninstalled, in order to be viable."

"Used kidneys," Stanley muttered.

Sims pursed his lips. "From a legitimate donor, let's say twenty to forty thousand dollars."

Corrigan whistled.

"And installed?"

"In a legitimate clinic or hospital, you're talking seventy thousand dollars."

"And from an illegitimate one?"

"Maybe twice that. Or, if you were to go to a developing nation like, say, India, you could score a kidney for, say, one-twentieth the American price — and maybe not even get hepatitis into the bargain. Plane tickets and gamma globulin extra. Although," Sims primly adjusted his glasses, "I am not immediately acquainted with black market pricing."

"So, supposing I could find one, it might cost anywhere from three thousand to seventy thousand dollars to replace my... lost kidney?"

Sims shuddered. "I'd *hate* to think of such a *delicate* operation performed by *untrained* personnel. *Hate* to think about it..."

"So don't think about it. How complicated an operation is it?"

"There are a lot of variables."

"How complicated, for example, was *my* kidney operation?"

Sims smiled thinly. "Not very."

"On the other hand," Corrigan interjected, "you're still alive."

"Which reminds me," Stanley said, "why am I still alive? Why didn't they just kill me and take both kidneys?"

"That's easy," said Corrigan. "They kill you, you're talking Murder

One with Special Circumstances — causing a death while in the process of committing some other crime — one of the surest ways to pull a capital offense. On the other hand, if they merely steal something from you..." He shrugged.

"Grand theft?" said Stanley hopefully.

"Or larceny. Not a particularly big deal, legally speaking. Hell, they didn't even use a gun." He glanced at Stanley. "Did they?"

"I told you," Stanley said, affecting a neutral expression, "I remember nothing."

"I heard you," Corrigan said mildly. "No guns, no witness... No wonder the Chief puts only the one guy on it."

"You?"

Corrigan grunted.

Stanley grunted. "How long do you think it took them?"

Sims raised an eyebrow. "A complete nephrectomy? Oh... two, maybe three hours, soup to nuts. Not including," he smiled, "outpatient care."

"You're referring to the five minutes it took to zip me into that sleeping bag?"

Sims smiled and nodded.

"Two or three hours for twenty thousand dollars. That's easy money."

"In your case it was probably more like twenty-five or thirty thousand," said Corrigan. "Your blood type is worth a premium. That's why they tapped you. If you go shopping for a new kidney, you'll find that out."

"You know," mused Stanley, "I had an old Ford truck once. Got in it one morning, started it up, put it in gear — and went nowhere. Turned out someone had stolen the drive-shaft. The drive-shaft! When I went to the junkyard to get a new one, I found out why."

"They were rare."

"Very rare. Extinct."

"There you go," said Corrigan. "In this case, there's a wrinkle, which is, O-Negative people are what they call universal donors. That is to say, with proper immunosuppression, almost anybody can accept an organ from an O-Negative donor."

"A maximum utility thing. So they get a premium price."

"Exactly."

"Wait a minute," said Sims, "I'd say they probably earned it. Think of the hard costs. Rent, the light bill, equipment, the anesthesiologist alone is a separate contract, and nursing staff, too. There's the girl to answer the phone..."

They all looked at him. His voice trailed off.

"Would you have to be a doctor to perform this operation?" Stanley asked.

"Oh, absolutely—," Sims began. He stopped and looked around him. From one face to another, he was met by skepticism. "I mean, one would hope that... No one in their right mind would submit... I mean allow... It isn't... It wouldn't be..."

"So there would *almost* have to be a doctor involved?" Stanley surmised. "But it's not necessary?"

Sims was at a loss for words.

Corrigan nodded thoughtfully.

"How about a veterinarian?"

Sims gasped.

"Try not to faint," said Stanley.

"Sure." Corrigan agreed. "But you'd want a real anesthesiologist. And probably a third party, a medical practitioner or trained nurse. The more help the better." He jerked a thumb at Iris. "Clamps, irrigation, sponging, drainage, supplies, monitoring, actually lifting the patient from whatever conveyance they use to get his Mickey-Finned ass from the bar to the operating table. And..."

"And...?"

Corrigan repressed a smile. "You need a florist."

"Very funny."

"And one more artist," Corrigan added.

"One more — artist?"

"You'd need the pickup artist."

"A pickup artist?" said Sims.

Corrigan's smile faded. He was looking at Stanley. "The pickup artist."

They all looked at Stanley.

"With, let's say, green eyes?" Corrigan suggested.

Chapter 8

A scream penetrated the hallway wall.

Followed by shouts and running footsteps.

The shatter of heavy plate glass, like restaurant crockery.

"The dispensary door," said Sims.

"Again," said Iris.

"Why do they keep telling us it's shatter-proof?" said Sims.

A long, piercing wail. Then a crash against the hall door, which shivered as if shouldered by a giant.

"Maybe this guy just got his bill," Stanley suggested.

Sounds of a struggle. Muffled curses. Fingernails dragging down the drywall. The ragged onomatopoeia of big zippers. A heart-rending ululation.

Sobbing.

The egg-timer ping of an arriving elevator.

Whispering. A distant shout. Diminishing sobs—abruptly ceased.

Stanley announced that he had more questions.

"So do I," said Corrigan, still watching him.

"I haven't seen any green eyes," said Stanley, meeting Iris' gaze. "Just violet ones."

Iris blushed.

Corrigan groaned.

Sims replaced his glasses on his nose and looked at his watch. "I've got seriously ill patients to attend to. If you people will excuse me..."

"How long before I'm out of here?" Stanley interrupted.

"Well." Sims cleared his throat. "A healthy man like yourself..." He cleared his throat again. "The fact is, at one thousand two hundred and fifty dollars a day — "

"*What?*"

"— you should get well very quickly."

"You've increased my pain."

Sims wagged a finger. "Morphine extra."

A corner of Corrigan's lip raised and exposed the tip of a gold canine, as if he could not help but stare, in sociological horror, at a crime vista exceeding his most grisly experience.

Sims stood at parade rest, the back of one hand covered by the palm of its mate, the clipboard vertical out of it, and regarded Stanley.

"*There but for fortune go I.* Is that what you're thinking, Doctor?"

Corrigan pulled at his lower lip and said nothing. On his face, however, revulsion lingered.

"I want mercy and an itemized bill," Stanley said.

"Mercy is Nurse Considine's duty," said Sims primly. "Itemization is standard."

The door to the hallway opened and a woman looked into the room. She was dressed more or less like Nurse Considine, but the little placard on her breast read Mary Blake, Pathology, and she carried a clipboard not unlike the one in Doctor Sims' hand.

"Dr. Sims," she whispered. "May I see you for a moment?"

"I'm walking out of here tomorrow," said Stanley.

Sims paused in the doorway. "Wheelchairs are down the hall." The door closed silently behind him.

"He's not a bad man," said Iris.

"Just a helpless cog in the system," said Corrigan.

"Helpless or hopeless?"

"The prices aren't his fault."

"Yeah," said Stanley. "A cog, the system, the prices. Good and evil have nothing to do with it."

"Listen, Stanley," said Corrigan. "That hooker's the last we know of your whereabouts last weekend. If you remember anything, here's my card. Call day or night."

The card spun over the foot of the bed and landed on the blanket. Stanley didn't even look at it.

"Inspector, does it even make sense to consider restitution? Or should I laugh, should I cry, should I kiss my kidney goodbye?"

Corrigan sighed. "Right this minute, your kidney could be anywhere from Geneva to Beverly Hills. It might even be in Redwood City. It might still be on ice, getting flushed with some stuff called Ringer's solution, what they call perfused by a special machine designed to keep the organ viable for as long as possible. But the odds are better that your kidney is already walking around again, installed in some clown who had the bucks to purchase a black-market body part. They've got only about three days to use it — five at the outside — after that, the organ is essentially dead."

Iris said, "I'd hate to think it's somewhere in this town."

Stanley considered this.

"You have to realize, Ahearn," Corrigan continued. "It's not as if a guy shows up at a hospital with a ruined kidney in his back and a new one in a jar. The legitimate scenario is, a patient is referred to a clinic that specializes in transplants. The recipient is dealt a number cross-indexing his blood-type, the urgency of his request, and, well..."

"The quality of his insurance coverage?"

"Don't be bitter," said Iris, patting Stanley's hand.

"They don't like to admit to that. Conditions vary all over the world. In an industrialized country with socialized medicine—"

"Which," Iris interrupted, "is all but two." She held up one finger. "The Union of South Africa, and," she held up a second finger, "The United States of America. These are the only so-called first world countries with no nation-wide system of health care — the same two, I might add, that remain committed to capital punishment. Coincidence? I don't think so."

"Lean and mean," said Corrigan.

Iris wiggled the two fingers. "The *company* we keep."

Corrigan cleared his throat. "Thank you, Iris. Although peacefully rolling back apartheid isn't a bad start."

Man, thought Stanley, a cop and a nurse discussing global socioeconomics. Now I know I'm still in San Francisco.

"As I was saying. In an industrialized country with national health care—"

"*Socialism*, mind you," said Iris. "The *shame* of it..."

"Nurse Considine—."

"I'm through," said Iris, taking up Stanley's hand again.

"...National health care... apartheid... what the hell was I talking about?"

Iris winked at Stanley. "Short-term memory loss, Inspector Corrigan. Brought on by jelly doughnuts, instant coffee, and non-dairy creamers."

"In an industrialized country with socialized medicine, everybody is supposed to be treated equally. In a market economy like ours, it's firstest with the mostest. In practice, the two systems average out. In the one the rich guys end-run the system, and in the other case..."

"The rich guys end-run the system," said Iris.

"Yeah, like that. But in the third world, it's really crazy. There're no controls, and it's capitalistic beyond our wildest franchises. As if we had no idea what 'capitalistic' means, here in the States."

"Meaning what?"

"Meaning we're moral about it," said Iris acidly, "and the underdeveloped ignoramuses aren't."

Corrigan rolled his eyes. "Meaning there are third-world clinics where poor people can sell an organ for more money than they're likely to earn otherwise in their entire lives. And who are we to say they shouldn't? But there are the shadier operations, too, into whose clutches these same peasants can fall, thinking it's a legitimate organ-for-cash deal, never to be seen alive again. When a body does turn up, it's a shell. Everything's been harvested and, needless to say, the donor didn't get paid. Another variation is the guy who takes a cab to a clinic for a hangnail and wakes up in a ditch with a nephrectomy. That's the difference between legitimacy and illegitimacy in the third world. The next step is an organization that buys and sells any organ you want. An organ broker. With overnight delivery. You place a purchase order for an out-of-stock organ and they guarantee to have the item for you by a certain date. The only questions asked or answered are when and how much. Forget whose it was and how it was 'donated.' It's half down, half on delivery; end of procurement phase.

"There are clinics from Cairo to Zurich to Bombay to Rio where you can get any organ installed, no questions asked. You can get them removed, too. You can get them turned upside down, exchanged, steam-cleaned. You can get your heroin-saturated blood drained and replaced with the blood of new-born babes. You can get bone-marrow that's been taken from children, sold by their parents. Liver transplants, eyeballs, hearts...."

Corrigan removed a pale white handkerchief from the pocket on the front of his brown jacket and mopped his face with it.

"I tell you Stanley," he said, blowing his nose, "I tell you Stanley…" he examined the kerchief for a moment, then refolded it and stuffed it back into the jacket pocket, "that kidney of yours is nothing."

"Oh, say, thanks, Corrigan," said Iris. "Try to cheer the guy up, why don't you?"

Corrigan raised an eyebrow. "Who, me?"

"No," said Iris disgustedly. "Decidedly *not* you."

"That's okay, Iris," said Stanley. "This is interesting."

"I'll tell you something else, son," Corrigan said darkly, pointing a finger at Stanley. "The supply of replaceable human organs will *never* meet the demand for them. It's a great racket to be in."

Iris read a small wristwatch strapped to the inside of her left wrist. "Personally, I think it's time for your next dose of morphine, Mr. Ahearn."

"Nurse, I —."

"Don't worry sweetie," she said. "In here, it's only nine dollars for fifteen milligrams. You can afford it." She patted his leg and stood up from the bed. "I'll be right back. Shall I get a nice overdose for Inspector Corrigan while I'm at it?" She pulled open the door and left without waiting for an answer.

Corrigan sighed. "Sassy little thing, our Iris. I went to Mercy High with her mother. Two peas in a pod."

Stanley was watching the door as it squeezed to nothing the vertical shaft of light from the hallway. "You've worked with her before?"

Corrigan walked to the window and looked down at the parking lot. "Eight times," he said to the glass.

Stanley looked at his back. "Eight?"

Corrigan didn't respond.

"I'm the ninth?"

Silence.

"Inspector?"

Corrigan filled his trouser pockets with his hands and shrugged. "We figure Iris might pick up something from the victims that might otherwise elude us. She's been the nurse on every case."

"Were they all kidneys?"

Corrigan nodded.

"They all survived?"

He shrugged.

"You've solved none of them?"

Corrigan ducked his chin and scrubbed one cheek on the shoulder of his jacket. It sounded like someone cleaning upholstery with a wire brush.

The door admitted Sims. This time he had two clipboards with him, and a disturbed look on his face.

"Mr. Ahearn."

"Why, Dr. Sims, at last you seem upset."

"What's the matter?" said Iris, following him into the room.

"Maybe they socialized medicine," said Stanley.

Corrigan turned away from the window.

Sims took a deep breath. "I've just been handed this report from Pathology."

"Yes?"

Sims looked as if he were about to faint.

"So?" said Stanley, annoyed. "Is something wrong? I mean, is something *else* wrong?"

Even as he said it, everybody in the room realized that, yes, something else was wrong.

Sims opened his mouth and moved his lips. No sound. His face turned red. He shook his head and moved his lips again. No syllables emerged.

Summoning what remained of his resolve, Stanley said weakly, "Out with it!"

"Mr. Ahearn," Sims blurted. "How long have you had amyloidosis?"

Silence filled the room.

Finally Stanley asked, "How long have I what?"

"I'll tell you," said Sims, adjusting his glasses. He appeared to study one of his clipboards. Before long he realized it was the wrong one. He quickly covered it with the second clipboard and began the study over again.

"Don't be so nervous," said Stanley. "I might get the idea you made a mistake I can sue you for."

"One to two years."

"One to two years? For what?"

"You've had amyloidosis — or the condition that precipitates it — for one to two years."

"What did you call it?"

"Amyloidosis."

"It sounds like Gaelic square dancing."

Corrigan and Iris nodded.

Sims nodded morosely. "I wish it were, Mr. Ahearn."

Everybody waited.

"Just relax, Doctor Sims," said Corrigan soothingly. "Take your time. Take a deep breath. Maybe even walk around the block. Ahearn's not going anywhere. Just let him twist in the wind."

"Right," said Sims, snapping out of his humanistic reverie. "It's a chronic, underlying disease of the kidneys."

"Kidney," Stanley corrected.

Sims continued quietly, "It could be collateral with or systematic of tuberculosis — which we automatically ruled out when we let you in here — which leaves," he cleared his throat, "rheumatoid arthritis or multiple myeloma."

Stanley stared at Sims long enough to make Sims even more uncomfortable. Finally, Sims held up the two clipboards, and said, "On the bright side, you're HIV negative."

He didn't even smile.

"Oh, you *idiot*," said Iris.

Sims appeared very innocent.

"Why don't you just rub his face in it?" Iris continued.

"I just want him to feel better," said Sims lamely. "I thought…"

"Don't try to think," Iris shouted, "before you can crawl!"

Sims was truly puzzled by this remark. "Do you mean… emotionally? Crawl emotionally…?"

Iris stamped her foot in exasperation. "Oh!" she finally said, and, turning on the very heel she'd stamped, left the room.

The three men looked every way but at each other for a moment, in total silence.

Finally, Stanley made a suggestion. "Help me get this straight."

Corrigan advanced from the window, watching Sims.

"You mean to tell me, Sims, that my kidneys are… my kidney is… sick?"

"Kidney," Sims timidly held up a forefinger, "Yes. Singular, is… no good." He shook his head. "Bad kidney. No good…"

"Is this a puppy or a kidney, goddamn it? How no good?"

"Very no good."

"You mean, like, *completely* no good?"

"Potentially fatal."

A bolus of mucus seemed to be caught in Stanley's throat. His right ear was ringing. The room seemed to be tilting at an odd angle.

From beyond the door came the egg-timer ping of an arriving elevator.

"Sims. You can fix this?"

"I didn't say that."

"Can someone else fix this?"

"Maybe."

"Wait a minute," said Corrigan. "Could this mean the other kidney, the missing one, was diseased too?"

"Almost certainly," Sims confirmed.

"Correct me if I'm wrong," Corrigan said thoughtfully. "This means that these people who stole Ahearn's kidney have stolen something they can't use?"

Sims nodded. "That's exactly what it means."

"Good," Stanley said, through clenched teeth. "The bastards."

Sims adjusted his glasses. "It's not a good idea to open up someone to remove their diseased kidney and replace it with another diseased kidney, no matter how sick they are. Yes. A terrible waste of the patient's energy, not to mention the surgeon's. A waste of money too. Useless. It would be very like replacing a worn out fuel pump on a car with another worn out fuel pump. To take another example—"

"Okay, okay," grumbled Corrigan.

Stanley managed a grim smile. "That's a tough break for the bad guys."

"That's your point of view," Sims said primly. "What if the thieves didn't care whether it was diseased or not? Let's go one step further and ask, what if the people who are receiving the stolen kidney don't care whether they install diseased kidneys or not? All anybody's interested in is the money."

Corrigan shook his head. "Bad for business. My money says they're stuck with it."

"They couldn't spot the condition when they opened me up?"

"Not amyloidosis," said Sims. "You'd need a biopsy to detect it."

"You know," said Corrigan, "there's another interesting angle."

"What's that?" said Stanley.

"They let you live. They try to let their victims live. If they've lost a single patient I've yet to hear about it. Although," he added darkly, "that doesn't mean it hasn't happened. There are ways to disappear a body. But think of it."

"I can hardly think of anything else."

"To evade murder charges, they're taking a tremendous risk. What if the donor saw something, or remembered something?" He looked at Stanley.

Stanley looked at him.

"That's true," said Sims. "Patients often remember unlikely details from their surgical procedures."

"Is that so," said Stanley mildly.

"Yes," said Sims earnestly. "While theoretically unconscious, while machines are controlling their cardio-pulmonary functions entirely, patients are able to recall details that are surprisingly accurate. They remember that the anesthesiologist was a black man, or that the walls in the O.R. were green, or that the surgeon requested Mozart, or that a nurse was wearing pink sneakers. One patient filed a lawsuit because she overheard the entire surgical team discussing how fat she was while they were operating on her."

"You're kidding," said Stanley, as ingenuously as seemed credible.

"I never kid."

Stanley could believe that. "Did she win?"

"Are you kidding?"

"As much as possible."

"Hey," said Sims, "you're talking aggravated distress in the extreme. Beyond the pale. Not only could she hear what they were saying about her, she could feel the pain of the knife, too. But the partial anesthesia rendered her unable to move or speak."

"Jesus," said Stanley.

"Ouch," winced Corrigan. "What kind of surgery was it?"

"Full knee-joint replacement."

"My God."

"She won the case," said Stanley.

Sims nodded. "It never saw the inside of a courtroom." He shrugged. "The point is, under such circumstances inexplicably random, isolated details somehow filter in through the anesthetized senses."

"Little details like mind-searing pain," said Corrigan.

"But I would think," Stanley said, "in a case where they were stealing a part of the patient's body, if the patient were a victim, if he had obviously returned to consciousness, if he could see and hear the perpetrators, why then..."

"They'd have to ice him," concluded Corrigan, watching Stanley.

"Yes," Stanley agreed thoughtfully. "They'd have to ice him."

"They probably wished they'd iced the fat lady," said Sims.

The hallway door opened to admit Iris, who pushed a cart before her. "Okay you professional jerks," she said. "It's time to work on the patient's health. Everybody out."

Sims stood aside. Iris wheeled the cart up next to the side of the bed. "We'll keep feeding him, Iris," Sims said, "but the oxygen and the catheter can go. Did Nuñez put on the ascorbic acid?"

Nurse Considine scanned a pink clipboard on top of the cart. "Yes, doctor."

"Pedameth?"

"Yes."

He held out his hand. Iris handed him the pink schedule.

"Mmmm... serum... potassium... I reckon we can dispose of the hemoglobin, hematocrit, urinalysis..."

Sims made a few notes and, drawing blue lines down the front of his breast pocket, returned the clipboard to Iris. "I'll be looking in on you in the morning, Mr. Ahearn. Try to get better in the meantime." He assumed a smile. "After all, a sick man can't very well get to work and pay his bills." He stopped short. Iris groaned. Sims' smile faded. "We could use a few more tests — angiogram, maybe bone marrow just to clear up that business about the myeloma, a scintigram even, but," he shrugged, "you have no money." He grimaced. "Should get to the bottom of that amyloidosis, though." He looked up suddenly. "Had a physical lately? Who's your G.P.?"

Stanley stared into a middle distance.

Sims was shocked. "But it says here you're forty-seven years old. You've *got* to have a physical..." His voice trailed off.

After a silence in which everyone pursued his own thoughts—of mortality, of actuarial tables, of flexible sigmoidoscopy—Sims straightened, suddenly crisp. "Good day." He took the second clipboard and left the room.

"Guy's one of the biggest jerks in the hospital," said Iris before the door had even closed. "But he's a renal ace."

"I'll be around to see you again," said Corrigan. "While you concentrate on healing yourself, try to recall what details you can about last weekend. Also, are there any strange new people among your recent acquaintances? Any failed medical students? Anybody who suddenly has more money than they should? Any hookers dressed beyond their meager means?"

"Corrigan," snapped Iris firmly. "Out."

"Think on them especially," Corrigan said. "As my mother always said, you can't entirely trust a girl who spends all her time out of doors. Good night, Iris." He left.

"Like my mother still says," Iris said after the door closed. "He's all cop. Good for very little else."

The door opened again. "And consider this," Corrigan stuck his head and shoulders into the room and pointed a finger at Stanley. "Sometime this week or next, somewhere in this town, some poor schlub is going to go missing a kidney in exactly the same way as you have. And it's going to go on like that, week in and week out, until we stop them."

The door swung shut.

Iris busied herself with the cart. Stanley watched her. After a minute had gone by he said, "He told me he went to high school with your mother."

"That he did."

"Were they sweet on each other?"

"Nobody's talking. But after my dad died he was very attentive, very helpful. They go to the movies. Sometimes he stays over. It suits them to pretend I don't know."

"When did your dad die?"

"A long time ago."

"Your mother never remarried?"

"Never."

"Brothers and sisters?"

"Four."

"That's a tough road for your mother."

"She became a CPA and put three of us through college."

"Hard work."

Iris said nothing to this, but busied herself around the wheeled cart.

The room had long since darkened as evening closed down on the city outside the window, and now only the television and a light from the bathroom door provided illumination. The cartoon on the television had elided into a rehash of various Olympic highlights. Young girls cartwheeled on the balance beam, fireworks exploded, men and women and even claymation beer bottles swam above an underwater camera. The constant motion was enough to churn anybody's stomach, let alone Stanley's. He asked Iris to turn it off. She retrieved a remote control from a drawer in the nightstand and squeezed it toward the television. The picture died.

"Thanks," said Stanley, his face obscured by darkness. "That's a beautiful blank picture."

"It is," she agreed cheerfully. "But it's the morphine that makes you irritable. It's wearing off. I'll show you. First, let's get rid of this."

She peeled a bit of adhesive tape off his upper lip and removed the breathing tubes from his nose.

"Most people would complain about that," she said.

She took up a package from the top of the cart and began to unwrap it. The noise of tearing paper wracked Stanley's nerves. The little snaps and pops made by the latex gloves as she drew them over her delicate hands seemed unnecessarily loud.

"Do you have to make so much noise?" he said.

She smiled and held up her gloved hands. "All set." She retrieved a syringe from the cart and removed its needle's protective sleeve. "This is the morphine. The first of three injections."

"Three?"

"Three. Show me that arm. There's my hero."

"Don't call me that."

She dabbed at the arm with a cotton swab. "This one's intramuscular," she said, leaning over to apply the needle. "You don't have to watch," she said. Her eyes were about ten inches from his.

"What is it about you?" he asked.

"We have the same blood type," she suggested cozily.

"Is that true?"

"As a matter of fact, it is. I saw it on your chart."

"So our children are going to be perfect?"

She smiled. "Why don't you like to be called a hero?"

"Because I'm not a hero. Anyone would have done what I did."

"Maybe." She slid the needle beneath his skin, depressed the plunger, removed the needle, and swabbed the little wound with alcohol.

"Why do you hide your hands in those gloves?"

"Hygiene, silly. Why do you care?" She capped the used syringe, dropped it into a receptacle on the lower tray of the cart, and took up a freshly charged one.

"You have lovely hands. It's a shame to hide them."

She sat on the edge of the bed and swabbed his arm again. "This is an antibiotic. Also I.M." She smoothly injected the serum and swabbed the puncture. "I'll let you call my hands lovely if you'll let me call you hero," she said, dropping the second instrument into the receptacle. She added, almost wistfully, "My scarred hero…"

"That's not a fair trade," he said irritably. She turned back with the third syringe.

"Now what?"

"Vitamins." With her face turned toward him and away from the light her eyes gleamed in shadow, framed by the silhouette of her hair and cap. "What's fair have to do with it?"

The morphine had begun to socialize with his metabolism. "Okay," Stanley said, with a small sigh of relief. "I'll try to explain. Lovely hands are more or less permanent. Heroism is a transitory thing, a product of the moment that engendered it. You do it, then you've got to get on with the business of life. True heroism is not a spontaneous act but a continuous one, like getting up and going to work every day instead of blowing your brains out. Like what your mother probably had to do for you and your brothers and sisters after your dad died. I'm no hero, but I'll bet your mother is." He took one of her hands, peeled the rim of the latex glove back to the base of her fingers, and began to trace the delicate intricacy of the veins on the back of her hand. "A lot of people are heroic, or have heroic attributes. But not that many people have lovely hands." He looked up at her. She watched him. A moment passed.

"See?" Stanley said.

She suddenly kissed him.

Stanley was so surprised he didn't react.

"This is top-flight medical care," he finally whispered.

"No it's not," she said. "My hands are shaking enough to ruin you with this needle."

"Ruin me."

She did a fine job.

"Why did you kiss me?"

"I don't know. Maybe I take my heroes where I find them."

"That's no answer."

"I'll take it up with Stress Management," she said, dropping the third syringe into the disposal bin. "Speaking of which, we now remove the catheter."

"We what?" he said, gripping the bedclothes.

"Don't be afraid," she said, gently freeing the edge of the blanket from his fingers. "I can do it with my eyes closed." She drew away the edge of the blanket, along with the sheet beneath it, until it was below his knees.

"It's a boy," she said.

"I thought you said you could do it with your eyes closed."

"I can."

"I wish you would," he said.

"Why?"

"I'm shy, that's why."

"You don't look very shy."

"That was a dirty trick, kissing me first."

"It was not," she said. "Do you feel the morphine yet?"

"As a matter of fact, I feel like a man with a million dollars and two kidneys. Definitely delusive."

"The patient's irritation with slight disturbances seems to have turned into enjoyment."

"Why are we whispering?"

"You haven't the strength to shout." She stood up. "Well. This won't hurt so much."

She began to busy herself. The room had darkened considerably, illumined only by the light from the bathroom door. He closed his eyes. The sensation of his lids descending was as pleasurable as it was unavoidable. The morphine must have been doing its job, for all Stanley felt was the remote impression that, a certain distance away, somebody was boning a fish while it was head down in an umbrella stand.

He heard a clatter of equipment on the lower tray of the stainless steel cart. "There," Iris said. "All set." So pleasurable was the relief flooding his system that Stanley neglected to open his eyes at this news. Rather, he savored the distant clarion of retreat from the pain in his back. He heard the cart roll away from the bed. Realizing that she might be about to leave he forced narrow slits between his eyelids. Contrary to leaving the room, she had parked the cart directly in front of the hallway door. So that anyone attempting to enter would find the door blocked?

Her shadow moved back toward the bed, with a rustle of starched fabric. Reassured, he closed his eyes again. The bedclothes whispered about him, and the crisp hospital sheet nestled beneath his chin. Iris hadn't yet left him, he realized happily, she was tucking him in.

She sat on the edge of the bed, and new sensations began to communicate themselves to him. These, too, were remote, indistinct at first; but they were discernibly, pleasurable. Languorous, even.

When she placed one hand on his brow, and smoothed back his hair, he could barely open his eyes. The light from the bathroom door was blocked by her silhouette.

"You'll be able to use that thing in about a week," she said.

Chapter 9

The next day Hop Toy turned up at the hospital and paid for everything. Stanley let him, but only on the condition that Hop Toy get him out of there immediately. Dr. Sims assured Hop Toy that Stanley would be fine, if only he stayed in bed or a wheelchair for another week or two. Iris promised to look in on Stanley and keep his prescriptions current. So they let Hop Toy and his nephew Fong drive Stanley to Chinatown in the back of the delivery pickup, parked like a home-coming queen in a belayed wheelchair among sacks of onions and Jerusalem artichokes, thin-slatted crates of bok choy and lettuce, and the heaped fasces of asparagus spears.

Before Stanley left the hospital Corrigan dropped by to see if his memory had improved, which it hadn't. When nobody was looking Iris gave him a shot of morphine and a kiss that, later and often, would prove there was nothing wrong with Stanley's memory at all. When the little white hat got slightly askew her black hair fell down in ringlets.

Hop Toy had no intention of letting some strange professionals take care of Stanley Ahearn. He paraded Stanley straight through Chinatown to the apartment building on Brooklyn Place, where he'd installed Stanley three years before. All the way from Children's on California to Stockton Street, while Fong drove, Hop Toy talked out the back window of the truck cab, assuring Stanley that he needn't worry about his job, that it would be waiting for him when he got better, that

Hop Toy's wife Ruth would bring him three meals a day until he'd recovered, and that, as usual, the rent was a problem to be forgotten.

Much as he'd grown to appreciate the Hop Toy family, Stanley would have preferred to be alone.

But the Hop Toy family had other ideas. The shack squatted atop a narrow apartment building that faced Brooklyn Place. Hop Toy had tried to convince Stanley to take a nicer place a couple stories down, an actual apartment, but one look had sold Stanley on the shack. Originally built as a wash-house, the shed was a rectangular structure with four walls encompassing about three hundred square feet. Except for its tin roof the whole thing was made of unpainted wood long since weathered to gray. One long side of the rectangle was ten feet high and consisted of the entrance door and, from waist-high sills up to the modest header beneath the exposed rafters, a wall of windows facing east. On a clear day Stanley could see Mt. Diablo, forty miles away, and every other day he could be content with portions, allotted him by the fog, of the Bay Bridge, Berkeley, Treasure Island, North Beach, a large stretch of the Bay and, of course, the thirty or so top floors of the TransAmerica Pyramid, which tapered up from its block-square footprint a mere six blocks away.

Except on wash day. Being an enlightened landlord, Hop Toy had long since installed washing machines in the building's basement. Excepting Stanley, every single one of the rest of the building's occupants was Chinese. Some of them were quite old, having fled mainland China to escape the Communists or the Japanese, Yuan Shih-K'ai or Sun Yat-Sen or, for all Stanley knew, The Opium Wars. In Chinatown English was not a necessity, and since most of the elders rarely if ever left the vicinity, many of them had never bothered to learn to speak English.

Much as they clung to their language, many of these same elders shared a compulsion about drying freshly washed clothes in fresh air. They loved the machines that washed, but they sniffed suspiciously at the machines that dried, judged them a poor improvement, and insisted on carrying every load of wet wash five stories to the roof to hang them out in San Francisco's famous afternoon westerly—a sea breeze that can bluster to twenty or thirty knots, enough to dry a soaked bed sheet in fifteen minutes.

Hop Toy had no conception of privacy, but he went so far as to respect Stanley's desire for it. So Hop Toy declared Tuesday, and no other, Drying Day.

By noon or one o'clock every Tuesday Stanley's roof became a colorful, flapping cacophony of drying laundry.

Still, since he was at least a head taller than any woman in the building could reach to pinch a clothespin, even on Tuesday Stanley could stand on his roof and look out over the topography of his island of laundry and see the distant landmarks of the San Francisco Bay. From one of those landmarks he and his busy neighbors must have looked like a gang of pollen-bearers working the petals of a mutant, wind-blown flower.

The rest of the week he had the roof to himself.

A white-enameled cast-iron countertop ran the length of the south gable wall, surmounted by a four-burner butane stovetop and a plastic dishrack above an integral drainboard and sink. The north wall backed floor-to-ceiling shelves. The west wall, only eight feet, had foot-high clerestory windows above a platform bed. The furnishings consisted of two dissimilar caved-in Victorian easy-chairs, a bok choy crate with a small rabbit-eared television on it, and a nearly empty bottle of Bushmills planted on the floor next to the empty chair. The other chair was usually covered with *Chronicles* and *Examiners* drifting out from under a pile of laundry, because until his "accident" Stanley never invited any visitors to sit with him.

Outside, just around the corner from the front door, a five-gallon roofing-tar bucket covered by a Cadillac hubcap made do for the short trips to the toilet necessitated by whiskey and bad kidneys. The real toilet, with a corner-closet and a fiberglass shower cabinet with a mildewed curtain that looked like it had started out as the downhill half of a body bag, was one story down. Except for the curtain, the family of eight he shared it with kept the bathroom clean. And when one of them happened to run into him as he brought the bucket down to empty it into the corner closet, they would always smile, and ask him how the weather was.

And he always answered, "Beautiful, just beautiful."

And often he was telling the truth.

There was no elevator. Hop Toy and Fong and two others took turns in pairs dragging and lifting him and the wheelchair up the stairs, one flight at a time, with a cigarette break every flight.

"Hop Toy," Stanley said, to the shoulders of the man below them all on the stairs.

"Try not to speak," Hop Toy gasped. "You might tire yourself."

It had taken nearly all of the first year since Stanley had saved Hop Toy's daughter for the two of them to strike a balance between the generosity of Hop Toy's gratitude and Stanley's capacity to accept it. While the former seemed boundless, the latter was definitely limited. A job and a place to live, extended to a man who needed both, seemed more than fair to Stanley, and he'd said so. But now, with his needs so clear, Hop Toy found new opportunity.

They deposited Stanley on the roof. For the first time in ten days a stiff breeze freshened his nostrils. Then he saw his own bedsheets flapping from a clothesline, and figures moving about in his home.

Followed by Fong and the two others Hop Toy pushed the wheelchair to the door of the shack. The door was open, and inside stood Tseng, who was now eleven years old, and her mother, Ruth. They welcomed him, and he was glad to see them.

Tseng climbed into his lap and gave him a big kiss. She smelled of fresh mint and ginger and clean laundry. Was this Tuesday? He wasn't sure. Hop Toy wheeled them both over the splintered threshold and into position before the television set. Somebody had removed the two easy-chairs to the roof so that there was room for the wheelchair. The smells of garlic, peppers, chicken, rice, diced scallions, black bean sauce and even fried onion cake wafted through the room. The countertops around the stove and the little table before it were heaped with fresh vegetables and saucepans and cooking utensils. A wok stood over a butane flame next to a pot of rice and in front of a pot of tea and, even as Hop Toy parked Stanley in front of a Chinese news program chattering on the television set, Ruth, talking the while, began to spill spatulas covered with smoked ham and spices and chopped vegetables into the wok, where hot sesame oil made them sizzle. If these people knew all about making someone feel at home, they also knew how to work. The mother and daughter had swept the floor and washed all the windows. They had cleaned the kitchen and filled the shelves with groceries. They had found the extra set of sheets and made the bed with them and washed the old sheets, which Stanley probably hadn't changed in a month. They had done all his laundry and put it away, neatly folded. They had brought in the mail and complete runs of *Chronicles* and *Examiners* since he'd been in the hospital. They had planted flowers, Stanley noticed at last, in the neglected boxes that hung below the sills of the east-facing windows. Blooming pansies and geraniums nodded fitfully in the lee of the building.

People began to appear from downstairs. Several old folks walked in without ceremony, trailing grandchildren. They all spoke to Stanley and made him understand they were glad to see him home. The men squatted on the roof or sat in the two armchairs in the lee of the shack and smoked. The plumes from their cigarettes rose briefly and then shot away on the westerly, toward the Pyramid. After a while one among the men produced a deck of cards and dealt a hand of Pai Gow, the cards so creased and worn they drooped as if made of cloth instead of cardboard. The women came in and sat or stood around the table and gossiped. Someone turned up the television set.

Much of this commotion, including that on the television, was borne along on Chinese, a language of which Stanley had managed to learn very little in three years.

"Now that we've got you out of that hospital," said Hop Toy, switching to English for a moment, "we can care for you properly. The food in any hospital is no good. They take everything good out of it. Garlic, pepper, ginger — these things are good for a man. Can you imagine giving a man medicine, yet withholding from him his ginseng? There in the hospital, they act like they don't know that food is medicine. They cut you off from the healing power of good food. Good food keeps you well when you are well, and heals you when you are sick. Hospital food is no good."

Stanley agreed with him. The family that had brought Hop Toy to the United States as a little boy were from the Hu Nan province, whose food was reputed to be hot, spicy, and wholesome. But they eschewed nothing edible, so far as Stanley could tell; any kind of vegetable, fish, fowl or meat, the Hu Nan kitchen could countenance it, and prepare it well. Stanley had become a fond believer. The last time he'd had the flu, it had been a bad case, with vomiting, diarrhea, vertigo, hot and cold flashes, night sweats. A bowl of Ruth's hot and sour bean curd soup could stave off the symptoms for two hours.

"Tomorrow, a Chinese doctor comes to study you," Hop Toy said. "He will list herbs for tea and soup to make you heal quickly." He patted Stanley's knee. "You will soon be well."

Stanley looked around him. There were kids wrestling and squealing on his plywood bed. Bowls of food and rice stood steaming on his little round kitchen table. He may as well have been related to all of these people, so attentive were they to his distress.

Little Tseng came running up with a bowl of food. Before Stanley knew it Ruth's sister had tucked a cloth napkin under his chin and threaded a pair of chopsticks through his knuckles. The bowl was heaped with sliced carrots, scallions, bamboo shoots, boned chicken, and whole shrimp—all piled on a heap of steamed white rice, and shot through with short yellow skeins of fried egg flecked with bits of the red skins of hot cayenne peppers. The moment the fragrant steam rose from the dish and struck his nostrils his mouth started to water, and the aroma quickly supplanted the taste of ether-saturated mucus that had permeated his senses for the past week.

He chopsticked the hot, rice-covered morsels into his mouth Chinese style, a rapid one-two-three, chew and swallow, one-two-three, chew and swallow.

"Good?" said Hop Toy, his eager smile not ten inches away. "Hot?"

Indeed, the food was hot, both in temperature and spice. Tears sprang to Stanley's eyes as he swallowed. He chopsticked up another mouthful, and another, and another. Several of the old women around the kitchen table cooed their encouragement. Tseng stood before him and watched him eat. She wore a pink dress and her jet black hair was caught in blue ribbons on either side of her head, just above her ears. A bowl of tea appeared on top of the television in front of him, steaming with warmth and shimmering with the abruptness of its arrival. Hop Toy made a comment to Tseng, who laughed with delight, and showed her perfect teeth. And then Hop Toy fired a request toward his wife, who had begun to circulate bowls of food and chopsticks among the women around her. These objects began to move as if of their own accord toward the door and out among the men on the rooftop, and Ruth paused at the source of this brigade to retrieve a beer from the under-counter refrigerator beneath the drainboard. The bottle passed among the hands and over the heads of the chattering women to Hop Toy, who twisted off its cap and set it next to the cup of tea on top of the nattering television. Steam lifted off the surface of the tea. Beads of moisture trailed down and over Hop Toy's fingerprints on the bottle. Beneath them both, the television picture slowly rolled.

Stanley considered the two vessels. Various people considered him.

He transferred the bowl of food and the chopsticks to one hand and reached for the bowl of tea, but the sutures tugged and he drew back. At the table, two women stopped talking.

Stanley shifted in the wheelchair, stuck out his hand again, and retrieved the beer bottle.

The two great-grandmothers at the kitchen table murmured approvingly.

Stanley applied the mouth of the bottle to his own mouth and turned it up. The beer filled his mouth, surfed a shrimp down his throat, and left his tongue and cheeks tingling with spices and bubbles and coolness.

When he turned down the bottle he exclaimed, "Ahhhhh!" and smiled broadly.

Tseng, Hop Toy, his wife, the two old ladies at the kitchen table and Fong, watching from the open front door, cheered and applauded.

The last shot of morphine that Iris had kindly administered Stanley, just before Hop Toy had wheeled him out the door, was nearly worn off now, but the irritability that came along with its deliquescence was nowhere to be remarked. He had a few bottles of pills in a pouch slung over the side of the wheelchair, but he would take them only later, much later tonight, when Hop Toy and his wife and daughter and all of his neighbors and their children had gone home, when the pain of the unexpected incision in his lower back would come to reassert itself —along with the solitary habituations of whiskey, television, insomnia, now complemented by the enforced contemplation of his looming mortality.

The next week, maybe the week after, he wasn't sure when or how, but, one day soon, he would begin to seek a certain woman about a certain kidney.

Fucking Up
At Someone
Else's Expense

Chapter 10

Excepting a few props, the City Clinic for Sexually Transmitted Diseases looked like any other over-used and understaffed information dump run by a metropolitan government. Given the microfiche viewer and a few rolls of plans, the interchangeable bureaucrats and computers, olive drab wastebaskets and four-color cat posters, the water dispenser that sounds like the first aqualung, fluorescent lights that hum like a tramline, the vast indestructible linoleum floor that undulates over its post-quake substrate like the swell on a checkerboard sea, the ringing telephones, the mutter of a hundred hushed voices, monuments of paper, and the terrible clock staring down on it all—the clinic might just as easily have been the bureau at which to apply for a building or parking or parade permit, a dispensation from jury duty, or to find a map to any gas line in town.

Since the city wide ban on smoking in the workplace ("Effective February 1, 1994: To get help dial 1-800-QUIT NOW…") the waiting room to which smoking previously had been ghettoed had assumed the exhausted neutral air of a neglected solarium in a convalescent hospital, where a dying ficus drooped in a corner like a badly laundered shirt next to a rack of two-color pamphlets vaunting the appropriate issues—just about everything that can happen to a human body as a result of unprotected sex.

Waiting for test results without smoking while reading about how your appendages might be rotting from the inside out requires nerves of Kevlar. To alleviate suspense for the literate and ennui for the illiterate, the City Clinic for Sexually Transmitted Diseases had commissioned a videotaped lecture for its waiting patients, entitled "A Brief, Illustrated History of Sexually Transmitted Diseases," narrated by a noted Mark Twain impersonator.

But what distinguished this waiting room from those of other municipal bureaus was the litter of pink squares of paper strewn about its floor by day's end. Lending a distinctly parimutuel aspect to the room, without the smells of cigars and horse manure, these particular pink slips told a remarkably analogous tale of chance, misfortune, and the miraculous.

A preliminary interview between case worker and client precipitated such a sheet of pink paper, with a varying number of its pre-printed boxes checked according to the tests required. Upon concluding this interview, the patient carried the test requests to a nurse within the warren of examining rooms at the opposite end of the building—thereby passing again through the waiting room, with its street exit.

HIV testing had become a standard request on the form. Depending on symptoms described or exhibited there were many other tests, none no more unpleasant than the drawing of blood. But no test was so nerve-wracking as that for the presence of the human immunodeficiency virus, with its freight of imminent doom. Thus at the end of a given day, the litter of pink slips represented a sum-total of the persons who had lost their nerve at the last moment, who had decided not to follow through with the HIV test, spontaneously shedding the pink form and its onerous potential, preferring to hit the door to the street beyond which fresh air might be greedily inhaled, and with it the dubious comfort of an ambiguous future.

Stanley had been here three months before. Now he was back, because, until three weeks ago, outside of some functionary or computer inside this clinic, nobody else in the world could know that his blood type was O-Negative.

He had quickly divined the meaning of the pink litter. He'd made a little joke to himself concerning the cliché of what a pink slip meant to somebody who had a regular job, as opposed to what it meant to somebody about to discover his real job was called Life. He'd even had the time to wonder about the sense of humour of the bureaucrat who'd chosen the color. But, today at least, the pink slips reminded him not of the dozen or so people he already knew to have been killed by AIDS; rather, they reminded him of what it had been like, once, to have good health—of what it had been like to smell brisk salt air without wheezing, to piss but twice or three times a day and that without wincing, to drink all night and weep not at all.... Such was health, that condition most people don't realize they're in until they aren't in it anymore.

McAllister Street was the second or third location for this clinic in as many decades. Its very existence had once been predicated on the sexual mores of the late sixties. Stanley remembered those days, when sexually transmitted diseases were rarely more insidious than various more or less microscopic insects. When all was innocence mitigated by sympathy. And at some later midnight you'd meet your case worker, standing on line outside Winterland.

The next in severity were yeast infections, non-specific urethritis, syphilis, gonorrhea—most of them curable by a course of antibiotics concomitant with abstinence from sex and alcohol, usually for about two weeks. If taking yet another pill was cause for no surprise among one's peers, abstinence confirmed upon its victim a certain beatification. No social stigma accrued.

Toward the end of the war, diseases unknown to Western medicine began to appear. There were rumors of sprawling clandestine military hospitals in Japan devoted exclusively to the warehousing of Vietnam veterans with untreatable venereal diseases, and of devices like rotary-blade catheters and urethral-wart-cauterizers used to treat them.

"Cures were developed or they weren't," the videotape said. "Venereal warts were dealt with, but *herpes simplex* wasn't. Unless they wanted to pretend they were in the nineteenth century, and indulge themselves in mercury baths and tertiary symptoms (madness, arthritis, good poetry, bad philosophy, death), only through sheer neglect could a sexually transmitted disease kill a free-love hippie or a bathhouse homosexual.

"There were consequences, of course. Life is a series of consequences. Women, for instance, who had experienced variety and number in their sexual partners, later often encountered difficulty in conception...."

And scars on the soul? Stanley thought sourly.

"...By the middle eighties, Acquired Immune Deficiency Syndrome had changed American sexual behavior forever. Unprotected sex became the moral equivalent of Russian roulette, consummated with the fervidity of a pre-emptory funeral rite. The United States, the most developed country in the world, ironically found its official self reluctant to recognize the symptoms of AIDS, or to commit funds to study it. A coldly calculated political decision was taken. To commit resources to the virtually unrealizable proposition of using ground-based laser beams bounced off orbiting mirrors to knock down intercontinental missiles in flight—in order to protect less than 10% of the world's population—was deemed more important than undertaking to discover a solution to a plague threatening 100% of the world's population. For eight long years, the term AIDS was not uttered in public by a Federal official...."

Stanley's number was called. They used numbers here, at least at first, in order to preserve privacy.

Stanley limped down an aisle along one side of a field of shoulder-high partitions, within which hummed a colony of case workers, interviewers, health officials, nurse-practitioners, and perhaps, somewhere deep within, an actual doctor or two.

And perhaps a criminal or two?

The case worker wore a tie and a button-down collar beneath a sleeveless sweater-vest, was clean-shaven, Caucasian, his hair not so closely cropped he couldn't neatly comb it. Though he wasn't twenty-five years old, a little gold-rimmed pair of half-lens reading glasses perched on the tip of his nose, and from them depended a beaded lanyard.

"Ah, Mr. Fifty-six," he smiled, waving at an empty wooden chair in front of his desk as he peered over the top edge of Stanley's pink slip. "Ahearn, that is, what seems to be troubling you today?"

Hopeful. They always start out hopeful. A functionary such as this man, this boy, this boy above all, knew he might most immediately serve his client as a direct portal to damnation.

"Nothing specific," Stanley said, taking a seat. "I've, uh, got a new girlfriend and we've reached that stage in our relationship where we, uh, think it would be a good idea if we both got checked out for, you know... Everything."

"An excellent idea, Mr. Ahearn. And is your girlfriend with you today?"

"No," said Stanley, "she prefers to use her own physician. She'll probably get a little more thorough workup, fitted for birth control, and whatnot."

"I see. Here's a pamphlet on that very subject, Mr. Ahearn." He pushed it across the desk.

Stanley let it lay. "I thought I'd take some notes." He showed the clerk a pen and a little spiral notebook.

"That's fine."

"You're called...?"

"Oh, forgive me." The young man reached an open palm over his desk. "Giles MacIntosh."

"Hey," said Stanley, shaking the hand. "Like the computer."

"Well, it's spelled differently..." He spelled it. "But yes," sighed Giles, not smiling. "Like the computer."

"Oh, sorry," said Stanley, jotting the correct spelling. "I'll bet you hear that one every day."

"Apology accepted, Mr. Ahearn..."

"You can call me Stanley."

"Nice to meet you." Giles poised his hand with its mate above his computer keyboard. "And have you visited us before, Stanley?"

"Yes." Stanley adjusted his chair so he could watch the computer screen. "I was in here... Let me see..."

"No matter, Stanley," said Giles, his fingers flying over the keyboard. "Let's see what your name brings up."

"Wow," said Stanley. "You're a fast typist."

"A hundred and twenty words a minute," Giles said proudly. "I used to be a travel agent. Speed was everything."

Stanley radiated admiration. "With how many mistakes?"

Giles feigned a frown. "No mistakes at all, Mr. Ahearn. What possible good would a mistake be to a reputable travel agent? You wouldn't want to book a flight for Moscow and wind up in Puerto Vallarta, would you?"

"I believe I would."

"Ah ha. Very funny. Here we are. Ahearn, Stanley Clarke. You visited us about three months ago. Your case worker was a Ms. Dunkirk. Correct?"

"Yes. That sounds right."

"And your mother's maiden name, please?"

"Smith."

"Thank you, Stanley. Let's see. Measles, chicken pox, herpes simplex..."

Stanley shifted his chair, and the computer screen suddenly went blank. The whine of the hard drive lowered in pitch like a descending bottle rocket.

"Whoops," said Stanley.

"Oh, no," said Giles, his face falling in direct proportion to the rotational momentum of the disk. "What happened?"

"Damn, Giles," said Stanley, shuffling his feet beneath Giles' desk. "My foot's become entangled in the power cord. I fear I've unplugged you. Dreadfully sorry."

Giles pushed back his chair and looked under the desk.

"So you have, Stanley. Let's untangle it."

"I'm sorry. Here, let me…"

"No, no. I'll get it."

Giles crawled under the desk, uncoiled a loop of cord from around Stanley's ankle, and plugged in the machine again.

"I'm afraid I'm a little nervous," Stanley said. Suddenly rising out of his chair he began to limp about the small cubicle. "In between the last time I was here and today, I've had some *wild times*. This medical stuff makes me nervous. I get clumsy when I'm nervous. Ever since I was a kid… well… I hope I haven't hurt your computer. Have I erased my own records?"

"Now, take it easy, Stanley. I quite understand your nervousness," Giles said soothingly. "Although, if you'll permit me to make an observation, anyone who has the nervous energy you seem to possess usually doesn't have any serious health problems."

"Gee, thanks," said Stanley. "I'll accept that. A person with your expertise, who can type so fast…."

"I'm no doctor," Giles cautioned, reseating himself before the keyboard. "But I like to think positive." He looked sternly down his nose at the screen. "Flame on."

Stanley paused beside the desk, as if curious. "Is there a there there?"

"Yes…," said Giles. "It takes a minute for this machine to handshake the server. Then I have to log on myself."

"Password and all that," Stanley supposed aloud, with undisguised inquisitiveness.

Giles watched the screen. "It's no big deal. They make an effort toward security, around here. For confidentiality."

"I appreciate it. Though I must say, I remember when it was all on a first-name basis."

Giles looked over his shoulder and over his glasses at Stanley. "The sixties, no doubt."

"How'd you know?" Stanley said innocently.

"Oh," Giles smiled. "A little birdie told me."

"I wish one had told me," Stanley said.

"There, there," said Giles. "We're all young, once. Besides," he added, turning up the palm of one hand, "I thought the sixties were all rock 'n' roll and sex and riots and dope and stuff: you know, *fun*."

"I don't remember a thing, your honor."

"Well, you know what they say..."

"I'm hardly ever aware of what they say, Giles."

"They say that if you can remember the sixties, you weren't part of them."

"That much," said Stanley, "I can remember."

Giles assumed a puzzled look, then brightened. "Ah. Here we go." He tapped at the keyboard and spoke softly to himself. "Name... Password...."

As Giles tapped in his password, blank green boxes appeared on the screen, each corresponding to a keystroke. So, in attempting to steal Giles' password, Stanley had to read the fingers that tapped it in.

"I wish I'd learned to type," Stanley observed sourly, watching Giles' fingers. He took a couple of notes while the machine logged on. "Man," he said, limping back to his chair. "You are fast." Too fast. Stanley had managed to catch only *fome*—two letters short of the complete password.

"Actually," Giles said, "I'm very fast on a typewriter, for which I trained. But the computer is more difficult. What with the function keys, non-standard keyboard arrays, and such." He brushed his fingertips over the keys, like a pianist sounding an *arpeggio*. "One gets slowed down a bit."

"Hey," said Stanley. "That sounded like a *guiro*."

"A what?"

"Do it again."

"Do what again?"

"Run your fingers over the keyboard."

"Like this?"

"That's it. That sounds just like a *guiro*. It's a Mexican musical instrument. They hollow out a dried gourd or piece of wood and carve parallel ridges into the exterior surface, see? And when a musician runs a twig or drumstick over the ridges he has a percussion instrument that sounds a lot like a giant male cicada."

"A what?"

"You've heard one," Stanley continued enthusiastically.

"A giant male cicada?"

"No, a *guiro.* Janis played one in the intro to *Piece of My Heart.* I think it was *Piece of My Heart...* It's on that album, anyway. You know, the song that—"

"Janis? Janis who?"

"Janis... Joplin. That's... She...."

Giles' interest faded with his smile. "Do tell."

Amazed that this kid had bought the geek-hippie act for as long as he had, Stanley let his voice trail to nothing. "Sorry."

"Quite all right," said Giles mildly.

"We made do with what we had, in the sixties..."

"I understand."

"I mean, maybe she wasn't no Fine Young Cannibal or Mazzy Star or nothing," Stanley added, somewhat disconsolately. "But, still, she could sing like..."

"I know, I know," Giles interrupted, holding both hands aloft. "Although mother and I lived on a commune in Costa Rica, she had to have her record collection."

"Oh really? You had electricity?"

"A water wheel in the creek ran the generator, so we could listen to subliminal tapes. Every Saturday night we played records. Wenatchee John said it was all right."

"Wenatchee John?"

"He was our leader. At least for a while."

"Isn't that the guy who got cooked and eaten by some pissed-off splinter group of his own followers? About 1974?"

Giles pulled off his glasses and sucked on a temple bar. "We were gone by then, but, yes. He wasn't such a bad guy. Just another control freak."

"A control freak."

"Have you seen the video?"

"No," Stanley said tonelessly. "Should I?"

"Mother's still living off the residuals. At any rate," said Giles, replacing the glasses, "all *my* disposable income goes into a balanced portfolio of penny stocks and mutual funds, not records and tapes. But in stocks, as in communal living, diversity is the key to growth." He cleared his throat and adjusted his chair. "Now where was I?"

"Your password."

"Oh yes," he retyped it without thinking.

The computer beeped.

"Oh," said Giles. "I already did that!"

"Did what," said Stanley innocently, making a note. The last two letters were *n* and *t*—the password was *foment*.

"Never mind."

"Say, look…"

"Yes?"

"I can see you're on a network, here. But do you share information with other facilities?"

Giles typed for a moment before answering.

A logo filled the screen. Stanley made another note. The clinic's venereal software was called BUGTRAK.

Giles spoke somewhat distractedly as he typed. "Only statistics. We share statistical information with the National AIDS Data Project, also with a network of blood and organ banks, and a couple of other, similar outfits."

"Really? Blood and organ banks? Just like that? What if I want to be buried in one piece?"

"Then we don't list you as a donor."

"No names?"

"No names."

"What kind of statistics?"

"Every kind. Blood types, age groupings, sex of course, sexual preferences if volunteered, stuff we glean from the workup."

"Histocompatibility?"

Giles turned and looked at Stanley over his glasses.

"I know what you're thinking," said Stanley ingenuously. "What's an old hippie like me who gets his foot tangled in computer power cords know about the Major Histocompatibility Complex?"

"Yes," said Giles. "What does he know about it?"

"Nothing," Stanley shrugged. "He is just curious."

"In fact, Stanley, we don't normally do histocompatibility panels here. I mean, so far as I know, nobody ever consulted a histocompatibility panel before having sex—or afterwards. And, let me assure you, we've heard it all in here. Besides, we don't do the actual analyses."

"You send out to a lab. A subcontractor."

"Exactly. But the lab we send out to doesn't work up histocompatibility either."

"Could they? If you wanted it, I mean?"

"Oh, yes, they're a full-service medical laboratory. They can do just about anything with a blood sample."

"There's just one lab?"

"For us, yes."

"They work for other people?"

"Sure. Doctors, clinics, hospitals, the police. Say…"

"Yes?"

"You know, just last week another clerk was telling me about this detective who came in, asking questions very like the ones you're asking."

"Cops are known to be curious."

"And old hippies?"

Stanley looked at the clerk. "That's the second time this month someone has taken me for a cop."

MacIntosh shrugged. "No offense."

"The more interesting question would be, has anybody besides a cop been here asking these sorts of questions?"

"That's another question the detective asked." Giles studied Stanley. "If he comes back and asks it again, I can tell him yes."

Stanley shrugged. "I'm just a guy anxious to go to bed with his new girlfriend, and she's a little nervous about his past."

"Ah, yes," said Giles. "The girlfriend." He returned his attention to his computer screen. "I guess that makes *hetero* your sexual preference." He tapped tentatively at a key. "Unless…?"

"Hetero's fine," said Stanley.

"Yes," Giles smiled, hitting the key. "This is now and that was then."

"And what would you know about it?" Stanley asked archly.

"My mom talks about it all the time. Mom always says there was about a three-year period when she would sleep with anything with buttons on it."

"She didn't mention *guiros*?"

"Not that I recall."

"A woman doesn't want to tell her son everything."

"Not unless she wants to drive him mad with desire."

Stanley smiled.

"But as we were saying, only the AIDS survey gets your statistics without your permission. The data submitted are anonymous, involving HIV results, gender, sexual preference, income level, age, geodemographic stuff like that. Obviously, in an organ or blood donor database, the information can't be anonymous. But for that we get your explicit consent."

"I don't remember that woman, Ms...."

Giles glanced at the screen. "Dunkirk. Ms. Dunkirk."

"I don't recall her asking my permission to divulge such information."

"Then it probably wasn't granted, Mr. Ahearn."

"Okay," Stanley agreed thoughtfully. "So it wasn't granted."

Giles' casual glance at his screen became more concentrated. "But it says here, Mr. Ahearn, that it was granted."

It was a moment before Stanley answered. He recalled the other case worker asking the question. *If, in case of an accident, do you wish your intact organs to be put to best use?* No, Stanley had replied, *I don't.* He'd been assuming, at the time, that by the time he died he'd either be HIV positive from messing around with hookers or too pickled in alcohol for his organs to benefit anyone.

"Negative, Giles. Permission was not granted."

Giles was silent for a moment while he studied his screen. He typed a key. He tried another. "Hello...," he muttered softly.

Stanley waited a bit before he said, "The computer says that my permission was given, doesn't it. Giles?"

"Permission for what?" Giles asked nervously.

"Permission to share information."

Giles looked up from the screen. "Yessir, Mr. Ahearn. According to your file, sir, you gave your permission to share organ donor information."

Stanley watched Giles for a moment.

"Oh, well," he said suddenly, breaking eye contact with Giles as he did so. He sat back in his chair, heaved a sigh and looked up at the ceiling. "This Ms. Dunkirk, or somebody else, must have slipped up. Maybe the computer burped." He allowed his eyes to find Giles' again. "Right?"

Frowning, Giles turned to his screen. "Right," he said.

"Still, I refused it."

"Yes sir, you said that."

"It didn't have to be her mistake, did it?"

"Pardon?"

"Ms. Dunkirk. She didn't have to be the one making the mistake, did she? Somebody else could have made it. No? What's the matter?"

Giles stared at Stanley for a moment, then looked back at the screen. "I don't like mistakes," he said simply.

"Oh, a perfectionist, eh? Well my boy, I'm with you there. Used to be quite a perfectionist myself when I was your age. Had to give all that up, of course. I saw a bit of the world and gave up on perfection. Now it's your turn. Welcome to the club. Perfection isn't how it works. Perfection isn't what the world produces. Perfection is only something it eats, not what it shits out. Get my meaning? Give up on perfection, Giles. Perfection will only stick to your shoes and bring you heartache. See?"

"I never had a father," said Giles, staring at his screen.

"Besides," Stanley said, ignoring this remark. "Was this Ms. Dunkirk the only one with access to this file? Obviously not. You're sitting here and looking at it. Let's suppose, if she didn't make the mistake, maybe somebody else made it. Then we'll get on with our current business."

Giles remained silent, tapping a key thoughtfully.

"Is there a record of accesses?"

Giles brightened. "As a matter of fact, Mr. Ahearn, there is a record kept of something like the thirty-two most recent accesses to a given file."

"Thirty-two? Why thirty-two?"

Giles shrugged. "It's the fifth power of two. Binary computer stuff. They have to put some limit on these little conveniences or risk a drain on memory, which could lead to a crash..."

"So? Look them up."

"I don't have access to that information..." Giles shook himself again, as if out of a reverie, and frowned at the screen, renewing his concentration. "Besides, it might not make any difference."

"How's that?"

Now Giles studied Stanley for a moment. Stanley studied him back. Giles looked like a nice kid, raised by a mother of Stanley's age. A nice kid with something bothering him. What bothers a kid who grew up swaddled in a rebozo hanging from a tree limb on a commune in Costa Rica?

"Ordinarily, Mr. Ahearn," Giles said thoughtfully, "I shouldn't be exposing internal procedure to the scrutiny of a client. But this is a public agency. And, as my mother taught me to believe, most of what public agencies do and how they do it, especially the information they accrue, should always be accessible to the public. Moreover, since that police officer was here, I've been fooling around with the computer."

"So?"

"So I've noticed a little... anomaly."

"A what?"

Giles cleared his throat. "A glitch."

"A glitch."

"I remind myself that these are your data we're talking about here, Mr. Ahearn. Not belonging exclusively, as some people would like to think, to the clinic, but to you as well."

"That's an admirable sentiment, Giles. Easily worth a cup of coffee, along with a buck."

Giles smiled. "Yes. Well, step around my desk for a moment, if you don't mind."

Stanley limped around the desk.

"Is your hip bothering you?" Giles asked solicitously. "Mom had a hip replacement just last—."

"I stepped on a nail," Stanley said coldly.

"Oh," said Giles. He turned back to his monitor. "Okay. Take a look at this."

Giles' computer screen showed the agency's computerized form, requesting the client's name, address, phone number, age and sex, along with considerable additional information. The data in this particular form were Stanley's from his previous visit. Up in the right-hand corner was a long alphanumeric case number.

"You don't mind if I make a few notes," Stanley said, jotting down the number.

"I think it's your right to have any and all information involving your own case file," said Giles. "Most of the people who work here agree with me, although not all of them. And conditions being such, I'd appreciate your treating this matter in full confidence."

"Mum's the word, Giles."

"See that box holding the cursor?"

"Yeah."

"How's it labeled?"

"*Share info (Y/N)?*"

"That's right."

"Meaning, I take it, has this client given his or her permission to share his case information with other agencies?"

"That's correct."

"So?"

"What's it say under the cursor?"

"*Y*, meaning *Yes*, which is a damnable lie."

"That's true. Ms. Dunkirk asked you whether you were interested in getting on a national list of blood or organ or bone marrow donors. That's her job, she's supposed to ask you that, all of us ask our clients that. And you said *NO*."

"Okay. So far so good."

"Watch this."

Giles typed a *y* on his keyboard. "You get an upper-case *Y* no matter which *y* you input."

"So great," said Stanley. "But *Y* isn't my answer."

"Precisely," said Giles. "Your answer is *N*, for *No*."

"That's right."

"So type it in."

"Me?"

Giles slid his chair away from the desk. "Go ahead. Upper or lower case."

Stanley searched the keyboard until he found the *N* key, and tapped it.

"What's it say now in the answer box?"

"It says... It still says *Y*."

"Precisely. Try an upper-case *N*. Hold down the shift key and hit the *N*."

Stanley tried an upper-case *N*.

"It's still comes up as *Y*."

"That's right. Still a *Y*," said Giles. "No matter what the input your answer is positively *Yes*: you want to be on national lists of organ donors."

"Nobody's noticed this before?"

Giles looked evasive. "It's the first I've heard of it."

"What are you guys, asleep around here?"

Giles ignored this. "A typical case worker would be asking the questions rapidly and filling in the answers as he or she watched the keyboard. Not only that, the blood type and test results are filled in weeks later, after the report has come back, and not by the interview clerk but by data-entry personnel. The latter are all touch typists: they watch the data sheet they're recording from, and only occasionally glance at the screen to make sure they're on the right page. What I'm trying to say is, it's entirely possible that nobody's ever noticed this quirk before."

"Quirk? You call this a quirk?"

"If anybody else has noticed it, they haven't told me."

"Skip it. Somebody wants my info in their database."

"If you rule out a quirk, that's an interesting idea."

Stanley looked at Giles. "I'm ruling out quirks."

"Okay." Giles shrugged. "Somebody wants your info in their database."

"Or some part of me."

"Beg pardon?"

"Nothing."

"But why?"

"More to the point, who?"

"Maybe it's a cabal of intergalactic hippies, trying to stay in touch with their ever-fewer brothers on earth."

Stanley looked at Giles a moment, tried not to smile, then looked back at the screen, which he now read in its entirety. A lot of medical stuff.

He put a finger on the screen. "Giles, my man, you see that blood category, there?"

"Sure."

"See the blood type?"

"It says you're type O-Negative."

"So I've been told. Change it."

"Change it? What for?"

"Just change it. You can change it, can't you?"

"Sure." Giles rolled his chair back under the keyboard. "Change it to what?"

"How should I know? What's your blood type?"

"AB-Negative."

"So type in AB-Negative."

Giles changed the blood type to AB-Negative.

"Now Giles," said Stanley, "go back up to the consent box and put in a positive answer."

Giles arrowed the cursor back up the screen to the consent box and typed a *Y*.

"Now look…"

"It says Y. I just typed *Y*."

"Put in a negative answer."

Giles typed an *N*.

"Look at that!"

"It says *N*."

"Yes…?"

"Works just like it's supposed to work. That is interesting, isn't it.

Now how about changing the blood type back to O-Negative?"

Giles arrowed back down the screen and changed the blood type.

"Look at that, Giles…"

"The N changed back to a Y!"

Just to check, Giles arrowed up to the consent box and typed in a lower-case n. The upper-case Y remained unchanged.

"It's keyed to the blood type!"

"Which is filled in after the tests come back. Right?"

"That's correct. No less than two weeks later. Usually three."

"So the case worker filling in the form wouldn't even notice the wrong answer appearing in the consent box. The Y only appears in the consent box after a blood type O-Negative is entered two or three weeks later by other personnel. The clerk's got no reason even to look at the consent category."

Giles considered the screen. "But what does this mean?"

"Giles," Stanley said, standing up straight and scratching his shirt over his scar. "It means that somebody is interested in people with a certain blood type."

"I guess so. Say, are you sure you're not a policeman?"

"Yes."

"What exactly is your interest in this?"

Stanley considered Giles for a moment, then countered with a question of his own. "Could you get me a list of the accesses to this file?"

Giles nodded thoughtfully. "The sysop is a friend of mine. Tommy's the only one I could go to who would have enough security clearance to read the list. In fact the reason I haven't mentioned this Yes/No anomaly to anybody is that I figured it was some little game that Tommy was up to."

"Well?"

"Well, but now I see that it's keyed to the blood type…."

Stanley waited.

Giles tapped the keyboard. "It couldn't be Tommy. It's not his style. Anybody with enough programming know-how to finagle this information form would be able to access the results without leaving a trace."

Stanley considered this. "How well do you know this sysop guy?"

Giles thought for a moment, until his eyes widened and he exclaimed, "No way!"

"You sure?"

"No way Tommy would.... Why should he?"

"Money. Think about it, Giles. Is the guy in trouble? Paying child support? Driving too nice a car? Does he gamble?"

Giles shook his head. "Tommy's highly overpaid as it is. He likes to work at night. We hardly ever see him. In fact, he's not on the regular payroll, he's here as a consultant. He works for about ten government and corporate offices like this one. Does it all. Wires the place, sets up hardware and software, writes custom modules and subroutines, does network maintenance, installs upgrades.... He's a re-seller, too. Guy's smart and he's good. No." Giles shook his head. "He doesn't need money. As far as I know, he doesn't even care about money. What he cares about is computers. In fact, if he knew there was somebody fooling around on one of his systems, he'd go ballistic. Right through the roof. I guarantee he wouldn't sleep until he figured it out. That's the kind of guy he is."

"You trust him, then."

"I trust him."

"And me?"

Giles looked at Stanley a moment, then looked away. "I've eaten a lot of goat-cheese pizza with Tommy," he said. "He's not like most of these other clowns around here, always goofing off, just waiting to get home and smoke some pot and watch *Star Trek*."

"What do *you* do after work?"

"I go to the gym. Work out."

"Yeah. What about this guy Tommy?" said Stanley. "What's he do after work?"

"Other than eating pizza, I have no idea."

"Okay. So you don't really know what he's up to, outside of his business and his pizza habit."

"But messing around with this computer system, we're talking about a couple of people's jobs, here. This is a government-sponsored clinic, after all. There's about ten watchdog agencies that will come down on this place like a ton of bricks if they think something funny's going on."

"There'll be a time I'd like to see that," said Stanley coldly. "But not just yet."

"Really?"

"Really."

"But... Mr. Ahearn, I guess my question is... supposing that you're an honest man... why is this important enough to you to ask me to risk

Tommy's and my job for you?"

"Forget about me. What about that little glitch we've just discovered? Doesn't that make you wonder?"

Giles glanced at the computer screen. "That's a start."

"So?"

Giles turned to face him. "It definitely makes me curious."

But it wasn't quite enough. Stanley thought about this for a moment.

Then he took a step backwards, raised his shirt, and turned his back to Giles.

"Jesus Christ," said Giles, almost inaudibly.

"There used to be a type O-Negative kidney under that mess," said Stanley, watching Giles' expression over his shoulder. "I want to find the people who took it."

Giles was very pale. "They… They didn't ask?"

"No. They didn't ask."

"I don't feel so good."

Stanley dropped the shirttail. "Neither do I."

Giles inhaled deeply, gripped the armrests of his office chair, and swayed slightly. His eyelids fluttered. For a moment it looked as if he might pass out.

Stanley let it ride. The fluorescent light over his head hummed like an electric razor. The recycled air was full of the voices of people speaking in undertones. A telephone rang. Stanley stood head and shoulders above the office partitions, but only at the opposite end of the huge room, far away, did he see another human being.

After a minute Giles said, "This is what that cop was looking for."

Stanley nodded.

"Why not tell him?"

Stanley watched Giles. "Sure. Why not?"

Giles squirmed in his chair, then swiveled back to face his computer. On its screen, the cursor blinked over the Y in Stanley's donor-info box. Giles tapped the Y key, then the N key. Y, N. Y, N. The Y in the donor-info box persisted.

"Okay," he said finally, after a thoughtful sigh. "Let's see what Tommy can come up with. At the very least he'll put a stop to this bogus data-sort, here." He frowned at the computer screen. "Or whatever it is…"

"You on the Net?"

"Sure."

"Got an address book?"

"Of course."

"Bring it up."

When Giles had his net addresses on the screen, Stanley showed him Fong's mailbox address, written on a page in his notebook. FIRE-BIRD@SWEET.COM.

Giles typed it in.

"E-mail me anytime," said Stanley. "Make sure it's private, and ask for a receipt."

He extended his hand.

Giles shook it.

When he reached the waiting room, Stanley realized he still had the pink form in his hand. He paused for a moment, gazing at the form without really seeing it. Was this kid Giles what a cop would call a break? And so what if he was? Stanley was still out one kidney, and half out of the other one.

Glancing up from the pink test request, Stanley found himself looking into the eyes of the last customer of the day. He was an emaciated man with deep-set eyes, seated in a corner, who had just raised his chin from the mallard's-head crook of a walking stick he'd been resting it on. His clothes hardly fit him, they drooped as if they'd been cut for a much larger man. His hair was thin. The bones of his skull showed clearly beneath the drawn, parchment-like skin of his face. While it was not the face of an old man, the eyes belonged to one.

The informative videotape muttered quietly from the opposite corner of the room.

The young man's old eyes glistened, wreathed in shadow, hollow, careworn, haunted.

Stanley let the slip of pink paper flutter to the floor and limped out to the sidewalk.

Chapter 11

Giles was a lucky break.

The question now: what to do with his information?

Information was the wrong word. A trick in a computer program wasn't information, it was a trick in the information, that is to say, it was a clue. But it wasn't information.

So somebody screens the patients of a sexual diseases clinic for O-Negative blood. Then what? What do they do with this information?

For that matter, having diddled the software, why just one clinic? Why not several? And if several, what more would it take to diddle the entire DonorNet? Just a computer freak with a phone line? Was it so easy?

An organization? Organ-ization. At last Stanley gets the joke. Stendhal declared murder and puns incompatible; but what about puns and nephrectomy?

An organization could bring a computer freak on board, somebody to finagle the health clinic's software. But what kind of guy could write software and perform nephrectomies too? No kind of guy, probably. It would be difficult to believe there could be one such person in the entire world. A character with the skills necessary to trapdoor a big software program and perform nephrectomies on the side wouldn't have to break the law to make all the money he could possibly use, no matter what his tastes.

So that left an organization with at least two highly skilled members.

A national database of organ, blood and bone marrow donors would have access to, and be able to be accessed by, its users, which in turn would mean other nets, which in turn would mean telephone lines and hackers. Security would be a consideration; perhaps not a top priority, but important, because the people in charge of the donor net wouldn't know about the pirate harvesting scheme. If they knew about it, security would be tight. If they knew about the scheme and security wasn't tight, it would follow that not only would the people running the donor net know about the harvesting scheme, but they would be in on it.

Pretty complicated. A big organization. A big organization means leaks. It means mistakes.

But if the information were freely given by the members of the database? With a little coaxing from some finagled software, of course...

Security wouldn't be a problem.

Think of it. You sit down to a computer terminal. You log on to, say, America Online, Prodigy, CompuServe, or the World Wide Web. Via scientific or medical databases or university computers you find your way to the donor database, you log on with Giles' password...

By virtue of the mere fact that you've been able to log on, the database has accorded you professional status. As a professional, you seek certain information. As host to a professional database, the computer's job is to give you that information.

Say you work for a drug-testing firm. Done with horse and goat cultures, you are now ready to try out your new AIDS vaccine on a human control group. This group should consist of, say, 250 HIV-positive ARC or AIDS patients with T-cell counts between 200 and 500, who have never taken any retro-viral vaccines or drugs, who have never had any form of radiation therapy, who show no signs of other viral diseases, and whose taste in underclothing runs to untanned leather.

National database, do your stuff.

Or let's suppose you have an interest in kidneys.

Healthy kidneys. Kidneys that test HIV-negative, show no other signs of disease, the leather issue's neither here nor there, it's no sweat if there's no histocompatibility workup available...

We'll work out histocompatibility later.

After we get to know the patient a little better.

After we've taken a kidney from him.

In post-op, there's all the time in the world.

Especially if somebody else is paying the bill.

But say, Database, while you're in there sorting thousands of

patients, cough up boys and girls between 20 and 50 years of age with
no discernible health problems, HIV-negative of course, that's very
important, we could even specify that they be heterosexual and live in,
let's say, the San Francisco Bay Area.

Because, let's speculate, we've got a really good guy out there in San
Francisco. A fine surgeon. Other than whatever it is that allowed us to
persuade a talented surgeon to sign on with the likes of us organ
pirates, who sail for renal plunder, there's only one problem with this
talented guy: Talented Guy doesn't like Federal Heat.

So dump onto the A: drive — Drive Not Ready, Christ, insert the
floppy —: all God's children on this database who fit the criteria and
who also live in the greater Bay Area, so our man doesn't have to travel, and so we don't have to get into any kidnapping raps, crossing state
lines with criminal intent, bringing down the FBI on our bad selves,
that kind of stuff. It's always messy, to cross state lines to commit a
crime. Probably need an ambulance, portable generators and portable
refrigerators, all kinds of drugs, tools, glassware and an operating room
in a Winnebago; a good map of camping facilities with water and
sewage hookups in the host states; gunsels with steely eyes slouching
against the roll-out awning who flick a contemptuous cigarette toward
the campfire singalong at the next site over; nurses who look like grandmothers; ice-cooled perfusion machines, tubes and wires, a fake gas
tank for the Ringer's solution, attendants, coordination, organization
— and *still* a gun in the glove compartment. What would all that trouble and expense get you? A federal rap, curated by the FBI.

Get a grip, Stanley. Leave camping and the FBI out of this. Stick
with a local scene, the local cops. Stick with understaffed police depart-
ments with low budgets and we don't have too much to worry about.
We might even have one or two of them on the payroll…

But, hey, Database? There's just one more thing, one more little favor.

Put a little asterisk next to the names of the candidates who come up
type O-Negative. Would you? Thanks so much.

Those type O-Negative kidneys, they bring a much better price.

Cough 'em up, Database.

Put 'em on this diskette.

I got a habit to support…

Iris Considine lived in the back of a six-unit building just below the
University of California Medical Complex, a block south of the jog in

the streetcar tracks at Carl and Arguello. There's fog at that intersection when the sun's shining everywhere further east, its gloom assisted by the towering hospital parking garage, and when the streetcar rumbles across Arguello from Irving and turns onto Carl in a thick evening fog, its inside lights turn its passengers into a horizontally scrolling *tableau vivant*. People reading their papers, sleeping agape against the windows, standing and staring with their backs to each other, gazing fondly up and down at one another, all of them in that peculiar daze municipal transport puts people into—the whole drifts past like installments in serial monogamy.

The neighborhood has a lot of medical types living in it. Clerks, janitors, hematologists, radiologists, nurses, doctors, residents and whatnot. It was a neighborhood Stanley rarely visited. It had one or two of the tall buildings that he liked to know were around him at any given time, but the structural and population densities were altogether too thin for his nervous system; he preferred the crush of Chinatown. The spiritual cleanliness usually termed *anomie*, scrubbed by the bath of the crowd, achieves a special purity when the crowd you're taking your bath in is chattering in a language you don't understand. Chinese made Stanley very comfortable—as would any other language in the world excepting English, including Klingon; it left him alone with his thoughts, and thoroughly anonymous.

Take medical jargon, he was thinking, as he rang the bell of Iris' apartment. For a guy who had not darkened the door of anything more medical than a tattoo parlor for the better part of his adult life, Stanley was really having the tour. The up side of the tour was that all the medical jargon he was hearing made him feel nearly as anonymous as Chinese did. Except he reckoned Chinese as much more mellifluous. Medical jargon reminded him of nothing if not sea lions barking, in an environment characterized by a lot of funny smells, people dressed in white, and mucus that tastes like puréed herring.

The down side of the tour was its cost: one body part.

A second streetcar rolled through the intersection at the top of the block, heading in the direction opposite the first one. Nearly empty, its illuminated interior hovered in the night and fog, parallel to the nearly invisible street below it. Something must have gone wrong, Stanley thought. That's too many streetcars this late at night. Too much service at the wrong time.

The front door buzzed, and he let himself into the lobby, a fluorescent box painted and tiled in earth-tones with a quiet, waterless fountain, a nest of aluminum mail boxes, and, next to a jacaranda tree in a redwood tub, a chair nobody ever sat in. Posture long since ruined by the low ceiling, as if cowed toward its grave by the implacable radioactivity of the acoustical ceiling's twinkling gypsum, the tree crouched in its corner like a tall old functionary, stooped from a lifetime of deference, an incontinent stain spreading from beneath its tub like a secret revenge on the master who took it for granted.

A flight of carpeted stairs, its blended-tobacco color designed to conceal decades of quotidian drudgery, lifted him up to a third-floor hallway. The twin strains of lavender incense and *Haunted Heart* as interpreted by Jo Stafford invited him to limp on in, through an open door at the back.

Iris stood in the kitchenette, making a drink.

The entire place was decorated in blue. The floor was wall-to-wall dark blue carpet, deep and fuzzy. The walls themselves were a few shades lighter and the ceiling probably lighter yet, though it was too dark in the apartment to make it out. Any daylight that penetrated the place would have to find its way through a large tank of fish that stood between the viewer and a glass sliding door that led to a narrow outside deck. But there was no daylight, and Iris hadn't gotten around to putting on any more lights than she had clothes.

She came around the corner of a little built-in bar wearing a clinking glass and a kimono. There's white-belted, there's brown and black-belted; but then there's loosely-belted, which has been known to defeat them all.

"Hi," she piped cheerfully, handing him the drink as, redolent of soap, she brushed past him. "Did I ever tell you about the American in Paris who tried to ask for a straw and got a blowjob?"

"No. We just met, remember? What about it?"

"Beats me. I just like the story."

She closed the door behind him. "Is the patient okay with whiskey?"

"If the patient is alive, the patient is okay with whiskey." Stanley limped into the living room, trying not to trip over anything in the gloom. The incense boded emphysema.

Iris stood very close to him. "I was wondering when you were going to show up."

"I don't get that many invitations," said Stanley. "It takes me a long time to react."

The loosely wrapped kimono was a beauty. When she turned to

retrieve a cigarette from a hollow glass bust of Sigmund Freud, a red-eyed dragon of indisputable gravity flared its green nostrils and splayed silver talons across her back: a carp-whiskered malevolence, poised atop a golden-scaled tail that coiled possessively about her.

The whiskey was interesting, too. Stanley judged it a single-malt.

"I don't give that many." Iris sat on the couch against the wall at right angles to the bookcase and crossed her legs, which split the front of the kimono all the way to her hip.

"Straws?"

She smiled and patted the cushion next to her. "Invitations."

Stanley gently let himself down into the cushions, which were very low. He made it down okay, but he wasn't sure he could get up again without tearing his sutures.

She handed him a green butane lighter. "Still hurting?"

He stared at the lighter a moment, then turned it in the gloom. The logo of some medical association was stamped on it. He shrugged and lit her cigarette. "Since when does a nurse smoke?"

She exhaled smoke into his face and sat back on the cushions. "Since she discovered she likes to sin a little while she's away from the office. About twenty years ago."

He put the lighter on the coffee table and watched it. "I just thought a nurse ought to know better."

"Hey," she said, "it's not like I just walked in front of a bus."

"True."

"Just two a night," she added with a smile. "One before… And one after."

"*Star Trek*, you're referring to. That's judicious." He tore his eyes away from the lighter. "Could I borrow your phone?"

"Sure. Going to call your mother?"

"To hell with her."

She produced a cordless phone from somewhere within the cushions of the couch and handed it to him.

Stanley dialed a number he'd written in the little spiral notebook. Iris caught his eye and they stared at one another, he listening, she smoking. As the number picked up, she blew a smoke ring his way.

The high-pitched squeal of a modem assaulted his ear.

He cursed, disconnected, redialed.

While it rang Stanley stared at the lighter.

Fong answered at the fourth ring.

"Fong. Stanley."

"My white friend. What's cooking?"

"I got a name and a password."

"What, no phone number?"

"You can probably get to this outfit through any Internet gateway."

"What outfit?"

"It's a national database of living-will-type organ, blood and bone marrow donors called DonorNet."

"Yuck."

"Think positive. The organ they donate might be your own."

"Or yours."

"Very funny."

"So what am I looking for?"

Stanley gave Fong a rundown of the glitch he and Giles had discovered.

"Oh," said Fong. "That explains this wacky sexgram spamming my in-basket, here."

"What sexgram?"

"Standby."

Stanley could hear Fong's fingers driving a keyboard, chording fistfuls of keys like it was a piano. Another touch typist. Where did they come from?

"Check it out, and I quote:"

> Old Hippie,
>
> We overlooked it just now (need to test this address anyway), but, given type O-Negative, turns out if change _Sex_ category from (M) to (F), donor info remains as selected (Y)es or (N)o. But, given O-Negative, if change (F)emale to (M)ale donor info automatically goes to (Y)es if already (N)o. In other words, the trapdoor's only interest is in type O-Negative Males.
>
> Hmm. Just had a thought. Right back...
>
> Back. I was right. Changing category from (M)arried to (S)ingle does the same thing.
>
> They're after _single_ O-Negative males.
>
> Will be in touch.
>
> Guiro

"Go, Giles," said Stanley. "Is there a return address?"

"Yeah."

"E-mail him back. Mark it private and say, 'Go Guiro Go'."

Fong typed. "What does this mean?"

"That's our inside boy, whom you're in place to cross-check. And it means he's on the case."

"Hmmm. He's got menu-driven software acting like this?"

"It's possible the whole network is rigged."

"In my entire Mah-Jong career," said Fong, "that's the most brazen bullshit I've ever heard of."

"It's worked on at least nine victims so far. Giles got interested in the problem on account it impugns the integrity of his data."

"Is that a fact? We'll have to run him for President."

"It could have been a put-on, but I don't think so."

"Stanley, you are paranoid."

"In normal people, excess paranoia is filtered through a system of paired kidneys."

"You mean, to halve the number of kidneys is to square the amount of paranoia?"

"Axiomatic."

"And all this time I think to myself, that Stanley, he's not learning a word of Chinese."

"So I'm thinking it might be advantageous if you continue with your inquiries, despite this guy MacIntosh's apparent interest. Double up on him, so to speak."

"Sounds good to me."

Stanley gently freed his hand from Iris' and took up the little spiral notebook. "The phone number there is 255-2289. The password *foment* in combination with some or all of the name *Giles MacIntosh* should get you on for starters."

"Hey," said Fong, "like the computer."

"Not quite." Stanley spelled all three words, holding his notes up to the dim light. "I want a sort off the organ database. Query for everybody on it who (1) is male, (2) single, (3) lives within fifty miles of San Francisco, (4) has type O-Negative blood, (5) is HIV-negative, (6) has tested negative for any kind of renal dysfunction or kidney disease, insofar as they are listed or considered, and (7) has been a client of the San Francisco Clinic for Sexually Transmitted Diseases in the past two years, whose modem number you now have. A list of everybody who works in the joint would be handy too, particularly the names of whatever computer consultants and sysops you can come up with. Look out for one with first name Tommy."

While they were talking, Iris had worked the toes of both her bare feet under Stanley's hip.

"You got that?"

"Sure." Fong repeated the filter specs. Stanley listened in silence, staring at Iris, who wiggled her toes and blew smoke between Stanley's face and notebook pages.

Fong said, "Should be easy, man. How'd you get that guy's handle?"

"I just limped in and asked for it. This kid's so sympathetic, I'm surprised he's got time to feed himself."

"Anything else?"

"Yes. Isn't there a newspaper database on CompuServe?"

"Sure. It's one of the handiest things on it."

"Does it have both the *Chronicle* and the *Examiner*?"

"Yep."

"Good. Query both papers for any mention of the black market in human organs, organ theft, illegal trade in organs, etc. Go back two years. Emphasize kidneys, kidney theft, illegal transplants, mysterious women in bars. We're particularly interested in any local case of a guy with blood type O-Negative meeting a smart and sexy woman in a bar and going home with her, only to wake up in Golden Gate Park missing a kidney."

"What if there are no such cases in the papers?"

"Then we'll have to see what the cops have in their computers."

"Now we're talking fun," said Fong.

"While you're at it, see if you can download any articles about California surgeons or internists cashiered for egregious malpractice."

"Man, you *have* to be egregious to get cashiered."

"Call me," said Stanley, holding Iris' eyes with his own.

"Where?" said Fong.

"I'll be at…"

"Five six six," said Iris quietly.

"Five six six," repeated Stanley.

"Two two three zero."

"Two two three zero."

"Got it." Fong rang off.

Stanley had to take his eyes off Iris to find the button to turn off the phone.

"You'll have instant access," Iris said. "That phone can go wherever we go."

"What if we stay right here?"

"It'll do that, too."

He set the telephone on the floor.

She moved a little bit closer.

Stanley put his arm around her shoulders. The kimono was silk, and now it parted over her knees, which were just under his chin and against his chest.

She kissed him.

He kissed her back.

She nipped his lip with her teeth.

He asked her, "Why me?"

She traced the lines of his mouth with a fingernail.

"You've been hurt. I'm a nurse."

"That's not enough."

"You're a hero."

"Still not enough."

She shrugged. "I've never kissed a hero before."

"You're not kissing one now."

She smiled and snuggled. "I'm getting pretty close, though."

In the dim gloom each of her eyes reflected a tiny candleflame.

"No more than that?"

"Well...," she said. "You really want to know?"

"Yes..."

"There's that scar."

She giggled.

"Scar? What—?"

"This scar," she said, pulling at his shirt.

"That scar," he said, grabbing her hand. "What about it?"

She stopped tugging and locked eyes with him.

"May I see it?"

"You've already seen it."

"I want to see it again."

"What for?"

She snatched the shirttail out from under his belt.

"Okay, okay," Stanley said. "Ouch."

"Just relax," she whispered. Her voice had gone a little husky.

"Who, me? Sure, sure. I'll relax."

She plucked at the buttons on his shirt. "I can't see the whole thing. Lie down."

Stanley relaxed against the cushions of the couch.

Iris worked on the clothing problem.

"Ohhh," she said after a while. "It's beautiful."

"Thanks," said Stanley staring at the floor. "Though I feel I might well have gotten through life without it."

"Oh, Stanley," she said. "But now you have it, and it's a beautiful scar."

Stanley sighed loudly.

A moment passed, and another. He could hear her breathing.

When she spoke, he realized her mouth was inches from his hip. "May I... touch it?"

"Iris," Stanley said. "Why...?"

She blew little puffs of air over his flesh.

He suddenly acquiesced. "Of course. Of course you can touch it."

She ran a finger along the line of still-fresh sutures. The edge of her nail ticked them off slowly, like the tang of a zipper passing over its teeth.

It tickled, it itched, it felt very strange, but Stanley lay still for it, until he involuntarily shivered.

Iris permitted herself a profound sigh.

The scar began to feel better—or at least different. Stanley had to admit, it felt better than it had felt in quite a number of days.

She moved the fingernail back the other way.

"Iris." He tried to sit up.

"Hush," she said, pushing him back onto the couch. "I want..."

"What do you want?"

"*Scarlingus.*" It was a whispered hiss. A dragon's exhale.

Before Stanley had time to believe his ears she added, "Also known as *cicatricio.*"

His mind helped out by supplying the image of a forked serpent's tongue straddling the scar of his recently acquired incision.

"God almighty," Stanley blurted aloud.

"She approves," Iris chuckled.

Stanley ran a mental finger down the index to his inner catalogue of acceptable social behavior. *Scar-licking, scar-licking...* The categories skipped from *Rorschach* to *Scintillant* — no *scarlingus*.

Stall. See if you can get another shot — with a beer back, an inner voice hastily advised.

She had her own advice. "Stick with me, brain-boy. You'll go far and come soon."

"Don't — don't you get enough of that... in the hospital?" Stanley stammered.

"What — sex?" She laughed. "You've got to be kidding."

"No. I meant scars, enough of scars."

"I originally thought that nursing would get me close to my most favorite thing in the world," she admitted simply, addressing, in fact, the scar. "Alas, it's a case of so near, yet so far."

"Scarlingus..."

"Yes. May I, darling? You'll like it. May I run the tip of my tongue along the entire length of your scar?" She laughed gaily. "You'll probably scream with pleasure. Go ahead. The old lady downstairs is deaf." He could feel her breath on his hip. "It's a beautiful scar. And so fresh. It's not even really a scar yet, you know. It's still... it's a *nascent* scar. It's a wound, really. No longer an incision, not yet a scar. A healing wound. A blessing. Deliciously ripe."

"I hadn't really thought of it that way, Iris."

"Licking is good for a wound. You know?"

"Dogs do it," he suggested.

"We should do it, too," she said. But she wasn't even listening to him anymore.

Iris rose to brush her lips lightly over his shoulder, nuzzled the hair at the edge of his scalp, and said moistly into his ear, "I want to touch the tip of my tongue to it, just to its edge. It won't hurt you. It might even turn you on."

"Go for it."

She didn't move. "Then you can do anything to me you want, Stanley..."

"I beg your pardon?"

"There must be something I can do for you, Stanley. Something... special...?"

"Special? Well, I—."

"I want to tongue the entire length of it! The entire length of your scar. Please, Stanley. After that... anything... anything you like. Please... your scar... I'll do anything for you, Stanley. May I...?"

"Well… well, hell yes, Iris," Stanley whispered. "Go for the scar."

Her tongue tickled the purpling tissue, as billed. It tingled. It felt… delicious.

You know what I really like, Stanley thought to himself, relaxing against the thick cushions of the sofa.

You know what's my favorite…?

Later, she said, "I have a surprise for you."

"Another one?"

"Let me get it."

She went away in the darkness and came back, pushing a wave of incense before her. "Here."

"What is it?"

"It's a bear."

"What?"

"It's a *special* bear."

Stanley maneuvered it in the gloom. It was a bear all right, stuffed, about six inches high, crafted in a sitting position. A fuzzy brown stuffed bear.

"Ah…what's so special about it?"

"It's a Get-Well Bear."

"You're kidding."

She wasn't. "And it's just for you."

"Oh, well, thanks."

She observed, "You can't see what it's holding."

"What? No, I… I'm not even looking at it."

"Look. In his little paws."

"It's a he?"

She struck the green lighter.

"See it now?"

"It's a flower."

"No, silly. It's an aster."

Stanley stared at it. It was an aster, all right. A purple aster.

"Is this some kind of bad joke?"

Even in the dark, he could see that she blushed deeply. "No, Stanley," she said. "It's a good aster. Not like that bad one we found sewn to you."

"A good aster…"

"Yes," she nodded. "A healing aster. Presented to you especially by Mr. Get-Well Bear. Mr. Get-Well Bear and his healing aster are going to make you all better."

He could see that she was completely sincere.

"Soon," she added, snuggling against him. "Get well soon."

Bartender, said the inner voice, deep in the tavern of Stanley's brain. *Hit me again.*

Chapter 12

I t took a month.

Fong's part, however, was accomplished overnight. Using Giles MacIntosh's name and password, Fong penetrated DonorNet immediately. The computer answered his call, accepted *foment* as a password, and invited him in. Except that it was good practice to figure where the files were kept and what they were called, Fong was almost bored. Within a couple of hours he had gotten the software available on the host computer to do everything for him, and had the information Stanley needed. On the way out Fong's evening was brightened by a browse through some interesting names, addresses and statistics in a file called PROSTIT.OOT.

DonorNet responded to Stanley's sieve with the names of twelve healthy, single, heterosexual, drinking men in San Francisco with type O-Negative blood.

Fong's search of the *Chronicle* and *Examiner* databases on CompuServe yielded nine notices of kidney predation.

Six names were on both the DonorNet and newspaper lists.

Chronologically, the six duplicate cases succeeded the three previous incidents.

One of the duplicates was Stanley Clarke Ahearn.

Though the newspaper articles made no mention of blood types, Stanley had little doubt he had stumbled onto at least one of the means by which the thieves selected their victims. This left him with three avenues of approach.

First, he could canvass every bar in the city looking for a woman who liked to drink a Tom Collins and always carried a lime.

Stanley rejected this approach because of its obvious needle-in-haystack type of, uh, fruitlessness.

Had he been a cop, Stanley figured, he might have taken apart the Center for Sexual Diseases, department by department. No personnel or file would escape intense scrutiny. He would put everybody in the place under the bright light, one at a time, from the janitor to the philanthropist who put up the matching funds. Simultaneously he would have looked into the company that wrote and maintained DonorWare for the DonorNet, as well as the agencies involved with the collection and distribution of data on donors and sexual diseases and hangnails, too. Sooner or later a thread would emerge, and that thread would lead, eventually, to the Organ-ization.

If he merely wanted to *solve the crime*, all he needed to do was mention his discovery to Corrigan and wait.

Stanley rejected this approach as well. Of resources or time, he had little or none. And though there was an element of revenge in his quest, Stanley wasn't interested in how organs were being pirated, let alone who was doing it. Stanley was interested in a new kidney.

This left him the third approach, which he pursued.

He cross-indexed and eliminated the newspaper victims from the list of blood O-Negative clients. This left him with a list of six potential victims.

On a hunch, he eliminated four names because they were homeless, divorced, or inhabited the income bracket known as "below poverty line."

This left him with two names. He studied the available data. Both were single. Both made a living. Both listed "no close kin." Much of their data closely matched Stanley's. Single, employed, O-Negative, without immediate family.

He decided to have a look at them.

That's all it took. One look at the owner of the first name sent him to the second. Guy No. 1: a thirty-three year-old research economist at a bank. He wore a suit with suspenders five days a week, worked out at a health club three times a week, drove a brand new Saab Turbo convertible, owned his own home in the upper Haight, windsurfed at Crissy Field three evenings a week, and rented a garage off Capra Way in the Marina to store the windsurfing gear and a Harley Sportster he never rode anymore, but whose mere ownership kept him in touch with his inner fool. He had season tickets to the opera, cultivated five or six girlfriends all of whom earned as much or more money than he did; he wore a two-hundred-and-fifty-dollar pair of gold-rimmed eyeglasses when he read *The Wall Street Journal*, Barron's, Fortune, and a $1500-per-annum investor's newsletter called *Red Smith's Guide*, as well as everything published in hardback on the subject of personal growth as measured by money. He was never late. When at home for the weekend he wore the same pair of jeans he'd been able to get into for nine years, which gave Stanley pause for a thoughtful pat on the paunch, but the guy was never home on the weekends because he divided his leisure time between heli-skiing in the Canadian Rockies, alumni meetings at Stanford, and various girlfriend-owned time-share condos at Maui, Cabo San Lucas, and Stinson Beach.

And the man never, ever went to a bar unless there was a business deal in it, in which case he drank a bottled water he always carried with him.

One look at him was enough. Early the morning after staying up all night pondering Fong's data, Stanley parked the pickup in a bus zone across Frederick Street from Guy No. 1's address and waited. At 7:45 the guy and a blonde, both in business suits, with briefcases and wet hair, tripped briskly down the steep, fog-dampened steps of the guy's recently-painted Victorian. She opened the door of a year-old BMW nuzzled up behind the Saab, and sat into the safety harness. She started the engine, closed the door, powered down the driver's window, and leaned out to administer an adios with her lips. Before the kiss could become anything other than a technicality, the Beamer's telephone wheedled. From thirty yards up the street Stanley heard her say she had to go, even as she answered the phone. She backed out of the driveway, aimed the machine toward the financial district, and floored it. The BMW launched down Frederick Street and took the corner at Shrader without regard for the stop sign, its phone propped on its driver's shoulder even as she checked her makeup in the mirror on the back of the sun-visor.

Guy No. 1 stood in the driveway and watched her go, the front panels of his linen jacket drawn back under his forearms, the chamois forks of his duck galluses showing, his hands in the front pockets of his pressed linen pants, looking exactly like a man thinking about nuclear physics while waiting for his golden retriever to take a shit.

Guy No. 1 walked back up his driveway, pausing to pick up a cigarette-end someone had thrown there, and continued past his car to drop the butt into a trash can. As Guy No. 1 drove the Saab away—also aimed at the financial district, though his phone hadn't yet begun to ring—Stanley was already laying in the coordinates for Guy No. 2.

The second address was over a dry cleaner on Cortland in Bernal Heights. At 4:30 that same afternoon, Stanley was waiting for the 24 Divisadero to finish dispensing people so he could park in the bus zone when he saw a guy coming home from work. Guy No. 2 this guy had to be. He wore a blue and black checked flannel shirt with a black quilted insulated lining and gum-soled tan work boots. There would be white athletic socks inside the work boots and an ardent case of athlete's foot inside the socks. He carried a red and white insulated lunch tote with a tattered brown sweater, splotched white with dried joint compound, draped through its handle. His worn tee shirt was powdered white with sheetrock dust. So were his jeans. Their left rear pocket was ripped at the upper left-hand corner from clipping and unclipping a measuring tape all day long, eight hours a day, five days a week, 2,000 hours a year or for the life of the jeans or their wearer, whichever came first. He hadn't shaved in several days, and he was too old to be hanging sheetrock. Younger guys who hadn't hurt their backs yet would be giving him a run for his money. He'd already had a couple of drinks and anybody who hung sheetrock for a living, so far as Stanley was concerned, deserved theirs. Despite the drinks Guy No. 2 was walking gingerly. His work troubled his back, stiffened his hands, numbed his mind; but he worked hard so he could live alone, peaceful and unmolested, upstairs over a dry cleaner. Even from across the street Stanley could see that the man's cheeks were puffy from insomnia and drink. His nose was a little bulbous, his hair hadn't been cut lately, he was pushing forty, and that paunch straining the tee shirt would only be getting bigger, ultimately aggravating his back problem.

If he survived his forthcoming kidney operation, that is.

His name was Ted.

Ted Nichols crossed the street, went into a grocery on the corner next to the bus zone, and emerged from the grocery a few minutes later with a brown paper bag. The paper bag had the familiar rectilinear bulge at its bottom and the familiar red and yellow plastic sack protruding from its mouth: two six-packs topped by a family-sized bag of potato chips. Salt and alcohol, hops and starch; it's surprising how much of the nutrition that a guy like No. 2 needs to survive is contained in these two products. Hops and alcohol relax the back muscles. The mind as well. A man who sweats all day wants salt and carbohydrates. A man who works all day likes to hear the crisp crepitations of the humidity-free bag, the demolishing crunches of the three mouthfuls he stuffs the moment he has entered his apartment, before doing anything else, even before turning on the television, standing over the opened bag in his kitchenette, a familiar grammar damply punctuated by the pleasurable little explosion of the top torn off the first cold can of beer.

Was Stanley intimately familiar with the *genus* containing the species of Guy No. 2, or what?

Stanley could presume Ted wouldn't be going out tonight. It was early in the week, and Ted had his two six-packs, his chips, his television. Once his shoes came off he'd be lucky to desert the chair long enough even to bathe. If Ted planned carefully, he'd only have to get out of the chair to piss, the first time at beer 1.5, and once subsequently for each additional can. He might grab a quick shower on the way to bed, but equally, he might pass out in the chair. If Ted made it to bed in time to saw off a straight eight—less two for insomnia—it was because he hadn't passed out in his chair with a beer in his hand, the television on, his shoes and the light off, the flickering room slowly filling with the reek of his feet, the dank odor of beer, and crescendos of snoring and canned laughter. His blood-sugar, or a headache, or a particularly prolonged broadcast scream, would drag him awake in the wee hours, and maybe then he'd curl up in the quilt his mother bought off a Winnebago Indian in Wisconsin in 1946. But if the routine went like that he wouldn't bathe. Only if he went to bed at nine or nine-thirty would he turn off the set and take the shower. Between the sheets at that last moment of consciousness, and at only that moment, he always wished to be clean.

Ted Nichols wouldn't be going anywhere tonight, Stanley thought, watching the flickering blue corner window above the storefront laundry. But the next time Ted heads for a bar, I'll be right behind him.

Friday night, most likely.

Stanley blinked twice and looked down the street. The 24 bus was laboring up the hill from Bayshore, loaded with people coming home from work. A woman pushed a stroller toward him along the sidewalk. An old man in a limp fedora sat in a plastic chair in a doorway, his palms on his knees and his eyes shut against the evening light.

Stanley watched the side mirror. In it, two young men talked animatedly. Beyond them a car parallel-parked, beyond the car a guy locked the door of an appliance store. The woman pushed her baby carriage out of one side of the mirror's frame and into the other.

Who were they? What did they look like?

They were here. One or more of these people worked for them. Could he spot them? They looked just like anybody else, right? Regular people? They were motivated just like everybody else— right? They stole kidneys because they wanted a bigger television? Because the rent went up? Because their guns required pricey silver bullets? Because they wanted to continue to breathe the perpetually fresh, blue, salt-tanged, increasingly expensive air of San Francisco instead of the stale, brown, tangibly thick, if cheaper, effluent that passed for air in most of the rest of the world?

Oh, well. That's understandable.

These renal bandits are people, just like me, thought Stanley. When he found them, they would prove to be just plain folks.

Whether he could spot them or not, Stanley wasn't the only person on this street waiting for Ted Nichols to drink one too many in the wrong bar at the wrong time. Somebody else was waiting for Ted.

And Stanley was waiting for them.

He looked forward again, through the windshield. He had one advantage over whomever else waited for Ted. Even though "they" presumably knew what they were doing, and even though Stanley certainly had no idea what he was doing, "they" didn't know yet that, while "they" were waiting for Ted, Stanley was waiting for them.

He might get to observe their whole operation, unnoticed.

He swallowed one of the medicinal pills, of the type he might have to take every night for the rest of his life.

He watched Ted's flickering blue window.

This had to be the guy.

That night, Stanley almost quit drinking.

Chapter 13

I t took a month.

Camp Kill-Care looked like any of the bars Ted Nichols preferred.

As usual Stanley let Ted get his nozzle in, gave him a half hour to get started.

So long as Stanley could see the entry doors there was no particular reason to crowd the man.

Let him enjoy his last few weeks of renal tranquility.

The door into a bar is there for one of three reasons: It is convenient to people who want to drink; it is convenient to people who need to drink; it is convenient to people who have to drink.

Sometimes the crowds get a little mixed up, and you'll find a stone drunk with wet pants sitting in the catbird seat in a nice fern bar. To the catbird's advantage, some of the nicer clientele will be hobnobbing with him to prove they're congenial enough to countenance anybody. Then, when it gets to be ten o'clock, having had their two or three drinks, these latter types will leave a matrix of complimentary screwdrivers ranged in front of the guy with wet pants and go home. After all, these latter types have to go to work in the morning.

The guy in wet pants is already at work.

This is a lonely scene for the guy in wet pants, who is lonely anyway. But after he's mopped up the screwdrivers if he can still walk he'll go drink where drinkers more of his ilk drink. It's just natural to drink with people who drink like you do. Natural and less painful. It's part of the downward spiral.

Ted hadn't hit the wet pants stage yet. But, like Stanley, he had hit the phase where he liked to drink alone. Unlike Stanley, who wandered from bar to bar with no particular allegiance, Ted had it down to three or four bars in which he was a regular. If Ted went into a bar and saw somebody who might try to talk to him, he'd go right back out the door and straight to the next bar on his route. He hit these bars in the same order, and they were all peas in a pod, taxonomically speaking.

Camp Kill-Care was half full. Something passing for country-western music brayed from the jukebox, anthemic and hickly. Play it anthemic, Clint-I-forget-your-other-two-names, which means loud. Then modulate real stupid, like an S-curve in a gun barrel, and call it country. A huge, maybe priceless stained glass window was suspended by wires behind the bar. It always amazed Stanley that such a thing could hang in any kind of bar unmolested. It also bespoke the gentility of the premises, if tacitly and suspensefully. It seemed to him that, surely, sooner if not later, somebody would become annoyed with the placidity of this window—if only because it was there, let alone that it depicted a dove flying between Adam and Eve with an olive branch in its beak—and throw a chair through it. But nobody yet had.

Maybe tonight's the night, Stanley was thinking. There's always hope.

Then he saw her.

For just a moment Stanley had wanted a drink. Every night he followed Ted, it happened once or twice.

But the sight of her both stimulated and then almost cured his thirst.

She was sitting at the corner of the bar nearest the door with her back to it. Stanley was halfway down the bar, turning to take a seat, when he saw her.

Brunette hair, low-cut canvas sneakers, faded jeans clean and snug, a yoked cowgirl blouse with a couple of buttons open at the neck and nothing underneath. Light makeup and hoop earrings, the hair caught behind her ears by a tortoise-shell headband.

The eyes were just like he remembered them.

Favoring the healing incision in his back had taught him to limp, but now it was more a habit than anything else. As he changed course along the row of stools against the bar he realized that he liked his limp. It gave him a lot of time to study things while he was getting around.

He slid onto a stool at the far end of the bar, where he could watch her. The stool had a padded back, and he pressed his incision against it. Maybe if he held it there his guts wouldn't spill out. The incision no longer pained him much, but it still itched when he was trying to sleep. The firm lumbar pressure of the stool-back reassured him. Maybe if he held it there the scar would finish healing. Maybe if he held it there the scar would go away.

So, he thought. Her certainty of Ted's habitude allowed her, too, to lay for him at his first stop.

Around him various people chirped. He heard a whirring sound and, though he'd seen it before, looked up. A model train was making its way along the top of the back bar. He watched it. A red caboose disappeared behind the frame of the stained glass window just as a steam locomotive appeared from behind the opposite edge, emitting pusillanimous whistles. The engine began an oval curve in the track that would encircle the entire barroom, passing above the entrance door and below a large color television chained to the ceiling, over the tinted window to the street, over the video game in the corner, over the entrances to the rest rooms, over Stanley's head, over the bottles behind the bar, behind the stained glass again, over the jukebox and back to the TV, right after it passed…

He leveled his gaze.

…Over her. In between the jukebox and the TV.

He lowered his gaze to an ashtray on the bar in front of him.

What now, big shot?

He looked around. Nobody was paying any attention to the train. Nobody was paying any attention to him.

That included the bartender. This was a blonde woman wearing cut-off denim shorts and a cowgirl blouse tied in a knot over her ribcage. Her navel pouted outwards, a semaphore of great sexual prowess, to some. At least one of the men sitting near Stanley was drinking at this bar solely because this navel was to be studied here.

Just as Stanley was considering such a bartender as likely to be more concerned with the effect she was having on the customers than with setting a drink in front of them, she asked him was he thirsty.

"I was beginning to wonder whether anybody worked here," he said.

"Depends on what you call work," she said.

"You look terrific."

She drew the tips of both sets of fingers across her exposed abdomen. "Two hours a day at the gym. Every day. Year in, year out. Then I'll get a few wrinkles anyway and they'll fire me. Hopefully before that happens some fat real estate genius will come in here and slip a rock on my finger, tell the chauffeur to limo us up to his penthouse on Nob Hill." She rapped her knuckles on the bartop, twice. "For luck. And I do mean soon."

The man to Stanley's right stood uncertainly off his bar stool. "Thanks, Cindy," he said, throwing a ten onto the bar.

She looked Stanley straight in the eye. "You bet, Caesar." She turned to sweep the ten and the man's empty glass with its coaster off the bar. "See you tomorrow."

Stanley watched the man weave toward the front of the bar and shoulder his way through the door into the street.

"He sounds regular," said Stanley.

"Every night." She dropped the empty glass into a sink full of soap suds.

"Likes to drink, I guess."

"No," she said. "Not particularly. He's the father of my son."

Stanley stared at her.

"It hurts him deep to hear me talk about marrying somebody else."

Stanley blinked as he watched the street door close itself.

"I don't know why I told you that," the woman said. "I'm not that mean."

"I'm sure you're not."

"Look. You want a drink? You were doing all the complaining a minute ago."

Stanley paused. Then he said, "Bushmills. Over."

She got a glass and dragged it through a tub of ice beneath the bar.

"Throw out about half that," he said.

She did.

"They tell you to do that?"

She nodded. "Yes. But they don't water the booze." She placed the glass on a coaster in front of him and filled it with whiskey.

"Thanks." Stanley took a sip.

"Taste like whiskey?"

"Tastes like whiskey."

Since it was his first drink in a month, it tasted unfamiliar—a taste he would not have expected, a taste that did not coincide with the nostalgic succulence in his memory, wherein it resided in a file labeled *uisce beatha*, Gaelic for *breath of life*.

Cindy smiled a little smile and shelved the bottle.

Instead of going away she pulled a cigarette out of a pack that lived under the bar and showed it to him. "Mind?"

He plucked a folder of matches out of the ashtray and lit the cigarette for her. She inhaled deeply and leaned back into the corner of the bar, where it turned into the wall. Her first exhale sounded like a long sigh. They watched the room. The little train passed overhead.

"He always tip you?"

"Who?"

"Your husband."

"He's not my husband anymore."

"Ah."

"He just comes here to watch."

"I'm sorry I asked." He was, too.

"I'm sorry I married him."

"Nice kid?"

She smiled. "The greatest."

"Why can't he drink somewhere else?"

"Good question."

"It's not just a little weird?"

She shook her head. "The guy's completely harmless."

"Anybody ever suggest to him he's a little maudlin, too?"

"That too, what you said."

"Maudlin?"

"That's it. Harmless and maudlin. Worst kind of husband."

"Interesting combination."

"You think so? Maybe he should have met you first."

Stanley ducked his head and scratched his ear. She touched his wrist.

"I'm sorry," she said, leaning closer to him and lowering her voice. "Would you rather talk about the Giants?"

"No. I'd rather talk about the brunette sitting at the other end of the bar."

Her smile froze. For a moment Stanley thought she was going to slap him.

Stanley sipped his drink. "It's not like you think."

She stood up straight, not looking toward the brunette in question.

"Oh no?" She took a drag on the cigarette.

"No."

"You a cop?" she said, with renewed interest. "I just love cops. Those guns and that sense of propriety and all that dirt they get on them anyway."

"I'm not a cop. Why do people keep asking me that?"

"Maybe your shoes squeak."

"What's the brunette's name?"

"The guy talking to her calls her Donna."

"Donna what?"

"Beats me. I just heard that guy calling her Donna. When he calls her that, she answers."

"So what's the matter?"

"I don't know. She look like a Donna to you?"

He looked past her toward Donna. Now Donna had lit a cigarette, too, and was making a point to her companion by tapping on the bar in front of him with a green butane lighter.

Stanley couldn't see the gold stamp of the Reno casino. It was too far away.

But he was willing to bet it was there.

"How the hell would I know?"

"Well that's just the goddamn point, isn't it?"

Stanley brooded a moment. "What's she drinking?"

"Tom Collins."

She wouldn't have to provide her own lime in this place.

"She's a regular?"

"No. Last time I saw her was the first time I saw her."

"When was that?"

"What am I, a pocket organizer?"

He smiled and gestured toward her shirt. "A tie might help."

She glanced down at her cleavage, smiled, and leaned over the bar. The cleavage had freckles. "About two weeks ago. It was a Friday."

Stanley moved his drink just a little, so that his knuckles did not come in contact with her breast. "You weren't here last Friday."

"And you were?"

Stanley nodded.

"Last Friday Caesar the Second had the chicken pox."

"Chicken pox? Kids still get chicken pox?"

"Kids still get chicken pox."

"The germ pool at school, I guess."

"He's lucky that's all he caught. His best little buddy David came down with the crabs last year."

"Last *year?*"

She nodded.

"I'm almost afraid to ask this, but... How old is little Caesar the Second's best buddy David?"

She shrugged. "Same as Caesar."

"Twelve?"

"Eleven, when he caught the crabs."

"Frankly," Stanley said, taking a sip of his whiskey, "I'm shocked."

"Well if you think you're shocked, you should have seen little David's mother. He was naive about the crabs, at least. But that was about it for his naivete. Anyway, before he got around to asking her to help him figure it out he was just about eaten up."

Stanley smiled and took another sip of his whiskey. It was beginning to taste like he remembered it.

Cindy sighed. "For a while his mother went around thinking he and she might have been better off if he'd been born asexual, like his dad."

"Sounds like he's making up for it."

She smiled.

Stanley finished his drink. She moved to pour him another but he covered the glass with the flat of his hand. "Give me a bottled water. Any kind."

She appeared not to think twice about it. She put the Bushmills back on the shelf and uncapped a bottle of Calistoga.

"Just the bottle's fine."

She put the bottle on a fresh coaster and began to busy herself behind the bar.

"Caesar the Second," he mused, watching her wash a couple of glasses. "You called him that?"

She shrugged. More freckles. "He was paying the bills, at the time."

Stanley whistled softly. "You look great."

She didn't blush. "Thanks."

"You're too nice to be working here."

"Are you crazy? I take a grand a week cash out of this place. What's wrong with that? You think maybe I should get rid of the train?"

Stanley glanced at the brunette at the other end of the bar.

She draped the dish towel over a faucet and laughed. "Plus it beats hell out of that fly-speck town I started out in."

"Where's that?"

"New Mexico."

"Where abouts?"

"Little place called Kiva Junction."

"I have to admit…"

"You never heard of it."

"Pretty country, wherever it is, in that state."

"Not to propagate the myth, but there's nothing in that pretty country but cowboys and livestock and the pickup trucks they both ride around in."

"What's wrong with cowboys?"

"Everything."

"They're hetero, aren't they?"

"Who isn't?"

Stanley raised an eyebrow. "How long have you been in San Francisco?"

"Long enough," she said. She narrowed her eyes. "What do you mean? Is there a lot of queers in San Francisco? Where? Show me one."

Three people came in and took stools at the middle of the bar. Cindy went back to work.

Stanley worried the bottle of water for a while.

"Donna", Cindy had heard Ted call the brunette.

Donna Vivienne Carneval, did Stanley think? Portuguese and Swedish, did he think?

He stood off the bar stool, picked up the bottle of water, and limped down the bar. Reaching the corner to the left of the front door, he stopped to study the playlist on the jukebox. If nothing else came of it, maybe he could do something about the music in this place.

The machine took only paper money. Singles, fives, tens and, incredibly enough, twenties. Why not C-notes? If you're going to go to all the trouble to build a jukebox that only takes paper money, you might as well think big. To pass the time he fed it the most mangled single he had. The machine sucked it up as ergonomically as a junkyard dog inhales a Vienna sausage. He punched an alphanumeric without thinking. A digital display thanked him.

Why is it, Stanley wondered, as the jukebox sorted through its CDs, that these buck-eaters in bars will take any kind of wrinkled, twisted, or spavined bill at all, while a machine in a BART station or laundromat won't accept any but the most recently minted, if not ironed or dry-cleaned, tender?

He propped the bottle on top of the jukebox and pretended to get serious about a Rod Stewart selection. Donna and Ted were sitting directly behind him, close enough that he could hear both their voices.

"I guess that makes the human body capital-intensive," Ted was saying.

That's good, Ted, thought Stanley. You tape, I'll mud.

"Resource-intensive," Donna corrected him. "Take the United States, for instance. The United States makes a lot of claims about a free-market economy based on tremendous industrial and intellectual resources. But in fact it is a heavily resource-intensive economy. Or was, we should say."

The jukebox had begun to play the blindly selected tune. It was called *I'm Proud To Be An American*, and, as it caterwauled its nationalistic thesis, everyone in the bar realized that the guy with a slight limp drinking water by the jukebox must be the idiot who just spent a dollar on this truly awful song. Not a very efficient way to eavesdrop. Stanley raised his bottle of water in a mute toast to the bar behind him without taking his eyes off the playlists.

Ted Nichols shot an annoyed glance over his shoulder as he said to Donna, "Was?"

"Sure," she continued. "Was. The fish are gone, the trees are going. Copper, coal and other minerals are played out. Oil we can get, but at what environmental cost? We make a lot of noise about South America exploiting her natural resources, but all we really care about is inhibiting competition."

"But it doesn't make any difference."

"Correct. Soon enough our natural resources are going to be practically exhausted, and our civilization will be in the same relative fix as Europe, China, Iraq, or any other older, resource-exhausted country. We'll be buying everything we need from the developing countries. The balance of trade is biased 21% against us already." She paused to watch Ted sip his beer. "Ever heard of the Yellow River in China? Also known as the Hwang Ho?"

"Sure."

"Particularly the middle course, in the Shansi and Shensi Provinces, but mainly in the Honan Province — right?"

Did she mean Hu Nan? wondered Stanley, flipping past the Clint

Black catalogue. You say Honan, I say Hu Nan, let's call the kidney Off. Les Paul and Mary Ford?

"Um…," said Ted.

"Just say yes," Donna said.

"Sure. Okay, yes. Have you been there?"

"I have. But that's beside the point. The river's 3,000 miles long — that's the width of the continental U.S. Know why they call it the Yellow?"

"Ah… Because it's yellow?"

"Right in one. Know why it's yellow?"

Ted shook his head.

"An honest man. The river is yellow because it's full of topsoil, which is washed into the river by torrential seasonal rains that assault the watershed drained by the river."

"Do tell," said Ted, filling his mouth with beer.

"There's more. It's even to the point."

"It's your point," said Ted, carefully setting his glass on the bar.

That's interesting, thought Stanley. I can hear it in his voice. His tone says, *Why don't you leave me alone?* and, *I don't come here to solve the world's problems.* How's she going to handle that?

"The river drains so much topsoil because there's nothing to check erosion on the slopes of the watershed. Why do you think that is?"

"Lady, I don't come here to think."

"A spokesman for the race."

"So what prevents the topsoil from draining into the Yellow River?" Ted replied tiredly, with such disinterest that a stranger might have assumed Donna and Ted as married ten years already.

"Nothing. That's the point."

"But how much topsoil can there be?"

"Another interesting point."

"So?"

"Trees."

"Trees? Trees… I saw a tree just recently. Now where…? Yes. It was a big lone evergreen job in the lower Haight. I was rocking this used-clothing store…"

"What kind of lone evergreen?"

"How should I know?"

"God this song is awful."

Donna's rueful glance at Stanley's back caused his scar to crawl. "Patriotism's a lonesome business-like thing to do," she said.

Ted raised his glass. "Somebody's got to do it."

"Yeah." They toasted.

As Donna demurely sipped her Tom Collins, Ted drained his beer and signaled Cindy for another.

The song finished. While Stanley searched for a new selection an awkward silence lengthened at the bar.

"So what about this topsoil?" Ted finally croaked, standing off his stool to fish cash out of his jeans.

"Well, this topsoil has been draining into the Yellow River and making it yellow ever since a very specific event."

"Which was?" Sorting through a modest wad of bills, Ted suddenly tapped Stanley's shoulder with a folded single. "Hey buddy," he said, rather thickly. "Here's a buck. Play something decent."

"Sure, baby," said Stanley brightly, snatching the bill without turning around. "Any requests?"

"Something decent."

"Which was, the cutting down of the last tree in the watershed," continued Green Eyes.

Cindy put a beer in front of Ted.

"The last tree in the... You mean, there are no trees in the watershed of the Yellow River?" Ted picked up his glass and set it down again, half empty.

"Correct. As I said before, the Yellow's 3,000 miles long, and it drains something like three-quarters of a million square miles."

"You're telling me there's no trees in 750,000 square miles? What's the place look like?"

Mars, Stanley thought, punching up David Bowie.

"Mars," said Donna. "It's very beautiful, actually. Kind of morbidly fascinating."

"There must have been trees there at some time."

"Oh, there were. That's the point. The central course of the river was entirely forested. The forests had a lot to do with why Honan Province was the seat of the ancient Chinese civilization. Buildings, heat, doors, furniture — like that."

"Hey," said Ted, reaching out to touch Donna's forearm. "It was the days before sheetrock."

"Yes," she said, faking a laugh. "The halcyon days."

Ted walked his fingers to the inside of her elbow. "So what happened?"

"The Chinese cut them all down."

"When?"

She shivered and looked at Ted's fingers, which had almost reached her shoulder. "When they were resource-intensive."

"When was that?"

"The earliest records keeping track of the river's doings date back to the third millennium, B.C."

"Jesus..."

"About the same time as Iraq."

Ted was picking it up. "Back when Iraq was... What did they call Iraq before, you know, before they called it Iraq?"

The Garden of Eden, thought Stanley. At last: Roy Orbison, *I'm Falling*. Q-32.

"Paradise," Donna said.

Ted looked deep into her eyes. "The Garden of Eden?"

"That's what they called it."

"Have they called it that lately?"

"No. Not lately. Even Saddam Hussein hasn't called Iraq the Garden of Eden lately. The garden part is now a vast marshland."

"You been there, too? To paradise, I mean?"

"Yes."

"But I haven't?"

"No," she smiled. "Not yet."

Ted nearly drained a full glass of beer.

"Which is the point."

Stanley suddenly realized that Ted and most of Donna were almost perfectly reflected in the glass encasing the playlists in the jukebox. He watched Ted squeeze his eyes closed with the fingers of one hand, then squint at 'Donna' from beneath the shade of its palm. Ted was a tired man. "But of course... So the big question is..." Ted sighed wearily. "What *was* the point?"

"You said it was to get drunk and put some moves on me."

"I said that? We don't have to get drunk. I would like... But no, really, this is... interesting. Your arm is... soft. What was the point? I forget."

"We were talking about the fragility of resource-intensive economies."

"Ah. No wonder I forgot."

"Ever read a book called *At the Edge of History*, by G. Irwin Thompson?"

One play left. Instead of punching it up, Stanley watched the reflected Ted lower his hand to his glass, pick it up, up-end it, set it down empty. Maybe Ted really was trying to keep up with her, but it was obvious that his interest was cooking down to a good night's sleep. A recalcitrant pigeon for Donna.

Ted said, "Suppose I haven't?"

"Then you've missed a very interesting remark he made," she answered, "which is, 'The human body is the romantic landscape of the twentieth century.'"

When it became obvious she wasn't going to keep talking, Ted tried to repeat the words, moving his lips soundlessly. *I Fall to Pieces*, which had replaced the piece of tripe about America's pride in her workers, was coming to an end. The spiders from Mars must have gotten lost somewhere. Ted was having trouble willing himself to keep up with Donna's conversation, and had put his palms flat on the bar, the better to sway along with the music. Stanley could see that he was bored, had had a hard week, had nothing but hard weeks. He probably had one or two other things on his mind besides the Yellow River and resource-intensive economies—like whether he'd missed *Deep Space Nine* yet—or maybe he had nothing on his mind at all, and wanted to keep it that way. But it was Friday night and he'd done all he could do for one week, and Donna was certainly attractive enough to make him try to ignore his weariness, so long as she was easy. And, thought Stanley bitterly, Donna, who could play men like Paganini played the fiddle, would know exactly when to play easy. For the opening of her allegretto she had brought up the human body. Gamely Ted rallied to ask, "What is this to do with…"

"Thompson's point," she interrupted him, "is that there are fewer and fewer of any other landscapes available. Like, say, a nice riparian habitat, with trees and undergrowth and birds and babbling tributaries — all growing out of topsoil that's a hundred thousand or so years old because it hasn't been washed out of its watershed. His is a radical view, of course, radical-poetic you might call it. One could probably do quite all right for romantic landscapes along the Alaska Highway, for example, or in Siberia or James Bay or Patagonia. Come to think of it, in the case of James Bay you'd better hurry. But for the vast majority of humankind, who are city dwellers, the scope of the romantic landscape narrows considerably, is limited to the one in which they might find pleasure in watching, touching, interacting. After riding the subway to work and back, and spending all day in a building whose windows don't open, breathing air from which has been filtered any taste of spring…."

"Recycled air fit only for breeding vicious Legionnaire's bacteria," put in Ted, with a ridiculous flourish of his hand. "Ah," he sighed dismissively, and made the bold move of feinting two fingertips, nearly touching them to her lips, before, with a flourish, he took up his glass again.

She had moved her lips to meet the touch, but his fingers, falling short, retreated. She pouted as he repeated, "A taste of spring…" into the mouth of his beer glass.

"*Voila,*" she said, as if proud. "To one accustomed to such an environment a nude companion writhing with pleasure in twisted sheets and semi-darkness is about as romantic a landscape as one might realistically expect ever to see."

This got Ted's attention. "Or touch," he managed to say, awkwardly brushing the work-swollen knuckles of two fingers along the cord of her neck. Stanley winced. He remembered the cord of that neck.

"Or taste," she whispered.

"Oh, yeah," Ted uttered thickly.

A charming flush of color did not rise from her shoulder to her cheeks. But she agreed with him verbally, repeating, "Taste," and softly encouraged him by catching his hand in one of hers and bringing its fingers to her lips.

And now — who could ask for more? — Roy Orbison began to sing *I'm Falling.* Who, indeed, thought Stanley, touching their reflections on the neon-illumined glass with his own fingertip, as it weaved down the playlists.

Donna folded her own fingers into Ted's fist. "So," she concluded. Without another word she dipped a fingertip of her free hand into her Tom Collins and touched his lower lip with it. "Can you guess the next step?"

The poor guy took the fingertip between his lips. Stanley imagined the taste of Tom Collins and, quite strangely, sensed a twinge of… Was it jealousy? Remorse? Nostalgia?

"At the moment I'm, like, totally incapable of pursuing a logical thesis," Ted admitted, fitting the words around the tip of the glossed nail. "Help me."

"Can you stand the notion of the human body as the *industrial* landscape of the twenty-first century?" she responded gaily.

She dropped her hand and slid its fingers along the denim inside his thigh, pausing just as her fingers reached his groin, and moved her lips close to his ear, so that their cheeks touched. "If ever there were a resource-intense economy," she whispered, "it's the human body. The last natural resource remaining to be exploited in a devastated world."

She pushed his leg aside and slid off her bar stool, so that she stood up between Ted's parted legs, and within his tentative embrace. She breathed a sigh into his ear, and followed it with her tongue. Stanley stood close enough to hear the click of saliva. He watched as her free hand swept up under the tail of the sheetrock taper's flannel shirt, over the pale roll of fat, his ribs, onto his lower back, coming to rest where, had it been Stanley's back, the palm would have encountered a line of stitches.

He wondered if she smelled of lavender and acetone.

"It seems that you have already entered the resource market," she said into poor Ted's damp ear. "This market is demanding. Does your schedule afford you a proportionate amount of... leisure time?"

He pushed her to arm's length. "You mean, like, trips to China?"

She forced a smile. "Since you bring it up..."

"No fucking way," Ted Nichols said, a little too thickly. "China my ass."

One for the landlubbing proletariat, thought Stanley.

Donna laughed, a little too loudly, and ruffled her victim's hair. "Silly boy." Then she grabbed two fistfuls of his hair and shook his head as if it were a drying gourd and she needed to hear if any of its seeds were loosened yet.

Ted winced and raised both of his hands to covers hers, but said nothing. They stood like that for just a moment. She, her eyes burning, held great thick tufts of his hair, as if on the verge of getting his attention by really hurting him. Well, she was. A fascination etched into her features what, even by the luridly backlit reflection in the jukebox, could only be the result of her own amazement that this specimen might subconsciously think she might let him get away, as he had from every other woman in his life.

And Ted, covering her fists with his own two hands, grimacing, not entirely sure what had happened, still interested in only one or two things, said "Ow, shit," in a gentle, good-natured, softly confused voice.

Donna softened her smile. She freed one hand and, not releasing the other's grip on Ted's hair, pulled his face very close to hers, flattened her palm against his cheek, and whispered, "How about San Francisco, then? My place. No plane tickets involved," and kissed him full on the mouth.

Startled, Ted was slow to respond, but when he did he came on with everything he had. Poor Ted must have been sitting in front of that television over the dry cleaner for a long time. Probably ever since a redhead with gray eyes had thrown him over for a rich drywall contractor, Stanley thought bitterly. At any rate, tired as he was, Ted was hungry and eager. He pushed Donna against the bar and kissed her hard, and she let him do it.

What a gig, Stanley thought.

She waited until Ted released her.

Ted Nichols stood back a step, weaving just a bit. A tuft of hair stood straight out from one side of his head. As he turned aside the stub of a pencil dropped from behind his ear, bounced off his shoulder, and fell to the floor. He was breathing as if he'd just run a block to tell everybody in the bar that a swarm of killer bees had cornered the mayor with his pants down in his executive bathroom and stung him to death.

Ted reached for his drink but couldn't find it. He tore his eyes off Donna long enough to locate the glass and turn it upside down over his mouth, even though the glass was empty.

"Sure," he said, dropping the glass to the bartop and wiping his mouth with the back of his sleeve. "Your place."

Emboldened by drink and the sixty-second kiss, Ted had finally taken the initiative. As she started to turn back to the bar he took her arm in one of his hands and turned her back towards him.

"First your place," he said. He moved his eyes very close to hers and lowered his voice to a husky whisper. "Then maybe we'll see about China."

Donna laughed straight into his face.

Stanley left the bar.

By the time Donna and Ted had paid up, Stanley would be sitting across the street in the pickup, ready to follow them.

There was little time to feel sorry for Ted, for Guy No. 2, with his weary eyes and flannel shirt. But if Stanley made a mistake, Ted was on the spiral to being Guy No. 10 on a different list.

Chapter 14

It was nearly midnight. Traffic was intermittent. Most of the store-fronts had long since darkened, and fog had begun to isolate the street-lights along Geary Boulevard. The temperature had dropped with the intrusion of a layer of cool marine air. There was a taste of salt in the fog, and every couple of minutes the big bass foghorn groaned from the south tower of the Golden Gate Bridge, beyond the Presidio.

The truck was parked across the street from the bar, headed west. Stanley had jaywalked across Geary and unlocked the driver's door by the time the sporting couple exited *Camp Kill-Care*, heading east on Geary. They walked arm in arm, huddled against the cold of the fog, each with a hand in the other's opposite hip pocket, as lovers will. Stanley quietly rolled down the window of the truck, adjusted the side-view mirror and followed their image in it. As they approached 4th Avenue, a tractor pulling a forty-foot Safeway trailer slowed for the light and stopped, blocking his view. He gave up on the mirror and turned to watch the intersection. Though there was no other traffic and the truck was obviously going to go straight on after the light changed, the couple did not jaywalk across 4th Avenue. A foghorn sounded. A car slowly hissed along the middle of the damp three-lane boulevard and passed him, headed west.

The light facing north changed from emerald to orange to ruby. The Safeway truck grunted, then pulled through the intersection, its diesel whistling between gear changes. The trailer's receding taillights revealed no loving couple. They had turned up 4th Avenue.

Stanley started the truck and pulled diagonally across west-bound Geary. He U-turned through a breach in the cement median —a sign forbidding left or U-turns briefly glared in the headlights—and drove diagonally across east-bound Geary until he turned right and south, up 4th Avenue. At the top of the block he saw the couple just jaywalking across Anza Street.

He motored slowly uphill, as if looking for a parking space. When he got to the intersection, fog blew straight through the lights, right to left, west to east. It was a four-way stop and he stopped for it, leaning over the wheel to look west, south and east. In fact there was no parking to be seen. Nor could he see his quarry. As he sat there wondering what to do about it, a police cruiser suddenly burst into the intersection from the south, opposite him, all its blue and red lights flashing, its siren silent. Stanley hadn't seen or heard it coming and jumped three inches—exactly the distance allowed by the vertical clearance between his head and the headliner of the little pickup. The black and white braked briefly enough to dip its front end and emit a brief whoop from its siren. Then, its carburetor moaning for air, it leaped across Anza and passed the truck with a sound like a sliding door violently slammed shut. Stanley watched it descend the block in his rear view mirror, slough whooping and sideways through the intersection at Geary, and straighten out enough to head west.

Silence and fog descended again on the Avenues.

Stanley turned left through the intersection and proceeded slowly along the line of parked cars. Four slots in front of him a car turned on its lights. He braked to a stop and waited.

The car was a new BMW. It was late in a quiet neighborhood. There was no one else around. The BMW almost certainly had to contain Donna and Ted. Possibly Ted Nichols had never been in such a car before. As its lights came on its radio antenna telescoped up out of its sheath in the rear fender. After a moment the white backup lights came on, its front wheels turned toward the curb, and the car backed until its bumper nudged the car behind it. Then its front wheels cranked outward, the backup lights turned off, and the car inched forward.

He waited, not dimming his lights as politeness might suggest, until he could see the silhouettes in the BMW. When the car pulled into the street he caught a glimpse of long hair and a flash of earring as the driver racked the steering wheel and glanced to her left and then, aha, he saw her passenger's shoulder draped in square-checked flannel. The license plate was California DDT 301, which he copied onto the top page of the little notepad with the red Chinese logo that rode on a stalk held to the truck's windshield by a suction cup.

He dimmed his lights and pulled in front of the parking space as the BMW rolled to the end of the block. He even put the truck in reverse for appearances's sake; but as soon as the BMW reached 3rd and turned left, Stanley threw the pickup in first and took off after it.

The BMW was a creamy white with gold alloy wheels cast in a geometric pattern. Its dashboard glowed reddish-orange, like a fire in a distant canyon. It wasn't the car that Stanley remembered Donna driving six weeks ago. But, six weeks ago, Donna hadn't been the green-eyed brunette's name either. She had been called Vivienne Carneval then, practically an homage to his credulity, and she drove Stanley to her Excelsior apartment in a navy blue Pontiac station wagon. He'd found that address again, three weeks ago, its red and white FOR RENT sign visible from a block away.

At the time Stanley had thought the Pontiac remarkable, not only because he hadn't been inside a non-Japanese vehicle in something like ten years, but also because it enhanced his vision of Ms. Carneval as an angry divorced or estranged up-scale housewife who would demonstrate in bed more desperate tricks under Stanley than the CIA under Casey.

Short of scarlingus, that is.

Had Stanley been paying attention, this thought might have given him pause. Supposing scarlingus—voluntary, nay, *willful* scarlingus—treatment superior to that which he had received from the deceitful tongue of the green-eyed Donna, would Stanley not be well-advised to allow the BMW's taillights to fade into the night? And having done so, would it not be prudent and civic to then drive straight to Iris' apartment; telephone this BMW's license number to Corrigan; let the cops do what cops do best; and finally surrender to the fanciful elaborations of the nurse's fetish, as the present and more-than-equable resolution of his fate?

Prudent, no doubt. As well as civic. Safe, too.

But Stanley was paying attention to other concepts. Revenge, for one. To inflict injury upon he, in this case she, who has injured thee. Actual sex with Green Eyes, as additional compensation, for two. The possibility of continued good health by virtue of a new kidney, from the vantage of which he might resume drinking himself to death without any further help from disinterested parties, thank you very much, for three.

Stanley eased his foot off the brake, and let the truck drift downhill to the intersection.

His story to Corrigan notwithstanding, Stanley remembered a great deal about that Friday six weeks ago. His memory of the events that led up to the subsequent three-day blank might even be described as relentlessly vivid. Making Donna, for example, had been no trouble at all: The green eyes, of course, brunette, 5'9", 130 pounds, northern Midwest accent—possibly from Detroit, which at the time he thought might explain her taste in cars.

Now he surmised that her cars were stolen, one per job.

He remembered a lot more. The expert way she'd psychointellectually manhandled Ted varied little from the way she cajoled Stanley into going home with her. She'd smoothly parried, without deflecting entirely, Ted's amorous intentions with a story about global ecology, not unlike one she had foisted on Stanley. Different theme, though. One theme per job. At the time he'd assumed that she was sounding his politics, that if he weren't liberal enough, she wouldn't sleep with him. No doubt Ted was thinking the same way. Subsequently her aggressive kiss came as a welcome surprise to a man too worn out from a week's work and too disarmed by drink to fly very high in the blue skies of the eco-theoretical.

She turned east on Geary.

Stanley followed.

About now she would be suggesting that Ted take a look in the glove compartment. There he would find a pint of excellent brandy, a three-pack of lubricated prophylactics, and a short-handled whip. Then she would ask him if he thought he would mind handling all five of them, and her, too.

This query would make Ted thirsty.

While he took a sip of brandy, her right hand would drop to the inside of Ted's left thigh, high up, and gently knead where no woman had lately kneaded.

Gosh, Ted would be thinking, I could have stayed home and watched any one of the three versions of *Star Trek* currently available to viewers everywhere—approximately what Stanley himself had thought six weeks ago.

He was still thinking it.

The BMW swung off Geary, up the ramp to Masonic, and turned south. Stanley let the choppers of a couple of Hell's Angels already on Masonic merge in between his truck and the Beamer, which wasn't driving particularly fast, nor were the two Angels, who were biking one-handed, passing a joint back and forth over the blacktop between them.

At Turk Street the BMW caught the red light and stopped. All four vehicles sat in a row, idling comfortably in the cool night. A single car drifted across the intersection from the west and continued downtown. Two cars waited northbound on Masonic.

His partner declining the roach, the other biker stubbed out its coal on his own tongue, then swallowed it.

Stanley was just thinking how quiet it was for a Friday night, when the light changed to green. The two Angels simultaneously twisted the throttles on their Harleys and caused a tremendous roar to engulf the two idling automobiles as completely as a grouper swallowing a brace of guppies. The two motorcycles split around the BMW and blasted across the intersection before the woman at the wheel even had time to take her foot off the brake. The rider on the left, his teeth clenched like a skull's in rigor mortis, jetted across Turk Street and down the hill perched on the rear wheel of his scooter, its front wheel high in the air above and barely before him, with two and three foot flames belching out of the bike's parallel exhaust pipes, bathing the asphalt beneath them as if to melt it. The other bike bolted forward while almost perpendicularly sideways to its vector of travel, straddled by its rider as if with intention to brand it, just as soon as it could be wrestled to the pavement. The machine switched and wallowed across the three southbound lanes of Turk Street, the beam of its headlamp sweeping every direction within ninety degrees of straight ahead, purple smoke spewing from its nearly tractionless rear tire. This rider's left elbow came perilously close to tearing the right side mirror off the still motionless BMW, and the steel-clad heels of one or another of his boots spewed rooster tails of blue sparks as they skidded along the pavement.

Within just a few seconds the motorcycles were completely out of sight, though still audible. Only a swirling blanket of blue smoke remained, the visible component of the distinctive paraffin reek of Castrol. A few seconds after that, the cars opposite Stanley and the BMW began to move north. Still the BMW did not move into the intersection. A car behind Stanley sounded its horn. Stanley quickly moved his left arm across his face, as if to adjust the rearview mirror. Whether or not Green Eyes glanced into her mirror he could not tell. But the BMW began to move. As it did so, the signal went to orange. A Volvo abruptly passed Stanley on the right, charging through the intersection as the light changed to red. Its driver honked his horn and raised his middle finger as he passed the BMW.

Watch it, buddy, thought Stanley, running the light; you might wind up the victim of a drive-by nephrectomy.

Crossing the Panhandle and upper Haight the BMW zigged right onto Frederick and zagged left onto Clayton, not two blocks from the address of Guy No. 1. What a coincidence.

Green Eyes was up to her eyeballs in blood group O-Negative demography tonight.

The white Beamer crossed 17th Street and Clayton, dropped down onto upper Market, and headed west. Up the hill at Clipper, the BMW turned left, cruised a few blocks along Diamond Heights, U-turned through the median at Duncan, and drove slowly back the way it had come, past a scenic vista high above the fog-bound nocturnal city. From here the occupants of the BMW, and anybody else, could view roughly a quarter of San Francisco, along with the lights of the Bay Bridge and the East Bay hills from south of San Leandro clear up beyond the Richmond Bridge, twelve miles away. The bank of fog that had begun to blanket Geary Street now stretched all the way downtown, swamping the skyscrapers of the Financial District like spilled cement perhaps twenty stories high.

It's a lover's tour of the city, thought Stanley. How come I didn't rate this?

Maybe the guy balked at using the quirt on her. Maybe she misjudged his character.

Maybe she thinks she's being followed.

Maybe this is the wrong goddamn white BMW.

Stanley pulled to the curb and killed his headlights. Fifty yards further the BMW slowed, but did not stop completely, crawling along behind the cars of lovers parked where they could hold hands and gaze down on the midnight lights of the city and contemplate a future without jazz radio.

At last the BMW moved off. He waited until it had surmounted a small rise in the street before turning on his lights, allowing another car to fall in between himself and the object of his surveillance before he pulled back onto the street.

The BMW turned east on Portola and drifted slowly along the shoulder of Twin Peaks, which also affords panoramic views of the city. Emphasizing this, there is a neighborhood just west of Twin Peaks in which the streets are named Panorama, Starview, Gladeview, Knollview, Skyview, Cityview, Longview and Mountainview—not to mention Aquavista—and for a while Stanley thought it the BMW's destination. But the white car abruptly turned right, into a little cul-de-sac called Parajito Terrace.

Stanley knew the neighborhood well enough to avoid following the BMW all the way into the dead-end. He pulled over at the top of the street, lights doused, to watch.

The BMW descended the steep short street and drove three-quarters of the way around the cul-de-sac, counterclockwise from six to eight. Just as Stanley was about to become convinced the car had deliberately led him here, so as to identify him and his truck, it pulled up next to a van in front of a dark stucco house and parked.

The BMW's lights extinguished. After a minute both its doors opened. Stanley rolled down his window in time to hear a man and a woman sharing a laugh.

Again, Stanley experienced a little twinge of jealousy. Was some part of him so eager to suffer?

Dark figures exited the car, two doors slammed, and a car alarm squawked twice as the figures moved toward the house.

A stolen car with a car alarm. How civilized.

A wooden ramp led from the street to the garage and front entrance of the stucco house. Stanley plainly heard the lighter footfalls of Donna's sneakers on the wood ramp as she walked past the step-van parked on it. Ted's rubber-soled work boots made heavier, less-frequent thumps behind her. Ted's steps were erratic, hesitant. Ted was drunk.

There was another sound, of something moved sharply through the air. For a moment Stanley couldn't place it. But, the third time, he recognized it.

The whip.

Ted was carrying the whip. He was playing with it, tentatively snapping its split thong against the leg of his pants. He was getting a feel for it.

Ted said something that Stanley didn't catch, followed by a swoop and a soft snap. The woman gave a little yelp and laughed. Ted, neosadist, was dispensing a little taste of the lash. Emboldened, was he?

What had he said to make her laugh? Gee, it's dark out here? It might be too dark to hit you some place where it might feel good? Whap! Yipe! How was that? Was I close? Pretty dark, though. I want to watch. You got any candles? Only if you beg. You like hot wax on your nipples? Oh, you dog. Yes, I always been a quick study.

Your turn to mud, Stanley thought, while I tape.

They began to whisper together at the door. She would be giving him some business about not waking the nosy widow who lives across the way. Then she dropped her keys. They clattered when they hit the deck. They jingled as Ted hastened to retrieve them. Mademoiselle. Oh, you speak French. And Greek. Giggle. Haw. Bark like a Chihuahua. Whap! Yipe! That's it…

Stanley considered. All this noise seemed too obvious. Was it a signal? A stall?

The front door was finally opened. For a moment Stanley could see the lights of the city twinkling through a window at the back of the house, beyond the narrow entry hall, then a light came on over the ramp.

There she stood. Green Eyes. Watching the night.

The door closed. The light went out.

At least he had the right party. And a couple of big brass twos nailed to the wall between the entrance and the garage door beneath the light had declared the address.

He made a note on the darkened pad, below the BMW's license number: *22 Parajito Terrace.*

An address that would be good for maybe another hour.

Plenty of time, never a more perfect time, to call Corrigan.

A thought struck him. They wouldn't do the operation here — would they?

He dismissed the idea as too complicated. A reasonably equipped operating room couldn't be easily portable. So, he concluded, she would drug Ted here, then move him. Maybe switch vehicles, too: that would seem like a good precaution.

So, to wait.

Good luck, Ted.

Stanley released the parking brake. The truck coasted soundlessly down the hill toward Parajito Terrace, and he swung it into the first driveway at the mouth of cul-de-sac.

The driveway led uphill, to the right, more or less opposite the car deck. As gravity slowed the truck Stanley pulled the hand brake with infinite care, click by click until it held, avoiding the footbrake so as not to illuminate the cul-de-sac with his brake lights.

In the silence that followed he began to detect the little neighborhood's audio environment; the whispers of the fog passing through the boughs of a grove of eucalyptus ranging up the bowl that formed the south and west sides of the cul-de-sac; the riparian flow of the perpetual traffic of upper Market Street, a hundred yards up the hill, over the bowl's lip.

Stanley peered up at the building in whose driveway he'd parked. It was a tall apartment building, of several units terraced up the west slope, eventually rising almost as high as the looming berm of Market Street. The views would be magnificent. The wide garage door just beyond his hood would open up to the entire ground floor. The building was dark and silent. Everybody was snug for the night or gone to Tahoe for the weekend.

The whole neighborhood was as if asleep, buttoned-up, or abandoned. A single-engined airplane droned overhead, drifting toward the Bay until its lights were no longer distinguishable from the myriad bulbs of Oakland, its drone silenced by the distance.

The fog had begun to froth down from Twin Peaks, cooling the slope as it came. From the glove compartment of the pickup Stanley retrieved a pint of whiskey. It had been in there for five or six weeks, untouched since his last tour of the Tenderloin. He twisted off the cap and treated himself to a slug. Antifreeze. He replaced the pint in the glove compartment, and, thinking that he'd never been able to comprehend how any hooker could manage to look cozy while half-naked on a freezing street corner, he slowly zipped up his jacket against the cold.

He concentrated on keeping the zipper quiet.

But it was loud enough to prevent him from hearing the back door of the van open.

Chapter 15

He'd been looking at the house for at least a couple of minutes before he abruptly realized that someone had opened the back door of the van before he'd started watching. It may even have happened while he'd been capping whiskey. The thought brought a prickle to the back of his neck. He should be a little more alert. Otherwise the next person he tried his smile on might be a coroner.

So Stanley didn't move. He almost stopped breathing.

A lighter flared in the back of the van. Igniting two cigarettes, its flame clearly illuminated the faces of a black man and a white man. The lighter went out. Two orange dots floated around the dark mouth of the van door, like fireflies in a cellar.

If these two smokers were looking out the back door of the van at all, they were looking directly at the open driver's window of Stanley's truck. The street was plenty dark, but the least movement on Stanley's part would certainly betray his presence.

Stanley was twisted sideways in his seat, unmoving. He wasn't unthinking, though—thoughts like, two guys quietly smoking cigarettes in the back of a van on a quiet street in a quiet neighborhood of a quiet San Francisco midnight could quietly mean nothing, right?

Wrong.

Now what?

Kick down the door with two guns blazing.

Right. Call Corrigan? Right. Too late to call anybody, now.

How about another license number?

No problem. The license plate was hanging right underneath the two fireflies. One of the fireflies even had a lighter by which Stanley could read the tag—along with the make and maybe even the year of the van. Very helpful, such a lighter. Guy holding it might even offer to get a hose, siphon a little gasoline out of the tank, and set Stanley on fire, just as soon as Stanley assured them he'd committed the license to memory. Whoosh. Recite it to Shiva, baby. Maybe light up Stanley right here in Hop Toy's pickup truck. Not only does upholstery kill dogs that eat it, it burns good.

A puff of smoke appeared over the van's door and billowed straight up. Stanley thought he heard someone talking, but the talk wasn't any louder than his own heartbeat.

Even so, he realized, he must now be seeing the chapter he'd missed six weeks ago.

Donna had taken him in a different car to a different house, in the Excelsior District. Drinking and flirting as they had been, polluting sips from the pint of excellent brandy with gargles from a quart of Lucky Lager, toying with the little quirt at stoplights, Stanley hadn't taken proper notice of the address of her apartment. He was still in San Francisco, after all. Historically speaking, he could wake up anywhere in town and find his way home. It had been an apartment, that much he remembered. And he recalled her taking an involved route from Geary Street to the Excelsior, probably to disorient him. But he recognized quite well the environs of the Excelsior District — who could miss a whole series of streets named for the great cities of Europe? London, Paris, Lisbon, Madrid, Edinburgh, Naples, Vienna, Athens.... Not only that but Hop Toy had an aunt who lived out there, and Stanley took her a box of produce once a week. Which reminded him, he or at least his truck had to go to work at 4 a.m.... Come on, he hadn't even named her street yet. European cities: Moscow, Munich, Prague... Prague was the aunt's street — and then... Dublin. What a jump.

Stanley remembered most of the Excelsior's streets, more or less in their correct order. This brand of serial memory was a hangover from when he'd worked in a vast plumbing-supply warehouse in the late seventies, and had been forced to learn long lists of the *non-sequitur* concept-names of different models of toilet: The Butler. The Carrera. The King and the Queen. No Knave, but a Baron and a Duchess, and also a President. And then there were the colors: a Buff President, a Mocha Queen, a Manhattan Granite Duchess, and so forth.

For the record, one of the lines of concept toilets coincided almost exactly with another neighborhood of Excelsior street names: Dartmouth, Cambridge, Yale, Harvard, Princeton, Amherst... And so forth.

One of the two smokers cleared his throat and spat. The bolus of mucus arced out of the darkness in the back of the van and caught what little light there was at its apogee, about ten feet above and halfway across the street, before it descended onto the canvas top of a Jaguar convertible nosed into a driveway not ten feet from Stanley's truck.

Stanley heard a soft chuckle. A disembodied voice drifted out of the darkness. "Good thing the man left his top up."

Another chuckle, different from the first. "Ever boosted a Jag?"

"Once," answered the first voice. "I might as well put a sign on my back says, 'Arrest this dumb member of the Negro race.' A big mistake."

"In this town? Are you kidding me? Just wear a suit and show the calling card of your law firm."

"I tried all that. More mistakes."

"It's the details, bring a man down."

"True story."

"What was it this time?"

"Give him the wrong card."

"Which card was that?"

"My bail bondsman."

"True story?"

"I am a little fucked up at the time."

"Who goes your bail?"

"Jerry Barrish."

"*Don't perish in jail — Call Barrish for bail.* My man."

"I make him rich."

"What does the heat say?"

"The man squints at Jerry's card. Then he squints at me. Then he squints at the Jag. It's a nice one. Twelve cylinders, leather interior, walnut dash, top of the line and brand new, too. So new it's still got the dealer's plates on it. He squints at Jerry's card again. After a while he shows me the card and says, 'Aren't you getting a little ahead of yourself, sir?'"

"Sir," the other man chuckled softly. "Respectful, like."

"He said, 'Just step out of the vehicle, sir, and keep your hands where I can see them.'"

"Oh, man. Away we go."

They both laughed grimly.

After a short silence: "That was it for me and the Jaguar thing."

"Not to mention the freedom thing."

"From then on, I just stick to keepin' wheels under Sibyl."

"Just enough to keep your hand in."

"That's right. A Beamer here, a Pontiac there. Mix it up. Nossir," the man sighed, "it don't pay to be any more particular than you can afford to be."

After another, longer pause, the same voice added, "That's a damn nice car, though. Damn nice car."

The other voice grunted.

The two fell silent.

Higher up the hill a motorcycle on Market revved its engine at the stoplight perpendicular to Parajito, getting ready to instantly accept the green at face value. Stanley realized he had created a crick in his neck by holding still for so long. Yet he didn't move. He had no doubt that the two men with the disembodied voices, reclining comfortably in the back of the van, were staring directly at him, whether they knew it or not. Waiting for something.

Stanley had long since grasped the key ring dangling from the ignition switch, ready to crank up the truck and back all the way out to Market Street if anything went wrong. His fingers were cramped. He even refused his eyeballs permission to move in their sockets.

Kick down the door with two guns blazing.

Right.

The motorcyclist redlined the engine and dumped the clutch. The machine took off, and its rider speed-shifted all the way up Market Street, snapping the clutch just enough to toe the gear change, not backing off the wide-open throttle at all. Stanley listened to the machine go through four or five gears until the sound had diminished into the ambient mutter of the city.

The two men in the van were listening to the motorcycle, too.

"Man," one of them said. "Must be something he wants bad, down the road."

"That, or something bad wants him up at this end."

While they chuckled, Stanley finally permitted himself to move his eyes enough to make a startling discovery.

The front door of the stucco house was open.

She was standing there.

There was no light. But he could easily make out the unmistakable figure of the brunette, silhouetted in the darkened doorway. Against the plate glass window on the other side of the house she was a complete darkness, outlined by the twinkling lights of the city.

The figure didn't move. How long had she been standing there?

She, too, must have been listening. But to what? The motorcycle? The conversation?

Stanley tried to remember whether he'd moved at all in the last twenty minutes. Had he done anything that had betrayed his presence to her?

The drink. Had she been there long enough to have seen him take the goddamn drink?

A convulsive movement of his sweating fingers caused the key ring to click against the steering column, and he stopped breathing. It seemed like the loudest sound he'd heard all night— louder than all motorcycles put together.

The woman's figure disappeared from the doorway. A moment later it reappeared at the back of the van.

A brief, whispered conversation ensued, cut short by a final, sharp whisper from the brunette.

"Can't you two keep quiet for a minute?"

"Aw, Sibyl, we was just —."

"Shut up!"

They shut up.

Sibyl, thought Stanley. The name clicked into place. Sibyl. Baby. How'd your date go with the helium-voiced anesthesiologist?

More to the point, how's your date going with Ted?

Sibyl made a sharp gesture with her arm and stepped aside.

Two men materialized in the gloom at the back of the truck.

Using a very conversational, ordinary tone, speaking noticeably louder than before, Sibyl said, "I hadn't realized you two had arrived already. You should have knocked."

One of the men replied, "Yessum."

"We was just takin' a break, lady," said the other man. "Been at it all week long."

"Well. Anyway, I appreciate your coming all the way out here at such an ungodly hour."

"Yessum."

"I'm sure my husband will make it worth your while."

"Thank you, ma'am."

"Now let's get this over with. You have the new one?"

"Yes ma'am."

"How do you want to manage it?"

"Well… How about we just bring in the new one and bring out the old one?"

Nobody said anything.

"Ma'am?"

"What? Well of course. Let's get on with it. It's getting late."

She led the way toward the house, followed by the shadow of one man dragging something out of the van and, a moment later, the shadow of the second man, taking up the end of the something. Between them stretched a horizontal shadow, about eight feet long and a couple of feet thick.

The woman entered the house first. The vista of city lights beyond darkened and reappeared. After a moment a light came on in the entryway, and Stanley could see that the two men were carrying a rolled carpet with fringe along its edges.

The front door closed behind them.

Someone locked it. The sound of a deadbolt sliding home was clearly audible.

The porch light went off.

Stanley blinked.

Then he lifted his legs over the Toyota's gear shift, transferred himself to the passenger seat, and gently pulled the latch on the passenger door. The dome light blinked on. Stanley barely restrained a loud curse as he pulled the door to. This was the first time the dome light in this truck had worked in two years. He thumbed a switch on the light's bezel. Then, taking a deep breath and ignoring the tingle in his lower back, he slid out of the passenger door.

Keeping low, he scuttled silently to the rear fender of the Toyota and peered beyond the tailgate.

The fog bank now spilling down off Twin Peaks rustled the grove of tall eucalyptus behind the house at the very end of the cul-de-sac, to Stanley's right. Otherwise, all was quiet. Directly in front of him, the front door of the stucco house remained closed. No light shone from within.

As quietly as he could do it, Stanley ran across the circle of asphalt and slid into a crouch at the back of the van. The open back door exuded odors of stale cigarette smoke and foam carpet padding, transmission fluid and... an essence he couldn't place. He hesitated.

What was that odor?

He shook off the query. He didn't have time to think about it.

It was dark there, darker than he'd thought possible. He had to put his nose to the license plate and actually trace the raised metal to figure out its letters and numbers. This took time. 1E...L...T0...36. It could have been a zero or the letter 'O'. No matter. A commercial license plate. 1ELT036. He could remember that: One El To Thirty-six. Like directions to a party in Chicago. Some party. Doubtless a California tag would attract the least attention. Even in San Francisco, two guys delivering carpet at midnight with a truck registered in Minnesota might look a little artless. He grasped the rear corner of the door and half-closed it. For this the light was better. A chrome script showed on the door panel: Ram. That would be a Dodge. Centered on the door above the model name was a magnetic sign.

CABRINI CARPET

Sales
Installation
Service

1338 Mission St
San Francisco
415-864-2825

Cabrini. He could remember that. Nice Italian name. Probably Florentine. Also, Cabrini Green is an infamous housing project in the heart of Chicago. And the phone number — forget the phone number. This sign was obvious bovine scatology — it had to be. It was the license number he needed to remember. He eased the door back to its open position. What was it? One El To Thirty-six. The EL runs in Chicago, where Cabrini—. He heard a sound. The deadbolt. A door swung open.

A woman's voice announced, "Well, that was painless."

"Yessum."

They were coming back. He wasted a look of pure nostalgia on the Toyota, but the truck may as well have been a mile away across open country in broad daylight.

Stanley backed away from the van, keeping its mass between himself and the front door of the house, backed across the asphalt in a direction at right angles to the one he would rather have gone, until he found himself in the shadows under a staircase. Just as he crouched toward a pair of plastic garbage cans a man appeared behind the van, walking backwards. Stanley ducked into the shadows behind the cans and watched the ground, his heart pounding.

Shoes scraped grit on the pavement behind the van. The two men grunted as they hadn't before.

"Damn Afghans is heavier'n them Persians," a man's voice said.

"They got a tighter weave and a better arms deal with the Great Satan," chuckled the other man.

"Maybe I should have kept it then," said the woman icily.

"Oh Lord, lady," said the second man. "Don't change your mind now."

"Hey!" hissed the first voice.

"Shit."

"Oh my," said the woman's voice. But through the velvet tone of those two words passed a core of steel, like the tang of a knife through its handle.

"Ahm... Sorry lady. Vince is just... tired."

"That's... quite all right. The streets are... clean around here. Just don't let the good side become... soiled. More soiled than it is, I mean. There might be... oil or something... where the cars park."

"Yessum."

"Pick it up, Vince," she snapped.

"You heard the lady," grunted the other man.

Stanley peered through the crack between the two garbage cans. He could make out several pairs of legs among the figures standing behind the van, though none of the torsos supported by them. The *dramatis personae* hadn't changed. It was still two men and a woman.

Green Eyes was called "Sibyl," when she wasn't called "Ma'am." The black guy was called Vince.

The two men were trying to get a carpet into the back of the van and, although they were talking about switching Afghans for Persians, it looked like the same carpet to Stanley, fringe and all.

But the black guy had dropped one end and now it splayed on the ground, partially unrolled. The white guy, unable to heft his end into the back of the van, still held his end of the carpet waist-high, and was muttering imprecations designed to encourage his partner to get his end aloft again.

As the black man stooped to gather up the spilled end of the carpet, Stanley glimpsed an extra hand there.

A white hand.

The hand was quite motionless, too. Its fingers folded an edge of the carpet against its palm, much as a sleeping child's might cling to the hem of its favorite blanket.

As briefly as Stanley glimpsed this hand it was gone, crushed against the belly of the black man as he heaved up his end of the roll and, with the other guy, manhandled the whole thing into the back of the van.

The white guy climbed in after it. The black man closed the door behind him and, wasting no time, walked briskly to the front of the van and climbed into the driver's seat.

The van's lights came on, its engine started, and it backed out of the driveway and across the cul-de-sac, directly toward Stanley. Less than ten feet from his hiding place the van stopped, its brake lights turning the underside of the staircase a brilliant scarlet. A gear lever on an automatic transmission clicked twice, the brake lights extinguished, and the van recrossed the cul-de-sac, heading up the hill toward Market.

The woman stood in the gloom of the front porch, watching the van until it was out of sight.

Crouched under the staircase behind the two garbage cans, Stanley was almost talking aloud to himself, ordering, willing the woman to go back into the house, shifting his eyes from her shadow to the pickup to the empty street at the top of the hill and back.

Still the woman lingered in the doorway, as if savoring the night air.

Stanley watched her in despair.

Finally she turned and went into the house. Stanley crouched toward the edge of the shadow beneath the staircase and waited, the fingers of one hand touching the asphalt just behind the shadow line, like a sprinter at his starting block. But he did not hear the front door close, nor the deadbolt slide home.

Straining for those audio cues, he waited. At the top of the hill you could drive east on Market, downhill, or west, up hill. If he sprinted to the truck, and if it started right away, and if the traffic up above wasn't too dense, and if the van wasn't driving too fast, and if the light wasn't red — he would have a fifty-fifty chance of turning the right way to catch it.

But if the brunette heard the truck start now she would become suspicious. After all, they had been in this cul-de-sac for nearly an hour, and beyond the three vehicles involved in this game, not a single other car had come or gone. Surely she would think it odd that a car would start up and leave immediately after the departure of the Cabrini Carpet van?

She was clever or perverse or both — wasn't she? — to tarry, as if to take the night air, while the van went on its way, while the van disappeared, into the big city. Just in case she wasn't alone here, she waited.

Or maybe she really *was* taking the night air. Right.

Stanley crouched behind the garbage cans, immobilized by her delay.

Then he heard the front door close, and the deadbolt shoot home.

But just as he put his weight on his forward foot, all set to sprint for the truck, he heard a thump on the car deck. Then another.

It was a sound he'd heard before. He froze.

A car alarm squawked. A car door opened. A foot scraped. The car door slammed.

A starter ground and the motor caught.

The BMW.

Bright white light spilled around the black cylinders of the two garbage containers, and Stanley made himself very small behind them. The light moved, the shadows moved with it, and he receded along with them, until he and the garbage cans were cast into complete darkness again, as, with an application of horsepower, the BMW swept around and suddenly accelerated out of the cul-de-sac, up the hill, and was gone.

Stanley shot out from behind the two garbage cans. At the second step of his sprint a sharp pain tugged at his lower back, but he kept on. It seemed to take him forever to cross the asphalt circle, as if he were trying to catch someone in a dream. In the renewed darkness his left knee glanced off the rear bumper of the now-invisible Jaguar. Another inch or two to his left and he would have exploded his patella. He kept on. Gaining the white Toyota at last he fumbled at the door handle until it opened, and fell into the driver's seat. The ignition key was still in the switch, and he twisted it. The engine turned over and caught.

Breathing heavily he fumbled at the headlight switch, inadvertently pulling its stalk down so that, as he backed out of the driveway, the headlights came on and the left turn-signal began to blink. The passenger door was still open. He backed straight across the mouth of Perego Terrace, onto the wooden parking deck of the stucco house. He placed the gear lever in first, let out the clutch, and the rear wheels lost traction on the wood deck and squealed. The passenger door slammed itself shut as he accelerated out of Parajito Terrace and threw the little truck into second. The engine bogged. The old Toyota didn't have quite enough moxie to make the grade in second. He forced the gears back into first. The engine revved up and the truck crested the hill at Market.

His light was red. Market Street flowed both ways beneath it, a solid barrier of fast traffic. Seeing no choice, Stanley swung right, grabbed second gear, and accelerated down Market Street. Brakes squealed and a horn sounded behind him. The street wound to the left around a tall median wall and back to the right. He punched the truck into third. There was no sign of the BMW. The mouth of a street flashed by on the right. Avenue of escape. He pulled it into fourth. No van — what was its license number? He'd forgotten it! No. He hadn't. No, he wouldn't. He concentrated. The intersection of Clayton passed by on the left. Another avenue of escape. One. That was it. One, EL, yes, T0, 1ELT0...

He was doing fifty now and the mouth of other streets shot by, left and right. Market Street was straightening out, the median wall had tapered down to nothing, and traffic was visible in both directions. He coaxed the stub of a pencil out of the ashtray and wrote the license digits on the vibrating note pad without looking at it, in large figures, remembering them as he drove. Commercial license plate, should be seven figures. Alphanumeric mix. Standard California pattern, a numeral followed by three letters followed by three numbers. OneELT... that would make that naught a zero, 1ELT0 — gotcha: 36. Thank you, brain. A brown Dodge Ram, license number Cal 1ELT036. As he scribbled this he heard the expanded metal grid of the BART air vents growling under his tires and realized he had descended nearly all the way to the intersection at Castro. He looked up. The light was red. Traffic and people were already streaming through the intersection, directly transverse to his line of travel. He slammed on the brakes with both feet, and his front wheels skidded to a halt, two feet into the crosswalk. A big leather queen with a bleached crewcut and a naked beer belly framed by a black vest patted the Toyota's right fender, smiled, and kept walking.

People were everywhere. Not dull, Castro Street on Friday night. He was in the left lane of three, completely hemmed in by cars and pedestrians. A two-ply wall of gridlocked traffic inched across Market, heading south down Castro toward 18th Street. Hundreds of people thronged in the crosswalks in front of him on both sides of the intersection, and he dimly registered that, sixty yards away, the Castro Theater had just released a large audience.

He was stopped.

He scanned every vehicle. Every face. There were plenty of each.

No Dodge van. No white BMW. No certain white guy, no particular black guy. No exact brunette. No hapless sheetrock taper, either.

He'd lost them all.

Stanley placed his elbows on the lower rim of the steering wheel, tented his fingers before his face, and scrubbed his eyes with the balls of his thumbs.

"Ted," he said. He peeled his hands down his unshaven cheeks and looked up at the windshield, no longer seeing the traffic and lights beyond. "I'm sorry, Ted."

Chapter 16

Corrigan was sitting in Stanley's rented wheelchair in the doorway of the shack, watching the pyramid.

"Come in," said Stanley.

Corrigan didn't move. "Never spent time in a wheelchair before. It's pretty comfortable."

"Yeah? You look about as laid back as a goldfish on a porch swing."

Corrigan cast his eyes beyond the rooftop, toward the distant hills of Berkeley. "It's true that a badge is somewhat alienating," he conceded. "What's your excuse?"

"I don't like being forced to join clubs I never heard of."

"That includes the human race?"

"They look like me, they walk like me." Stanley shrugged. "Maybe that's why I hate them."

Corrigan produced his palm-top computer, held it up to the moonlight, and thumbed the ignition. "If you should become a statistic tonight, it'll be because you got run over while walking the white line down the middle of the information highway."

"Not because of a bum kidney?"

"As the good Doctor Sims says, you keep taking those antibiotics, you'll be fine." Corrigan pecked two thumbs at the tiny keyboard. "M-O-R-P-H-O-L-O-G-Y. That right?"

Stanley threw up his hands.

"Return," said Corrigan, thumbing a final key.

They waited. Down on Brooklyn Place a car horn honked. An east-bound whisper from the ever-cool marine layer flirted with the thread-bare wires draped over the alley, bringing with it hints of dialogue from a Chinese pornographic video, and the faint tintinnabulations of wind chimes.

"Ah." The two caustics of Corrigan's eyeballs reflected tiny mono-chrome rectangles. "*Branch of biology that deals with the form and structure of organisms without consideration of function.*" He glanced up. "I'm a nickel-word man."

Stanley sighed raggedly. "Well that's just nickeliferous."

Corrigan clicked his tongue. "That's a good one."

"You got *mono-renal misanthrope* in there?"

Corrigan didn't even flinch. "I got one right here in front of me. Why waste batteries?" He snapped the lid closed. "Batteries is money, you know."

Stanley wedged himself sideways between the wheelchair and the doorjamb, but before he got over the threshold Corrigan slapped a fat envelope under his chin and said, "When you get a light struck, have a look at these."

Stanley dropped the envelope next to the sink. "Coffee? Codeine? Whiskey? Antibiotics?"

"Column A," said Corrigan. He folded his hands over the palmtop and contemplated the view. "Quite the location you've got here."

"You should see the parties I throw," Stanley said, filling the black-ened bottom half of the espresso-maker with water. "I feel I should warn you, Corrigan."

"Warn me, Ahearn."

"This espresso machine is aluminum, and they say aluminum accel-erates your Alzheimer's."

"That's okay, Ahearn. You should see what we drink out of at head-quarters."

"Ah yes, the public trough." He tamped an inch of Safeway's cheap-est into the machine's bail. "Styrofoam, I presume."

"Actually," Corrigan replied mildly, "it's galvanized zinc. You pay rent here?"

Stanley set the machine on the stove and scratched a match.

"It's worth at least three hundred a month, isn't it? Four hundred? I'm curious. My career insulates me from some of the crueler facts of life."

The propane ring bathed the base of the coffee machine in a soft blue flame. Stanley waved out the match and dropped it in the sink. "Come on Corrigan," he said. "You know exactly what goes on here."

Corrigan's eyes were following the thin stream of headlights flowing west over the upper ramp of the Bay Bridge. Whoever decreed the upper deck of that particular bridge as westward-flowing really knew what they were doing. "Yeah, I guess I do. You pay no rent. No garbage or utilities, either. You have no telephone service. These practically add up to positive cash flow, in this world we are deconstructing for ourselves — or, as a cop I should maybe say, that other people are deconstructing for us. Still, it makes you pretty independent, being phoneless; hard to get in touch with; toward which, as a professional misanthrope, you are naturally inclined."

Stanley poured milk into an enameled metal cup. "What is this, Corrigan? You got a hole that needs a pigeon?"

"I like to categorize people, I guess. Define them. You could say it was a *cop-ly* thing to do. But, as an American, you might prefer to look at it as *individuation*."

"You tried astrology?"

"The girlfriend looks after the eldritch side of things."

"Iris' mother?"

Corrigan said nothing.

"Damn," said Stanley after a while. "I haven't come across that word since I read H.P. Lovecraft."

"That was his favorite word, I believe," mused Corrigan, without missing a beat. "Lovecraft used 'eldritch' like Kerouac used 'sad.'"

"That's a lot of authors for one cop."

"Only two."

"You consider astrology eldritch?"

"No," said Corrigan mildly. "I consider it bullshit."

Stanley pushed open the window sash next to the door and sat gingerly on the sill. If he'd suspected he'd torn open his incision before, his thoughts were definite on the subject now. It stung, and it was damp. He pointed north. "You know there's an alley named after Kerouac, right over there?"

"I know," said Corrigan. "It used to be called Adler Place. Specs' bar is still there, though."

Stanley nodded his head in the dark.

The Love Boat was parked at Pier 19, all lit up. After a few moments of watching it Stanley said, "You think Lovecraft will ever get a street named after him?"

"Sure," said Corrigan. "Later. In the space station nostalgically named after San Francisco."

Stanley frowned thoughtfully. "We're nearly the same age. You and I...?"

This personal question, too, Corrigan avoided answering. But, Stanley realized, Corrigan was only three or four years older than he was.

Two minutes of silence passed, during which an entire floor of lights suddenly became extinguished in the TransAmerica Pyramid, and steam began to percolate through the works of the espresso-maker.

Corrigan heaved a sigh. "Take a look in that envelope, will you?"

"Why should I?"

"I'm afraid there's an excellent reason."

"Let's have coffee first."

"Suit yourself. I was just thinking the other day about how I was getting too much sleep lately."

The espresso-maker's sound announced that all its water had boiled away. Stanley pulled the machine from the flame and replaced it with the tin of milk. Soon enough, he had two steaming mugs of *café au lait*.

"Sugar?"

"Nah."

He handed a cup out the window to Corrigan, then showed him a fifth of Bushmills. "Nudge?"

"No thanks."

"Sweater?"

"What is this," Corrigan growled, "a goddamn camp-out? Take a look at the motherfucking pictures, why don't you?"

Stanley nudged his own coffee, tasted it, then set his cup on the counter. "What I like best," he muttered, more or less to himself, staring at the envelope, "is a nice Irish coffee with the midnight mail."

Somewhere a garbage truck hydraulically yawned, upended a dumpster over itself, and redeposited it on a sidewalk with a crash.

Stanley snapped on the light over the sink.

The envelope was plain manila, 9 by 12 inches, with a button-and-thread fastener. Stanley hadn't seen such an envelope in a long time. He studied it. The string looked like waxed dental floss except, like the two buttons, it was the color of dried blood. Other than its model number and size, printed along the sealed seam opposite its flap, the envelope was unmarked.

"Aside from the fact that I associate it with you," said Stanley, still not touching the envelope, "What's bothering me about this?"

"I'm sure I don't know," said Corrigan. He sipped his own coffee. "Unless you already have an idea what's inside it."

Stanley frowned. "How the hell would I know that?"

"Beats me," Corrigan admitted, blandly ingenuous. "Foresight would imply you had brains. But," he added, "your interest in hookers — let alone what that envelope contains — proves you in short supply."

"Fuck you, cop."

"Ahearn," said Corrigan tiredly, dropping his eyes off the bridge and staring at the gravel at his feet, "thanks for the cup of coffee. Now, I don't want to be rude. It's not in my nature to be rude. But as soon as you get over your cozy clairvoyant qualms and have a look inside that envelope there, we're going to have a chat for real. You know it, I know it. I'm being nice about it, and you're not. You apparently have all night, but I don't. So quit stalling, get it over with, and let's talk. Because starting right now, if you don't take a look at that envelope, like, immediately, I'm going to drag you by your ears down to my office on Bryant Street, and nail them to a desk. Then for sure we'll find out who's got all night. Now, how's the audio? Is this clear?"

"Keep your shirt on."

"I'm done with that: hop to it."

Stanley unwound the thread and opened the envelope.

Pictures, all right. Like Corrigan said.

Colored pictures.

The first one was of a purple sleeping bag.

It could have been the one he himself had been found in, six weeks ago.

Something was inside it. Something that tapered from one end, possibly the feet, a yard up to what might have been hips, to shoulders, abruptly to what could easily have been a head.

There was a hand showing at the seam. Its fingers curled around the edge of the nylon, like… a sleeping child's might curl around the edge of its quilted comforter. This disconcerted Stanley. Had he not seen just such a hand in just such a pose not two hours ago? He looked up momentarily, but resisted a glance over his shoulder. Had Corrigan found Ted? Already?

Get a grip, he told himself: that's impossible. Green Eyes isn't done with Ted yet. The sleeping bag comes later.

Stanley lingered over the first photo. What struck him about the shot

was that the hand seemed outsized, adult, too large for the apparent
mass of the body inside the sleeping bag, which could have been that
of a child. The apparent mass seemed... diminished.

A fringed, green blur across the top of the photo was probably a tree
limb.

So. A sleeping bag in a sylvan setting.

A park, maybe.

He set the first photograph aside.

The second picture was... disconcerting.

The setting had changed. Now the subject was brightly lit, with no
shadows or blurred details.

The subject was a human head.

Face up, the head stared straight at the camera. But the stare was
sightless.

The head had no eyes.

The lids were there, but there were no eyes behind them. The lids
were sunken, like two little graves.

The head lay against a stainless steel table.

Obviously, the head belonged to a dead man.

A man whose eyes had been removed.

For better or worse, the head seemed to be still attached to a body. A
sheet was pulled up beneath the chin.

Beside the head, parallel to its vertical axis, lay a child's one-foot ruler.

Stanley hesitated over this photograph for a long time.

To be sure, it was fascinating.

Certainly there was additional detail to be had from a prolonged
study of the image. But Stanley hesitated because something about it
disturbed him.

Stanley also hesitated over the second photograph because he had a
distinct foreboding.

Caught between these two sensations, Stanley was pretty sure he did-
n't want to see the third photograph—let alone the fistful of others that
would follow it.

So stalled, Stanley's mind ground almost to a halt. Yet his hands,
operating external to his will, inevitably dealt him the third photograph.

A torso, hips to neck, naked and the color of lead.

And the ruler, again. It was yellow.

Mute and shocked, Stanley mechanically shuffled the second picture
back over the third, checking.

It certainly looked like the same ruler.

He set the second photograph aside, face up.

Though the skin looked like that of a young person, and though it was male, the torso was pale and shrunken. The breasts looked shallow, emaciated.

But those details struck Stanley only later. His immediate perception was of the large, coarse sutures that transected the gaunt trunk like the legs of a pair of flattened millipedes. Their black so coarse as to render almost invisible the sparse clumps of fine body hair, the gleaming threads contrasted with the blanched skin as impersonally as the ebony mensurations embossed along its bevel contrasted with the ruler's yellow plastic. The livid, orthogonal incisions formed two meandering puckers, their bilious discoloration flowed along the pallor of the flesh into which they had been gouged. These, like nave and transept wickedly inverted, dissected the torso vertically, from groin to throat, and horizontally, along a line grazing just below the twelfth rib.

"That's called a radical cruciate abdominal incision," Corrigan said over Stanley's shoulder.

He hadn't heard Corrigan come inside. Emanating from the shadows Corrigan's voice blasted Stanley's concentration as thoroughly as that voluminous sneaker wave had blasted little Tseng's rock at Land's End. Stanley jumped as if snatched by the scruff of his neck, straight up. The pictures tumbled to the countertop as he whirled with a balled fist and a torque at his incision and yelled "Goddamn fucking sneak-ass gumshoe cop!"

"Tsk," clucked Corrigan, ignoring the fist and regarding Stanley, as if from afar. "Are we nervous about something?"

"I was fine until you showed up," Stanley snapped. Too loudly.

Corrigan allowed the faint trace of a sour smile to be replaced by a not-so-faint contempt. "And that poor son of a bitch in these pictures was fine until you showed up, Ahearn." He pointed at the photos on the counter. "Radical enough to be called butchery, that incision. Usually, it's practiced exclusively on cadaver donors."

Stanley blinked. "What?"

Corrigan moved his face until it was a foot from Stanley's, and curled his lips in disgust. "There wasn't enough left inside that kid to feed a dog with."

"What," Stanley muttered feebly, "are you talking about?"

Corrigan bored in. "He was alive, when they gutted him. He had to be."

"He had to be what?"

"Alive! So they could harvest his vital organs!" Corrigan shouted. "What do you think they took?"

Stanley was confused.

"*They* again?" he croaked.

"Both eyes, both kidneys, his liver, the heart, and both lungs. Get it? The works! Everything they can sell! Look at him!"

Corrigan swept up the photographs from the counter and shook them in Stanley's face. "There's nothing left of the poor bastard," Corrigan shouted. Abruptly, recognizing the expression on Stanley's face, Corrigan's own face changed into an incredulous, almost cruel leer, accentuated by the bad light.

"You didn't recognize him," Corrigan realized. "You don't know him."

"Know who?"

"You think so?" Corrigan continued, not listening. "You think you don't know him?" He answered his own question. "You just didn't recognize him. Here. Have another look!"

Corrigan dealt the photographs one after another, in rows, like cards in a game of solitaire. There were at least twenty of them; twenty autopsy photographs of a disassembled corpse, of exposed vertebrae, of an empty ribcage hastily laid open by power-sawing the ribs, of abruptly terminated arteries, of a yawning, eviscerated abdominal cavity.

"You see." Corrigan's face was contorted by horror and disgust nearly matching Stanley's own. But, unlike Stanley's, Corrigan's expression was steeled with disdain. "Now take another look at this one."

Corrigan plucked up the second photo Stanley had looked at, that of the victim's eyeless head, shook it in front of Stanley's face, and threw it back down on the counter.

Stanley glanced at it, then looked away.

"I saw that one already."

"But you didn't recognize him," Corrigan said. "Look again."

"Rec...?" He looked at Corrigan.

Corrigan looked at Stanley. At that moment, Corrigan's face could only be described as carnivorous.

Stanley forced himself to find salients in the picture aside from the eyes. The lips were well-defined, but appeared soft. The nose was almost cute. They might almost have been the features of a girl. But, still, his mind wouldn't place them.

"The name was MacIntosh," said Corrigan at last. "Giles MacIntosh."

Chapter 17

A fire engine emitted a preliminary wail as it left the station house on Stockton Street, two blocks away.

"That's number ten," Corrigan said, pointing to the eyeless head of Giles MacIntosh. "But it's not meant as a statistic for the newspaper." He shuffled the photos and chose one. "Have a look." The ghastly photo displayed the trunk reopened, its sutures unzipped. Corrigan took a pen from his pocket and touched its tip to a small object resting inside the eviscerated cavity.

"See that?"

Stanley's esophagus was surging with bilge. "No. What is it?"

Corrigan chose another shot, a close-up.

"Recognize it?"

"It's a flower."

"What kind of flower, Ahearn?"

"How should I know?"

Corrigan just perceptibly smiled. "You'd think a guy with your experience would know a purple aster when he saw one."

He actually hadn't recognized it. Or maybe he just hadn't wanted to. For a guy Corrigan hadn't yet laid a glove on, Stanley was feeling pretty worked over.

"But why?" he managed to ask.

"It's meant as a warning."

"To who?"

Corrigan's eyes showed the certainty of death. "To you, of course."

Stanley stared at the photo of Giles' eyeless face. First Ted, now Giles. Come to think on it, the proper order must be the other way around — first Giles, then Ted. He felt sick. Should he tell Corrigan about Ted, soon to become number eleven? Maybe Corrigan knew about Ted already? If not, maybe there was still time to... Abruptly he dissembled: "A warning to me? Why me?"

"Come off it, Ahearn. You telling me you didn't know this guy MacIntosh? Really? If you think these pirates are playing mumblety-peg for bottle caps, take another look at this kid's eyes. Maybe, really, you don't get it. Did your back heal so fast? There're plenty more photos. Here's a good close-up. Have a look."

"No, I —."

Corrigan gathered Stanley's shirtfront into a bunch, twisted it until their faces came together, and said quietly, "Look at them, you spineless fuck."

Stanley stared at Corrigan in disbelief. Weren't there laws about police officers getting physical with crime victims?

Corrigan released Stanley just as suddenly as he'd grabbed him.

Stanley smoothed his shirt while Corrigan, breathing like an asthmatic, carefully redistributed the photos over the counter. It was a gruesome collage.

"The short version is this," Corrigan said, adjusting the photos so that few overlapped. "Sometime Tuesday night your friends picked up MacIntosh and took him for a ride."

"*My* friends?"

"His, too. It's almost certain he knew who they were. His apartment showed no signs of forced entry or a struggle. No signs of chloral hydrate in what's left of his system, either. There was an appointment time penciled in on his calendar. Just a time. No name." Corrigan jerked his head toward the room behind them, not looking at it. "His crib was in much better shape than yours. He was expecting to be home in time to cook supper for his mother. When he didn't show, she called us."

The word *guiro* suddenly popped into Stanley's head.

"A homeless guy found him in the park."

Rebozo. Guiro and *rebozo.*

"Another guy is missing too, one of MacIntosh's buddies. A colleague from the Center for Sexually Transmitted Diseases, where they both worked. Kid was the systems manager."

Stanley pulled himself away from his sentimental reflections. "A contract guy? Worked mostly nights?"

Corrigan fixed Stanley with a look, and there passed between them the silent awareness that there was no longer any reason for Stanley to maintain some lame fiction about his connection to Giles MacIntosh.

"Name of Tommy?" Stanley added, his voice barely audible.

Corrigan touched various of the photos. "Tommy Quinn. Nice kid, they say. Bright. About twenty, light build, tall, thin, sandy hair, brown eyes, talks with a slight stutter. Been making it as a contract programmer since he was sixteen. You seen him?"

"No. MacIntosh mentioned him to me, but I never met him."

"And so now I get to ask how you knew MacIntosh."

Stanley told him everything he knew about the clinic — almost everything.

Corrigan shook his head disgustedly. "We go over that place with a fine-toothed comb, and you're telling me you just walk in there and finger the one guy who can open up this case like a can of okra?"

"I don't know from computers, Corrigan, but this kid MacIntosh does — did. He found it by accident. He knew about it when you were there, but he hadn't made the connection. That, and you didn't actually talk to him. He thought the glitch was some game or scam his hacker buddy Tommy was up to."

"His hacker buddy needed a scam. His hacker buddy has been shorting the stock market, and is currently experiencing the flexible sigmoidoscopy of the IRS."

"Why am I hearing about that everywhere I go, lately?"

"You must be in your forties."

"So?"

"So what about you and MacIntosh?"

"He happened to tumble to it while I was there, that's all. I was following the only lead I had."

Corrigan's face darkened. "Which was?"

"Which was, I got myself an HIV panel there a few months ago, and that was the only blood test I'd had since they took my tonsils out in 1954."

Corrigan nodded nastily. "The type O-Negative would have turned up both times, but only the recent — computerized — one counted."

"That had to be it. Otherwise, out of all the lushes in town, this outfit picked me by chance. Okay, maybe that's possible. Given the amount of time I used to spend in bars, I had a lot of exposure. But the O-Negative thing couldn't be a coincidence. You gave me the idea yourself. It's the donor blood type most in demand, and that makes me more valuable than most other people to organ thieves. So the clinic had to be the connection, and something or somebody in the clinic had to be connected to the connection. It was simple. Anybody could have figured it out."

"Sure," said Corrigan acidly. "All they needed was a little information."

"Yeah. And some luck."

"So how come you didn't provide your local police force with this lucky bit of information?"

"I didn't think of it until later, and even after it checked out, I had no proof."

"You didn't think of it until later, and even when it checked out, you had no proof."

Stanley shrugged. "Morphine dulls the senses."

"That's okay, I got it all memorized. But morphine doesn't necessarily make you stupid into the bargain."

"Who said anything about stupid?" Stanley said stubbornly.

Corrigan held up one of the photos.

After a while Stanley said, "I can't even tell what that is."

Corrigan reversed the photograph and held it at arm's length, turning it to the light. "That's a tight shot of the inside of the kid's abdomen with the flower removed. What they found when they undid those quick sutures in the cruciate incision, see, was nothing. A lot of severed wires. It looks like a car with the engine snatched out." He touched the photo with the pencil. "See the vertebrae?" He dropped the picture onto the countertop, face up. "They took anything they could sell."

"Oh, boy," Stanley cleared his throat.

"Yeah," said Corrigan, watching him. "Even his heart."

Stanley avoided his eyes. "So what's that tell you?"

"It tells me you were stupid. It tells me the kid let you sucker him. So far, he's picking up the tab for both of you. That's the warning. Of course," Corrigan added, "they might not know who you are."

"Huh?"

Corrigan shrugged, but he was watching Stanley. "The kid might not have talked."

Stanley squirmed. "I don't get it. It was just a hunch. I just wandered

over there like I was in a dream or something. I had no idea it was
going to pan out. And when the kid said he'd get his friend the programmer to look into it —."

"Tommy Quinn."

"—get Tommy Quinn to look into it, I figured, well, let's just see
what happens. Really, I never in a hundred years would have thought
these guys would come up with anything we could use. Let alone get
themselves killed."

Corrigan's lip curled. "We?" he said. "We? What the hell you think
I am, a fourth for pinochle?"

"No, no. Hell, I know this is serious. But I figured if this kid came up
with something, I'd be sure to tell my friend on the force, Inspector
Corrigan, all about it. I just didn't think it would pan out, that's all. It
looked like a fluke."

Corrigan built a quizzical frown with his face. "What are you thinking about, Ahearn? You playing movie shamus, here?"

"No," Stanley shook his head. "No way."

"I guess not. Nobody's that stupid. Even you. Not now, anyway."
Corrigan jabbed a finger at the photos spread over the kitchen counter.
"But you must have been thinking about trying to play footsie with
these guys. What for? Revenge? Get back at the guys that rummaged
through your guts? They say it's like being raped. They say it hurts in
ways that sneak up on you years later in your sleep."

Stanley dismissed this line of reasoning with a wave of his hand, but
Corrigan had the bone, and he wanted to worry it.

"Maybe trip them up enough to reveal their whole operation? Make
them so confused they turn themselves in? Maybe make them feel
guilty about what they do? Haunt them until they get nightmares and
give themselves up? Until they come to me and beg me to lock them in
a cell, hide them from daylight, hide them from the street, from the
awful, the odious, the gore-encrusted, the dripping-fanged, the venge-
ful destroyer Ahearn, put them where Stanley Ahearn won't be able to
get at them, won't be able to run them over with his monster truck —
for so much as thinking of harvesting a kidney from him? Him, of all
the drunken jerks?"

Stanley's face was burning with shame. Everywhere he looked, the
autopsy photos glared back at him.

"No, Corrigan. No, I—."

"You're crazy, Ahearn. It's that simple. Should I get the bruisers in fairy slippers to come zip you up and give you a shot? You want a scrip for Prozac? How about a ten-day free all-expense paid vacation in our new panoptical jail? You get to wear an orange jumpsuit and if you're good we'll give you a window so you can watch the suckers walk by on the sidewalk five stories below, enjoying their freedom. You might look at it as a vacation. Or maybe you're so fucking deluded you think on account your stellar detective work I should be hiring you to give the annual Hercule Poirot Forensic Deduction Lecture at the Police Academy?"

"No, I—."

"Not you, *me*. I got *news* for you, lush. You have just fucked around and got a guy killed. Maybe by now it's even two guys." He threw a photo against the dishrack. "*You* did that. All by yourself. Get it?"

Stanley blinked. An awful moment passed while he added it up. Two guys. It was hard to get around that. Probably impossible. But what enabled him to set his jaw and look Corrigan dead in the eye was the thought that maybe, by now…

Maybe it's three guys.

"Don't come on to me," Corrigan continued, "about how you didn't know what you were doing. *I* know you didn't know what you were doing. But the problem is, you don't believe it. You think you did know what you were doing. Or at least, you *thought* you knew what you were doing. One has hopes that these photographs might change your opinion of yourself. You knew goddamn well that HIV test was a potential lead. Yet you deliberately withheld the information from the very people who might have been able to do something with it. Now one guy — practically a kid, for chrissakes — has been gutted alive. Since you forced our friends to play for keeps — as if they weren't already playing for keeps — they figured they might as well make some money out of it. So pour that over ice and suck on it. Moreover, if I can use a polysyllabic adverb on a fucking moron like yourself, *moreover*, that is to say, beyond what ugliness has already been stated, it's very bloody likely that MacIntosh's buddy Tommy, as you call him, was either in on MacIntosh's dismemberment and has blown town on the proceeds, or has himself experienced the joys of the harvest. In which case not only is that *two* guys you've done for with your little deductive fling, but you've pissed away our only leads into the bargain."

Abruptly Corrigan looked at Stanley as if he had just seen him in an entirely new light. He cast a contemptuous look around the shack.

"How long have you lived in this dump, Ahearn, feeling sorry for yourself? How long have you been taking advantage of a hard-working stiff who has real people to support, people who are related to him, people who perform actual meaningful emotional and physical labor on his behalf — letting him carry up food for you, this bum on his roof, rent you wheelchairs and pay your doctor bills and even provide you a vehicle to go get your willie sucked every Friday night? Huh? How fucking long? You sorry little sack of shit, you sniveling twit, you forty-seven-year-old delivery boy, when's the last time you did something for somebody beside yourself? I'll tell you. It was three years ago — three and a half! Christ. The most miserable cop on the beat does more for people in an afternoon than you've done but once in your entire fucking life. Hasn't your little reward thing gone on long enough? Has the booze infantilized you completely? I'll bet there was so much ethanol in your kidney those thieves didn't even have to sterilize it. Christ!"

Corrigan is getting a little carried away on the question of turpitude, Stanley was thinking, as he watched the detective. So what's this tack? In his unusually animated rage Corrigan had allowed his features to become exaggerated and distorted, cartoon-like was the term that occurred to Stanley. A cheaply produced cartoon from Hong Kong or Seoul, where they omit two cells out of three to save money, so the completed sequence has this wooden, time-lapsed quality — although, he reflected, quality has little to do with it. Inevitably, as Stanley knew from years of watching Saturday morning cartoons as a kind of self-mortification involving hangover penance, bad animation was not put there to entertain you; the purpose of bad animation is to sell you something.

So what was Corrigan trying to sell him?

"That's why we got laws against withholding evidence," Corrigan went on. Stanley started to interrupt him, but Corrigan shouted, "I'm not finished yet!" and shook a finger in Stanley's face. "We got laws against clowns like you thinking they can sit on a piece of evidence long enough to turn it to their own advantage. I could book you right now. I could turn it into months of hassles for you, Ahearn. You hear that? Months! Shit. I go for accessory to murder, we're talking *years*."

Corrigan paced out of the circle of light, toward the front door, exhaled raggedly, looked at the Pyramid for a moment, then paced back. "But I'm not going to do it. No, I'm not going to run you in. You want to know why, Ahearn? You care? You give a shit?"

"Sure, Corrigan." But Stanley was thinking, go ahead and tell me, if you have to. Spill your guts, if it's going to make you feel better. But despite the fact that I just got one and maybe two and possibly three people killed, for some very particular reason of your own, you want to let me off the hook. "So why? How come?"

"I'll tell you why, Ahearn. It's because I feel sorry for you. That's why."

Stanley almost laughed.

"You little juice-monkey. I could give you a shot to that kidney incision that would wake your mother in heaven."

"No mothers," said Stanley coldly. "You were explaining my dispensation."

"I feel sorry for you. I really do. Sure, you saved that little girl's life. So what if it was three years ago? It's admirable enough. Not just any character would have done the same, either. But that was your moment, Ahearn. You've been living off it ever since, you're never going to do anything else for anybody again, and that's pathetic. That's sad. You've been sitting up on this roof watching television and drinking whiskey going on four years. What a life. Your only problem is that now you've only got one kidney to metabolize that booze with, and that kidney's sick. Isn't that right? Is that what you're afraid of? That you might have to quit all this? Isn't the drunkard's dream about to go up in smoke? Am I right?"

Stanley said nothing. He was waiting for the cop's weird reasoning to become clear, and, unlike Corrigan, he wasn't about to let this personal stuff obfuscate the issue.

"Then what, huh? When it's over, when you have to get sober, what are you going to do?"

Stanley frankly shrugged.

"Maybe that morphine scrip can be strung out for a few months," Corrigan suggested thoughtfully. "Maybe you can get off the booze and onto the junk." He gestured toward the door. "The stuff's all over out there. It might even be cheaper than the booze, initially. They say you live longer, too; though maybe that's not your idea of a plus. Of course, there's the social stigma involved, junkies are looked down upon, as if you care. For sure, though, you won't like the copping scene. A major irony is that while junk will turn you into even more of a misanthrope than you already are, you will become even more dependent on certain forms of — shall we say 'scum'? — way more dependent on certain scum-forms than when you were just a lush. That would be pretty hard on a guy with your personality. A guy who likes it easy. You get so bad off you can't negotiate a simple junk-for-blowjob deal on the street. That's you giving the blowjobs, now. No longer receiving them. For the money, you understand. For your habit. The contrapositive of your present Friday night which, like all your other nights, will become indistinguishably alike. They'll all merge into a spirit of misery, haunting the desperate husk of your former self. Of course," he dragged a palm back and forth over his day's growth of whiskers, sandy brown mottled with white, "of course, you get strung out enough you won't *want* a blowjob — on Friday or any other night. You won't be able to get it up, and you won't care. You won't even think about it anymore...."

Corrigan smiled and chucked Stanley's shoulder with his fist, a little harder than he needed to. "But hey," he said, "that bum kidney and your bum life will last a lot longer on junk than they will on booze."

Stanley jerked his shoulder away.

Corrigan paced to the front door and stood there, looking out over the wheelchair, as if peering into the heart of the darkened city. If so, the expression on his face suggested the metropolis was teeming with heartworms. He filled his lungs with fresh air and loudly exhaled. "And that guy, your landlord here." He inclined his head toward Stanley without looking at him. "What's his name?"

"Toy," Stanley answered quietly. He could see that Corrigan knew the name. He just wanted to get Stanley to say it himself. "Hop Toy."

"Hop Toy," said Corrigan, drawing out the last syllable. "Hop Toy's a good man. A family man. I had a long talk with him. You know Hop Toy?"

Startled, Stanley said, "Yes. I know Hop Toy."

"Hop Toy," Corrigan continued, "defends Stanley Ahearn down to the ground. There he is, in his wholesale grocery. The guy's knee-deep in ginger bulbs, or whatever they call them, and he's telling me he doesn't give a fuck about what you do, or how you live your life. He's *defending* you. All he knows is Stanley Ahearn comes to work most days, that Ahearn would never drive his truck while drunk, that Ahearn saved little... You saved little..."

Corrigan inclined his head toward Stanley, again without looking at him. "What's the little girl's name, Ahearn?"

"Tseng," said Stanley, his mouth tight around the syllable. "The little girl's name is Tseng."

"Tseng," repeated Corrigan, looking out over the city. "Little Tseng. 'Stanrey save my riddle girl's rife,' Hop Toy says. 'I take care of Stanrey.'"

"You don't have to—," Stanley began, his face clouding.

"It's the kind of thing we used to find on the walls of ruined temples in the jungles in Cambodia," Corrigan went on, ignoring him. "Chiseled in stone, with the whole jungle crowding in, tree roots busting through the masonry. The roof gone, the floor gone, the doors gone, the priests gone, the people gone...."

He turned and looked at Stanley, his face in shadow. "Moral instruction chiseled in stone, instructing nobody. You saved that kid's life, and Hop Toy's going to take care of you till some day he hasn't seen you for a couple days. It's going to come. Sooner or later, it's going to come. And so he'll climb up here. He'll find the door standing open, and the TV on, and something all burned up on the stove if you're still bothering to feed yourself. And there you'll be, stone dead in that easy-chair, with a bottle in your hand and shit in your drawers and seagulls standing on each shoulder fighting over what's left of your eyeballs. Then he'll be free."

"Who?" said Stanley, with a start. "Who'll be free?"

"Hop Toy will be free, Stanley." Corrigan had sweat gleaming on his cheek. "Who'd you think I meant? You? That you'd be free?" He laughed without mirth. "You have a point, I guess. Hop Toy won't be as free as you, at that particular moment. I guess, metaphysically speaking, that's true."

A moment of introspection passed between them.

"But," Corrigan abruptly continued, "Hop Toy will be free to start thinking about taking the money he's been spending on you and putting it toward Tseng's college education or her dowry or her first Mustang convertible or the good-luck firecrackers for her bat mitzvah — whatever. Something useful. Something important."

Another moment of silence.

"Which," Corrigan added, "Hop Toy will know would be the way you would have wanted him to deal with his new freedom — and your new freedom — with the resulting extra money. Respectively. He might even spring for your cremation.

"Hell," Corrigan smiled, showing teeth in the gloom. "Who else would?"

A longer silence. Even the man two stories down and across the alley, who apparently could not pass a waking moment without his pornography, had turned it off, or turned down the sound at least. There were the continual windchimes, a foghorn or two, and a far-away siren getting further away as they listened. A drip in the sink. The smells of cold coffee and scorched milk. The dank reek of geraniums. The city was giving itself and its citizens the gift of a pause.

Corrigan walked back to the counter. "Excuse me," he said, shouldering Stanley aside to gather the photographs. When he had them all in a stack he paused to study the shot of the body in the sleeping bag.

"Okay," the detective finally said, holding the photo so they could both see it. "You got any more bright fantasies about this case?"

"No," Stanley said, staring at the picture and chewing his lip. "I don't."

Corrigan fixed him with a long stare. Corrigan was worn out. Stanley could see that. His complexion was going gray and there were bags under his eyes. He needed a shave. His suit was rumpled and smelled like bus station upholstery. But the cop's stare was unrelenting.

"What about Iris?"

So that was it.

Stanley shrugged. "Iris is a nice girl."

"And?"

He gave it a moment. Then he shrugged again and said, "Don't worry, Corrigan. I know I'm not good enough for Iris."

"Excellent," the detective said huskily. "We understand each other. But one more thing. If I catch you making the least additional move in this case — any move at all, dumb, mediocre or brilliant — I'm going to collect your ass off this roof no matter what and put it where there's no view at all and no bottle to suck on, either. *Moreover*, you'll have to talk to people every day, my misanthropic friend — dozens of them, think of it — just to beg them to turn down their radios, just to kid them into liking you well enough not to shank you for kicks, just to stop them from stomping on your face till it looks like the sidewalk at Sixteenth and Mission, just to get them to stop *bothering* you, just to get them to desist interfering with the soul-deep yips brought on by your involuntary detox. You'll see more *Star Trek* than you ever knew existed. You'll listen to so many idiots discussing it you'll wonder whether there's an intact brain left on the planet. You'll wish I was your best friend. Even after you get over your d.t.'s you won't be able to change anything. Accessory to murder is not a light rap, and neither you nor the altruistic Hop Toy will be able to afford a lawyer good enough to get it off your shoulders."

Corrigan slid the photos into the mouth of the manila envelope. Then he raked Stanley across his neck with one edge of the flap.

"You get me, my misanthropic friend?"

Stanley surprised himself. He was a hair from slugging Corrigan. But then he suppressed a smile.

Iris. That much was plain. Of Stanley and Iris, Corrigan could hardly bring himself to think.

But maybe, just maybe, while Corrigan may have enough evidence to take Stanley in, he might not have enough to make it stick. It seemed more than possible. Corrigan had smoked out his relationship to Giles, all right. But that was no crime, really, and no proof that he'd really known what he was doing when he went to the clinic. For that matter, Corrigan would probably be hard-put to prove that Stanley had been there at all. What had Giles left behind? He hadn't had Stanley's phone number, just Fong's e-mail address. That hadn't come up, either. Which meant that Corrigan may not have figured out the connection. And what, after all, had Stanley done? It was Giles, not Stanley, who had surmised that the code for the info-sharing query had been tampered with.

And it was Giles who had paid the price.

It seemed possible that Corrigan wanted to goad Stanley into slugging him. All that stuff about "Stanrey" being a lush? Baiting him with ersatz racism? About freeloading and being a worthless citizen? And then, as if attacking him, the bureaucrat inflicts a paper cut? Was it just so he'd have an excuse to take him downtown and keep him for a few days? For assaulting an officer?

It seemed extreme. Ridiculous. Why didn't Corrigan just take him in on any old charge?

Maybe he was a straight cop?

"Don't worry, Chief," said Stanley, touching his neck where the edge of the envelope flap had nicked it. He drew his hand away and saw a thin streak of blood on it.

Corrigan saw it, too. His lip curled toward a smile, and there was a light in his eye Stanley hadn't seen before.

And, while he watched, as if in slow motion, he saw Corrigan set his weight back on his heels. The guy looked ready to throw a punch.

Corrigan really was acting the worried step-father.

"I'm all through with trying to figure out what happened to me last month," Stanley said, as carefully and evenly as possible. "I'm out. From now on, it's up to you."

Corrigan narrowed his eyes.

"That's the truth," Stanley emphasized. He gestured toward the photos. "Anyone can see I'm in over my head."

Corrigan relaxed his shoulders.

Stanley studied the trace of blood on the side of his hand. It wouldn't prove to be much more of a cut than he might give himself shaving. Definitely not worth slugging a cop for. Nor getting slugged back.

Without a word, Corrigan headed for the door.

"One more thing," Stanley said, as Corrigan crossed the threshold. "I just remembered something."

Corrigan stopped without turning. "What's that?"

"MacIntosh told me that he and that guy Tommy ate a lot of pizzas together."

Corrigan waited.

Stanley waited.

"So?" Corrigan growled.

Stanley shrugged. "That's it. You think it could be important?"

A knot rippled down the cord at the back of Corrigan's neck, like a rat swallowed by a snake.

He kicked the wheelchair out of his way and left.

Stanley stood just outside the circle of light in the shack, listening to the detective's footsteps cross the gravel roof.

Chapter 18

Stanley went to bed at dawn and slept the fitful sleep of the opiated mono-kidnoid. At eight the clock radio swelled into a bright racket of traffic reports until he aroused sufficiently to swat it into silence.

Getting out of the sweat-soaked sheets he pulled on some clothes and limped downstairs to make a call to an answering machine. Then he climbed back to the roof, took another pill, adjusted the timer on the radio, and went back to sleep. He repeated the drill at noon and three o'clock. With the six o'clock phone call he got to talk to a live person.

Bathing, he discovered eight or ten little flaps of skin where as many sutures had torn loose. After the shower he watched his hip in a mirror on the toilet tank while he snipped the dangling loops of thread with a toenail clipper, and pulled them out with a pair of needle-nose pliers.

It was the first time he'd actually studied the incision which, upon consideration, had the appearance of a lavender revision upon the white editorial of his neglected flesh.

Upstairs again and dressed, he sat on the roof in the wheelchair and watched the evening shadow of the city edge eastward over the Bay, while the espresso-maker forced steam through Safeway's cheapest. The three-star edition of the *Examiner* lay folded on the gravel. Poor Ted, he was thinking, as a few lights came on in Oakland. Where is Ted finding himself awake about now? If he is to be found awake at all, that is. Would it be a kidney they will have taken, leaving the guy unfortunate but alive? Or does the baleful demise of Giles MacIntosh presage a new order of predation and victimhood?

The *Examiner* made no mention of recent untoward nephrectomies. But, while unable to shoulder Bosnia off the front page, the MacIntosh case received 250 words toward the bottom of the Metro column, as a grisly unsolved crime with, unfortunately, no star-studded cocaine orgy attached. One could always hope.

So far as anyone knew, this particular outfit had killed nobody, until they killed Giles. They'd harvested nine kidneys and let their donors live. It seemed judicious, if miraculous. Murder attracts attention.

It also seemed judicious to expect that some day Green Eyes and her gang would snatch the wrong person off the street, somebody with a heart problem or epilepsy, somebody who would die from the chloral hydrate in Green Eyes' cocktail, or from an allergic reaction to the anesthesia, or from a jolt as the Dodge hit a pothole on the way to the park. How would such a gang look at this new development? As statistically inevitable? Tough luck? An embarrassment? A minor inconvenience? The cost of doing business?

Stanley poured a cup of coffee and thoughtfully added scalded milk until it attained the specific color of medium density fiberboard.

What if, he wondered, such a gang as this looked at Giles' death as a *windfall.*

Since Giles, apparently, *had* to die, they could harvest everything about him. A second kidney, two eyes, the liver. What else is recyclable? Gall bladder? Pancreas? Spleen? Heart…? Oh yeah. The heart.

Like a car with the motor ripped out, Corrigan had said.

What an outfit to work for. Make a mistake and you don't worry about getting fired, any more than you worry about getting bumped off: you worry about getting *harvested.*

Stanley set the saucepan back on the butane ring.

How many thousands of dollars worth of recyclable parts would there be in a healthy human body? Forty, sixty, eighty? A hundred thousand? Given a rare blood type or tissue match, maybe two hundred thousand dollars?

That's a lot of rent.

He settled into the wheelchair with the steaming cup of coffee.

So the temptation to go ahead and make a lot of money off a single victim must be large. But not so great as to be out of balance with, say, a certain well-known penalty for murder committed under special circumstances. Leaving people scattered around the parks of San Francisco missing their kidneys has its nuisance value, but it's not murder.

In the circumstance of Giles, the harvesters must have made the determination that, since they had to kill him, they might as well get paid for it.

The sun had set, pulling the day after it. But a half hour later the ultramarine sky above the Berkeley hills began to lighten, as the orange caustic of a large moon surfaced beyond them. The crown of the ridge cast a black shadow over the treeless blaze burned into its western slope by the great fire of 1991. Despite new construction, the path of the conflagration remained plainly visible, like an ominous brand on the flank of the summit.

He pulled a page of notepaper from the pocket of his shirt. Various bits of information were scrawled on it in pencil.

Cal DDT 301, new BMW — white
22 Parajito Terrace

Cal 1ELT036, brown Dodge Ram early '80s
Cabrini Carpet
4 digits on Mission St.
864+

Green Eyes; Brunette, Caucasian, 35ish — Sibyl
Vince: black, late 40s— early 50s;
jacket as car thief; stolen Jag—

White guy, 35-40 years ol—

Middle of 400 block Goettingen, even numbers

He studied this for a while. Then he retrieved a stamped envelope from a peanut butter jar half full of meager office supplies and wrote on it,

Lieut. Sean Corrigan
SFPD
500 Bryant St.
City

and placed the piece of notepaper inside without sealing it.

He was on his second cup of coffee when the door opened at the stair head. A light flooded a clutch of roof jacks sticking up out of the pea gravel of the composition roof, and a woman's voice said, "Thanks." The door closed, the light went away.

Footsteps approached him in the dark.

"I'll bet this is the first time you've been in that chair since you left the hospital."

"What makes you say that?"

She stood in the shadows beside the chair. "When you sit around all day you don't sweat so much."

"It's just that I'm glad to see you."

"You could do a little more than sweat."

She leaned over and kissed him. Her tongue flicked against his teeth. Before she pulled away she nipped his lower lip and whispered, "How's the scar?"

Stanley was noncommittal.

"I like kissing a man who drinks coffee," she said, standing up again. "It keeps me awake."

"Did Corrigan send you?" said Stanley.

"On the contrary," she laughed.

Stanley studied her eyes, gleaming in the moonlight. "Oh?"

"He warned me off you."

"Did he say why?"

"Sure."

"So? Why?"

"He said you were a loser."

So she had come on her own. "So how come you're here?"

Her reply was a monotone, conspicuous for its lack of inflection. "I have bad taste in men."

Deep down, Stanley agreed with that sentiment.

She changed the subject.

"How's the codeine?"

"Still some left."

"I brought some more."

"Hey. Thanks."

"Don't get in a lather or anything. You like them?"

"They're just great. They make me feel like I'm flying a kite from the bottom of the Marianas Trench. And sometimes, when the effects are really strong, I think that I or perhaps more correctly that ecclesiastical part of me that's so hard to put my finger on, that *soul*, that *distillate of spiritual essence*, that *whatchamacallit* we all desperately seek to fulfill, is the actual kite itself."

"Oh, my. No wonder they're regulated."

"How do you think I got so wet?"

She laughed. Her laughter reminded Stanley of sparkling ice cubes spilling into a faceted beaker on a toothed rubber mat.

"Codeine never does that for me," she pouted.

Stanley changed the subject. "How much does a new kidney cost, Iris?"

She didn't answer.

"Installed, I mean. Ten thousand? Twenty thousand?"

Still she said nothing.

"Come on, Iris. Tell me. I'm interested. I want to know how much it's going to cost me to stay alive."

She shrugged, then nodded. "Sure. You could spend that."

"You mean, if I had it to spend."

"If you had it to spend."

"Well I don't have it."

"So you're a good argument for socializing medicine."

"So great. While Congress is socializing medicine these little pebbles you see all over this roof are all going to grow hair."

She smiled. "You're really cute."

"Thanks."

She smoothed his hair back from his forehead. "Is there anything I can do?"

Her touch felt good. He had to admit it. This in turn forced him to consider how wound up he was, how full of rage. Stanley wanted to turn his head against her hand, like a dog might do, and he resented it. The thing about being a loner is, there are these marvelously weak moments.

He persisted. "What's it take to remove a kidney?"

"Didn't Sims explain all this to you?"

"I was all doped up," he groused. "And what the hell: doesn't a man get to obsess on his fate a little bit?"

She sighed and scratched him behind the ear. After a moment she gave that up and shrugged. "A scalpel. Anesthetic. Some gear to keep you breathing and your blood circulating while it's done. Sutures when it's finished."

"What about blood transfusions and sanitation?"

"Blood would only be necessary in an emergency. A slip of the knife.

Sepsis isn't a high priority because the kidneys are retroperitoneal —
they're outside the sack that contains most of your vital organs."

"Liver, heart — like that?"

"Like that."

"How complicated is it?"

"As surgery goes it's very simple. There's three plumbing connections
— the ureter, which comes from the bladder, and the renal artery and
vein, through which blood makes the round trip from the heart."

"That's all? Just three?"

"Three. After that there's only the connective tissue, which holds it
in there. The bed of fat it sleeps in."

"Is the process reversible?"

"Good question."

"What's that mean?"

"Well, obviously it's done. But a transplant is ideally performed with
both donor and recipient immediately to hand. There's two incisions,
the removal, the installation, two closures."

"So, let's say, incision, removal, and closure take place today. Then,
let's say, an incision, installation, and closure take place at a later date.
Next week, say, or next month. Would that make it more difficult?
What about transportation...?"

"When Corrigan has solved this case," she interrupted him pointed-
ly, "we'll find out about all that stuff. You sure you don't want to make
love?"

"Sure. I mean, later. Right now my libido's a kite in the Marianas
Trench, and the rest of me wants to talk about kidneys."

Iris sighed determinedly. "It's always more difficult to go in through
old scar tissue. The longer you wait the harder the scar tissue becomes.
But the larger problem is the quality of the original work. If the plumbing weren't properly terminated in the first operation, re-installation of
a functional kidney becomes that much more difficult."

"What about artificial parts? Plumbing, I mean."

"You mean, like, cannulation?"

"What's that?"

"It's a kind of pasta."

"Quit fucking around."

"Oh. Aren't *we* serious."

"Serious and humourless."

"Well," she pouted stubbornly, "it's not that far-fetched. Cannula and cannelloni have the same root in the Latin word for cane, reed, or hollow tube."

"Jesus Christ, Iris."

"I tell you this to make it easy for you to remember."

Stanley scowled. "I guess it's always possible I'll forget."

"Sure. Cannelloni are a tubular pasta, and cannula are plastic tubes used to replace sections of arteries or veins. The procedure is called cannulation. See?"

"They can do that?"

"Sure. One of my favorite stories of the medical profession involves a Glaswegian doctor. Everybody who worked at the hospital knew he was mad. A typical staff in-joke. His hygiene was such a mess it counted for nothing, the nurses practically had to keep him in diapers. But he was a brilliant surgeon, and the management let him carry on. He was particularly good at anastomosis and cannulation — sewing in bits of plastic tubing to veins or arteries at angles or end-to-end. Very meticulous, intense labor, but he just loved to put cannulae in place of ruined or even merely damaged vessels."

"So what's the point?"

"Well, they finally had to let him go."

"Why?"

"The staff had noticed long since that this doctor would cannulate at the drop of a hat. But, finally, well, this girl came in with a broken arm, see…"

"What would you cannulate for a broken…. Oh. I get it. While setting the arm, he somehow worked in a little cannulation."

"Not a little, a lot. He replaced a few inches of her left renal artery with a few inches of plastic hose."

"He opened the girl up? He operated on her?"

"That's right."

"For a broken arm?"

"Right again."

"That's insane!"

"Exactly."

"So what'd they do to this guy?"

Iris shrugged. "Let him go."

"What? They fired him?"

"They fired him."

"They didn't bury him alive in some scorpion-infested pile of stones two hundred miles inland from Abu Dhabi?"

Iris half laughed, half frowned. "No way. This is a surgeon we're talking about. Surgeons are to the medical profession as jet pilots are to the Israeli Air Force: from the cradle their destiny is to serve the Greater Good. Allowances for deviation in character are liberal. They're special."

"What do you mean, 'this is a surgeon'? This is a criminal, too. What he did to that girl... They should cannulate on him and see how he likes it."

Iris shrugged. "It's easy to see you haven't spent much time around hospitals."

"As little as possible, which is too much already. Enough to make me want to spend the rest of my life somewhere else."

"Anyway, this guy from Glasgow," Iris said matter-of-factly, "they just put him out to pasture. Farmed him out to some golf condo with a pension. If he kicked about it, they would have been forced to suspend his license to practice in the UK."

"You mean they *didn't* suspend it?"

"No way."

"Christ..."

She folded her hands together, as if in prayer. "You know what a *fasces* is?"

"What are you, some kind of on-line dictionary?"

"No. I just pick up a lot of Latin and Greek in my profession, and Corrigan does the rest with his etymological software. Then there's the *Chronicle* crossword. I do that every day. It's better than the one in the *Times*..."

"Don't forget the Italian deli connection."

She smiled. "Italian used to be Latin, about 2,000 years ago."

Stanley shifted uneasily in the canvas seat of the wheelchair. "Yeah. Sure it did."

"Although these days," she pointed out, "Rumanian is the closest living language to that spoken by the Caesars and Catullus. Kind of like how what they speak on Ocracoke Island, off the coast of North Carolina, is closer to what Shakespeare spoke than what's currently heard in England." Iris used the Spanish pronunciation of Shakespeare, Shock-eh-spe-ahr-ray. "Isolation is the usual explanation. Both Ocracoke and Rumania are relatively isolated from the flow of modern history, see, and —."

"Hey, hey, hey!" said Stanley, waving both hands as if warding off a hornet. "What's this got to do with insane doctors?"

Iris stopped mid-sentence, frowned, then nodded her head once, a second time, then a third, like a waitress recounting forks for a dinner party. "Oh," she said suddenly. "*Fasces*. Well." She folded her hands again. "Bundle of sticks gathered together. Symbol of Roman strength. You remember the parable. Take out one of the sticks, it breaks over your knee with ease. Two sticks, same deal but a little more difficult. A few of the sticks, much more difficult to break them. Take all of the sticks together and call them, let's say, the Glaswegian Medical Association, and try to break it over your knee with a sudden downward motion — whammo," she mimicked this, "— broken knee."

Stanley nodded.

"Put another way," she added, "'United We Stand, Divided We Fall'."

"You're saying that doctors stick together."

"Like migrating pelicans."

"So," said Stanley, who could cling to a subject with the best of them, especially when that subject concerned his health, "cannulation is a reality. If the ana— anasto—."

"Anastomosis."

"What you said, if the vein is frayed or badly trimmed or whatever, they can cut back the damage and cannulate to a new organ, or wherever."

"Exactly."

"I see. But we're running up a bill, here, aren't we?"

"Yes."

"And there's only one way to determine if the site will be easy or difficult or feasible at all, which is to go in and look?"

"That's right."

Stanley thought about this a moment. "Might as well have a kidney on hand when you go in, then. Along with some can... cannula?"

"It would be a good idea."

After a silence Iris said, "This can't be very pleasant for you to talk about."

"Are you kidding?" said Stanley. "It's fascinating, my beautiful caregiver. It's like watching a snake that's been run over by a car but remains unkilled. And—get this—inside that snake's head is *my brain*."

"Oh, please!" she exclaimed. And she suddenly knelt beside the wheelchair and concealed her face against his chest. "If there're two things I hate in this world," she said into his shirt, "it's snakes and kites."

She looked up and added, "Since the end of the Reagan Administration, it's just the two."

She buried her face against his chest again.

This unexpected levity put Stanley's dour self-concern at a disadvantage. He still had a coffee cup in one hand and the envelope in the other. After some hesitation he placed them both on the roof beside the chair, and tentatively put his arms around Iris' shoulders.

"You're shivering. Are you cold?"

Abruptly she turned her head against his shoulder, so he could look down at her face. Tears glistened along her cheeks, like twin freshets over a moonlit glacier.

"No," she said. "Yes. I'm cold."

"You're crying, too," he said. "That joke wasn't that bad."

She buried her face against his shoulder again. "No I'm not."

"I thought nurses could handle this stuff," Stanley said uncertainly. "I mean, who else could I ask about —."

"Look." She raised her face and looked into his eyes.

"Yes?"

"Can we go to bed now?"

"I beg your pardon?"

"It's been a month since I've seen you naked."

"So?"

"So your scar is healing by the minute."

"Why don't you love me for my personality?"

She shook her head. "Better you should be thinking, *I am scarred, therefore I am.*"

He smiled and touched her hair. "It's only been three days since I've seen you at all, Ms. Considine. And I —."

"Three days? Stanley, it's six."

"Okay. Six."

"You're avoiding me."

"No way."

"Go on," she said. "Protest."

"I'm busy."

"Say it."

"Very busy."

She shook her head and opened her mouth, so that he could see the tip of her tongue playing along her teeth as she carefully pronounced the word. "I want you naked. Say it."

"N-n..," he said.

"Come on," she coaxed.

"Naked," he said.

"That's it," she whispered, taking his head between her two hands and kissing him on the mouth. "Naked."

"Naked," he said into her mouth.

She held his face so that their eyes were a few inches apart. "Now can we go to bed?"

Her eyes were beautiful. The fully risen moon hung to the east of them, as brilliant and big as a spotlight in a boxcar, as big as moons get in a night sky. Its light suffused her hair with an opalescent aura. Her fingertips pressed against his temples. It was not like she was asking him to join the army or give blood or submit to a flexible sigmoidoscopy. Besides, scarlingualists aren't that numerous. It's hard for them to find each other. It's not like it is with, say, the San Joaquin tarantula, the male of which goes looking for the female every October, and she's out there waiting for him, or another tarantula like him, and that's that. Scarlingus is not that simple. The code is not that formalized. Not so biologically preordained. Not so Calvinistic. He was barely breathing. His mouth was dry. He was interested. He was caving in.

The door to the staircase grated open.

Chapter 19

Even as Stanley struggled not to utter the word "cyberspace" instead of "I love you," the door at the head of the staircase threw a trapezoid of light across the rooftop gravel, and Felix Choy stepped into it. Fong followed him.

Given a place sturdy enough to hang him from—an A-frame, say, of the type generally used for removing engines from Caterpillar tractors—you might stretch Felix Choy to five foot six in gravity boots. There was some hope that his weight had topped out at 250 pounds when he turned fifteen years old, but that was only a few weeks ago and time would tell. He wore unlaced thick-tongued high-topped $250 air-cushioned sneakers (a dollar per pound, he liked to say), impeccably custom-seamed jeans fabricated in an uncle's 100-machine sweatshop, a snakeskin for a belt with a Pentium chip and its socket for a buckle, a bright red wool warm-up jacket with leather sleeves and a patch on one shoulder that read *Voice = Data* and a campaign button on the other shoulder that read *Hackers for Choice*. Underneath the jacket he wore a Hawaiian shirt, also custom-tailored, in emerald, mauve, white and black, with pink buttons, its mutant pineapples faded, possibly, by cathode rays. He also wore fingerless chamois batting gloves, their forgotten logos a souvenir of some over-capitalized Silicon Valley startup's one-season foray into B-league softball.

Altogether, Felix Choy affected the essence of the cyber-sartorial. The warmup jacket had a fur collar, too.

An elegant piece of carry-on Bangkok pigskin, tanned to the color of perfectly fried onion cake, hung from a lambskin strap looped over a fleece pad on his shoulder. Day or night, as ever, Felix wore a $150 pair of Porsche sunglasses, to the wearer of which everything appears in a hepatic or post-nuclear ochre. On the inside of his left wrist gleamed a $32,000 Seiko analog wristwatch that, along with the correct time, could explain everything non-cybernetic (less and less) in terms of its registered owner's mother's biorhythms—password-protected, of course— guaranteed impervious to amniotic fluid.

Behind Felix came Fong, lugging two bags of groceries and a brief-case-style computer tool-kit that resembled the slim valise favored by uptown cocaine mules.

"Greetings, my white Anglo friend," hollered Fong, adding in a stage-whisper, "self-righteous Protestant spawn of Nordic fish thieves and the all-acquisitive fur-bearing octopus of European culture." He closed the access door with a backwards kick.

"Geez," said Iris, not bothering to get out of Stanley's lap. "You are?"

"Are we interrupting anything?" said Fong eagerly, stopping within inches of the wheelchair. "And, if so, may we watch?"

When nobody said anything he added, "It's okay. Felix here, being a Buddha of the 10th grade, can work under any but the most non-electrical conditions."

"Felix," said Stanley, "this is Iris."

Felix raised one corner of his mouth until it caused the baby-fat cheek above it to collide with the lower frame of the sunglasses.

"I'm Fong," Fong reminded Iris politely. "We met at the hospital." He rustled one of the grocery bags. "Care for a cherry Coke?"

"Sure," said Iris. "Is it diet?"

Fong laughed.

Felix held out a beefy hand. Fong filled it with a 12-ounce can of Cherry Coke. Felix grunted. "Okay, okay" Fong said. He retrieved the can, popped its top, and put the can back in Choy's hand.

As Fong opened one for Iris, Felix took a sip and looked around. He walked to the edge of the roof, toward Berkeley, and looked over it. His bulk nearly obscured the lower half of the full moon. He strolled halfway back.

"Like standing on the edge of the world, huh Felix?" Fong prattled. Felix said nothing.

"Huh, Felix?" Fong coaxed. "Here, Felix," he added, as if calling a recalcitrant cat.

Felix considered the shack. The other three humans on the roof might just as well have been orphaned TV antennas.

Felix upended the Coke can and emptied it into his upturned mouth. Then he crushed the can in his pudgy fist and hooked the dripping wreckage over his head to Fong.

"A genius," Fong said, catching the crushed can in the grocery bag, and not bothering to suppress a note of awe from his sarcasm.

"Good spot," Felix said, in the unmistakable near-falsetto of a teenager. He unrasped and rerasped the Velcro strap on the back of one batting glove and said, "Chairs and a table, outside, facing the moonlight. Where's the phone?"

"Downstairs," said Fong.

Felix made a face. "Pulse?"

Fong dialed circles in the air with his forefinger.

"Pulse. Well," Felix sighed, "come on. I got to go to school tomorrow morning."

"Too many absences this month already," Fong said, as an aside to Stanley and Iris.

"You passing anything?" Stanley asked.

Choy flicked his hand sideways. "I pay guys."

"First thing in the morning?" Iris looked at the little watch on the inside of her wrist. "It's not even nine o'clock."

"I'm only fifteen," said Felix, demurely shooting his cuff for a glance at the Seiko. "I need my sleep."

"You should watch all that sugar," suggested Iris, indicating the can of Coke. "Sugar makes kids crazy and gives them insomnia."

"Real-time behavior," said Felix, ripping and re-ripping his Velcro, "is deceptive."

Carrying the tool-case, Fong led their way downstairs.

"Cyberspace," Iris said, watching them go. "I'm sorry I confused you with them."

Stanley grunted. "Fong is good; but, he says, Felix is better. Fong says Felix routinely visits NASA, BitNet, CompuServe, all the major banks, most government systems, telephone company satellites and credit databases, not to mention Lawrence-Livermore, White Sands, Los Alamos, the Institute for Advanced Studies, the Fermi Lab — and the Feds have never gotten near him. Not to mention DataBAsia."

"Which is…?"

"A profound database concerning Asian martial arts films and hacker bulletins. Nobody knows who runs it, where it is, or how to access it."

"Wow. I think."

"Also, he flies cataclysmic Flight Simulator."

"Oh boy," said Iris, with some disdain, "skills for the millennium."

"Level 10."

"Are you certain that Flight Simulator is really going to come in handy?"

"Are you kidding? Just cooking the books for Hop Toy brings him in two hundred a week. Takes him about two hours on Saturday morning."

"Is that why Fong carries his valise?"

"Fong carries his valise because they're friends. Fong respects Felix. Besides, Felix is too young to drive. He pays Fong a hundred a week plus mileage and burgers to drive him to school, his jobs, his tailor, the computer store, and like that."

"Jobs? Plural?"

"As far as I can tell, between school and jobs, the kid is at it about fourteen hours a day. He's a type A — driven, single-minded, millionaire-by-the-age-of-twenty type of kid, Felix is."

"Friends," said Iris.

"It's symbiotic. Felix knows computers and Fong wants to learn. Fong's got the Firebird with the *Flammenwerfer* sound system, and Felix likes to ride and sing along."

"Associates."

Stanley shrugged. "Fong was dealing dope until Felix got a hold of him. Felix was taking taxis until he met Fong. It's a beautiful thing."

"So what do these guys owe you?"

"They're related to little Tseng."

"Tseng's the girl you rescued?"

Stanley shrugged again. "I was with her when we were both rescued."

"If you're so modest about the recompense, why do you continue to take advantage of it?"

He leveled a gaze at her. "This question seems to be getting around."

She looked at the moon. "As questions go, it's kind of an obvious one."

"Wouldn't you?"

"Wouldn't I what?"

He indicated the view. "Take advantage."

She leveled her gaze at him. "Depends on the reason."

"How about life or death? Would that be good enough?"

She watched him for a moment, then looked away.

"That's my reason. Those organ-buzzards have left me no choice."

"That's kind of changing the subject, but you mean you feel that you're left with no choice but to break the law?"

"Who's breaking the law?"

"If you aren't doing it yourself, you're going to get these two kids to do it for you. What are you going to do? Send them out for a new kidney?"

Stanley looked at the moon. It was getting smaller as it got higher. "I wish. If it were that easy, Hop Toy would have done it already."

"You mean it's not possible?"

"How would I know? On one hand there's no doubt that it's some-how possible. On the other hand, it's not feasible — financially, I mean — for me to get a legitimate kidney. Hop Toy's a good guy. He's done plenty for me, and would do more. Tseng means everything to him. Because of her he's given me a home, a job, a truck to drive. If I'm hungry, day or night, his mother or his wife feeds me. They do my laundry, they let me use their phone, they get me the best hacker in the neighborhood and pay his expenses. But they don't have what it takes to procure and install an uninsured kidney. It's too expensive, and it's too complicated, it's very illegal, and, you might be interested to know, I'm not asking."

"What do you mean, complicated?"

Stanley shifted uneasily.

"It's not the procedure that's complicated. It's the Hop Toy family's relationship to authority that's complicated."

"Authority?"

"Yeah," said Stanley. "Authority."

She frowned.

Stanley sighed loudly. "IRS? Do I have to spell it out?"

"Oh. I get it. You mean if he suddenly comes up with too much money…"

Stanley nodded. "Little bells go off in big computers." He waved his hand. "But, bottom line — Hop Toy has done plenty for me as it is."

Iris touched his face. "Too bad we're not married. My insurance might have covered this…"

Stanley looked at her. "Married? I hardly know you."

She replied softly, "The scope of the subjunctive."

Stanley blinked. "Beg pardon?"

"Condition contrary to fact."

"Ah...: Yes...?"

She shook her head. "I came across a couple of lines, once, on just that subject, by Tom Raworth. He's an English poet. Perhaps you know of him?"

"Yeah," Stanley sighed wearily. Was there no end to this woman's discursiveness? "Perhaps I know of him."

She smiled an inward smile, and quoted the lines.

each day
repeated
he lives
for ever
he thinks
alone
in the honey
comb o
the subjunctive
that riffle
of the deck

She ruffled his hair. "That didn't flood the noggin too badly, did it?"

Damn, Stanley brooded. *This woman's smarter than I am.*

The metal door to the staircase opened with a crash and the light flooding out of the portal was eclipsed by the bulk of Felix, who stood aside for the much thinner frame of Fong, walking backwards to let a wire peel off a spool between his hands.

"What's this?" said Iris. "It looks like they're going to blow up the building."

When Fong had cleared the door Felix kicked the wire into the corner of the threshold and closed the door on it.

Fong trailed wire off the whirling spool until he'd arrived by the arm of Stanley's wheelchair. Then he set the spool in a flower box on the windowsill and disappeared into the darkened shed. A few minutes later he reappeared with the bok choy crate that normally lived beneath the TV. He set it to the right of the door and went back inside.

Felix Choy stood the briefcase full of tools on the pea gravel beneath
the spool and geraniums, turned his back on the shed and studied the
layout. After a moment he moved the wooden crate a couple of feet
toward Berkeley. He stepped back for a moment, shaded his eyes
toward the moon, then stepped forward and adjusted the angle of the
box.

"What's he doing?" Iris whispered, as if Felix were on stage.

"Shh," said Fong, from the darkness beyond the door. "He's aligning
the table for optimum Chih energy."

Iris giggled.

When Felix was ready, Fong produced a folding camp stool and
stood it on the pea gravel between the bok choy crate and the window
box. He placed a fresh can of cherry Coke next to the stool and went
back inside the shack.

Felix stood the pigskin bag on the crate, unzipped it, and pulled a
small plastic case out of it. Even in the dark, the case looked like a
computer. Not much of a computer, Iris judged, as it seemed to be
about the size of a box of chocolates. On the other hand, Sean
Corrigan carried a much smaller one that seemed impressively powerful. The edges of the black plastic case were sleek and rounded, and
three sides of it bristled with buttons, slots and connectors. Felix set
the computer on the box and pulled two more plastic boxes, two wires
and a curly-cord out of the bag. Fong came back outside trailing an
extension cord, and traded the female end of it to Felix for the pigskin
shoulder bag, which Fong zipped closed and placed on the floor just
inside the door of the shack—not without a certain tender reverence
for the bag's quality.

Sitting down on the canvas stool, which creaked ominously beneath
his weight, Felix Choy pulled the crate toward his stomach as far as it
would go. The effect was similar to that of a bumblebee refueling a
gnat. He picked up the computer and plugged a wire into it. Then he
set the machine down to plug the other end of the wire into a transformer, and plugged the transformer into a multiple-outlet strip. This
in turn he plugged into the extension cord. Then he carefully stood a
portable printer on the tool valise, beside the table, and plugged its
power cord into the power strip.

He picked up the computer again and held it to the moonlight,
peering at one edge of it. Having reappeared from the interior of the
shack with another chair, Fong handed him a loose end of the tele-

phone wire from the spool on the windowsill. This Felix plugged into the computer as well, along with a cable from the printer.

Finally, Fong lit six sticks of green incense and stuck them into the dirt among the geraniums.

"Flame on," Fong said softly to himself, taking a seat where he could watch the screen over Felix's shoulder.

Felix fingered a lock and the whole top of the computer opened up, revealing a screen and a keyboard. He touched a switch. The machine beeped, and a little green light winked in the darkness. With miscellaneous clicks and whirs the machine spun to life. The screen lit up a bright, deep blue, casting an eerie glow over the features of Felix who, as soon as the machine had booted, began to stab at the keyboard with all ten fingers. His typing style was a graceful, assured blitz, quite unlike anything else evinced by Felix's teenage demeanor.

His typing style reminded Stanley of Giles MacIntosh.

"You want to sit down?" Stanley asked Iris, taking his eyes off Felix. "This might take a while."

Still sitting on Stanley's lap, Iris realized he was talking to her. "Am I too heavy?" she asked.

"No. I was thinking of your discomfort."

"Oh, Stanley," she said, and put her head on his shoulder.

Felix took a long pull on the new cherry Coke. "Got the data?" he said to no one in particular, and made a low scooping gesture with his free hand, beside the camp stool. When his hand came up empty, an expression of unmitigated petulance darkened his beardless features. "Hey."

Fong dropped the front legs of the straight-back chair down to the gravel and went inside the shed. They could hear him rooting around in the shopping bags.

Stanley plucked the folded piece of notepaper from the envelope and handed it to Felix.

A jet liner sloped in over the city from the northeast, with a long decrescendo of turbofans. The night was so clear they could distinguish every round window on the starboard side of the aircraft, like the stops on an ocarina.

Fong came back out of the shed to place an opened family-sized bag of potato chips next to the bok choy crate, well within reach of Felix's questing hand.

"There's no paper in the printer," said Felix, digging deep into the bag.

"Salt plus hydrogenated palm oil equals smarter already," muttered Fong, uncharacteristically humble.

While Fong bent over the little printer, carefully stacking and loading ten or fifteen sheets of paper into its feeder, Felix happily filled his mouth with chips once, twice, and a third time, each mouthful sluiced by a long draft of cherry Coke. The crunching sounded like a herd of reindeer migrating across the gravel roof.

Felix thoroughly crushed the soda can between two meaty fists. When he tossed the can over his shoulder, calling, "Recycle," Fong caught it and replaced it with a fresh one.

"Department of Motor Vehicles," said Felix, eying the slip of paper as he sipped at the third cherry Coke. "We'll start there." He slipped a corner of the paper under an edge of the computer, where he could read it by the light of the screen, and attacked the keyboard.

Fong leaned forward, his hands on his knees, to watch the screen over Felix's shoulder.

"First," Fong narrated, "a free, untraceable phone line."

A dial-tone hummed within the little computer, then its modem dialed a long series of digits, each proceeded by the variable-length clicks of rotary dial access.

The clicks stopped. A telephone rang once. The line picked up. A modem from cyberia emitted a squeal and a chatter. The computer's modem squealed back. Various messages flashed on the screen in front of Felix. Iris and Stanley watched the play of light on Felix's face. The modems reciprocated each other with chattering trills, like mechanical birds. The devices agreed on something, data began to flow, and the modem speaker fell silent.

"Now," said Fong. "Accessing somebody's account. Needing a password."

After a minute or two Fong let out a low whistle. "Would have took me all night, just to do that," he said appreciatively.

Felix let his fingers fly over the keys as he watched the screen. Stanley pulled on the wheels of his chair until he'd maneuvered himself into the doorway of the shack, Iris still in his lap, so they could see better. In Felix's hands the computer might well have been a grand piano.

Felix, Stanley realized uneasily, typed faster than Giles MacIntosh.

Fong broke into a grin. Simultaneously, Felix frowned.

"This person's password is Poontang," muttered Felix. "What's that mean?"

Iris blinked and looked at Stanley. Stanley looked at Fong.

"Island off Borneo," Fong said quickly. "Very obscure."

"Oh yeah?" Felix said. "I got a pop-up atlas in here somewhere..."

"Skip it," said Fong. "Sticking to the mission."

"Never hurts to learn," said Felix petulantly.

"This is an illegal phone connection," Fong reminded him. "Not to dawdle."

The computer beeped. "Account accessed," said Fong. "Calling Department of Motor Vehicles in... how about... Duluth, Minnesota?"

Felix hunched a shoulder and typed. "Duluth... Minnesota."

Before long Felix was inside the California DMV's main computer, accessing its vehicle registration files via the Minnesota Highway Patrol's main computer, which for reasons best known to Felix Choy was acting under the impression that Felix was a patrol car making a routine check on an out-of-state vehicle while cruising the beltway engirdling Duluth. Within a few minutes he had the name, address, and serial numbers of outstanding parking tickets credited to a registered owner for the license number Stanley had taken from the BMW the night before. As Felix was about to hit the key to print this information, he sat up in his chair, nearly upsetting the table.

"Hey. The California computer is getting excited." He waited a minute. "Oh, wow. Way cool. The Beamer is stolen." He dragged a fistful of potato chips out of the bag and stuffed them into his mouth, still watching the screen. "Are we surprised?" he said through the mouthful of chips.

Fong and Iris looked at Stanley, who had told them nothing of the night before. "No," he said. "We're not surprised. But get the info anyway."

Felix hit a button. "Printing data." The little printer below the table began to zip and snap like a tiny welder.

"What about the van?"

"Checking...," said Felix. He consulted Stanley's slip of paper and tapped in the figures.

Stanley had never had much hope for the Beamer, but he held out some for the van. It seemed obvious that they might think it important to steal Green Eyes a different car every week. Her vehicle was the more exposed. But the van would be a much more intrinsic part of the operation, too difficult to readily replace.

A moment passed, then two, then three. A sailboat, motoring through the still night with all sails dropped and a single light atop her mast, emerged from beneath the Bay Bridge, hard against Treasure Island, cruising silently north, unremarked by the party on the roof.

"Got it," said Felix. "It's not stolen."

"Don't sound so disappointed," said Fong.

"Hey," said Felix, brightening.

"What's up?"

"I'm not disappointed anymore."

"Why not?"

Felix pressed the key to print the screen and the little printer came to life again.

"It's registered to a funeral home."

He happily filled his mouth with chips.

Chapter 20

The columbarium was in Oakland—not far from where the grass grows greener on account of all the leaky sarcophagi.

Bay Memorial Vista was a beautiful if blunt *memento mori* by moonlight. Surmounted by the perpetually lit and windowless Mormon Tabernacle, the marble garden draped over the slopes of a low pair of adjacent hills like a silk blouse over the shoulders of an immortal concubine, providing its eyeless denizens a thorough overview of the phantom trace of the Cypress Freeway, felled with a loss of 62 souls by the earthquake of '89, and the shadowy landfill flats of West Oakland (called Ghost Town by the locals because of its murder rate). Beyond lay the velvet darkness of the Bay, the intermittent twinkles of Treasure Island and the catenary path of yellow bulbs following the Bay Bridge to San Francisco, a vista stretching fifteen miles and more. Between Ghost Town and the edge of the Bay glowed the crane derricks and slab-sided hulls of the container port. The quartzite mauves and ochres, their geometries set quivering by distance, seemed a bright, complex world built and maintained by robots, entirely enclosed within the prolate globe of a mercury lamp balanced on the palm of Oakland's outstretched hand.

The Chippendale O'Hare Columbarium, Crematorium, and Funeral Home didn't actually border Bay Memorial Vista. It was a low, rambling building several blocks north of the cemetery, with a discreet sign that should have made it hard to find. But lofting from the far corner of the premises, its snub muzzle of painted bricks like the handle of a four-story nightstick, the smokestack gave it away.

Number 34, Avenida Del Fumador. The numeral was etched into a brass plate screwed high up on a brick pilaster. A slight breeze occasionally lifted the shadow of an oak limb off the plaque, so it could be feebly touched by the light of a street lamp.

Stanley slowed the truck long enough to confirm the address, then accelerated past it. At the second cross street north he made a U-turn and drove slowly back, to park just below the crown of the hill overlooking the hollow that contained No. 34, where he could comfortably study the layout.

Aside from Chippendale O'Hare, the neighborhood seemed strictly residential, and older than those by which more recent development had encapsulated it; its cozy bungalows had been built between the Depression and the end of World War II, when the labor demands of the naval shipyards attracted many new people to Oakland and San Francisco. At the end of the war, one of these bungalows could be had for five thousand dollars; the payments on a 20-year, four-percent loan bequeathed by the G.I. Bill came to $27.84 a month. But the shipbuilding had ceased long since. The massive naval force that had steamed in and out of the Golden Gate, all through the war, now rotted in row after row of mothballed hulks in Suisun Bay. The sailors' and welders' families that had occupied the bungalows were all grown up and scattered.

A disjoint abutting of slabs whose horizontals were delineated and emphasized by clerestories, Number 34 would have been very modern in 1956, an architectural innovation. Now dated by its design, a few windows cracked, some plywood paneling warped, enveloped by neglected oaks and acacias, it projected seediness. A tall pyracantha hedge paralleled the brick perimeter wall, the two entirely enclosing the compound. Behind the buildings a tall Monterey pine stood almost as high as the smokestack.

A leaf-covered driveway swept into the entryway between two brick columns, broadened to encompass a carport and parking lot, then spilled steeply through a pair of locked gates onto the street demarcating the back side of the block.

And it was quiet in this neighborhood.

Dead quiet.

The northern building seemed to be of one story. But a row of low windows along its north side were only about a foot off the ground. Studying the structure, seeing certain vents and gratings, Stanley realized that another, subterranean level must extend all the way from the row of windows, beneath the carport, to the southern building. The complex was actually two stories, and would encompass perhaps six or seven thousand square feet.

The three-dollar digital clock integral to the notepad stalk depending from the inside of the windshield said it was a quarter to two. How late do mortuaries stay open?

This one looked closed. In fact, the more he studied the place, the more Stanley wondered if it did any business at all.

The parking lot was deserted. The trees and the hedges had a shaggy look to them; certainly, much time had passed since they'd been attended to. Pine straw was drifted up in windrows along the edges of the parking lot and the roofs of the buildings. With a little rain all that detritus would cause a lot of trouble with a drainage system. Surely, bad drainage wasn't a good idea in a building intended to display urns containing ashes of the dead?

The upper branches of the trees suddenly filled with angular beams of light. A car topped the hill behind the truck and Stanley slouched in his seat as the cab flooded with swift shadows. The car accelerated downhill, trailing fumes and music, passed the Toyota, nominally braked for the stop sign at the corner, and with a squeal of tires was gone.

Silence ebbed back into the sleeping neighborhood.

After a while Stanley could hear a breeze passing through the upper branches of the lone Monterey pine. When the breeze ebbed he could detect a similar whispering, almost a mutter, from the freeway, nearly two miles away.

At the bottom of the hill, across the intersection, a light came on in a window of a bungalow. It was a small window with a frosted, translucent pane.

Stanley shifted his eyes above the window and its roof, to the lights twinkling south and west of the field of pale obelisks. Just as a pain asserted its identity in his lower back, a discreet cluster of lights lifted above the horizon. The lights assumed a path that took them up at an increasingly oblique angle, drawing them further away from their landlocked brethren until they passed beyond the darkened side of the hill to Stanley's right, on route to Portland or Seattle, Vancouver or Anchorage.

The pain was not occluded, but grew. He gripped the rim of the steering wheel, concentrating on the light in the frosted window at the bottom of the hill, and pulled himself straight in the seat. Beads of sweat broke the surface of his forehead, and cooled there.

On the seat beside him was a small backpack. He opened it, taking care with the noise the zipper made. From it he withdrew a small flat tobacco tin. He snapped its lid open and studied its contents by the diffuse glow of the streetlight. He selected three pills. One was a Codeine tablet, of 60 milligrams. The other two were Dexamyls, each capsule bearing 15 milligrams of dextroamphetamine modulated by about a hundred of barbiturate.

One pill to kill the pain, two more to keep him alert in its absence.

He snapped the tin closed and set it into the catch-all molded into the plastic behind the gearshift. From the backpack he drew a bottle of beer. The cap made only a slight hiss when he twisted it off, and a couple of clicks when he threw it into the passenger foot-well. He took a sip, hiked the pills into his mouth, chased them with another sip, and another.

The bathroom light went out at the bottom of the hill. By the time he finished the beer the pain in his back had diminished to the far-away call of a coyote in dense, snow-filled woods.

He sat in the truck with the empty bottle resting on the lower rim of the steering wheel. The pain in his back almost a memory, his vision lucid, his mind awake, he felt better than he'd felt in nearly two months.

He knew it was an illusion. He knew he was a sick man, but, just now, he didn't feel like one. At the moment, he felt, he might manage to take charge of his own destiny.

Perhaps this illusion was particularly cohesive because he was sitting under the wheel of a pickup truck. One always feels at least partially in charge of one's destiny, at the wheel of a pickup truck. Stoned on a cocktail of speed, essence of poppy, a barbiturate, a beer, and — what's that? a touch of fear? — he, Stanley Ahearn, felt as if he might be taking charge of his destiny.

What a joke.

He laughed grimly, without mirth.

His eyes hardened. Fuck the facts.

He considered the Chippendale O'Hare setup.

Stanley didn't even know if he was going to be able to get inside the building. He certainly had no idea what he was going to do if he did. He didn't know what he was going to discover. He didn't really want to discover anything.

What he wanted was his life back. He wanted to be able to sit on his rooftop and sip whiskey out of a bottomless quart, go to his little job in his little salt-rotted pickup truck and make his little wage and eat marginally nutritious meals and get back up on the roof in front of his little shack and sit in front of that magnificent view and drink his little life away with no help from anyone else, thank you very little.

Corrigan had him pegged there.

He visualized Green Eyes, as she watched her goons load poor Ted into the van.

His face burned with shame as he thought of her. She was a beauty, all right. And she had cleaned his clock. He could clearly recall his feelings as he sat next to her at the bar. After so many drinks he'd practically given up on talking, just to stare at her. She had a mouth that taunted him, challenged him, laughed at him, invited him, did everything but inhale him. And those lips. Even in their natural rest position those lips drew him to her as inevitably as a sun draws its satellites through thousands of millennia of captivity toward absolute, certain doom.

Then she'd touched him. It had been a long time since a woman had touched Stanley for free — for free — hah! What a laugh! For *ten thousand dollars* she'd touched him.

It had been a longer time since he'd really wanted, *desired*, to be touched by a woman. And it had been an even longer time since he'd touched a woman he desired to touch, and whom he desired to touch him back, and who, moreover, desired to be touched by him and to touch him back too. These things, it seemed to him, were very delicate to arrange, almost impossible, a matter of coincidence and spontaneity, and, let's face it, close to miraculous and maybe even worth the risk of rejection.

They were not to be taken lightly.

They were not to be betrayed.

He wondered if they'd found Ted yet.

Green Eyes had taken his, Stanley's, hand, and guided it to where she wanted him to touch her. Right there in the bar. He'd had to put down his drink to do it.

He wondered whether they'd found Giles' friend Tommy yet, dead or alive. Maybe even now Corrigan was interviewing Tommy or Ted in a hospital. He wondered if Corrigan had taunted Ted about picking up women in bars, yet. He wondered if Iris had...

He tightened his grip on the beer bottle.

He wondered if Ted had any insurance.

Maybe it was different for Ted. Maybe Ted had a regular enough job with a regular enough contractor who carried regular enough insurance to cover a decidedly irregular catastrophe. Maybe, Corrigan would say, maybe if you just tell me everything, Ted, how it happened, where you were, when you got there, when you left, what kind of car she was driving, which way you went when you left the bar, where she... you know... touched you...

Maybe Ted would have the answers that would enable Corrigan to solve the case. Maybe put Green Eyes out of business. Maybe soon...

She'd put his hand between her legs. Right there at the bar. It was warm, between her legs. And she'd pressed herself against him and sung along breathily in his ear with *I Fall to Pieces*, by Patsy Cline. Then she put her tongue in his ear, all wet and, uh, sexual. Stanley had heard the ocean: had Ted heard the ocean? Then she took her drink and rolled the tall glass over the front of his pants, over and over, like the glass was a rolling pin and his abdomen was a marble pastry counter and she was rolling out sourdough for that great day in the gold fields and she whispered, "Oh, my, Stanley." She whispered, swaying back and forth in front of him, her forehead touching his forehead, the bottle between them, the both of them watching it, she had whispered, "Maybe it's time to get out of here..."

He'd not forgotten her sympathetic psychology. On the contrary, he remembered every word of it. Completely. But not until he overheard her laying it on poor Ted, sex in the guise of radical ecology, had he grasped the masterful scope of her duplicity. He remembered every syllable of it, and might never shed the mortification of having been so thoroughly taken in by this woman's deception.

And those green eyes, too, of course. There was some compensation in them, wasn't there? Wasn't it better to be taken in by one's delusions of feminine beauty than one's susceptibility to an unexpected intelligence?

Why unexpected?

Because it was possessed by a woman?

He threw the empty beer bottle into the foot-well of the passenger seat, with a little too much force. It took a few ricocheting thumps to settle down there.

The breeze picked up again. Across the street, the top of the Monterey pine swayed. Above it a few of the brighter stars were visible. A single star twinkled through the tree's branches. It must have been a hundred, maybe even two hundred years old, that tree. How much had it seen?

And that smokestack next to the tree. The atomized corporealities of how many souls had risen into these breezes, to be sifted through those same branches as their last contact with things of this earth?

Ted?

Are you alive, Ted?

Tree? Have you seen Ted? Touched him? *Sifted* him?

Stanley reached into the daypack and pulled out a thin black penlight. He held it under the dash to twist it on and off. It worked, and he slipped it into his hip pocket. Then he reached into the daypack and pulled out a blue steel automatic pistol.

It was an old one. The neglected bluing had long since blistered off the muzzle and breech. The sweat of forgotten hands had long since corroded the shellac off its walnut grips.

This was Stanley's secret quality-of-life insurance policy. When the going got too rough, when the pain became unendurable, when he'd become hopelessly incontinent, he'd blow out his brains. Simple as that.

He'd always planned it that way. He'd bought the gun, learned how to shoot it, and filed it away in a drawer.

Just like any other insurance policy.

Better, call it quality-of-death insurance. Or *assurance*, like they say in Canada. Quality-of-death *assurance*.

The assurance that he wouldn't die in a hospital, quilled by needles and tubes, speechless, pissing the rubber sheets, undrinking, a corpse animated by pharmacology and shame and the ability to wiggle its toes in response to yes/no questions.

Forty-five caliber quality-of-death assurance: only $150. Plus tax and bullets. A single-payment policy. A short waiting period, only ten days. No physical examination. No flexible sigmoidoscopy.

Until recently it hadn't occurred to Stanley that this insurance tool, this handgun, might come in handy for anything else.

But now…?

He turned the butt up and looked at it. The clip was still missing, so it hadn't loaded itself in the dark. You laugh. Guns do things like that.

He rummaged in a side pocket of the daypack until he came up with two clips. The dull tips of the fat slugs shone in the gloom like two stacks of inquisitive maggots.

He dropped one clip into the inside breast pocket of his jacket. The other he slid into the butt of the automatic until it locked into place.

He held the pistol down below the steering wheel and jacked a shell into the chamber.

A wave of nausea passed over him. He leaned his head against the rim of the steering wheel, the gun pointed between his feet.

When the nausea passed he gripped the pistol with both hands, its muzzle aimed between the clutch and the brake pedals, and let the cocked hammer gently down onto the firing pin with both thumbs, and set the safety. This operation had always made his hands sweat, and the hammer, though serrated, never seemed properly curved to accept the pad of a single thumb. Not like in the movies, bub. Which was why he always used both thumbs and a neutral target like the floorboard of a pickup truck when he cocked or uncocked the .45.

Though nobody died when it happened, he had learned this bit of gun control the hard way, and blown a great hole in the side of a perfectly good refrigerator in the process.

Gray Eyes found the slug a week later, when she thawed one of her dietary linguini dinners.

They'd shared a bottle of wine over the linguine and stuck the cork in the bullet hole in the side of the freezer, where it stayed until they split up.

Those were the days.

He released the clip and fished an extra cartridge out of the back-pack. He thumbed the shell into the clip, replacing the round now advanced to the firing chamber. Ordnance topped off, he fed the clip back into the handle of the pistol until it locked into place with a single, metallic click.

Stanley quietly rolled up the truck window, staring past the edge of glass as it passed between him and the mortuary.

Across the street the Monterey pine swayed in the breeze. The shadows of its limbs played over the linear taper of the smokestack. The heat from the stack would make the air dance above its mouth: the dance of Adios.

It was time to go in.

The
Fusion Vipers

Chapter 21

At the north end of the building the steep slope of the hill gave access to the brick perimeter wall, and from there it was an easy scramble onto the roof.

The brick wall stretched away from the building to the east, cornered, and ran south until it encountered the rear access gate. This right angle enclosed a small meditation court, complete with overhanging acacia and a whispering spruce tree, stone benches, and a small pond with scattered lilies. Against the far corner of the court a stand of cattails clicked softly.

Walking the parapet wall, the garden to his left and the gravel roof to his right, Stanley approached a clerestory that rose no more than five feet above the south end of the roof. This would let north light into a room below, perhaps a chapel or reception area.

The six rectangular frosted windows were in a line, and illumined from within. Standing on the parapet, eighteen inches above the first roof, his head was about a foot above the second roof, topping the clerestory. Beyond the skew, dark plane of the upper roof the Monterey pine and the smokestack loomed side by side.

An irregular ticking turned out to be a wire, which the breeze caused to tap the rusted stanchion of an old TV antenna.

He stood there for a while, getting used to it.

Just as he had stepped down to the roof in order to try the nearest window he heard a rustling sound.

He strained his ears until all he could hear was the ringing induced by the drugs he had taken.

Something was unmeditatively making its way through the cattails, diagonally across the garden from him.

He stood with his head four feet above the parapet, an excellent and disconcerting silhouette to anyone who might look up from the court-yard below.

The rustling abruptly ceased.

He collapsed onto his haunches, one hand on the scored grip of the .45 in his belt. But for the codeine he'd taken, the pain of his incision would have made this position untenable.

A minute passed, then another.

The cattails rustled. He strained to locate the source of the noise in the darkness. Then he saw two bright yellow eyes, looking right at him.

His mind nearly stalled, then raced. It was way too soon to pull out his cannon and blast the neighborhood, but he was tempted.

Framed by the gently waving cattails, as if peering out from under a giant fright-wig, the eyes blinked.

Raccoon.

Stanley exhaled a puff of air and sat down. After a dazed moment he leaned back against the wall. Despite the dose of speed in him, he was thoroughly fatigued. He unclenched his hand from the butt of the .45 and stared at the fingers. They quivered.

Chickenshit.

If a fellow were to set himself up in the business of stealing human body parts, wouldn't a funeral home provide a perfect cover? He won-dered if Corrigan had thought of it. Even if he had, there must be a couple of mortuaries for every, what, 50,000 people? Which would net, let's see, long division in the middle of the yellow-eyed night on several drugs and a rooftop with a gun in your hand, carry the two, 120 of them in the Bay Area alone. It seemed perfect. For one thing you, like Death, having no documented respect for Time, could keep weird hours. For another, a fully equipped operating theater might not look at all out of place in a funeral home. Don't morticians remove organs and pump fluids with the best of them? And who would will-ingly snoop around a funeral home? Anybody would assume that, behind any given door, corpses slept. What snoop needs to see that?

The grounds around him backed up this supposition. At first, Stanley had been surprised by the evident lack of security surrounding them. That bench on the south side of the building, for example, underneath a cypress tree. A perfect place to sit and smoke a joint — right? But no. The place was too creepy. Sooner than later, the awareness of what was going on immediately around him would leak into the pothead's little mind. Very quickly, the stoned party wouldn't be having fun anymore, would instead find his thoughts adrift along dark and maudlin shoals, his lee shore eerily lit by funeral pyres and obscured by an acrid smoke that hung close to the dark waters, an atmosphere difficult to breathe… The stoned party would shove off to vistas less moody.

No. Nobody would visit this place unless they had business here.

So, what's with Yellow Eyes?

Stanley peered over the parapet.

Yellow Eyes had disappeared. Maybe with good reason? Stanley slowly trained the automatic over the cattails.

Nothing. The eyes were gone.

Then he heard a splash.

He looked straight down.

A very large raccoon stood on its hind legs, waist-deep in the lily pond, looking directly up at Stanley. It was as if the creature had been waiting for him to look over the wall. Its front paws were dripping, and a gleaming orange fish writhed futilely in their grasp.

Now, both Stanley and the raccoon waited.

If Stanley was afraid of the least noise, the raccoon seemed afraid of nothing. The raccoon after all was minding its own business. It had come for a nice, fat carp.

Depleted, Stanley leaned back against the vertex of the parapet and clerestory walls and sighed as raggedly as the necessity for absolute silence would allow. His shoulders shed tension like a steeple its bats at dusk. But for the codeine every joint would have ached. Sweat gleamed on his face. He clutched the checkered butt of the pistol between his sweating palms, its barrel between his drawn-up knees.

He sat for a long moment, watching the stars to the north and breathing the cool night air. Sapped by his nerves, his strength was waning. If he didn't move soon he wouldn't move at all. What the hell was he doing on the roof of a funeral home at two o'clock in the morning with a gun in his hand?

The water thrashed in the pond beyond the wall, and the raccoon blundered hastily into the cattails.

"You see?" said a voice. "I told you. It's that old bull coon."

Stanley froze. *I know that voice.*

"I guess it was," said a second voice.

A beam of light swiveled through the lower branches of the acacia and played along the clerestory wall, just above Stanley's head.

"How'd he get down from the roof so fast?"

"Same way we got out here so slow. Put that heater away."

"Man," said the first voice, "I don't care how much money I make here. I don't care how much time I spend here. This place gives me the willies like a airborne ball of snakes."

"What's your problem? It's just a raccoon. I thought you grew up in the country."

"I did grow up in the country. The *wine* country."

They shared a knowing laugh.

"Lettin' a old bull coon throw a scare into you."

"It ain't the coon. It's this goddamn funeral home, and that god-damn Djell. The man's nuttier than Telegraph Avenue."

"His money spends just like anybody else's, don't it?"

"Don't it," the other sighed. "Don't it."

The light left the corner where the parapet met the clerestory and swept through empty space.

"Vince," said the second voice, "that old coon's got these carps about thinned out."

Vince chuckled. "Have to get him some more. Kinda fond of that old coon."

After another moment the light went out, and the two men walked around the side of the building, talking as they went, until their voices faded.

"Bet he'd like trout better."

"Or perch."

"Okay. Perch."

"Where in hell you get perch...?"

A door slammed directly behind the wall against which Stanley had flattened himself, and he realized that the two men had entered the room onto which the clerestory allowed daylight. Beyond the glass, a chair scraped on a tile floor.

Paydirt. He recognized both those voices.

When they weren't feeding raccoons they delivered rugs.

Vince and his buddy.

He'd found the right funeral home.

This would be an excellent opportunity to telephone Inspector Corrigan. Never better. If it hadn't been for that raccoon Stanley would have opened the clerestory window practically on top of the two thugs, and Stanley would have found the end of his trail. Next time there might not be a raccoon hanging around to save him.

What would the end of the trail mean around here?

He needn't speculate. All he had to do was recall those photographs of Giles MacIntosh. Or what was left of him.

They should change the name of this joint, from Chippendale O'Hare to Trail's End.

Or Chippendale O'Negative.

Har de har.

Guy could just laugh himself to death around here.

Stanley stood on the parapet wall and tiptoed back the way he had come. He took the long step down to the brick perimeter wall. He shot a glance across the street, where he could see his truck. He should get out while he could still walk. He should call Corrigan. He knew it.

He could read the name of Hop Toy's business on the door of the truck. Even though it was in Chinese.

Then he saw a green butane lighter and a pack of cigarettes hit a polished bartop, and before the memory could roll its first reel his face burned with shame.

He turned his back on the truck and headed for the cattails.

Where the brick wall cornered, the cattails were very high. He crouched behind them and listened. Nothing. Just the wind passing through conifer boughs.

Stanley gently parted the cattails, and obtained a line of sight past the chapel building, straight across the driveway, to a sunken loading dock.

The brown van was parked there, backed up to the loading dock with its back door open. If he had seen it earlier, he would have been as certain about the true business of Chippendale O'Hare as he was when he heard Vince's voice.

He ran along the crown of the brick wall like a rat, keeping as much of the landscaping between himself and the compound as possible.

The wall ended in a brick pilaster at the rear gate. The gate was closed and the ground outside the wall, to his left, fell away sharply to the street. If he chose to use the cover of the outside slope to cross the mouth of the drive it was doubtful he would be able to climb back inside.

A pool of light flooded the asphalt between Stanley and the loading dock. To his right and slightly behind him stood the building behind whose clerestory roof he had just been cowering. In its lower corner stood a gray metal fire door, through which Vince and his partner must have passed. The door was closed. Twenty yards in front of him, just inside the wall, the big Monterey pine swayed, creaking gently. Little else stirred. Stanley waited, breathing deeply. The cool air had a salty tang to it. He, Stanley Ahearn, about as introspective as a claw hammer, now discovered within his soul a sudden nostalgia for sea air, cool and damp and salty. He should have taken more walks on the beach, when he had the leisure.

He touched the extra clip in the lining of his jacket and thought, *Fine, motherfucker; let it be the last time I taste salt air.*

When the breeze picked up and the big pine began to creak and sigh he dropped off the wall, stood up, and walked across the pool of light, as casually as a man making certain his golf clubs were in the trunk of his Mercedes, ready for tomorrow's early tee-off. When he reached the pine he stood in its shadow, its rough bark under the heel of his gun hand, the right front door of the van not ten feet away. Still he saw no one. A magnetic sign on the door panel said,

CHIPPENDALE O'HARE

Your Complete Funeral Service
Genteel & Dignified

Funerary Articles
Transport & Display
Refrigeration
Cemetery & Interment
Crematorium
Columbarium
Music & Oration
Memory Garden

** Free Estimates **
24 Hours

34 Avenida Del Fumador
Oakland
510-836-4796

'Since 1941'

He stepped to the passenger side of the panel truck and had a look in the window. On the seat lay a second magnetic sign.

Stanley knew what it said, but he turned his head to read it anyway.

CABRINI CARPET

Sales
Installation
Service

1338 Mission St
San Francisco
415-864-2825.

The thing about magnetic signs is, they're cheap. Why get just one?

A large garage door at the back of the loading dock was closed. A trash can stood to its left. The van was headed out, its back door stood open. Beyond the garage door was another, smaller door. Closer to Stanley, five or six narrow concrete steps led up from the asphalt to the loading dock.

He took these steps two at a time, crossed the loading dock, and tried the door.

It opened.

There was no light behind it. He went in anyway.

Closing the door behind him he pulled the pencil flashlight from his hip pocket.

The place looked very much like what Stanley would expect to find beyond any loading dock, like the warehouses of any number of places at which he daily picked up produce.

It didn't smell like produce, though.

This loading dock had another exceptional detail.

There was a carpet on the floor.

It was a nice carpet, too. Oriental job. Fringe.

Against the far wall stood a gurney, much like those Stanley had seen during his recent stay in the hospital. This one had a couple of seat belts dangling from it. Beyond the gurney was a glass wall that looked on to a sort of control room. It would be from in there that the flame and the conveyor and other aspects of cremation would be controlled.

Stanley clicked off the flash and stood in the dark. As he grew accustomed to the darkness he could hear the distant hum of machinery. A compressor perhaps. Refrigeration.

Then he discerned a line of light. He watched it for a long time, but it didn't move. It didn't get bigger, and it didn't get smaller. It was just a horizontal line of light, floating in the darkness in front of him.

Not in front of him, exactly. More like below him.

He clicked the penlight on again. To his right the beam found a concrete ramp behind a pipe railing, leading down. At the bottom of the ramp was a wide double door.

He clicked the penlight off. The sliver of light reappeared, right where the threshold of the double doors would be.

He watched the line of light as his dilating eyes allowed it to reappear, and listened. Other than the distant hum of machinery, the place was as quiet as a globe full of falling snow.

He thumbed on the penlight and followed its thin beam down the ramp. When he reached the doors he doused the penlight and listened. Nothing.

He pocketed the light and clicked off the safety on the pistol.

With his other hand he pushed gently at the door.

It moved. A vertical slit of light appeared before him, and the sounds of compressor motors became louder. There was a smell, too. A smell he recognized but couldn't place. He applied his eye and the gun barrel to the slit. Nothing stirred beyond the door. It looked like a corridor, pale green and brightly lit. The door swung easily, about fourteen inches away from him. He was about to step through it when the door crashed violently backwards, throwing him down on the concrete ramp.

He lost the gun as he fell, and for some reason it didn't go off in his face. He expected to be attacked, but nothing touched him. Something kicked the doors from the other side. The doors shivered but didn't open.

"Oh! That was a nasty trick to pull on me. But I've got you now!"

Still, nothing touched Stanley. No light came on over the ramp. The doors did not open.

There were sounds of a struggle, followed by the deep laughter of a woman, and assorted kicks and thumps against the door.

The woman screamed, and fabric was torn.

"Hah!" said a man, and something was torn further. "Jezebel!"

"Monster!" she screamed. "Beast!"

As Stanley rolled away from the door he also rolled over the automatic.

"Oh, God!" shouted the woman, amid the rending of cloth.

"Mine!" screamed the man. "All mine!"

Stanley retrieved the pistol, sat up, and pointed it at the closed doors. Loud thumps and grunts sounded beyond it.

"Jesus!" the woman shouted. "Christ!" The man responded.

The man puffed and rhythmically grunted, as if he were driving a stake with a twelve-pound mallet.

"Mother of God!" the woman screamed.

"Hippocrates!" he screamed.

As Stanley crouched toward the doors, he could smell natural gas and some kind of solvent, maybe formaldehyde or ether — strange industrial odors.

Preceded by eight inches of pistol he pushed open the door.

Sweeping the gun to his right he saw an empty corridor, with closed double doors at the far end, perhaps thirty feet away.

To his left a pair of slim rails, let into the concrete floor like railroad or trolley tracks of a narrow gauge, paralleled beneath and past him and disappeared under steel double doors at the other end of the hall a mere ten feet away. These were secured by an iron bar.

Dead center between the two rails, pinned against the bar, Green Eyes struggled. She wore a nurse's uniform, or what was left of one. Her dark hair was in disarray, spilling over one shoulder, with a little white nurse's cap clinging to it by dint of a single bobby pin.

The green eyes were open and looking right at Stanley. But her mouth was open, too, and she was rhythmically moaning. The sound upset Stanley deeply. Blocking most of his view of her was the bulk of a large man, draped in a white coat not unlike the uniform of a lab technician. But this man's tweed pants were pooled around his ankles, which were encased in a pair of argyle socks. From the paired V's of their garters the stems of two hirsute, pale legs disappeared up into the drape of the white coat. With all of his weight, with all of his energy, this monstrosity was slamming his body into that of Green Eyes. She was pinned between him and the double doors of the crematorium, the iron bar across the small of her back. Yet, far from resisting or even letting him do it, she was helping. She was reciprocating.

When Green Eyes saw the gun her eyes widened, and she faintly smiled. Then she raised her right leg, the one toward Stanley, who stood not ten feet away, and lodged her foot firmly in the small of Lab Coat's back. The coat caught on her heel so that, had he had any doubts before, Stanley could plainly see that everybody was mostly naked beneath.

Naked except, on Green Eyes' part, a white garter belt and two torn white nylon stockings.

Torrid, thought some part of Stanley's mind. They are filming pornography in here. But the sexual aspect of this scene commanded only part of his attention.

Equally riveting was the syringe taped to the inside of Lab Coat's naked forearm.

"Ach!" screamed Lab Coat, raising his face toward the ceiling. "It is close!"

"Is it close?" coaxed Green Eyes, lapsing into apparent passivity despite the fervent jactitations of the man who had her pinioned against the door, while her eyes, though glazed, never left Stanley's.

"Jah!" screamed the other. "Jah jah! It is close! Ever so close! Minutely, incrementally, Angstrom close!"

"Say when, darling," said Green Eyes, and she moved one hand to the syringe.

So fascinated had he been by the two circles of white adhesive tape, holding the stem and the barrel of the syringe firmly to the inside of the doctor's forearm, for the first time Stanley noticed a length of coffee-colored rubber tubing knotted around the arm, just below the biceps, and just above where the point of the needle had entered the man's skin.

"When! When!" screamed the man, lunging against the woman with such force that the firebricked doors behind them boomed with the impact. "Now is when!"

Despite the ride she was getting Green Eyes managed, with considerable adroitness, and not taking her eyes off Stanley for so much as a second, to loose the knot in the surgical tubing, and, even from ten feet away, Stanley saw a bright trace of scarlet jet into the glass of the syringe with the abrupt suddenness of a moray eel starting after its prey.

"When," she gasped, and "When," the man whimpered, and Stanley could see that if, a moment ago, he had blown the spine out of this man theoretically assaulting Green Eyes, as he'd originally considered, she might have torn him, Stanley, limb from limb. For this was a consensual act he was witnessing. It would have been like a cop interrupting a fist fight between man and wife, only to have them both turn on him.

The man was grunting, huffing, laboring toward some invisible peak of ecstasy, one arm hooked under his partner's shoulder, the other with its syringe suspended mid air, as if from an invisible subway strap, the fist opening and closing. He could barely master his voice sufficient to croak, "Now! Now my bitch, my angel, my nurse, my whore! Now Now Now…!"

And Green Eyes, clutching the forearm with both hands now, sent the plunger home, not with an abrupt stab but with a deliberate, even pressure of her thumb, a disconcerting vector, harrowing to witness, for all its thoughtfulness.

"My God!" the man screamed. "My God!" And his head rolled back between his shoulders, and his eyeballs into his head.

Green Eyes released the syringe and clasped the man's hips to hers, taking her eyes off Stanley for the first time, closing them in fact, and closing with her shuddering partner, convulsing with him, whispering nonsense to him, stroking, encouraging, joining him in the anguish of these frantic devotionals, to which they, she and he, had obviously gone to such great lengths to achieve.

Stanley let the door swing to behind him. His gun hung unaimed at his side.

It seemed banal to think that the steel doors behind the couple led into the furnace. So the rails must lead from the furnace to the chamber wherein the bodies were prepared for cremation. In a chamber where bodies could be prepared for cremation, they could be prepared for other things….

"Oh," said the man, sobbing now in the woman's arms, she stroking his hair, their clothing as if the wreckage of the cocoon from which they'd just emerged. "Jesus, Joseph and Mary..."

Before Stanley could consciously detect the absence of the door's mass and the draft that had replaced it, tiny cool pricks arrived, nearly simultaneously, at the hollows beneath each of his earlobes.

A voice behind him, as falsetto as a child's, said, "If you move, you'll die."

Chapter 22

$\mathbf{T}$hose green eyes had fooled him again.

Even as the spent customer in the white coat sagged in her arms, Green Eyes watched Stanley. Like a cat in a window watching a bird's nest, she studied him. She'd used her eyes to hold Stanley while some guy with a voice like broken train wheel slipped up behind him.

She'd fooled Stanley again.

Green Eyes let her ankle fall away from the small of her partner's back. As her dress fell with it, Stanley caught a glimpse of pale thigh and despite the circumstances felt himself momentarily blanked by loathing and desire.

He moved his head.

"Tsk," clucked the man behind him. "There's a hollow stainless steel no. 14 point aimed at each of your eardrums. A penetration will destroy your hearing. But you'll never hear the sound of silence. *Hello darkness hello pain...* Eh? Eh?"

Oh, perfect, thought Stanley. I'm going to be Simon and Garfunkeled to death.

"But," the helium voice continued, "there's enough sufenta in these two syringes to enable you to walk through the fires of Hell without feeling a thing, if you get my meaning."

Green Eyes smoothed the front of her skirt.

"I've never done it before," the high voice assured him. "But if you're up for fuel-injected audio, I'm willing to watch — get it? Get it?"

The guy was hysterical. "Take it easy," said Stanley. "I get it."

"So. Let's dosey doe, down to the floor, and let that heater go."

Stanley bent his knees slowly.

The needles followed him down.

"This is like dowsing," said the helium voice. "Dowsing for disarmament."

Stanley laid the pistol on the floor in front of him. *The safety is still off,* a little voice said inside him.

Oh, Stanley responded. *All I have to do is kick backwards, catching this helium freak in the nuts and rendering his voice a full octave higher, pitch myself forward as he convulsively stabs himself in each of his wrists with the two needles intended for my eardrums, taking up the pistol as I roll, and come up one gun blazing.*

He opened his hand over the pistol, as if releasing a set trap.

Still and all, he thought, with a longing look, the safety is off.

"Good boy. Now, up. Up."

Stanley, the needles, Helium Voice—they all stood up.

The man in Green Eyes' arms had begun to collect himself.

Savagely, he tore away the circles of tape holding the syringe. Two pale bracelets of depilation encircled the forearm, indicating repeated applications of adhesive tape.

Green Eyes was working on her appearance. She raised the dress in order to straighten the garter of first one stocking, then the other. Then she dropped the hem of the skirt and demurely smoothed it over her lap. She glanced over one shoulder, then the other, inspecting the white line of the seam of each stocking, tracing the apogee of each calf before it tapered into the upper of a well-tailored nurse's shoe.

The guy in the white coat, his pants around his ankles, penis dripping, blinked as he plucked the needle from the vein inside his elbow. There was dried blood on the front of the smock.

"What was in that?" Stanley asked suddenly.

Helium Voice chuckled. "Doctor's little cocktail...."

The man in the white coat looked up, as if noticing Stanley for the first time. His upper lip twitched. The eyes were bright as marbles.

When the guy suddenly smiled, Stanley clearly saw that he was absolutely, disconcertingly, hopelessly sane. As sane as a television newscaster, as sane as a vacuum cleaner salesman, as sane as any politician. As sane as the man with the sledgehammer, who, all day long, every day, coldcocks horses for dog food.

The smile was a death's head. Nourishment had clearly become a problem. The teeth were dark, their gums receding. The skin was sallow, like old paraffin. The man was gaunt, and he looked older than his years, perhaps sixty-five. The hair was thinning on top, receding in front, spotty in back. Reddish blotches had appeared on the forehead and about the throat. A modest pimple directly over the carotid artery had become infected. There was an abscess over the inside of his right elbow, too.

This climax-injection thing has been going on a lot, lately, thought Stanley.

The man held his arm aloft, massaged the inside of the elbow, and grinned a rictus, if comradely, salute. "Speedball," he said proudly, through clenched teeth. "Finest veterinary quality."

And then the man laughed.

His laughter was a hideous combustion, mechanical and vapid, as of a John Deere tractor chained to an unyielding stump, or the *wap wap wap* of a biplane climbing into a stall.

It was the laughter of a man who'd always known that everything in the world had been put there either for his annoyance or for his amusement, and for no other reason. Nothing was funny, and everything was funny, it was all up to him. It was the laughter of a man whose entire being had been subsumed by turpitude, who could not distinguish between pain or joy in others, who lived only for the depravity that he might deploy upon them. His philosophy would preach a freedom of indulgence as the true test of liberty, but he would believe in it only insofar as it enabled him to debase. Rare, indeed, would be the partner who might share his perverse delights, compete for them while maintaining the delusion that their shared equity would always rejuvenate amusement.

Green Eyes seemed to have taken on the job with all four paws.

Indubitably damaged, his super-ego—if the term even applies— keelhauled after walking the plank, the doctor's intelligence would not be in question; it would be as inspired as it was debauched.

All this Stanley grasped in a moment, even as the doctor held the syringe aloft for him to admire.

"Injected just milliseconds before orgasm," said the physician dryly, "It is, as they say, way, way cool." He made a broad sweeping gesture with the side of his hand. "It is like passing the medical boards all over again." The hand came back to lay its fingers at his temple. "And now, of course," he bulged his eyes, "I am *wide awake!*"

That laughter again. Automatic, impersonal, deadly laughter.

The safety is off, thought Stanley, on this guy, too.

He allowed his eyes to fall, rather fondly, onto his gun, on the floor perhaps two yards away.

The doctor's eyes followed his. "U.S. Army," the doctor said. "Caliber .45. Big slug with a lot of momentum, designed to stop armed Filipinos on betelnut."

"Well," said Stanley, "I only wanted to blast doped-up avarice on the hoof."

The man with the needles tittered behind him. It sounded like air escaping from a pinched balloon neck.

"All I can hear right now," said the doctor mildly, touching two fingers to each temple and narrowing his eyes, "is little tiny Yuppies kayaking my white corpuscles."

Oh, man, thought Stanley. And I thought I could speak English.

The doctor suddenly stooped and stood up again, dragging his trousers up to his waist and cinching them.

Stanley heard a door open behind him, and the sounds of rubber wheels on linoleum.

"Comin' through," said a familiar voice from the far end of the corridor. "Outta the way."

"Turn around," said Helium Voice. "And don't make no funny locomotions."

Stanley turned. Vince and the white guy whose name he'd never learned advanced down the hall, rolling a gurney between them.

On the gurney was a purple sleeping bag.

"Step aside," said the black man, passing Stanley.

On the sleeping bag lay one of those plastic signs most often seen hanging from motel doorknobs.

OCCUPADO

No Lo Perturbara

"Hello, Vince," Stanley said.

The black man stopped so abruptly that the white man drove the gurney straight into his thigh.

"Hold it!" said Vince. "I said hold it!" he repeated, and gave the gurney a kick.

The sleeping bag groaned.

"Hey," said Helium Voice. "That guy's in Recovery."

With hardly a glance at the needles gleaming under Stanley's ears, Vince demanded, "How'd you know my name?"

"Why, Vince," chided Stanley. "I saw you on Upper Market just last night. Little cul-de-sac called Parajito Terrace? You were humping carpet with your partner, here." He indicated the white man. "I didn't catch his name? But, say," he swiveled his eyes back to Vince and smiled. "Didn't you do some time for rustling Jaguars a while back?"

Vince's mouth twisted. "Who the fuck is this guy?"

"His name is Stanley."

Everybody but Vince turned to look at Green Eyes.

"Friend of yours?" said Vince, his hideous grimace now inches from Stanley's face.

"Vince," said Green Eyes indulgently. "Try to think."

"I'm thinkin'."

"Cast your mind," she suggested patiently, "back."

"I'm casting."

"A month ago. Maybe two."

"That's asking a lot."

"In your case," quipped the doctor, "maybe you should cast your mind forward."

"Very funny."

"It was the night we used that place in the Excelsior. I've forgotten the address."

Vince's expression didn't change. "Goettingen," he said. "The house was on Goettingen, and the car was a Pontiac wagon."

"Bingo," said Green Eyes. "Vince, you're amazing."

"Navy blue," Vince concluded.

The white guy shook his head. "Can't add two and two, but he can remember the stupid stuff."

"Hey," said Stanley. "I got that kind of memory, too. The car you stole this week, for example, was a BMW."

"Shut up," said Vince.

"It was white."

"Stanley," said Green Eyes coolly, "was the one who gave us that bad kidney."

Everybody looked at Stanley.

The doctor stopped twirling the spent syringe between two fingers. "The kidney that came up amyloidosic? This is the guy?"

"This is the guy."

The doctor floated down the hall as if he were on wheels, stopped in front of Stanley, and contemplated him as if he were a smear on a slide. "Remove the needles."

The icy epifoci of Stanley's being went away.

The doctor slapped Stanley's face with an open palm. Not a tap.

"Swine," the man said, not raising his voice. "Do you know how much work you cost me?"

He backhanded Stanley this time, considerably harder.

"An entire night — wasted!" He was yelling, now. "Do you have any idea what that cost?"

Stanley lifted his knee into the man's spent testicles.

The doctor screamed and fell into a fetal position on the floor, both hands gripping his crotch. Vince watched him writhe there for a few seconds, not without pleasure, then planted a meaty fist directly in Stanley's right eye.

Vince didn't throw the fist far—a foot, maybe. But when it connected with Stanley's eye it made a sound like somebody trying to bat a fungo with a toad.

As he went down, Stanley lunged for the .45. But Vince planted a foot squarely between Stanley's shoulder blades and pinned him to the floor.

Helium Voice, laughing, his two syringes gathered into one hand, gingerly picked up the pistol by its barrel.

The doctor sat up, rather breathlessly, and held out his hand. "Give me that."

The room went still. Helium Voice handed over the pistol, butt first. The doctor took it, inspected it, aimed it at Stanley's head. Then he turned and, despite a shriek from Helium Voice, discharged the weapon in the direction of Green Eyes, who was leaning, rather languidly, against the two steel doors at the end of the corridor.

The detonation filled the hallway with smoke and noise. The spent shell spun on the floor, right in front of Stanley's nose, like a game token.

"*Sheis*," the doctor said, in the awed voice of a child, "this thing kicks." He touched the inside elbow of his gun arm. "Damn near popped the scab off my abscess."

Helium Voice squeaked like a stepped-on rubber toy. "Sibyl, are you... Are you...?"

Stanley rolled his good eye up from the floor. *Sibyl, we are introduced at last.*

Everybody was looking at her. Ten inches above her little nurse's cap, now neatly replaced onto her marvelously tousled hair, a puckered hole smoked in one of the metal doors. The green eyes stared them all back, insouciant.

Damn, thought Stanley. *This is a woman to die for.*

Give it a try, a little voice cozened inside him. *Die for her: see if she cares.*

"Sibyl...," repeated Helium Voice weakly. "If anything happened to you, I... We..."

Helium Voice couldn't countenance the thought.

The day something happens to her, declared Stanley's inner voice, *is the day this operation is over.*

"Gun-shy she will never be," declared the doctor proudly. He handed the pistol to Vince. "Yes, my little aster. The day something happens to you, is the day my *weltanschauung* goes up in flames like a Sioux tepee in December, 1890."

"So," said Green Eyes, jerking her chin toward Stanley. "Where's that leave this guy?"

They all looked down at Stanley.

"Leaves him on de flo'," said Vince.

Everybody laughed at Stanley.

"Get him up," said the doctor.

Vince picked him up as easily as he might raise the lid off a saucepan.

The eye hurt. *Go for it*, a little voice prompted him. *Start early.*

"Look," Stanley asserted, though he drooped from Vince's fist like a rain-drenched shirt. "Except that you're a bunch of perverts, I got nothing against you guys."

"Do tell," said Helium Voice.

"I do. I'm not here to bring this place down around your ears. If I'd wanted to do that, I would have told the cops what I know."

"And, my amyloidosic friend," said the doctor, setting and unsetting the safety on the pistol. "What is it, exactly, that you think you know?"

Stanley squinted his ruined eye at the doctor. "How about we start with Giles MacIntosh?"

The doctor frowned, and didn't reset the safety.

Vince and his white friend exchanged a look.

Helium Voice looked at Green Eyes.

Green Eyes watched Stanley.

Stanley looked at as many of them as he could. "He hacked that glitch in DonorWare right off the bat. It's amazing it went undetected as long as it did. Face it. If hadn't been me, or him, it —."

"The fact is, Mister —."

"Ahearn," said Green Eyes. "You can call him Stanley." She used his first name like she would her quirt.

Despite hating her, Stanley felt himself blush. He was flattered to hear, to see, his name on her lips. How abject was this going to get?

He tried to stick to his point. "The fact remains, I didn't go to the cops."

"Suppose we believe that. Then what?"

"Then there's Ted Nichols. And Cabrini Carpet. And Chippendale O'Hare. Not to mention Parajito Terrace, Vince, Sibyl, and the good doctor here, who was educated in Germany, emigrated to the United States after the war, passed the California Medical boards, and, ultimately, lost his license for cutting on little children without due process. Or something like that."

"What's that?" said the doctor, casually fitting the gun to Stanley's nose.

"I'm just making it up," Stanley said hastily, turning away from the gun. "But it can't be that far off, either. The point is, I didn't tell the cops what I found out. Instead, I came here." He looked from face to face. "To you."

They waited.

"I need help," said Stanley. "I need at least one new kidney. Or...."

Still they waited.

"...Or I'm going to die."

Silence.

Keep it up, urged the little voice. *Negotiate. Give them something to think about. I'm okay you're okay. Don't stop now.*

His mouth dried up, however, and the eye felt like a tuned drum head somebody was bouncing quarters off of. *Go go go,* insisted the little voice. Stanley cleared his throat. "I figured, if I was to ask you folks real nice, and promise never to go to the cops with what I know, maybe you'd give me the kidney I need to... to..."

"To quietly drink yourself to death." Green Eyes said complacently.

"That's...." Stanley began. He looked at her, looked away. Then he looked at her again. He'd forgotten that this crowd would know at least as much about him as they knew about Ted Nichols. "That's about the size of it," he admitted, "though it's none of your business."

Nobody spoke.

"I figured the gun might help you see things my way," he added lamely.

Silence. Then Helium Voice, his ferrety eyes darting from face to face, could contain his mirth no longer. He giggled his helium giggle.

It might have been involuntary. He tried to choke it off. The silence returned, but only for a moment. Now giggles eddied after the silence as surely as seagulls following a laden trawler into port.

The laughter was contagious. Vince chuckled, low and mellifluous. The doctor joined in with his mechanical, percussive coughs. The white guy laughed, whooped, and then slapped his knee, like a rodeo cowboy whose bull has just been turned out of the chute.

Altogether, it was an unguarded moment. Even Sibyl, watching Stanley, allowed her lovely green eyes to sparkle behind their long lashes, and her nose to wrinkle, and finally her face to dissolve into a beautiful, becoming, *genuine* smile. In the general hilarity this smile quickly elided into an open-mouthed laugh. She modestly covered her mouth with one hand, while casting a covert glance in Stanley's direction. Seeing him staring at her, and her alone, she looked away, then back. She covered her mouth with both hands, but this could not conceal her amusement. She stooped her shoulders as if perhaps physical effort might contain this spontaneous jocundity. But finally, with an incredulous double take in Stanley's direction, she dissolved into helpless laughter.

This is good, Stanley thought hopefully. If a fellow can get them laughing, a fellow has a chance.

After a while the laughter died down. Once again, silence began to fill the corridor, interloped by the odd chuckle.

"So," said the doctor, as disconcertingly sane as ever. He handed the .45 to the white guy who, despite this responsibility, could not stop smiling.

"Careful, Sturgeon," the doctor said. "It's loaded."

This remark provoked a new outburst of hilarity.

Vince still held Stanley by his collar, from behind. As the laughter died again the doctor stepped up to Stanley and, not unkindly, plucked at the lid of, not the rapidly swelling eye, but the uninjured one.

Stanley jerked his head away, like a horse refusing the bridle.

Vince grabbed Stanley's head by its hair.

"Now, now…" said the doctor, revealing a certain gleam in his own eye, its frigidity spreading like a skim of ice over the pinpoint pool of his stoned iris. By pinching the lashes between thumb and forefinger he succeeded in raising the lid on Stanley's unpunched eye. "Ah," the doctor said, turning his head to peer within, his face inches from Stanley's. "Very good." He released the lid and stepped back, leaving Stanley blinking amid a compounded reek of gun powder, rubbing alcohol, and semen.

The doctor nodded.

"We'll begin with the eye."

Chapter 23

As the little procession followed the narrow-gauge tracks down the hall, Doctor Djell admonished Vince.

"How many times have I told you," he said, enumerating his fingers. "Don't hit them in the eyes, the kidneys, the spleen, the liver. Don't break their ribs either, because their lungs get punctured. Lungs are expensive."

"But Doc," whined Vince, "What's left?"

"Just administer him a concussion, like I showed you…"

Just explode, the little voice said to Stanley. *That'll do it. The shrapnel will kill them all*. He flung his arms outward. His hands made a grab for the doctor's throat. He kicked somebody.

Vince expertly blocked Stanley from the doctor, as easily as anyone else might have restrained a child.

"Be careful," said Djell, from behind Vince. "Don't let him hurt himself."

"Lemme at a meaty vein," said Helium Jaime.

"That's the idea," said Djell. "Pre-op the monkey."

Stanley unleashed a feeble kick to the side of the gurney, which still blocked the hall.

"Hey," said the white guy. "That's an outpatient."

"Well, Sturgeon?" said Djell. "Give a hand, there."

Sturgeon caught one of Stanley's flailing arms and twisted it high up his back, until the wrist was between the shoulder blades.

"Can you turn that elbow outward?" Helium Jaime asked.

Sturgeon obliged, eliciting a yelp from Stanley.

"A few milligrams of fentanyl." Djell suggested, watching disinterestedly as the three men pressed Stanley face-first into a wall. "Skip antibiotics, skip the anti-immune course."

Sturgeon yanked the collar of Stanley's jacket backwards over his shoulders, pinning his arms to his side.

Vince showed Stanley the business end of a scalpel.

"Look at this," said Sturgeon, disentangling the extra clip of bullets from Stanley's jacket.

"Loaded for bear, were we?" said Vince, as he used the scalpel to slit the jacket's sleeve to expose the inside of Stanley's elbow.

Jaime expressed a jet of fentanyl from his syringe onto the wall about a foot in front of Stanley's face.

"That's very professional," said Sturgeon, admiring Vince's work with the scalpel.

"It's analgesic," said Jaime to Stanley, as they both watched a thin rivulet of fentanyl run down the wall. "It's an opiate, too. You'll be conscious until we put you under, with no pain. I'm sure you're all jacked up about the humanitarian angle. Don't worry. You'll be docile as a New Age symphony."

Stanley was getting weak in the knees.

"What about the enema?" inquired Sturgeon, his mouth emanating a foul odor an inch from Stanley's nose.

Djell smiled. "He'll never miss it."

"Bummer," said Sturgeon.

Upon feeling the sudden coolness of an alcohol swab on the inside of the exposed forearm, Stanley kicked feebly.

"Why anesthesiology's a specialty," said Djell, observing Jaime swab the arm, "I'll never know."

"It's just somebody else they can sell insurance to." Jaime moved the needle aside as Stanley struggled. "Fucking Class Five insurance driving me bananas."

"Something you know too too much about," said Djell.

"Insurance?"

"Bananas."

Vince laughed.

"I could miss with this and hurt you badly," said Jaime, showing Stanley the hypodermic. "My insurance policy tells me so. So hold still."

Stanley struggled more than ever.

"Save the isometrics." Vince bumped the back of Stanley's head with the palm of his hand, bouncing Stanley's forehead off the tiled wall.

Through the stars that ringed his vision Stanley could see Sibyl standing behind Djell, watching them wrestle, with cool detachment. He caught her eye. *Come on, baby,* he thought as loud and stupid as he could think. *Get me out of this. We could make something out of ourselves, you and me...*

A sharp prick announced itself against the skin at the inside of his elbow, and the needle sheathed itself in the vein below.

...Then I could kill you.

"Ahhh..." said Sturgeon, watching with satisfaction as Stanley's type O-Negative plumed into the barrel of the syringe.

Stanley strained every fiber of his musculature, but could not move. The two gorillas held him to the wall and he twitched feebly there, like a moth webbed to a twig.

"Damn. You are good at that, Jaime," Sturgeon whispered.

"Shit," breathed Jaime, steadily depressing the plunger. "I used to lie in my bunk when I was in the Navy. The high seas would pitch that tin can like it was in the bathtub of an epileptic. First you'd see lightning and the undersides of thunderheads, then the porthole's rolled two fathoms under. Me, I'm in my bunk with one foot on the bulkhead, the other on the floor, banging the mainline with morphine sulfate, just for the practice. Force Ten's nothing to these hands. Steadier than what El Señor Malpractico has got going, over there..."

"Wait till you're my age," Djell said, petulantly rubbing his abscess. "Then we'll see who's got shaky hands."

Stanley watched Sibyl watching him. She was waiting for the drug to hit him. Stanley realized he'd seen this look before. And suddenly his memory recovered an image and slipped it into his mind as neatly as a slide slots into a projector.

It was late. Sibyl and Stanley stood in the shadowed living room of the bungalow on Goettingen Street. He was drunk. Not too drunk to note to what part of town she'd driven him. He'd expected Nob Hill. He got the Excelsior.

And not too drunk to recognize the tune she'd taken the trouble to cue up, on a portable boom-box type CD player, a common device, too common for its portability to be suspicious—but portable it was and suspicious it should have been. The tune was Chet Baker's cover of *Everything Happens to Me.*

Black cats creep across my path
until I'm almost mad
I must have roused the devil's wrath
cause all my luck is bad...

The ultimate in jazz-age self-pity, it could have been Stanley's theme song. A solipsism in a minor key; a chestnut of misfeasance, afloat in a Tom Collins. Grotesque, overstated, lyrically ham-fisted; yet in Baker's hands, everything happened to him, who spoke for Stanley. Artistic empathy. Existential squalor.

...I make a date for golf
and you can bet your life it rains
I try to give a party
and the guy upstairs complains...

He'd even sung along with it, what a sport, lamentably off-key. If she loved him, she wouldn't mind. And why shouldn't she love a lonely, self-indulgent drunk? He'd even flattered himself that she'd gone to the trouble to intuit his taste in music—the fool doubled down.

...I guess I'll go through life just
catchin' cold and missin' trains...

If he was drunk enough to suppose she played it just for him, he was right for the wrong reason. It was annoying and embarrassing and not a little disconcerting to have discovered that his pathetic psycho-portrait would be so obvious to such a beautiful predator, that she could handle him as easily as a bright kid handles a new video game.

Ev'ry-thing hap-pens to me-ee...

Ev'rything got poured into him, too. No food, of course, with a comely apology, having to do with a lack of interest in shopping, late-

ly—too depressed, she admitted simply. Nothing solid to which a man
might anchor his belly against the tsunami of intoxication that charac-
terizes alcohol and chloral hydrate poisoning.

> *I never miss a thing*
> *I've had the measles and the mumps*
> *And every time I play an ace*
> *my partner always trumps...*

Besides, you don't want your patient to be eating solid food within
twelve hours of his nephrectomy.

The copious liquor selection, of course, like the boom-box, she
would always carry with her, from house to house, victim to victim.
Normally plenty paranoid, he'd been too drunk to even cough up that
preposterous an idea, let alone assess it. No blame there. Obviously,
he'd prefer to believe that she wanted him strictly for his innate sex
appeal. It would have been paranoid to think anything else.

> *...I guess I'm just a fool*
> *who never looks before he jumps...*

Sitting on the very comfortable couch, littered with fat down pillows
covered in silk, he'd patted one of them with the handle of the little
quirt. His way of saying he wasn't really into flagellation, but he'd settle for the missionary position. What an idiot. The prop department of
this operation must be quite something to see in action, Vince and
Sturgeon ranking with the best stage managers, their fealty to illusion
up there with that of the highly skilled stagehands who can gaff a tour-
ing set for tonight's show in less time than it takes to say

> *Ev'ry-thing hap-pens to me-eee...*

He'd been too drunk to notice her slip his dose of chloral hydrate
with the ice into three ounces of whiskey, and too enamored to notice
the modulation in taste of a brand of booze he'd been drinking every
night without fail for three years...

And he'd been too drunk to remark upon, though not too drunk to
remember, the curious way she'd begun to watch him after he'd swallowed about half the drink. She had watched him then the way she was

watching him now, as if he were some kind of curious dinoflagellate her dishwasher had failed to scrub off the rim of the crystal punch bowl, a repellent life form, perhaps leaked down from the columbarium, onto which she had lavished a sixty-second jet of insecticide, whose toxicity guaranteed the dissolution of the nervous systems of anything from red-headed soldier ants to translucent scorpions; yet the creature languishes; and now, having a bit of time on her hands and a curious mind, she would watch it writhe until it died: unless the phone rang; unless the mundane interrupted the banal; or *vice versa.*

Green Eyes on her post-coital death watch. Her cheeks flushed with blood, her lips swollen and gleaming, her eyes emitting more light than they were collecting.

"Okay," he heard Jaime's helium voice say, muffled by great chemical distances and an extraterrestrial wind. "He's a pussycat now."

I'm a pussycat now, Stanley thought to himself, watching himself watch her watch him. *Why don't you float on over here and transmogrify this whole deal into some kind of fantastic sex trip? Let's leave together. Sexodus? Because,* he endeavored to articulate the formula, whose words he'd always had trouble saying, the mantra he'd never been able to utter at the right time, never been able to say aloud at all, *because,* he'd always found it so hard to give tongue to it, he'd practically choked over giving it full throat, but he thought he might say it right now *because* they were the right words for her, and this is the right time, and this time he did it. He pulled it off. He mumbled: *Because... Because...*

"...I love you," quite audibly.

Sibyl started. Shock and amusement vied for a holiday with the nerves and muscles beneath the surface of her face.

"Woo-ee," said Vince, relaxing his grip on Stanley. "I got to try me a snootful of that stuff my own self."

"Do you know," piped up helium-voiced Jaime, "that one of my colleagues wanted to manufacture lollipops spiked with this fentanyl? For kids?"

"You shitting me," said Vince.

"Git the fuck outta here, Jaime," disparaged Sturgeon. "Lollifuckingpops." He, too, had now relaxed his grip on Stanley, relaxed it enough so that it could no longer be called restraining, but not relaxed it entirely, so it could still be called supportive, so Stanley wouldn't sink to the floor like a suit falling off a hanger.

"It's true," said Jaime proudly. "I have sucked the prototype."

This elicited a number of catcalls.

"How come you leave the needle in, like that?" Sturgeon asked when the fun had died down.

"I just think it looks cool," said Jaime. "Unbutton his shirt."

They turned Stanley around, and Vince unceremoniously tore Stanley's shirt open. Its buttons ticked onto the floor.

"Pipe down, Help," said Jaime. "I'm trying to get a heartbeat, here."

"Who you calling Help?" bristled Vince.

"You," Djell barked. "Shut up."

I could save you the trouble, thought Stanley. *Heartbeat's all I can hear, in here. Ba-boom, ba-boom...* It was true. His heartbeats came to his ears like a stylus darts to the spindle at record's end.

"Huh," said Jaime. "Heart's going like crazy."

"He's in love," said Vince.

"He's scared," said Sturgeon.

"Must have more sense than I thought," said Vince.

"I got... high blood pressure," Stanley croaked-and-drooled, lying for the hell of it.

"Man," said Jaime. "One kidney, amyloidosis — which could mean rheumatoid arthritis or TB or even myeloma — and on top of that he's an alcoholic with high blood pressure. Liver's probably damaged, too. You sure you want to mess with this mess?"

"Certainly," confirmed Djell.

"Don't look gift giblets in the mouth," chuckled Vince.

I'm stoned on speed and codeine, too, thought Stanley. *Maybe that's an edge. Maybe I'm gonna puke. Maybe this time I explode for real.*

Stanley's mouth was moving, but no sound came out. A little bile did, though.

"You could use a good doctor," Jaime said to him, as if in confidence.

Stanley agreed, his voice thick on his tongue.

Can't you hear my heart beat, Baby, he sang softly to himself. *Give me a narcotic and right away I'm hearing* Herman's Hermits. Sibyl was talking to Djell about something. *Lookit that ass on that woman. I'm going to fuck her. Then I'm going to kill her.*

"Look out," said Sturgeon. "He's lurching."

"Okay," said Jaime softly, throwing the bell of his stethoscope over one shoulder. "Just a little more. Not too much..."

You know, Stanley was thinking, noting with detachment the renewed pressure at his forearm, *I'm just groused about my kidney... I'm not a con-*

trary guy. How come you wanna mess with me...?

"That's the part you like, isn't it," said Vince. "The needles."

"Actually," said Jaime, "it's the far-reaching humanitarianism of medicine that got me into the profession."

"There's some dope left," said Sturgeon.

"Not for him there isn't. Not with that pulse."

"I wasn't thinking about him."

"He's all yours, Manny," said Jaime. "Actually, Vince, the part I really like about this profession is it enables me to afford that condo at Tahoe. Now, the wine cellar is in pretty good shape. Mostly California reds, and some French; but there're some very tasty Sauvignon Blancs and Chardonnays for your swishy types to drink. Just as soon as the hot tub gets plumbed and the birch switches come from Colorado and I can get my hands on an ounce of pink Peruvian flake, I want you and Sturgeon to come up and spend a little time with me there because, frankly, I just don't see enough of you guys around the mortuary, here."

"Aw, Jaime," said Vince. "You mind I bring a mess o' catfish?"

"You embarrass me in front of my guests, I'll lock the wine cellar and swallow the key."

"He means he hasn't seen enough of us because we keep our clothes on," cautioned Sturgeon.

Vince shook his head sadly. "We just ain't goin' to be relaxed around each other, you can't get wid a mess o' catfish."

"If you insist on keeping up that bogus patois," said Jaime, "I'm going to bust you one in the patella with my little pink hammer."

"*Whoa*," said Vince.

"Watch it," said Sturgeon, grabbing Stanley. "He's sliding down the wall."

"Like a mess of catfish," said Vince, helping.

"All right, boys," said Dr. Djell from the end of the hall, raising his voice out of his conversation with Sibyl.

"Oh, shit, look out," said Sturgeon. "The boss has a plan."

"Let me swab that arm," said Jaime, removing the hypodermic. "Don't want any sepsis."

"First," said Djell, pointing to the gurney, "Take this sheetrock taper up to the garage, roll him up in a carpet, put him in the van. Crack a window so he gets plenty of fresh air. Lock up and keep your eyes peeled, somebody else might come snooping. Bring a gurney down for Bum Kidney, here. We harvest Bum Kidney, cremate the dross, enshrine the ashes… We get all that done before dawn we'll be lucky."

Ashes…

"Then we drop the outpatient in the park and make the perfusion delivery, see, but we only take one run to do it."

"That's good task flow," said Vince.

"Hold him," said Sturgeon, turning Stanley loose.

"Hey," said Jaime, dropping his syringe in order to catch Stanley.

Sturgeon backed through the double doors toward the loading dock, pulling the outpatient gurney behind him.

Stanley hugged the coolness of the tiled wall. *Purple sleeping bags*, he thought hazily, watching the gurney pass between himself and Sibyl *They must have gotten a deal on them.*

"Guy's heavy," said Jaime, groping with his portion of Stanley. "Like he's dead already."

"Exercise is good for you," said Vince. "Be showing less carbs in the sauna."

Jaime shouted gleefully, "Aieee, Chihuahua!"

"What about the cremains," Vince asked.

Djell shook his head. "We get this harvest squared away, then you take off. Sibyl can call in the delivery while you guys dump the outpatient. We'll deal with the ashes here. By the time you get back, we'll have them shared out among any number of grandmothers, upstairs."

Cremains… Stanley heard a subway train, rushing from one side of his head to the other, all its cars lit and completely empty. It didn't stop for him, though. It went on down the tracks, its wheels counting off the odd loose tie under a curve in the rails.

Djell rubbed hands in anticipation.

"Uh-oh," said Vince. "The Doc is scrubbing early. Big casino: money-night."

Vince and Jaime high-fived.

"Nocturne of filthy lucre," Jaime squeaked.

"I could get used to this," Djell agreed. "We're looking at eighty or ninety kay, here. Depending on how good this louse has been looking after himself."

"You know," said Sibyl. "That's a point. That other kidney should be amyloidosic, too. Almost has to be."

"Son of a bitch," snarled Djell. "That's correct."

"So we skip the nephrectomy," said Sibyl.

"Just go for the big stuff," Jaime agreed.

All of Me, thought Stanley, *please, take all of me...* The hits just kept on coming. Despite Green Eyes still taking the time to cast him a curious glance once in a while, he drooped between Vince and Sturgeon like a windless flag. *Everything Happens to Why Not Take All of Me...*

"Fine," said Djell. "It's going to be all night as it is."

Sturgeon returned with the empty gurney. Within a few minutes they had Stanley strapped onto it and were wheeling him toward the double doors at the far end of the corridor.

Why? thought Stanley, casting euthanized-puppy eyes and silently beseeching lips at Djell, who walked beside him. *Can't we talk this over? Can't we pause this video?*

"What's that?" said Djell, cocking an ear in his direction.

"Can you hear me?"

Djell shrugged. "Sure."

"Why?"

"Why what?"

"Why didn't you send Giles up the stack? Isn't that what you're going to do to me?"

Djell looked down at Stanley for a moment, then shrugged. "We didn't know who you were, and we couldn't get him to tell us."

"You're kidding."

"I guess he had a lot of experience with drugs."

"You didn't torture him?"

"What do we look like," Djell scowled. *"Barbarians?"*

"Well..."

"Skip it. We couldn't figure out who you were. He obviously wasn't trying to blackmail us or something stupid like that. He didn't have a venal bone in his body."

"How could you tell?"

"I looked."

"Jesus Christ."

At the head of the gurney, Vince snickered.

When his queasiness had passed Stanley asked again. "So why did you leave him in the park?"

"So you'd hear about it."

"Me?"

"It was a warning. We knew you weren't the cops. The cops wouldn't have thrown MacIntosh to the wolves like you did."

"What do you mean? I didn't—."

"So we figured somebody was out to cash in on us, move in on our operation. Who would have thought...?" Djell laughed. "Who would have thought it was some guy that wanted his *kidney* back?"

Vince and Jaime laughed aloud.

Stanley choked down a bolus of bile. So Corrigan had been right. Poor Giles MacIntosh.

"You see how well it worked," Djell added.

They were through the doors now.

Chapter 24

It was an operating room, simple as that. It may at one time have been used for preparing corpses for burial. It may at one time have been used for serving tea.

Nephrectomy, necropsy—the room didn't know the difference and didn't care. Stoned nearly senseless on a smorgasbord of drugs, Stanley saw the room as a coyote trap with no exit, starring himself as the coyote.

A large, circular light looked down on an operating table. There were smaller, wheeled tables, each covered with a clean white cloth, each cloth displaying a neat array of stainless steel instruments. There was a cart packed with electronic gear and looms of wires, and another cart with cylinders topped with valves and gauges. On a table against the far wall, opposite the pair of double doors, stood a boom-box and piles of CDs.

The personnel bustled around this equipment, each individual focused on some function, very team-like.

Vince, Sturgeon and Helium Jaime wrestled Stanley off the gurney and onto the operating table. Djell and Green Eyes stood aside—holding hands, yet. Even upside down, as Stanley momentarily saw them, they appeared a cute couple. About as cute as a nuked atoll.

"This guy," grunted Sturgeon, who carried Stanley's legs, "is heavy like he's dead already."

"You say that every night," said Vince, who carried Stanley's shoulders.

Producing his scalpel, Vince neatly severed Stanley's leather belt. Sturgeon began to tug at the cuffs of Stanley's jeans.

"It's gonna be c-c…," mumbled Stanley. "Cold."

"You don't know the half of it," said Jaime, parting the buttons on Stanley's fly.

Sibyl's going to see my dick, Stanley thought to himself. *And when I'm scared it's real small. Oh, please, don't let Sibyl see my….*

"Look," said Sturgeon, as Jaime and Vince lifted Stanley's hips off the table, so the jeans would come off easily. "Goddamn hippie wears no goddamn underwear."

"Roll him onto his side."

"Whoa."

"This guy has definitely been here before."

"He's been giving those sutures a workout."

"Any sign of the aster?"

"He must have transplanted it."

"Hardee har har."

"Ragged from stress, but healing nicely," said Jaime, tentatively touching Stanley's nephrectomy scar. "As clean as a cat's forepaw."

As the boys rolled Stanley onto his left side he reestablished contact with the green eyes. These eyes, surrounded as they were by the clinical horrors zeroing in on him, yet persisted as some treacherous salient of beauty to Stanley, the first to have broached his emotional perimeter in a long time.

And, once through his defenses, what had she done?

What *hadn't* she done?

There she stood, receiving caresses from another man as Stanley watched.

Well within shooting distance…

And now, to his mortification, Stanley felt a double twitch in the glans of his penis, and its length began to stir.

One pulse for lust, *two* for pure hatred…

His pulse counted off the cadence of his humiliation like ratchet clicks on a windlass hoisting a yardarm.

One for pure sex, *two* for loathing, *one* for fornication, *two* for murder…

Oh, no, he protested silently, giving an order to his body, something he hadn't troubled it with in some years, perhaps never. *Not now. Not here.*

One for itch, *two* for scratch. *One* for life, *two* for death...

His concentration protracted the silence, in which the three men finished stripping him. For some reason they left his socks on.

One for no, *two* for yes...

"Hey," said Sturgeon, absently feeling his way through the pockets of
Stanley's pants. "Check it out."

The little voice in Stanley's head looped a string of blasphemous gib-
berish over the waters of his mind like a casting fly line. *Not now, of all
nows...*

"How's that?" said Vince, who was likewise meticulously rummaging through the pockets of Stanley's jacket.

Please...

"He's gettin' a hard-on," said Sturgeon. "Check it out."

"Pre-op tumescence," said Helium Jaime. "Happens to me all the
time."

To hell with it, Stanley thought suddenly. Lights, camera, masculinity.
Pump it up, motherfucker. I hate you, I hate it, I hate everything. Concentrating
his gaze on Sibyl's eyes, Stanley let himself go. He beamed hatred and
lust directly at her, like an underfunded observatory desperately prob-
ing an empty universe for any sign of life.

Vince followed the gaze. "Hey. Guy's got a hard-on for Sibyl."

"Join the club," cooed Jaime.

It's for you, Stanley thought furiously, hopelessly straining to bring to a
glow certain telepathic capacities within vast unexplored areas of his
brain that he had never doubted didn't exist at all. *See how much I love you.*

"Tighten that strap."

Agitated by fear and embarrassment, Stanley tried to buck himself
off the table. But the drug they had given him made it a languid gesture, as if he were merely practicing the backstroke with an erection in
a sea of mercury. Vince and Sturgeon, at opposite ends of the operating table, restrained him easily, while Jaime tightened the various seat
belts. And still Stanley did not take his eyes off Sibyl, who, along with
Djell, had approached for a closer look.

"Man," said Sturgeon. "Guy's hot for your old lady, Doc. Look at
that."

"He touches her I'll kill him early," Djell said matter-of-factly.
"Cover that disgusting display."

"What do you say, Sibyl?" teased Jaime. "Want to kiss it goodbye?"

Well? thought Stanley, experiencing a groinal twang at the idea.

Sibyl's eyes suddenly twinkled with malice.

He's right, you know, Stanley persevered. *It's for you my body makes a fool out of me.*

Without breaking the connection between her eyes and Stanley's, Sibyl picked up a pair of surgical scissors from a nearby table. She held them vertically next to her fixed smile and, still not breaking eye contact with Stanley, she made the scissors go *snip. Snip snip.*

Sturgeon laughed uneasily. Sturgeon knew Sibyl better than Stanley did, and the tone of his disconcerted, half-hearted laugh communicated to Stanley that Sturgeon was giving her a fifty-fifty chance of following through with the gesture, the *snip snip*. Like a diver who has just achieved the top of his arc, Stanley's erection hesitated at the very brink of its maximum potential, poised for the acceleration into spent kinesthesia.

"That's enough prurience out of you, Lopez," snapped Djell. "Cover this guy up and let's get on with the job."

Sibyl thought Stanley, watching the green eyes. *Sibyl, you are so silent. Why don't you speak up? Get me out of this. All you'd have to do is say the word, and we—. You wouldn't cut me, would you? Would you?*

Hah.

"You know," said Sibyl suddenly, breaking the lock that her gaze maintained with Stanley's long enough to glance at his throbbing penis. She placed a hand on Djell's shoulder and scratched his day's growth with the closed point of the gleaming scissors. "No surgeon should have to go through this sort of debasement. The patient should have been prepped long before you even stepped into the O.R."

"Sheeit," Vince hissed under his breath, moving a table. "This guy is never worked nowhere else *but* debasement."

Jaime tittered.

Djell clasped the hand bearing the scissors and kissed it. "Exactly, my dear." He watched Stanley's penis with a long-suffering sigh. "It's unseemly. But with such help as we have been able to scour off the sidewalks, well—" he shrugged "— one must monitor every aspect of the operation. Otherwise," he smiled, "the patient might suffer."

"Of course," Sibyl said solicitously, her eyes again meeting Stanley's. "You're always right about these things."

Oh, Sibyl, thought Stanley. *You wanton sycophant, you fucking bitch.* In the confusion arising from a bloodstream full of drugs, his illusions struggled with his reason. This woman saw him only as property, a collection of assets, a job description; yet some part of Stanley insisted on wanting to possess her; while, equally desperately, it wanted to filet her with her own scissors. No amount of humiliation seemed sufficient to quench this twin desire. And yet, and yet...

Somewhere deep down Stanley knew, and he could see it in her eyes, too. Deep down in those cruel green eyes Stanley could read that, given the chance, given the opportunity to have her, given the moment to seize her, and despite the manhood yet rampant on the operating table, despite a thorough ravishing...

...He would fail to touch her.

Those eyes would render him impotent. Even as he mauled her, he would never touch the evil that animated those green eyes.

Even as he thought this thought, his manhood withered like a napalmed silkworm.

If he'd been paying attention, six weeks before, this realization might have saved him a lot of trouble.

Sibyl smiled. Her eyes intuited a kill. Anticipating triumph, they glittered.

Stanley's eyes dimmed in defeat.

And, finally, Stanley looked away.

"Tape him," said Djell. "On his back, as he is."

The rasp of a length of two-inch wide tape, torn from its roll. A sudden adhesion, as the strip was pressed to his naked thighs.

"Shit," said Sturgeon. "Got it crooked," and he tore the tape away. The strip brought with it a sparse mat of crisp hair, yet Stanley felt only a tug. *Wow*, some fraction of him registered, *I'm more stoned than I know, here.*

Sturgeon peeled another length of tape off the roll and carefully reapplied it, as before, across the thighs. He laid another over the shins, and taped down the ankles individually.

Vince continued to hold down Stanley's shoulders as casually as he might lean over the back of a couch to watch television.

Sturgeon abruptly re-cinched a nylon strap over Stanley's chest. He restrained each of his wrists, too, with Velcro cuffs.

Far away or close by, his perceptions increasingly unreliable, Stanley could hear the hum of compressors. As Vince and Sturgeon worked on him, the anesthesiologist gathered the tools of his trade. He wheeled up the cylinders and a rack of electronic equipment. At the periphery of Jaime's endeavor, Sibyl broke a fresh surgeon's smock out of its hygienic plastic packaging and donned it. She broke out another and helped Djell into it. Djell was careful not to touch anything with his hands.

Sturgeon laid the last strip of tape across Stanley's brow, about half its width in his hair and about half on his forehead, and thus fixed Stanley's head to the table.

"Can you move your head?" said Vince kindly.

Stanley blinked his eyes once. No.

"How about wiggling your ears?" laughed Sturgeon.

Beads of moisture mottled Stanley's brow.

"Goddammit, Sturgeon," squeaked Jaime. "Veins up — *veins up.*"

"Oh, yeah," said Sturgeon. "Sorry." Sturgeon un-Velcroed Stanley's right wrist, turned it palm up on the table, and re-Velcroed it.

Jaime came into Stanley's narrowed field of vision. He had donned a pale green smock and a mask, the latter held in position over his mouth and nose by four strings tied behind his head. His hair was neatly tucked into a mint-colored shower cap. Vince rolled a chrome IV pole to the side of the table. Various tubes and plastic sacks hung from its upper arms. Some of the tubes had clips on them. Some of the clips were stainless steel, some of them plastic, the plastic ones had different-colored hand-written labels, da dee da dee da dee…

It's the little things that will drive a man crazy, knowing that they ultimately conspire to cut on him.

The light above the table suddenly came on. Stanley squinted against the glare.

Shades, he thought stupidly, *I want my shades…*

Jaime positioned a smaller table behind the IV pole. He unstoppered a bottle, let its contents saturate a cotton swab, and replaced the stopper—all with one deft hand. The odor of ethyl alcohol wafted over Stanley's nostrils.

Stanley heard the clink of instruments, the whirring of the small fans that cool electronic assemblies, and now, Chet Baker in the background.

"Vince," Sibyl said. "I need a couple of French drains, sponges all sizes, the big clamps, all the hemostats we have, Ringer's solution — stand by: Manny, we're skipping the nephrectomy, right?"

"Correct, my pet. It's probably damaged, as you so keenly observed."

Pet. His pet. Will you get over this, demanded a snappish little voice. *Why bother now? Oh, Sibyl…*

"Skip the Ringer's, Vince."

"Yessum."

"...Couple boxes of gauze, start the autoclave..."

"Yessum."

"Will you stop with that yessum drivel?"

Despite his slim build, Jaime loomed over him. Jaime had his eye on the inside of Stanley's forearm, over which he made a pass with the alcohol-soaked swab. "Okay, my friend," he said, his kind tone belying his insidious diction, "we begin with a local. You'll feel a mild prick."

Stanley felt a mild prick.

Another pass of the cool swab.

"Let that take hold..."

And then, among the clink of instruments, the closing of doors, the chatter of casters over the tiles, and the distant strains of Chet Baker, Stanley heard a very familiar sound.

It can't be, he thought. *Now I know I'm out of it.*

But his ears did not yet betray him. Someone was chopping cocaine.

"Jesus," said Jaime. "Didn't you get enough of that stuff in the mainline?"

The sound of a rush of air, drawn inward by the lungs, pulling with it a line of granulated cocaine through a straw and into the maxillary sinus.

"Never," came Djell's reply, in a strained voice. "Never enough blow, never enough money, never enough Sibyl..."

"Or type O-Negative donors," threw in Jaime.

Sibyl's green scrubs flitted through Stanley's peripheral vision.

Come a little closer, my vampire, thought Stanley, *and I'll spit in your eye.*

"Well, let's have some of that blow, you pig-valve host."

"Certainly, Jaime, since you ask so nice. Anyone else?"

"Yo," said Sturgeon.

"Uh-*huh*," said Vince.

Everything stopped while somebody laid out six or eight lines, and the entire staff took their turns at the straw.

"If any rhinoviruses can hear me," said Jaime in a strained voice, "Now is your moment."

"Fret not, this surface is sterile."

A lot of snorting followed. It sounded like a Doberman pinscher trying to worry a Barbie doll into wetting its pants.

"Hey, that was *my* line."

"There's more. Be cool."

"Ach," said Djell, beyond Stanley's vision. "I'm operating now. I'm an operating fool."

"Sheeit," drawled Vince. "When Manny was born his pappy jump back and say, Look out, Mama, he's got a straw in his hand."

"Scalpel," Djell corrected him archly. "Scalpel in his hand."

"Will you use it to cut out that lame country shit?" barked Jaime. His bark sounded like a Chihuahua's.

Someone sneezed violently.

"Ach-shit! Ach-shit! Ach-shit!"

"Sturgeon," said Djell. "Try to sneeze *away* from the work."

Jaime reappeared, rubbing his masked nose with the back of a gloved hand. "Now I'm going to install a couple of IV catheters," he said to Stanley. "You should only feel a little pushing."

Stanley felt a little pushing inside his left elbow.

"All set, baby?" Jaime said over his shoulder.

The head of Djell appeared within the corona of the overhead light. On his other side appeared Sibyl. They, too, wore masks, caps and smocks.

Her eyes were radioactive, above her surgical mask.

He focused on them.

If he spit very carefully…

He tried to muster a missile of spittle. But his mouth, or that part of him he could still discern as his mouth, was dry.

No, his mouth wasn't dry. He just couldn't find it.

"Wh-wha…" he tried to say.

"He's doing that guppy-against-the-side-of-the-aquarium thing," observed Sturgeon.

"The eyes," said Djell, not without satisfaction. "One of them anyway. Which one did you strike, Vince?"

"The right one. His right, I mean." A black hand flitted over Stanley's face. "Here."

"If you like," said Jaime, all business with his gentle manner, "you could try counting backwards from one hundred."

Ye gods and little guppies, thought Stanley, *No: One hundred indistinguishable gods and just the one guppy, ninety-nine sex gods and ninety-eight single guppies, ninety-seven Christs Velcroed to ninety-six crosses…*

Sibyl wrapped the cuff of a sphygmometer around Stanley's left biceps and snugged it up. Those goddamned eyes!

"Ninety-five," Stanley whispered, attempting to clear his throat. "Ninety-four, ninety-three...."

She pumped the rubber bulb. He could barely feel the constriction. There was not pressure in his mouth sufficient to spit. Pure sand, maybe. Individual grains of sand rolling down the inside of the inverted cone of his mind's mouth, to where the spider waits... He could barely breathe. The green eyes were caught in a band of flesh between mask and cap, like bearings in a race. Frictionless exit. Those green eyes would be the last things he would ever see.

"Blood pressure?"

"Ninety-two over ninety-one, ninety, eighty-nine...."

Not so bad. Painless. It could have been an an episode of *Star Trek* he'd never seen before...

"One-ten over eighty."

"Ninety... one ...ninety ...three... eighty-ninety...."

"Ready, steady..."

Spit in them eyes, man. One last defiance. Hawk it! Those two eyes. One last gasp. Ready? Three, two, one...

"Three," Stanley breathed, with all his strength, the words barely audible. "Two, one, every, every..."

Ev'rything hap-pens to

me-eeee....

Chapter 25

At first my heart thought
you could break this jinx for me
that love would turn the trick
to end despair...

Green eyes.

...but now I just can't fool
this head that thinks for me
I've mortgaged all my castles
in the air...

She had never loved him. She had never even wanted to fuck him. She reserved that favor for the junkie that was about to cut out Stanley's liver and sell it for enough dough to take her to Cabo San Lucas. Stanley had been to Cabo San Lucas, with Gray Eyes, once. The first thing he saw when they got off the plane was a 250-lb. guy, maybe 5'6", short, wearing a white tee shirt with capital letters on the front of it spelling SHUT UP in black letters and BITCH in red letters twice as large as the black ones. Stanley immediately concluded that someone had transplanted Las Vegas to Baja, and he made Gray Eyes get on the next flight back to the States. They never left San Francisco together again, and she never forgave him for it. And he'd thought he was being sensitive. The next time Stanley left San Francisco was to take delivery of his first drive-by fellatio, in a truck-stop outside of Reno, six months after Gray Eyes left him. It took him that long to become, uh, social, again. The next time Gray Eyes left San Francisco was with a coke dealer who took her to Cabo San Lucas—five days after she left Stanley. It took her that long to become, uh, social, again...

I've telegraphed and phoned,
I sent an Air Mail Special too,
your answer was "good-by",
and there was even postage due...

Sibyl worked the first pair of eyes to strike gold in Stanley since Gray Eyes, and there you had it. There was nothing for it. It was incontrovertible. Facts speak to realists. Caged radium spoke to Stanley. Twin novae witnessed through the chartreuse phlogiston of swinging Venus, a loner's horoscope. A lithium caldera beyond the grotto of her skull holes. Tantric awareness.

Then those green eyes had betrayed him.

One day, maybe he would be watching the curious effects of moonlight filtered through the eyeholes that had once been hers.

Maybe he could keep her skull on top of the television as a reminder, maybe with a little sign that reads: Always pay for it.

Pay in advance. Because, brother, if you don't pay now, you're going to pay later. You get what you pay for, especially when you know what the price is. Especially when the terms are clear. Why is it, that we retreat to cliché, in extremis?

You mean, time heals all wounds.

That's right, baby. But first I have to inflict some wounds of my own.

Maybe later.

Right now, goddammit, before it's the other way around—again.

Time wounds all heels — especially if your name is Achilles.

Yo, Patroclus, pass the Bushmills.

Listen, boss. For the last time, I'm telling you. Don't Hector me.

Ghostly Greeks dead 5,000 years laughed in his head, until, abruptly, they turned into a canned TV audience. Time heals all wounds.

But seriously, folks, does Time heal Death? I'm not talking about your beloved mother's death. I'm talking about your own death. Does Time heal that?

A single Hah! *from high up in the cheap seats, beyond the blinding lights.*

All right. Try the clank of instruments.

And that pressure, on your face. On your face, Stanley. That pressure on your far-away face.

But first, an etymological aside.

One pleasant evening, in the midst of an escalating session of scarlingus, the tip of her tongue having just lifted off the ridge of Stanley's empurpling scar, Iris said, "Tsssss."

"Tssss?"

She parked his erection between her breasts and repeated the sibilant.

"Tssss," said Stanley, with the complicity that often overwhelms a lover. "What?"

"That's the sound of a stereotype, getting quenched," Iris announced.

Her breasts were white and taut, each nipple a cupola of a distant city sighted halfway around a very round world.

"Stereotype," Stanley murmured vaguely.

"To make a stereotype, pour liquid metal into a mold. Then cool it in a bucket of water. The result is a plate you can print with."

"Like a blacksmith would do with a horseshoe?"

"Exactly. Once the stereotype is quenched, it's immutable."

Stanley moved his hips a little.

Iris lowered her shoulders and rocked forward, back, forward again. She aligned a set of fingertips atop his scar, and dragged them along its entire length. "Tssss. The French verb is clicher, whose past participle is cliché: which, the fanciful etymology would have it, is the sound of a stereotype being fixed in steel forever."

"Tssss," Stanley whispered.

Iris reversed the tickling along the crest of the scar, trailing her nails along his ribs, over his chest, up his throat and chin to his lips, and then her eyes were very close to his, and deadly serious.

"Do you think sex with me is stereotypical?" she asked.

Before he could answer she moved her mouth past his lips, not pausing for even the briefest kiss, and rammed the tip of her tongue into one of his nostrils.

"Yow!" squirmed Stanley. "No way!"

While he scrubbed his nose Iris slathered the side of his face with the flat of her tongue, over his cheek, the wincing eye above it, his forehead, his hair, until Stanley's nose cleaved her two breasts like a manatee breaching in a trough between swells.

Iris clasped the breasts together with her two hands until each of his nostrils was as if corked by an erect nipple.

"Tssss," she hissed. "We pour the new stereotype..."

"Tssss," said Stanley, by way of surrender. "Tssss, already."

"Tssss," she said, sliding her hips down on his belly, "we quench it..."

"Tssss," hissed Stanley, rising to the challenge. "Tssss," driving upward.

Later, despite lying with Iris in the dark, Stanley could only concentrate on two things, both of them green.

Those eyes.

How he hated them. And yet...

And at that moment he realized that Sibyl's green eyes had replaced Mary's gray ones in his pantheon of desire. Desire in the sense of craving... in the sense of possession, of dominance, of triumph, of remorse...

In his heart, *now that he knew the score, Stanley wanted a rematch. That's a good word. Heart.*

He wasn't sure how it happened. He hadn't noticed the transition. All he knew, lying there, Iris' violet eyes slumbering next to him in the dark, was that, after three years — three years! — gray eyes had gone, and green eyes had arrived.

The violet eyes revived him, provided him with transitional, mid-arc moxie. But the trajectory was from gray eyes to green.

It wasn't the same, of course. Gray Eyes was domestic, ambitious, silent, unintellectual, distracted, driven by her thirty-ish biology. Her one concession to uncivilized behavior had been — still, doubtless, was — to remain untamable in bed. She was wilder than Stanley could handle. Her screams embarrassed him, made him wish he'd never unzipped her dress; he couldn't meet his neighbor's eye in the morning. The scope of her orgasms always seemed out of proportion to his sensibilities, to what he himself was experiencing, to his skills as a lover, they seemed to be happening to somebody else. Well, they were *happening to somebody else...*

Green Eyes, on the other hand... Green Eyes was shrewd, ruthless, criminal. Green Eyes was cold, logical, dangerous, and wily. She was a winner in a game played by losers.

And she'd never even let him get close.

Why should she bed a loser?

And Iris?

Mainly because they would never entertain the idea of doing it with someone as bad off as they are, losers often wind up with nothing but contempt for the people who deign to go to bed with them.

After three years of burning incense in the shrine of Gray Eyes, of grinding his teeth at the thought of rich men lavishing cash on Gray Eyes in exotic locations, Iris had come along and shaken Stanley out of his complaisant indulgence, his emotional stagnation, his alcoholic infantilism, his stalled healing, his three years of rent-free addiction to television and alcohol and solitude and a dumb job. Iris was kind, generous, unconventional, a self-starting professional, benevolently kinky, she had violet eyes — she even liked him.

But Iris wasn't what Stanley wanted.

Love doesn't stick on the rebound, Stanley told himself. Not even lust does. Iris is transitional. You know you know, little voices told him, chronologically speaking you met her second; Green Eyes was first. No, no, he argued, chronology means nothing. Casuistry tells me so. Even after three years, love won't stick on the rebound. While there should always be a transitional figure between two great loves, why would chronology matter? Chronology is a mere technicality.

In any case, as regards Green Eyes, he'd never had his way with her. Worse: She'd had her way with him. The best to be hoped for is a merciful terminus, the final putre-faction, so the spirit is freed at last — if one believes in spirits and freedom. Short of that, one can always hope that the switch on the Love Machine is thrown to OFF, and one can make certain efforts to keep it there. Drink too much, for example. Watch tele-vision until one's brain turns to silage, for example. Throw oneself into the sea in an apparent attempt to reverse an apparently irreversible situation, to rescue a drowning child caught by a hopeless undertow, to die there with her. For example.

But the Transitional Figure. Willing to cope with recalcitrance, aggressive enough to cope with passivity, understanding enough to tread gently. Willing to breathe life into the cryogenic sensorium.

Of course, there's one really egregious flaw in this fentanylated weltanschauung, *which is, nobody had bothered to inform Iris of her status as Transitional. Iris thought she'd found herself: (a) a mutt to rescue, (b) a reluctant hero, (c) a nice, fresh scar.*

Like any number of male clowns in similar circumstances, Stanley had never uttered word one about his emotional makeup. Not to Iris. Not to himself. Not to any-body. He considered his ready compliance concerning prophylaxis as more than meet-ing any woman half way.

But knowing Iris as he did, having slept with her at any rate, did Stanley think she would sit still for an attempt to deprive her of himself?

Someone slammed a big metal door.

He woke up. His head throbbed. The features of his face floated awry, adrift on a subdermal film of acetone-saturated mucus.

Acrid smoke drifted between Stanley's eyes and the bright light over the operating table. He turned away from it.

And saw Sturgeon, sprawled on the floor like a parachutist in free-fall, dead.

A trickle of blood meandered from beneath the corpse toward a floor drain. As he watched, its scarlet vanguard dipped into a grout joint; filled it up; climbed out.

"Just to give you sons of bitches something to do," Iris was saying, "why don't you harvest your thug, there? Make a night of it."

Iris!

Djell, Sibyl, Vince, and Helium Jaime Lopez stood quietly around the corpse, as dumb and feckless as twilit livestock clustered around a salt lick.

Stanley stared at the operating table for a full minute before he realized he was no longer strapped to it. Instead, he was lying on a gurney across the room, against the wall, just beside the twin entry doors.

"You heard me," scowled Iris. "Hop to it."

"Uh…," said Djell, speaking as if shell-shocked. "You… heard what the lady said."

Vince and Jaime gazed forlornly at the dead Sturgeon. Djell, too, looked dejected.

"I loved him, you know," Djell glared at Iris. "This man was my friend. My colleague. He—."

"Oh for Christ's sake," Jaime snapped, clearly on edge. "Shut up, Manny."

Not distracted by this exchange, and even though she watched Iris like a cat watches a mousehole, Sibyl was the first to notice that Stanley was awake.

She turned those eyes on him. Detestation and malice flowed from them, as twisted and pure as a thousand yards of new barbed wire. Stanley, however, saw a fire kindled. And he knew that she knew that he, and only he, saw it. She depended on him, on his illusions. A promising leer passed over her beautiful mouth, as fluid and supple as the hint of a cross-current over the caudal fin of a sea snake.

In his last bout of consciousness Stanley had witnessed Sibyl in per-fervid conjugation with Dr. Djell. There was little doubt as to her allegiance. The guy was her husband, after all. Yet despite this, Stanley's yearn to score, and to settle a score, with her and those green eyes had awakened with him, undiminished.

Lacking all number, structural integrity, sense, an irrational schema-

ta flooded his mind, projecting the result that, somehow, Stanley and
Green Eyes might abstract themselves from this nightmarish web of
other people's determinants—*and work it out.*

He seethed with hatred.

He was rocked by lust.

Neither could resolve itself fully into the other, unless—.

He tried to sit up. He failed. He tried again. He threw his legs over
the side of the gurney, nearly precipitating himself onto the floor. But
some inner gyroscope kicked in—its lurch against inertia nearly made
him puke—and the vertical perch held, leaving him teetering on the
edge of the gurney like a suicide on the edge of a roof. He was still
naked. His vision swam 450 degrees or so, and stopped on Sibyl. She
was watching him.

The drugs were powerful. So was the room full of eyes. How had this
all become his fault? He felt a sudden urge to detoxify; it expired just
as suddenly, an impulse that winked out of existence in a damp almost
inaudible snap: two or three watts of light atop a stem of drifting
smoke.

"Stanley." The interruption didn't go with the green eyes. It was Iris'
voice. "You're back."

"Yes. I guess I...." He stopped.

Finally, he'd noticed.

Though Iris was standing to his immediate right, at the foot of the gurney, an arm's length away, he couldn't see her. He could see Green Eyes,
who stood directly across the room from him, beyond a veil of gun-
smoke. But he couldn't see Iris, who must have fired the gun from just to
the right of him, well within the theoretical range of his peripheral
vision.

The gurney stood against the wall next to the double doors.

Now he noticed shreds of tape hanging from his wrists and ankles.

Blood caked the inside of his right elbow. A steel needle was still
taped there, its business end buried in a little bump above a vein. A wad
of blood-soaked cotton had been hastily tamped into its disconnected
bezel.

The blue fumes no doubt reeked of cordite. But his sense of smell
was thoroughly stymied by the acetone reek that suffused his saliva,
nostrils, sinuses, stomach fluids—all of him. It secreted from his pores
like the mephitic stench of a nightshade.

But what annoyed him was that he couldn't see Iris. He could see Sibyl—and Djell and Vince and Jaime and even poor Sturgeon —perfectly well, not twenty feet away, straight out in front of him. But he couldn't see Iris, who stood to his right, not three feet from his hand.

Something was in the way.

Something white.

Tape.

White tape.

And his nose. His too-pale nose. Down there, in the lower right-hand corner of his vision.

White tape on it, too.

White tape on his nose intruded between him and Iris like a wall, like a physical partition.

He turned his head.

There Iris stood, just as he'd seen her when he'd been lying down. Iris with a gun in her hand.

He swiveled his head back to the left. Green Eyes reappeared.

Iris went away.

He tried looking right again. Iris reappeared.

Again, he turned his head to look forward. Sibyl came back.

Finally he clasped one hand to the right side of his head, where it found a lump of gauze, with damp cotton spilling out from under it, and a large X of tape holding it in place.

"I got here as soon as I could," Iris said tightly, in a small, wavering voice, a voice barely under control. "I never killed anybody before…"

As he explored the bandage with his fingers, he caught Sibyl's eye. Something like a photon emitted from her and came at him. Something feral. Stanley had the sudden feeling he had found her in a dark cave, where the eyes were the only evidence of her presence, while all the rest of her lay concealed in shadow.

He covered and uncovered the right side of his face with the palm of his hand. No light waxed or waned. No shadow flitted through his perception.

"My eye," said Stanley suddenly.

Iris began again, shakily defensive, "I got here… as fast as I—."

"My eye…" Stanley realized everybody had been waiting for him to make this discovery, that he was a specimen on display, that, if his discovery were the first act, his reaction was the second.

"Look at it this way," said Iris.

"What?" said Stanley. "How?" He swiveled his head her way again, so that the horrible fascination in the green eyes was eclipsed from his sight, to be replaced by the kind, if sidelong, regard of Iris.

"You've still got the one." She moved the barrel of the gun uncertainly.

"One?" croaked Stanley, his voice a bushel of shards.

"One," Iris confirmed. "They took only one."

Chapter 26

"How does it feel?" she asked tenderly, not taking her eyes off the other occupants of the room.

"Like somebody wiped my ass with a puff adder," Stanley said.

"It hurts there, too?"

"It's mostly mental."

"Same thing." She laughed nervously.

Her gun hand was shaking.

"I got here as soon as I could," she repeated quickly. "It took a while to get Fong to tell me what was going on." She laughed abruptly, then stopped. "He wanted to talk about his car." Iris was scared. "He's awfully fond of that car," she added in a small voice.

"Want to give me the gun?" he asked.

She still wasn't looking at him. "I had to shoot that guy."

They all looked at the dead man. The new flower on Sturgeon's pineapple shirt bloomed a glistening red.

"Looks like you shot him, all right," Stanley said finally. "Better give me the gun."

"He didn't believe me," Iris continued in a monotone.

"You should give the gun to me," he repeated. But he was thinking, *they took my eye.*

"He walked right up to me like he was going to take the gun away from me. No. He had his hand out, like I was going to give it to him."

Green Eyes let them take it.

"*He* told him to."

Djell's mouth twitched.

She helped *them take it.*

"When he got five feet away from me — five feet away! — he said, 'Little girl,' he said, 'Lemme hold that rod.'"

Better to let me *hold it,* Stanley thought, and without speaking he extended his hand. It was the same hand he'd touched to the dark side of his nose, and there was blood on it.

"So I shot him. Loud in here." She kicked something in front of her, which skittered under the operating table with a metallic clink and spun there. A spent cartridge. "I made them turn off that stupid music." She glanced briefly at the hand. "You cut yourself?"

"No," Stanley said. He had to cock his head to one side in order to see her. "I just got a hole in my head."

"They were making jokes, too," she said, looking away.

"Jokes? About what?"

Her mouth was wrinkled, caught between a sad smile and a tremor of fear. Tears welled at the corners of her eyes.

"They talked about cauterizing your eye socket with a blow torch. But they were worried about the..."

Stanley cocked his head so he could see Djell.

Showing the grimaces associated with biting into an unripe persimmon, Djell was gradually positioning himself in front of Green Eyes.

"What stopped them?" Stanley asked.

"Take it easy, little lady," said Vince.

"Shut up, Vince," said Stanley, not looking at him. Iris glanced at Stanley, then at the extended hand. The room was silent. A distant compressor motor started, briefly dimming the light over the operating table. The autoclave bubbled in its corner. Something dripped. Remnants of blue smoke swirled before a wall vent.

"He had a fresh aster. Ready to go," Iris continued. She pointed the gun at Djell's gut. "Show it to him."

Djell looked surprised, but he didn't stop moving.

"And you," Iris said, her voice suddenly brittle. "Slide out from behind him or I'll nail you both."

Djell's eyes bugged slightly at this command, but Sibyl's stayed big, green and attentive. With the back of one hand she touched Djell's shoulder and moved him aside as if parting a curtain. And there she stood, in the green smock over her neatly pressed nurse's uniform, hem just above the knee, bloody swaths over her lap where she'd wiped her hands. Like Djell and Jaime, she still wore a pair of bloodstained latex gloves. Even from across the room, with one eye, Stanley could see the minute rusty speckling of dried blood on her white shoes. A surgical mask was pulled down under her chin. Magnificent, thought Stanley, this is a lot of nurse to get even with.

You ain't gonna have her a little voice said. *Take what the Good Lord's dropped in your lap and git the hell outta here.*

"Now show it," Iris said. An edge of hysteria was creeping into her voice.

Djell raised his right arm, turned the hand, and showed a single, purple flower, its stem pinched between his fingers.

If only Corrigan could see this, thought Stanley. Isn't this what they call circumstantial evidence? He surveyed the room. Operating table, four people on one side of the gun, two on the other, a dead man, the autoclave, lights, miscellaneous wheeled tables, cloth-covered trays, boom-box, tapes and CDs, stainless steel instruments, a purple aster…

Where was his eye?

"Say it," Iris hissed.

Stanley cocked his head to see her. "Pardon?"

"Not you." She gestured with the pistol. "Him."

Stanley cocked his head so as to see Djell.

Djell smiled ingenuously. "*Klein Aster?*"

"Say it!" she screamed.

Djell hastily launched into the recitation.

> *Ein ersoffener Bierfahrer wurde auf den Tisch gestemmt.*
> *Irgendeiner hatte ihm eine dunkelhellila Aster*
> *zwischen die Zähne geklemmt.*

Whoa, thought Stanley —

> *Als ich von der Brust aus*
> *unter der Haut*
> *mit einem langen Messer…*

— I'd forgotten this bit.…

"Yes," said Iris, "the long knife."

Djell's voice abruptly trailed off. Stanley shared his realization. *My fucking Christ,* he thought disconsolately. *She speaks German, too.*

"Finish it!" Iris said.

...Zunge und Gaumen herausschnitt,
muß ich sie angestoßen haben, denn sie glitt
in das nebenliegende Gehirn.
Ich packte sie ihm in die Brusthöhle
zwischen die Holzwolle,
als man zunähte.
Trinke dich satt in denier Vase!
Ruhe sanft,
kleine Aster!

Djell had assumed the pose of a Balboa discovering the Pacific Ocean. Aster held before him, posture erect, one foot forward, teeth gleaming in the theatrical glare, his smock smeared with blood, he declaimed his prize-winning poem.

"What the hell was that?" asked Stanley.

"It's a poem," said Iris bitterly. "Didn't you like it?"

Stanley shrugged. "It sounded like garbage sliding down a chute."

Jaime smirked. "I knew you would get us in trouble with that tripe. It was just a matter of time. I just knew—."

"Shut up," said Vince.

"That's his aster anthem," said Iris, smiling grimly. "It's about sewing up an aster in a corpse."

"I've heard it before," Stanley said.

"He wanted to sew it up in your empty eye socket."

Silence fell over the room.

"He recited the poem, which precipitated an argument." Iris pointed the gun. "*She* said that cremating the whole works was only smart. *He* acquiesced, but clung to the idea of sealing the flower into the urn. The gas man, there, thought of that idea as typical of the doctor's arrogance, of his predilection to tempt fate."

"You see?" said Jaime.

"Shut up, Jaime," Vince said irritably.

"Pretty cute, in any case," Iris concluded.

Stanley sat pillion on the gurney. While the poem and "the long knife" may have intrigued him, the sight of the aster had frozen his intestines. The circumstances of his last sighting of a purple aster trained through his memory, and ended in a long tracking shot of his hospital bill, zigzagging, page by fan-folded page, from the reception desk of the bursar, across the lobby floor, down the front staircase of the hospital, the last page with its bottom line unfolding at the foot of his wheelchair, just beyond that Get-Well Bear in his lap.

A purple aster in its little Get-Well paws.

He looked at Iris.

"That's what he was doing when I came in," she was saying disconsolately. A sob terminated what was left of her composure. The pistol barrel wavered. Vince, in particular, was watching it very carefully. "He was reciting it as he was… as he was…"

Don't ask for the gun again, thought Stanley. But now, suffused by rage, he felt as rigidly under control as he'd ever been in his life. Here he sat, naked. One kidney gone. One eye gone. The other kidney soon to fail. Not a hope or a prayer for mortal redemption, either. And these clowns were reciting poetry and handing out flowers and — he glanced at Iris — Get-Well Bears. He cocked his head to look at Sibyl. If Vince was watching the gun, Sibyl was watching Stanley. *Remember what she taught you about getting people to give you what you want?* Stanley thought: *Let them come to you, then take it.*

Instead of asking again for the gun Stanley asked what exactly the poem meant.

Djell didn't have to be asked twice. Proudly, one would have said, he resumed his declamatory pose, cleared his throat, and began again, this time in English.

Little Aster

> *The drowned beer-truck driver*
> *reposed on the slab.*
> *Someone had planted a lavender*
> *aster between his teeth.*
> *As I unzipped the skin*
> *over the sternum*
> *with my long knife*
> *to get to the tongue and palate*
> *I must have disturbed the flower*
> *because it slid onto the brain*
> *lying nearby.*

I transplanted it
into the excelsior
stuffing the chest cavity
before sewing up.
Drink yourself full in your vase!
Rest in peace
little aster!

Into the queasy silence that followed this recitation, Djell suddenly announced, "That's the greatest autopsy poem ever written," and bowed deeply.

"Damn," said Stanley. "There's more than one?"

Green Eyes and Vince suddenly applauded half-heartedly, their pairs of surgical gloves flapping like two flat tires.

Djell took a another, slighter bow in their direction.

Iris' gun hand was shaking as if she were trying to hold it steady against a strong crosswind. "That damned flower's all he cares about."

Stanley considered the surgical quartet, cocking his one-eyed head so as to take them all in. A trickle of blood chose this moment to dart out of his sideburn and launch itself off the lobe of his ear, falling onto the stainless steel of the gurney with a little tap.

"You going to shoot them?" he asked.

"Only if they make me," said Iris. "Although God knows they deserve shooting, and I'm tempted to do it."

"I feel like shooting them," said Stanley calmly.

Vince grunted. Helium Jaime whimpered. Djell looked like he would go to his grave happily now that he'd recited his poem.

Green Eyes just watched.

"I'll bet you do."

"But I'm not going to."

"Why not?"

"You must have Corrigan's home number?"

"Are you kidding? He's sleeping with my mother."

"Call him. Get him over here."

"Where's the phone?"

"Upstairs," said Djell with a smile. "On the loading dock."

"Oh," snapped Jaime. "Why don't you just dial the number for them, too?"

"Shut up, Jaime," Vince said evenly.

"There's not a phone down here?" Stanley asked suspiciously. "No cellular?"

"Oh, right," Jaime said with all due sarcasm. "Like we're gonna do business on a cell phone—"

"Jaime…," said Vince, his tone very ominous.

"This is a funeral home," said Djell derisively. "Who the hell's going to need a phone down here?"

"I don't feel up to the trip," said Stanley. "But if you wouldn't mind going, darling, it would give me great pleasure to tempt these animals into dying while you're gone."

This was the first time he'd called her darling.

"You think you can handle them?" Iris asked.

"If you hear any shooting while you're up there, run like hell. But," he added quietly, "there won't be any shooting. These are professionals. Professionals don't get themselves shot. They get themselves lawyers."

Iris moved closer. "Okay."

"In a line," Stanley said to the rest of the room. "All of you. Along this side of the operating table. Keep your hands where we can see them, and think Christian thoughts."

Nobody moved.

"Shoot one of them, Iris."

"Wh-what?"

"Hey," said Jaime uncertainly.

"You heard me. Do it!"

"Take it easy, man."

Iris moved the gun back and forth. "Wh-which one? I-I mean…"

Stanley locked his eye with one of the green ones. "I don't care. Just don't hesitate."

"I'm moving," said Vince, stepping around the foot of the operating table. Jaime quickly followed him. Djell already stood at the head of it with Sibyl.

Stanley turned his head forty-five degrees to his right, so as to take in his four adversaries and Iris' gun hand all at once.

Iris was right next to him now, ready to transfer the pistol from her control to Stanley's. She glanced at his hand. "Better wipe the blood off your paw."

To his left was a pillow. He placed it over his lap and scrubbed his hands on it until most of the blood was gone.

"Ready?"

"I guess," said Stanley.

Opposite, the four stood tensely; each, in his own way, measuring, calculating, studying the chances. Stanley would take but a second or two to get the gun from Iris' hand, but he might drop it. Though he was still naked, and the room was cold, his hands were sweating. Dropping the gun was a distinct possibility, and he had a sudden vision of the heavy .45 squirting out of his or Iris' hands. Of the two of them only Iris would be agile enough to go after it. Stanley was visibly woozy. But only Vince or Green Eyes would be possessed of enough alacrity to capitalize on such a mistake. Djell would hold himself above direct action, willing to stand by while even the most appalling events unfolded. Jaime was scared and nervous. Vince, a big man, was ready for action. And Green Eyes?

Green Eyes was watching every move Stanley made, attending her chance, abiding, confident in her prowess. All she had to do was wait, as patient and certain of ultimate victory as a spider, her perfect web spun between the ceiling bulb and a broken window in a rural summer phone booth.

So Sibyl was watching Stanley, and Stanley was watching Sibyl, when he said, "Okay. Give me the gun."

As she passed it to him Stanley did a funny thing, unexpected by anyone in the room. He withdrew his right hand and presented the palm of his left hand, into which the gun slapped as if the hand were a mitt and the gun a ball.

This simple change-up checked everybody.

"I didn't know you were ambidextrous," breathed Iris, taking a single step away from Stanley.

"I'm not," Stanley smiled, switching the gun to his right hand. "But how coordinated do you have to be to pull a trigger?"

Iris hesitated. "Should I make the call now?"

A prescient weakness seemed to have possessed her, a clairvoyant passivity that momentarily robbed her of the impetus of movement, even of the will to flee.

Sibyl saw immediately that something was up.

Stanley cleared his throat. "Okay." He pointed the gun at Sturgeon's corpse. "What's his blood type?"

Silence.

Stanley pointed the gun at Djell. "Answer the goddamn question."

Djell shook his head. "No idea."

"Tough," said Stanley. "What's yours?"

"AB-Negative," Djell said, without hesitation.

Stanley sighted the pistol on Sibyl. "Yours, Green Eyes?"

She regarded him malevolently.

Stanley tilted his head back a little more. A rivulet of type O-Negative coursed over his right temple and into his ear. "I'll kill you," he said simply. "Don't doubt it."

"I'm AB-Negative too," said Sibyl.

"That's an interesting coincidence."

She shrugged toward Djell.

Djell interjected, "We thought so too, when we wanted to have kids."

Stanley set his jaw. This information annoyed him. "This really brings you down in my estimation," he said to Sibyl.

Sibyl smiled contemptuously. "Your estimation is not even on my scope."

Stanley stared at her. He could shoot her now. It would be easy. And smart. It might even be defensible.

But his addled brain had formed a plan. Sibyl's contempt paled next to this plan because she had a part to play in it.

Two more to go.

"Stanley…," Iris began.

He trained the gun on the anesthesiologist. "Blood group?"

Jaime glanced to one side and another, then smiled nervously. "What is this," he squeaked. "A lottery?"

"If this were a movie," said Stanley. "I would cock this pistol. But," he showed it sideways to them and smiled. "It's already cocked." He pointed it at Jaime again. "Blood type."

"AB-positive. But I have low platelets—."

"Shut up. Vince?"

Vince shook his head and smiled. "I got no idea, boss."

Stanley believed him. There was a good chance the others were lying, but there was little he could do about it.

Besides, given the disposition of personnel, their skills and utility, their relevance to the surgical team, there were really only three people in the room he could use.

And only one he was sure of.

Well, said the little voice. *Is you or ain't you sick of this life, and everything good in it?*

He cocked his asymmetric vision toward Iris.

Iris backed away from him a step, toward the far end of the gurney and the double doors beyond. "I'll go make the call," she said hopefully.

He turned his head toward Green Eyes. "You'd better catch her," Stanley said, in a very tired voice, "Before she gets to that phone."

A stunned silence filled the room.

"He's bullshitting," yelled Vince, and he lunged toward Stanley.

Stanley shot Vince in the chest.

Vince embraced the vector of the bullet, like a gum wrapper speared by a nail on a stick, and wilted to the floor. The windowless chamber vibrated to the discharge like an oil drum struck by an iron bar.

Gun works good, observed the little voice.

The reverberations of the shock had hardly faded when Sibyl shouted, "Get her!" and sprang toward Iris like a mantis. She had to leap over Vince's body to do it. Jaime followed, side-stepping Vince carefully.

Iris was almost too stunned to react. She managed to turn half way around before Stanley stood off the gurney and neatly rolled it between her and the double doors, blocking her exit. Then Sibyl was on her, Jaime was clutching at her, and even Djell arrived at the margins of the fracas.

Iris fought back. She thoroughly clawed one side of Djell's face with her fingernails before Sibyl knocked her half over the gurney with a business-like backhand to the side of her head. It resounded so thoroughly that Stanley winced and shouted, "Don't hurt her!"

Subdued by six hands, Iris resigned herself to uncontrolled weeping and cursing.

"You bastard," she said, "I saved your worthless life…"

"And you're going to save it again, Iris," Stanley said. "Try to understand."

"Yeah," said Jaime, rolling his eyes incredulously. "Try to understand."

"But why?" she wailed, shaking her head. "Why?"

"That's easy," said Green Eyes calmly. "You two must have the same blood type."

Iris stared at her.

"Like me and Manny," Sibyl smirked.

"A match made in heaven," Jaime sneered.

Iris looked from Sibyl to Djell to Jaime to Stanley. "I've had you in my bed!" she shouted.

Stanley exchanged glances with Green Eyes. Hers said, *Oh, she has, has she?* Stanley's said, *If only I could test your blood.*

"Look at it this way," he said gently. "It'll be over in no time. Then you'll have your own scar to be fond of."

Iris cursed him.

Djell and Jaime gaped, looking from Stanley to Iris and back again.

"What deliciously low behavior," Jaime said admiringly. "I've never seen the like of it, not even in Polk Gulch."

Green Eyes was fascinated, too. "You want a kidney," she said, only half aloud. "You really did come here because you want a new kidney."

Stanley fixed her with a look. "That's all that's keeping you alive, honey."

This disconcerted Djell. "Look," he began. "Let's—."

"Shut your mouth," Stanley said. "Pay attention."

Stanley let Iris weep and curse for a while longer. Then he said, "One scar wasn't enough for you, was it?"

Iris ceased weeping as suddenly as if she had thrown a switch. A mad leer flashed over her mouth before she could muster enough sense to bluster, "You're crazy. You think I'd let you risk an eye operation under these conditions, just to collect a fresh…" She stopped.

"Say it."

"A fresh…"

"Yes? A fresh what?"

"Sc… Sc…"

Her voice caught in her throat.

"Put her on the table," Stanley said. "Let's get on with it."

"You're crazy!" shouted Iris.

By now Jaime had caught on.

"Wow," said Jaime, looking from Iris to Stanley and back as he held one of Iris' thrashing arms. "And this chick's a friend of yours?"

"She's more than a friend," said Stanley, fixing him with his one-eyed stare.

"She's a donor."

Chapter 27

Iris lay on her side. A padded device called a kidney rest, built into the table, enabled Djell to elevate her hip to facilitate access.

Her skin was beautiful, lambent.

Djell's scalpel pulled a red curve along the line of her twelfth rib, back to front, ending just before her navel. This was the first trace of the flank incision. Then, with surprising rapidity, while Sibyl expertly reflected the muscle layers and fascia, the knife progressively revealed the inner Iris. Djell's dexterity impressed Stanley, for whose visceral fascination a visceral revulsion competed. If Stanley had figured a sleazy criminal as incapable of anything other than ham-fisted surgeonry, he'd been wrong.

Djell announced that the girl's kidney was "low." Helium Jaime and Sibyl nodded.

"What's that mean?" Stanley asked suspiciously.

"Means he won't have to resect the rib," Jaime said, adjusting a valve.

"Forehead," said Djell. He inclined his head toward his wife and she dabbed it with a cloth.

"Ah, look, buddy," said Jaime, raising his hand. "We can see that the Doc's hands are shaking a little bit, and nobody wants no wiggy scalpel around the peritoneum. If you don't mind, I'm just going to start a conversation, here. It helps us relax."

"Sure," said Stanley. "But keep it down."

Jaime didn't hesitate. "Hey, Djell, you ever heard that Chicago slang for girlfriend?"

"No," Djell said, carefully adjusting a reflector.

"Rib," said Jaime gleefully. "Get it?"

"No."

"God took a rib from Adam to make Eve, see. And the Chicago brothers all know that, 'cause they got raised in church — right? Vince told me this…"

Nobody looked at Vince, so recently deceased.

"So one day this one linguistically mythical brother, he's in need of a new slang expression by which to impress his hipness upon his contemporaries. So, totally cool, he announces to the assembled, Hey, I'm taking my rib to the lake on Saturday."

"Rib, huh," Djell muttered behind his mask. "That's the proper order of things. Better than that chicken-and-egg stuff."

"You mean like who came first," said Jaime, "the chickenshit or his rib? How about he gets his divorce, see, and says 'I got my rib *resected*'? Ah ha ha ha…" Nobody laughed with him.

"Hey, Rib," said Djell, ignoring him. "Reflect that iliac vein toward you a little bit."

Sibyl applied herself to the work at hand.

Christ, observed an increasingly nagging voice in Stanley's weary head. *Whomever it was, who remarked on the banality of evil, he didn't know the half of—*.

"Arendt," said Djell, glancing over his shoulder at Stanley. "Hannah Arendt."

For a moment Stanley didn't understand. Then he asked, "Did I say that out loud?"

Djell, Sibyl and Jaime all paused to look at him.

Stanley looked at them.

Djell made two little circles in the air with the tip of a scalpel.

Stanley pointed the gun at him.

Requesting vacuum suction to clear the surgical site of blood, Dr. Djell made a small incision in the perinephric fat.

"Nice," said Sibyl.

"Little close to the pleura," said Djell.

"Steady hands," said Jaime toward Stanley. "Not bad for an old junkie." He winked and silently counted three latex-gloved fingers on one hand with the forefinger of the other, then nodded an exaggerated downbeat.

"Speaking of which," began Djell, looking up.

Jaime smiled as if to say, See? I have the refractory period of Djell's cocainization timed perfectly.

"Later," said Stanley sternly. "Keep at it."

"Speaking of later," Djell continued, unperturbed, "did anyone mark the time?"

"Three thirty-five, when she went under," said Jaime, consulting a gold watch on the inside of his wrist.

Djell peeled away perinephric fat until the kidney was reasonably exposed, which to Stanley looked like the chitterlings special at the meat market, with colors no Federal Inspector would permit. The blood required constant attention from Sibyl, who made careful passes, back and forth, with a little vacuum hose, or applied fresh sponges.

Stanley couldn't get close enough to see exactly what was going on, and didn't want to. He stayed on the gurney, which still blocked the door, and idly weaved the muzzle of the big .45 in and out of the transsecting loops of the lazy figure eight of infinity.

"The doctor always removes the upper pole first," narrated Jaime, watching Djell's work with a critical eye. He glanced nervously at the gun barrel, then at Stanley. "You interested in this?"

Stanley was feeling a little sick. A strange smell had come to permeate the atmosphere of the room—a malodorous cocktail of blood, ethyl alcohol, gun powder, corpse preservative, dead flowers, talcum powder, hydraulic oil, Ringer's Solution, benzene, iodine, acetylene, and the acrid fumes of what, if he were anywhere else, Stanley would have surmised to have come from a clutch of paper matches toasting the bowl of a crack pipe.

He'd never consciously attended a surgery, and it struck him as decidedly unpleasant. Aside from the prevalent odors, the room was tense with concentration, incongruous against the commonplace chitchat. Not to mention Stanley had just had an eye removed. Not to mention he'd just thrown Iris—a part of her at least—to the wolves. His system was swimming with anesthetics, antibiotics, adrenaline fatigue, pain, and—a sensation new to him—guilt. The combination went straight to his stomach.

"Yeah," he nevertheless said, if weakly, "I am interested in this. But not as much as you should be."

Jaime smiled and pointed. "That's the upper pole there, at that end. If he tries to get the lower pole out first, the upper end might slip up under the rib, there — see? Don't want that to happen."

Little slurping sounds mixed with the tinkle of instruments emanated from the nephrectomy site.

The room was starting to revolve around Stanley's head. When he tried to tighten his grip on the gun, he realized his palm was slick with perspiration. His mouth was flooding with acrid fluids, and his esophagus was choking up gas.

"So now he needs to identify the distal ureter," Jaime continued cheerily. "We're talking pee-pee here…"

"Shut up."

"We don't want—."

"Shut up," Stanley shouted, and he slipped and fell back against the wall, causing himself and the gurney to roll away from it and leaving him nearly supine.

Djell kept on operating, but the green eyes were on Stanley, and so were Jaime's.

"Nobody get inspired," Stanley said, covering them with the gun.

They worked. Stanley cleared his throat and spit furiously toward the floor drain. The effort caused his stomach to contract, but as he'd not eaten in a couple of days there was nothing to hold down.

Still, he was barely under control. His attention kept wandering, and his eye socket had begun to throb continually.

Then Stanley had an idea.

"Where's that coke?"

Djell continued to work.

Jaime's brown eyes exchanged a glance with Sibyl's green ones. "Ah… What coke you talking about, buddy?"

Stanley laughed sinister. "Hey Djell, *buddy*," he said. "You ever work without an anesthesiologist?"

Before Djell could answer Jaime said, "Oh — the cocaine! Why didn't you say so?" He slapped his forehead with the flat of his hand. "How could I have forgotten the coke?" He shook his head emphatically. "There's always a little coke around here…."

Jaime hustled around the end of the operating table, approached Djell as if stealthily, and plunged his hand into the man's front pocket.

Djell grunted disagreeably while quickly elevating his scalpel and a pair of needle-nosed pliers out of the surgical wound. Jaime rummaged beneath Djell's smock and came up with a fat bindle.

"I once thought he was Sibyl's not-so-little-secret," he smirked, "hung like a stallion. But turns out it's an eight ball." Djell swore beneath his surgical mask. Jaime winked at Stanley. "I mean, like, he's never without. Makes you wonder about those steady hands."

He made as if to carry the bindle to Stanley.

"Not so fast," said Stanley, centering the .45 on Jaime's gut. He stood off the gurney and stepped to one side. "On the gurney, there."

Jaime tentatively approached the far end of the gurney and dropped the bindle onto it.

White powder, rolled up in a plastic bag, about the size of a pig's foot. At least a quarter ounce.

"That ought to keep you awake for a while," said Jaime, regarding the bag skeptically. "This outfit rips through one of those every working evening."

Stanley looked at him incredulously.

"It's good stuff, too."

"Go back to work," Stanley ordered. "Is it milled, Djell? Hey, I'm talking to you. Is this shit ready to do up?"

Without allowing himself to be distracted from his work, Djell grunted.

"Are you kidding?" said Jaime, who hadn't moved. "He plays with it all day long. As my dead friend Vince used to say, in reference to recordings by Beniamino Gigli, the stuff's fine as frog's hair."

Djell grunted in the affirmative.

Jaime ignored him, still smiling at Stanley. "What say I lay out a couple fat ones?" he suggested softly. "Just for you and me?"

Stanley knew that Jaime was watching his right jaw, where beads of sweat were merging with the blood leaking from his empty eye socket. The two fluids commingled their way down the side of his face, along his neck, finally to spread in a thin film along the shoulder of his gun hand. Some of that sweat was even now stinging its way over the surface of the ball of his good eye, clouding its vision. Naked except for his socks and the eye bandage, draped in a blood-stained sheet, his head to one side so he could see to aim the gun, Stanley looked every inch a master of Butoh. Djell and Sibyl, too, were waiting for Stanley to fall flat on his face. *Fuck them.* They should be marveling at the stamina of a man who, having lost an eye to greed but an hour ago, not only refused to lie down and surrender to the powerful medicinal narcotics coursing through his system, or to the pain, or to his exhaustion;

who, rather, insisted on standing upright and naked all night in a funeral home with a gun in his hand in his attempt to wrest his fate away from the sinister forces attempting to co-opt it.

"If you get any closer to me," Stanley mumbled to Jaime, rapidly blinking salty perspiration out of his good eye, "my inner barroom is going to vote to ventilate you."

"Your inner...," the smile faded from Jaime's face, "...barroom?"

Stanley's head wobbled at an odd angle, as if it were mounted on a spring, the better to watch Jaime, the better to inhibit stinging fluids from flooding into his good eye. "The same inner barroom that voted to put Iris onto the table."

Jaime's jaw dropped.

"You may not hear the debate," Stanley advised, "but you'll hear the shot."

Actually there *was* a diminutive, unreliable part of Stanley's personality that had pirated all of his experience and none of its pain. It wasn't that part of his brain suffering from his remaining kidney's questionable viability, any more than it was the part that got the hangover headaches. This little part of his head had the exact same relationship to the rest of Stanley as the catbird seat has to a bar: it perched where it could see and comment on everything, get all the drinks it wanted without moving, and take none of the responsibility. This ethereal capacity was free to estimate any quality of Stanley's inner or outer existence with impunity, and to suggest the kind of snap judgment that made a difference in life, for good or ill, unbiased by pain, alcohol, unconsciousness, or even love.

So Stanley told himself, at any rate: in the hope that if he propped up these theories, they in turn might occasionally prop up him.

So he was telling Jaime, now.

But to speak of the Catbird Mind in public? To complete strangers? To strangers, moreover, whom one was looking to impress?

That's right, Stanley, said the little voice. *Baffle 'em with your bullshit. If they think you're crazy, you're way ahead of the game.*

Jaime recovered his composure enough to ask, "What did you say?"

But, as Stanley could see, Jaime wasn't sure of anything anymore. What had started out as bravado on his part, reinforced by his intimate knowledge of the pain afflicting Stanley, had now dissolved into uncertainty, deepened by the revelation that he was standing five feet in front of a man holding a cocked .45 who was not only enraged and desperate enough to have Djell perform surgery on his girlfriend, but was now also talking about a barroom in his head.

"Did you suggest," Jaime said, clasping his crossed palms like a solicitous *maître d'hotel*, showing his teeth in a forced smile, "that the, ahem, *inner you* requires two lines of the, ahem, *outer blow…?*"

Stanley thought better than to take issue with this. "That's a good way of putting it, Jaime," he confirmed, his voice slurred with menace. "Get us a straw and some kind of knife or a scalpel. Right now. Chop chop!" He forestalled Jaime with a raised pistol. "Hold it. Green Eyes!"

The eyes flashed above the seam of the surgical mask.

So she knew her name…

"Pitch this guy something with an edge to it."

She hesitated.

"Do it, honey," beseeched Jaime, watching the pistol.

She selected an instrument from a table behind her.

"Not over the goddamn site!" barked Djell, raising a hand to forestall her throw.

Sibyl stepped behind the operating table and pitched a long-bladed scalpel to Jaime, still in its sterile package.

She pushed the throw from the shoulder, like a feathery shot-put.

It was the most girlish thing Stanley had ever seen her do.

As if divining his thought, as if she'd revealed something to him she hadn't wanted him to see, her eyes flashed him a look of pure hatred.

Stanley smiled woozily, like a drunk holding up a stop sign. At last he'd scored, he thought, a miserable little point.

A relationship was developing.

"Unwrap it. Leave it on the gurney."

Jaime did these things.

Not turning around Djell made an impatient movement. "Can we get on with this? We were making good time, there, for a while."

"Straw," said Stanley, ignoring him.

"The doctor needs me," said Jaime.

Stanley shook his head and lowered the gun barrel a point or two. "A stall like that could cost you, Jaime."

"Oh a straw. A straw, he says. Right here. I got one right here. Christ, I can't believe I forgot I had one right…" Jaime raised an edge of his surgical cap and plucked three inches of a soda straw from behind his ear. He smiled.

The straw had a red and white spiral on it, like a barber pole.

Jaime placed the straw next to the scalpel.

Stanley wagged the gun at the gurney.

"Now beat it. Back to work."

Jaime side-stepped across the room, not taking his eyes off Stanley, passing sideways around the foot of the operating table. Once there, he picked up a syringe and began to fiddle with it.

"I see goose bumps," said Stanley suddenly. "Is she cold?"

Djell abruptly raised his head and looked around. "Who?"

Jaime's eyes panicked. He set the syringe down and wrung his hands wordlessly.

"Is she?" Stanley insisted. "Speak up!"

Djell and Sibyl exchanged a furtive glance.

"She's cold," snarled Stanley.

"Another sheet," Djell ordered.

Jaime opened his mouth, closed it, looked from Djell to Stanley to Green Eyes to the anesthetized Iris, then back at Stanley. "What do you —."

"Cover her!" Stanley screamed.

Without taking his eyes off Stanley, Jaime unfolded a clean sheet from a stack on a side table and covered Iris' legs with it.

"Okay…"

Stanley nodded warily.

"Okay," Djell repeated raggedly. "The distal ureter."

"Here," said Sibyl, her gloved fingers in Iris' guts.

"Ah," Jaime smirked. Drawn in by the surgical routine he resumed his station among his equipment, on the far side of the operating table.

Stanley positioned himself between the gurney and the double doors, with the notion that if any renal clowns rushed him he'd be projected through the doors instead of pinned against the wall. Somebody among this crowd almost certainly had a gun stashed somewhere. But given the various offices of the players, it seemed most likely that such an appliance would have belonged to either Vince or Sturgeon, both of which characters lay dead on the floor, their blood descending in various rivulets along the tiles until it commingled with Iris' in a drain beneath the operating table. There was getting to be enough blood on the scene to produce an audible gurgle.

The taste in his mouth reminded Stanley of an aluminum gum wrapper, but it was the taste of blood. He knew that the more he could taste the blood the more the drugs in him were wearing off, and the more his pain and fatigue were increasing. He had launched himself on an irreversible path. Though likely to be construed as self-defense, he had killed a man. He'd lost an eye in the deal. He was in the process of stealing a kidney from the only woman who had cared about him in years. She'd even slept with him.

No matter. The illness consuming his remaining kidney would have come to haunt him much sooner than the absence of half his sight, not to mention the loss of a girlfriend. He could still watch television. He could still lift a drink with one hand and zap a commercial with the other. If he could just get that new kidney, he could live out his days in peace, high atop Hop Toy's apartment building on Brooklyn Place, with its view of the Bay Bridge and the TransAmerica Pyramid and Treasure Island and the yachts of the rich and a thousand other great and small reminders of the entrepreneurial spirit of mankind.

And Stanley, too, might retain in his sunset years his own reminder of the entrepreneurial spirit, safely tucked away below his twelfth rib, expressing nutrients out of whiskey or whatever a kidney's job was.

And Iris, being crazy enough, healed enough, disembittered enough, might be that warm someone to tongue his scar for him.

Maybe he would bring himself to do the same for her.

Maybe not.

Holding the eight ball of cocaine against the bed of the gurney with the barrel of his pistol, he cut the plastic with the scalpel. The granules spilled over the stainless steel like a miniature talus of granite chips cloaking the shoulder of a Sierra cirque. Ah. On the big screen over the bar of his mind let's scroll Stanley's special memory of The Sierra Nevada, as seen from the window of the San Francisco-to-Reno bus known as the Gambler's Special. He often wondered why he hadn't moved to Reno. Was it because of his subconscious awareness of the beauty of all those Sierra cirques he'd be living within sight of? Cirques whose beauty would ever be too great for him to readily contemplate?

Or was it because there was no wholesale grocer in Reno willing to give him a job and a truck and let him live and drink and pass out on the roof of an apartment building for free?

Hah. Ask a hard one.

Loser, Corrigan had said — shouted. Oh yeah? Well, losers sat around losing. Losers went to a shitty job every day and came home to a braying wife and scrapping children. Losers made one smart move, and then walked around for the rest of their lives letting people call them *hero*. Losers let renal bandits harvest all over them....

Losers never fought back.

It was true that Stanley had lost or pissed away everything he'd ever been interested in. Mary, for example, the girl with the gray eyes — why not bring her up again? Any loser would. Then there were the six years he'd spent wandering around Canada instead of allowing himself to be drafted. Years spent bucking hay, driving tractor, nutting calves, picking apples, wrangling. By the time those years were over he was as lean and brown and hard as a hickory ax-handle, and what little idealism he'd started them with had dried up. The Carter Amnesty had let him off that hook, allowing him to return to the States as a citizen. Too, there were the more recent years of his life he'd spent as a drunk. Throw in a couple of years as a stoned hippie, for high school, for elementary school, for the time he'd passed letting his mother nurse him a little too long before she disappeared — it added up to a life.

Sadly, this shambles was not something he wanted to give up on. Not yet.

And if he had to lose, he was going to take a few others with him. Already had done so, it would seem.

He glanced up at the tableau that faced him across the operating room. Three alive, plus Iris. Two dead. He winced. Correction: Giles made three.

The word's not in on Ted, yet.

Or Tommy Quinn.

The clip in the .45 held seven cartridges. The chambered round made eight. Three, presumably, had been expended. One in the hall, two in the operating theater — he hardly even cared. Somewhere in the room was Stanley's extra clip. Somewhere in the room, come to think of it, were Stanley's clothes.

Of course, if he found it there was the problem of getting the second clip into the handle of the pistol, which actually succeeded the problem of getting the expended clip out of it, both of which preceded that of jacking a fresh shell into the firing chamber, all to be accomplished before his adversaries could rush him and plunge scalpels deep into his functioning anatomy, about which they doubtless knew plenty, and then drag him over to the operating table and extract a hundred thousand dollars worth of revenge out of his peritoneal cavity.

Well, they all knew the kidney was no good. Maybe the liver was shot, too. What about the lungs? Spleen?

And, oh yes...

His heart.

He clutched the sheet around him.

Stanley would like to have a look inside that one himself.

Djell rooted around in Iris' guts, assisted by his beautiful, blood-spattered wife and the neurotic anesthesiologist. "Okay," he announced, leaning toward Sibyl in order to facilitate her dabbing his brow with a sponge. "Ureter dissected." He took a deep breath and exhaled loudly. He rotated his head atop his spinal column, 360 degrees one way, 360 degrees the other way. His surgical mask had a dark moustache of perspiration. "Now," he finally said, "let's reflect the fat from the lower pole."

"Wow he's reflecting fat," Jaime blurted, smiling meaninglessly at Stanley, as if unable to contain his joy at the news. His nerves seemed to be getting the better of him.

The medical team's concentration renewed, Stanley buried one end of the straw in the cocaine and the other in his right nostril. The absence of his right eye presented no difficulty to this operation. *Although it would be nice,* a little voice observed acidly, *to be able to keep one eye on those bums and another on the blow.*

For a guy who doesn't exist, thought Stanley, you're getting mighty chatty, my catbird buddy. Coke getting to you?

An inner shrug. *It's just that you're getting so lonely.*

Within minutes two stout snorts of cocaine had alleviated many of the symptoms from which Stanley was suffering. Even the rising pain in his eye socket was tempered, and his nausea subsided. Above all, he was wide awake. The light above the operating table glowed like a flying saucer.

"Ligating distal stump," Djell said, and, as Sibyl mopped his brow, Iris moaned.

Jaime, who had been nostalgically watching Stanley snort cocaine, blinked and straightened up. Now he glanced at his instruments and shot a covert look at Djell.

"Not now, for God's sakes," said Djell, without interrupting his work.

"Get it together, Jaime," growled Sibyl, handing Djell a mosquito clamp.

Jaime twisted valves, rattled tubes, looked at dials.

"No," said Sibyl. "That's the gonadal vein."

"Right," said Djell. "You sure?"

"Christ," said Jaime. "How many do you have to see?"

"Shut up," Djell snapped. "Monitor the urine or something."

"You monitor that gonadal vein, O leader, and don't worry about me. Christ. Sometimes I don't think you know proximal from distal. Christ."

"It's true," muttered Djell, "that at the moment I'm not sure which end is up."

Jaime nodded in cautious agreement.

Stanley pressed a finger against the taped side of his nose and sniffed loudly.

"You really think he's going to go through with this?" Sibyl said.

Djell was busy, but he grunted, "He's off to a good start."

"Who is this woman, anyway?" said Jaime.

"His girlfriend," said Sibyl.

"Really? If that's the case, this is a pretty extreme example of pre-spousal altruism."

"More like pre-spousal abuse," Djell nodded. "My pet," he added.

"She's dedicated," said Sibyl.

"Not like some girls," said Jaime.

"Not like *this* girl," said Sibyl.

"What, my dove?" Djell protested innocently. "You wouldn't cough up the odd organ for the love of your life?"

"No more than you'd cough up one for yours," Sibyl said coldly.

"Why, my sweet, I cough it up for you most regularly."

"Ah," cooed Jaime, "geriatric *amour.*"

"Shut up," said Djell.

"I know why she gave it up," Jaime prattled on.

"Why?" asked Sibyl.

"He's good in the sack."

"Who, him?" Sibyl laughed. "Don't make me laugh."

Stanley stared at her.

For the first time, Sibyl's eyes lacked the gleam of superiority he'd always detected in them before. A shadow had appeared in them. A tincture of uncertainty. They reflected ugliness.

"Adrenal vein, Sibyl," said Djell impatiently. "Adrenal. Heads up, please."

Sibyl handed Djell a hemostat in whose jaws was clamped a pre-threaded needle.

After a while Djell announced he was freeing the renal vein.

A little while after that, Jaime dutifully narrated that Djell had started in on the adrenal gland, dissecting it away from the upper pole of
the kidney and its attendant arterial structures, a matter of delicacy
and finesse.

Stanley helped himself to two more lines.

As he was inhaling his second line a drop of blood appeared on the
crystalline pile, fallen from the soaked gauze over his ruined eye. After
a moment he caught himself staring, as its red stain spread through the
white powder.

He jerked his head up, his hand training the pistol barrel.

Jaime was watching him, and could not suppress a grin. "Surgery is
exhausting," he suggested. "It makes you soooo sleepy…"

Stanley could barely hear him. Some kind of aortal roar had co-
opted his sense of hearing. He shook his head like a wet dog. Drops of
blood spiraled onto the metal surface of the gurney.

"Hurry the fuck up," he growled.

"Right, right," Djell said without looking up. "Hurry the surgery and
fuck it up. Surgery costs money. Everybody's in a rush. And who pays
in the end? The patient."

"Well," put in Jaime. "This isn't exactly brain surgery, here."

"Piss off, Lopez."

"No," said Jaime mildly, glancing at a tube. "Diuresis is just about
right."

"Could use an arteriogram, here," muttered Djell.

"Oh, listen to him," Jaime said, addressing Stanley. "A hundred
nephrectomies, nearly all of them illegal, and he wants lab results. Why
don't you run upstairs and get them for us?"

All of them, thought Stanley, amazed. *One hundred…?*

"In a better world," said Djell, "this wouldn't be illegal."

"No, no," said Jaime. "They'd give you a medal shaped like a
BMW."

"Turgor," said Djell.

"Looks okay to me," said Sibyl.

"Why not ask me?" Jaime whined.

"Single vein, single artery," observed Sibyl.

"Spasm subsided," said Jaime.

"We're getting there," said Djell. "Ready for perfusion?"

Jaime made motions toward a sink-like device at the foot of the table.
The machine was on casters, with cables and tubes trailing after it.

Jaime said to Stanley, who was watching him warily, "I gotta do this."
"What is it?"

"It's a perfusion machine. To keep the kidney viable. *Your* kidney."

Stanley pursed his lips vaguely. He looked like a man getting off a plane in Nome who's almost remembered he left his stove on in Tallahassee.

"Vince was in charge of it," Jaime explained sadly. "Before he...." Jaime cleared his throat. "Now I'll have to handle it."

Stanley nodded his agreement. But he was becoming seriously disoriented, now leaning over the gurney for support, using both hands to keep the pistol trained on the surgical team.

Jaime rolled the machine around the table, next to Djell.

"Heparin."

"And now...," Jaime said to Stanley.

"This shit's not working," Stanley snarled.

"Have some more already," said Jaime. "You've a lot of negativity to overcome."

"What's in this stuff?" Stanley demanded. "I'm passing out." He drew a bead on the anesthesiologist. "Fix it. Fix it or I kill everybody, starting with..." his voice faltered, "with... you."

They just waited, watching him.

Stanley side-armed the scalpel at Jaime, left-handed, with all the strength he could muster.

"Ow, *shit!*" Though it glanced harmlessly off his upper arm before he could react otherwise, Jaime screamed and spun, ducked and hugged himself as if the tool had gone right through him, before it hit the radio and clattered to the floor.

Nobody moved. Jaime half crouched behind the operating table, looking around desperately for a place to hide.

"Don't make me get violent," said Stanley. "Reverse this chemical."

"Oh, dear," whined Jaime. "Oh dear oh dear oh dear."

"Jaime," said Djell, raising an eye toward Stanley. He pointed a hip toward the anesthesiologist. "Here."

"And bring back the scalpel."

Cringing and crouching, Jaime retrieved the scalpel and scuttled around the end of the operating table, muttering to himself. "That was the right pocket. Should it have been the left? I can never remember whether it's right or left... Oh my god," he shook his head with great exaggeration, nearly weeping with hysteria. "That was the heroinnnn...."

He plunged his hand into Djell's left trouser pocket, waving the scalpel with the other, an irrational expression on his face. The surgeon winced. Stanley had the impression that Jaime had pinched him viciously. Djell twisted away, but not before Jaime had extracted a second package. It, too, looked like powdered sugar or flour, wrapped in a clear plastic cylinder about the size of a polish hot dog. If it was cocaine, it was close to an ounce of it.

"As salaam Alikum," Jaime said timorously. Lowering his head and raising the ounce with the scalpel above his head, bowing, he approached the wheeled gurney. "With all due apologies, I bring you the contents of the left, that is to say, the correct, pocket...." He glanced up. "It's a mistake we make often around here."

He was ridiculous, and he was serious. This was an apology. They'd tried to drug Stanley so they could kill him. They had drugged him. They'd almost gotten away with it.

And now this guy was sincerely apologizing to him for their failure.

Stanley struggled with his temper. And his fear. He'd never seen anybody push the edge of destruction like this. He'd never even heard of it.

Jaime gently laid the ounce with the scalpel on the gurney, stooped low to the floor, and backed all the way around the foot of the operating table to his anesthesia post.

Stanley fiercely scalpeled the baggie and dipped a moistened fingertip into its contents. Jaime watched hungrily as he cautiously scrubbed a gum with the powdered finger.

"That's the stuff, eh boss?"

"If it isn't," said Stanley, his good eyelid drooping toward his raised upper lip, "you're dead." He sounded like somebody trying to have a conversation while flossing.

Jaime nodded happily.

The drug did, indeed, seem to be the real stuff. This powder was pink, shot through with large, flat flakes, and instantly numbed his gum. A couple of two-inch lines of this stuff in his face wouldn't counteract the effects of the heroin; rather it would collaborate with it on a metabolic concerto. It would also wake him up, numb his face, make him paranoid, encourage the grinding of enamel off his molars, and, in general, affect what passes for "high" among coke snorters, a notoriously discerning race.

It was in the nick of time, too. Stanley's head was nodding like a late-

summer sunflower on its stalk, his eyes were closing, and he was ceas-
ing to care, even as he tried to speak.

"Speedball, huh," said Stanley stupidly. He awkwardly raked a couple of fat lines of the new product onto the stainless steel with the edge
of the scalpel.

"To quote the septic bard—," Jaime began.

"If I pass out," Stanley managed to interrupt, flattening the gun on
the table so that it was aimed toward Jaime, "it's going to be in an
empty room, spiritually speaking."

He lowered his face to the pile and inhaled the first line, flakes and
all, and growled aloud.

"Could it be that our fair captor's sensibilities are impaired?" Jaime
whispered loudly.

"Jaime," said Sibyl, not laughing. "That was a stupid thing to do.
Shut the fuck up."

"You sew that nice nurse up," said Stanley, looking sideways at them
with his good eye, the bandaged socket not three inches from the surface of the gurney. "Then we'll shoot it out."

The cocaine did wake him up—although, he knew, it would take
more and more, at shorter and shorter intervals, to keep him that way.

But to keep him paranoid?

No problem.

Jaime shook his head. "This is getting expensive."

"Try to save me some," Djell nodded. "I'm intrinsic to this nightmare, yet I'm fading."

Stanley came up from his second line and looked at the surgical
team, tears flooding out of his good eye. As usual, Sibyl was watching
him, as was Jaime.

And Stanley's thought was, would Green Eyes dime her own husband to save her skin?

He winked at her.

She winked back.

Stanley felt a distant uptick in penile blood flow.

And his next thought after that was, how could he have doubted her?

This is perfect, said a little voice. *First these people try to gut you, then they
try to lay you low with junk, and all you can think about is sex. Each thought is
stupider than the one that came before it.*

Jaime caught the exchange of winks. Though excitable, he didn't
miss much. But for the first time he looked truly out of sorts.

Stanley couldn't let them kill Iris. He owed her that much. For the Get-Well Bear, he forgave her. Not to mention the new kidney, if things got that far, which betokened total redemption. But after all, what did he really owe her?

No answering argument was to be found or heard; the barroom of Stanley's soul was deserted.

That's great, thought Stanley. Get a nice little psychosis going and what happens? Nobody sticks around to appreciate it.

All these thoughts paraded before Stanley as if he were their proud father, home from three years at sea.

He was entertaining the illusion of lucid thought.

Picky bastard, aren't I, thought Stanley. So I must away under steam of my own counsel. And my own counsel declares I owe Iris that much. She won't see it that way, of course. Not at first. In fact, she'll probably try to kill me. Well, at least I'll still be alive to kill. There. That makes perfect sense. I can piss her off, but if I'm dead, what good is it going to do her? Besides, if *freshness* of scar really is her thing, she is about to be in high cotton. She can lick its reflection in a mirror.

No way I'm going to lick it for her. I'm stubborn that way.

As it had healed, his nephrectomy scar had diminished in scarlingual magnetism. But perhaps the renewed sex appeal of Stanley's freshly scooped eye-socket might appease her resentment. Given that, at any moment, he was prepared to blast Green Eyes to kingdom come; and given that, basically, he was a moral relativist, mostly innocent of the baser malefactions, a victim merely trying to cope; and given that Iris herself had killed on his behalf; given these things, he could probably make do with Iris and her violet eyes, her ebony hair, her predilection for a freshly scarred loser, he meant lover, and she with him. One in a million finds one in a second million. A match made in a stochastic maelstrom. Besides, she had a job. And a car. She probably had a couple of IRAs, the 401-K, social security, good benefits…

But, he was really thinking, his mind adrift like a holed barge, if he could get Green Eyes into the sack… Just once… Maybe before Iris wakes up….

Well, if not *in the sack*, maybe *on the gurney*….

Green Eyes, whom he hadn't *had*.

Who *owed him big*…

The doctor's wife. The wife of the man who'd stolen his kidney, to insult him by thus taking his wife, right in front of him, would be a greater revenge than Stanley had dared hope.

Those eyes.

Watching me. Always watching me.

He looked at the two piles of drugs.

There might be enough stuff here to get them all through it.

"Elevating…," Djell announced.

"The man is an artist," said Jaime. "A fucking artist."

"Clamp the renal, Sibyl."

"Clamping…"

"Okay. Jaime…"

Jaime darted back around the table to close the circle of endeavor around Iris' nephrectomy. The organ made little kissing sounds as it left the only home it had ever known. And before Stanley knew it, the kidney had been lifted like a Eucharist, gleaming, rust-colored, dripping, trailing *spaghettini*, and lovingly deposited into the machine to experience the joys of chilled perfusion by a heparinized electrolyte solution.

The surgical team heaved a collective sigh of relief.

"Okay, Green Eyes," Stanley said. "Come here."

Chapter 28

"Wait wait wait a minute," said Djell, flinging a forceps into a steel pan with a clatter. "Not her. Not my wife. She's got nothing to do with—"

"Shut up, mister," said Stanley. "I'm going to make you a deal so slick you could lubricate trains with it. Close up Ms. Considine's wound, there, and send your wife over here."

Nobody moved.

"Aw, shit," said Stanley raggedly, and sent a round straight through the package of drugs on the table in front of him.

The detonation was tremendous. The gurney rang like the first bell of a prize-fight and jumped a foot into the room as if jerked by a rope. Where the bullet went was anybody's guess, but it left a puckered hole in the stainless steel big enough to stick your thumb through. The air above it swirled with narcotic dust.

"She's coming, SHE'S COMING," squealed Jaime, looking out from beneath his arms, with which he'd covered his head. "She has to be going, Manny. SEND THE WOMAN OVER THERE. She's coming, buddy," he said, abruptly calm, to Stanley. "Take it easy with that thing. And for God's sakes, stop wasting the drugs." He drew himself up, paused, then exhaled loudly. "You know, I'm awfully tired. Manny's been working us like a MASH unit. And, really, in order to anesthetize at peak efficiency, I could use a blast of that blow, there, that you have been shooting at. You know? Please? Willya?"

"Bring her over here. Close the wound, clown, or your wife gets the next round."

"Closing, closing," said Djell, hastily pulling his mask back over his mouth. He traded a worried glance with his wife, and shook his head, no. She shrugged and, rolling a table full of surgical tools within easy reach of her husband, removed her own mask and approached Stanley.

"Bring along that roll of tape," he said to Jaime. He shifted the gun to Sibyl. "That's far enough."

Green Eyes was now three feet away from him, just on the other side of the gurney, the closest she'd been to him since the night they'd first met. Or, more properly, the night he'd been *selected.*

He could feel the pull of her, the magnetism of her physical presence, the heat of her, a spiraling vortex spinning so fast as to present the illusion of stillness and tranquility, of no motion whatsoever; yet she captured everything that came within her influence. Men, in particular, sank helplessly into her gravity, only to disappear into her brand of casualty management forever. It actually looked inviting.

She knew it, and stared at him accordingly. If she'd been a spider with eight eyes she couldn't have stared harder. Or more insidiously. Or more patiently.

"I had a puppy, once," she suddenly said.

Stanley winced as if he'd touched an electric fence. "What—?" He sighted the gun on Jaime, a step behind Green Eyes and to her left. Jaime said nothing, unexpectedly calm. He sighted in back on her. "You talking to me?"

"It was speckled, tan on brown, and it had little white feet, like sneakers. It was really a she. I called her Gabby because she liked to yap a lot. You know how puppies do. Yap yap, yap! All the time. Especially when she was alone. What is the sound of one puppy yapping? I'll tell you. It's your neighbor dialing the SPCA. The SPCA called me and said that if I didn't put a lid on that puppy they'd take her away from me. Take Gabby away from me! I said yes ma'am, I'd get right on it. I told Manny. That neighbor regretted that phone call, all right.

"I forget her blood type. The new one wasn't half bad. New neighbor, I mean. Said she loved puppies, especially since the grenade went off in her hand in front of a Bank of America in Santa Barbara in 1970 and made her deaf. Gabby yapping, she signed to me with her stump, *no hay problema.* So Gabby did fine with that neighbor. She and the neighbor used to hunt mice by feeling for vibrations in the walls. Caught plenty of them, too. Of course, you can't catch all the mice. Experiments have shown, it's impossible. There're always more mice. But after a while they get to know where the black holes are, mouse-wise, and avoid them. Unless you put out lots of birthday cake for them that is. Then the mouse authority sends one in, just for a test. May Jaime and I have some of that blow?"

Stanley had backed up a foot until he stood against the astragal of the double doors, the big pistol still hot from its recent statement held in both his hands and aimed right between beautiful green-eyed Sibyl's breasts.

"All work and no blow," Jaime pled, "make surgery a dull course."

"Sure," Stanley said quietly. "Have some blow."

Jaime fell to manipulating cocaine while Sibyl watched and narrated.

"So one day while she was eating her very first birthday cake with a single puppy-proof candle you buy them you know in any pet store they light but run on cold fusion or something so the puppy can't burn itself, little Gabby gets kind of sick. We thought it was from eating too much birthday cake and maybe from hyperventilating to blow out the candle — not Gabby hyperventilating but Manny hyperventilating and when he couldn't blow it out I was hyperventilating and then it turned out there was this tiny slotted rheostat on the bottom of the candle we hadn't noticed you could adjust it with a little screwdriver comes with every box, adjust its ability to be blown out, from it would hardly stay lit to you couldn't blow it out, but anyway by the time we got that snag worked out the puppy was going round and around, but we thought it was because she'd been hyperventilating so hard, see."

Jaime, having laid out six large lines, kneeled beside the gurney and rhinospirated two of them. Squinting violently, he angled the straw toward Sibyl without lifting it off the table. She leaned over it, apply-ing the upper end to one nostril, daintily closing the other nostril with the forefinger of her free hand. As in, how do *you* do cocaine, Stanley? Well, Stanley thought to himself, one difference is I don't show so much cleavage when I wear my little nursey uniform.

This maneuver put her head inches from the barrel of Stanley's gun, which followed her head as it dipped, inhaled, raised while she changed nostrils, dipped and inhaled again.

"So finally," she said, "whew, I needed that, so finally — hey Manny, there's a brace for you, too."

"In a minute," snapped Djell, obviously ill-tempered.

"Manny's hurtin'!" Jaime jerked a thumb toward the pile of corpses against the wall and explained, "Vince was almost shaped up to close wounds unsupervised."

"I can see what a loss that must be," Stanley said, not deviating the pistol muzzle so much as a millimeter from the center of Sibyl's chest.

"After wobbling around all over the house and really freaking out the new neighbor who couldn't even hear how the poor thing was whimpering and had the hiccups and all, poor Gabby just keeled over, you know? Dead as pressed flowers. I couldn't believe it. I cried and cried. Manny, though, he scooped her up and swept her down to his little hobby operating theater we used to have in the basement when we lived out in Piedmont on Hillside — "

"Placita," Jaime corrected her.

She frowned. "Hillside."

"Placita."

"Hillside."

"Maaaan-neee."

"Placita, I'm telling you. Why drag him into this? It was Placita I know because it was right up above that hot tub place where you and I used to go to, uh, relax."

Stanley blinked at Jaime. Was he serious?

"Okay, Placita. You're right. Manny took the dear poor little thing downstairs and put her on oxygen and that didn't work so he pounded on her little heart with a suction-cup dart from his dart gun like a miniature toilet plunger it was brilliant but it didn't work and he began to relish this I could see it but I was just hysterical until finally Manny tore the cord out of his favorite soldering iron. He quickly stripped an inch of insulation off the two conductors at one end and plugged the other end into the wall and *zap-zapped* little Gabby's heart no bigger than a plum as it momentarily turned out, he flattened the stranded copper against her little chest and — *yipe* — she yiped just like she always did, once for each jolt — *yipe yipe....*"

Just breathe from the diaphragm, Stanley told himself, *and you might not panic or throw up...*

"I mean it was just so life-like," Sibyl continued unabated. "But all it really meant was that her little puppy spirit was going backwards, of course, regressing through yaps to yips to whimpers. Manny persisted with his last-ditch Hippocratic electrical-cord thing until the air in the basement smelled like fritters, but until it was obvious there was no jump-starting that little Gabby's puppy heart."

Jaime held up a single finger. "They opted for electricity when they should have tried adrenaline. C-nine, H-thirteen, N-one, O-three: nothing like it. Adrenaline initiates many bodily responses, including most relevantly the stimulation of heart action as well as an increase in blood pressure, metabolic rate, and blood glucose concentration." He lowered his voice and rubbed his hands together. "Adrenaline has been known to save puppy-butt under very extreme circumstances."

"That puppy had plenty of adrenaline in its system from trying to blow out that joke-shop candle," said Djell querulously, raising a threaded needle high over the wound to snug a suture. "The very idea of that bungled triage with you in charge makes me stitch crooked."

"It was no use," Sibyl continued determinedly. "In the end, just at the threshold between this world and the next, she was just squeaking."

"Like a little rubber toy," said Jaime sadly. He emitted several toy-like squeaks. "Like one of those latex carrots you see zealous Weimaraners named Rilke trying to bury at the beach, too deep for their childless Yuppie surrogate parents to retrieve and make them fetch again."

Sibyl looked thoughtful. "Wasn't Gabby a Weimaraner?"

"No *way*," squeaked Jaime. "She was a Jack Russell Terrier."

"Impossible," said Djell, raising the needle shoulder high and snugging its thread. "Their hearts are smaller than their brains, which are smaller than plums."

"Anyway," said Jaime, "I want a kelpie next time."

"Well, of course," Sibyl shrugged, "it was hard to tell what Gabby had been, because Manny went right ahead with the autopsy. And you know what he found?"

Stanley by now had sagged against the doorjamb, more or less terrified. The gun muzzle was trying to keep up with his eye as it jumped from Sibyl to Jaime and back again.

Jaime and Sibyl knew this.

"Well?" said Jaime finally, turning to Sibyl, "What did he find?"

"A single kidney," Sibyl said, narrowing her green eyes at Stanley.

Jaime turned back to Stanley. "The little dear had come and gone through this veil of tears with but a single, forlorn kidney."

Sibyl allowed a smile to creep across her mouth, transforming the child-like ingenuousness of her narration into a maleficent leer of evil triumph. "The pathology of a single kidney," she cooed, "made all the difference when she was eating birthday cake. Mice? Mice were okay. But birthday cake?" She shook her head. Jaime nodded. "Nope. Cake bad. Mice okay." Jaime shook his head. "Cake bad," Sibyl repeated. Jaime nodded.

They looked at Stanley.

Stanley looked at them.

"You should watch out for sweets," Sibyl added softly.

Djell's pliers slipped from his hand. They landed with a soft thump on Iris' hip, and he cursed under his breath.

The hidden refrigeration, having stopped unnoticed, now started again, momentarily dimming the light over the operating table.

Somewhere something dripped.

Jaime closed one nostril with the side of a forefinger and snorted hard.

Sweat and droplets of blood made their ways, separate and commingled, over Stanley's right cheek.

"Djell," he said, watching Sibyl. "You finished?"

"Just adding the aster," said Djell, retrieving the pliers.

Stanley's mouth distorted into a figure eight and his upper lip twitched. He motioned to Sibyl with the pistol. "I like this devil-may-care mood we're in," he said through clenched teeth. "Open your mouth."

She parted her lips in surprise, then closed them.

"Wider."

The lips parted again. Her eyes had been taunting him, but now uncertainty crept in.

"Let's see those fillings."

She lowered her head a little, keeping him fixed with her green eyes, and let him see her fillings.

He placed one hand on the back of her head and neatly, uninterrupted, inserted one inch of gun muzzle into her mouth.

She jerked, but Stanley clasped her hair and held firm.

He was touching her for the second time ever.

"Careful," he said gently. "This thing is loaded."

Sibyl, of the green eyes, was almost up to the challenge.

Never taking her eyes off him, she pursed her lips around the gun muzzle and moved them, ever so slightly, out, in, out...

For the first time in almost two months, Stanley smiled.

Death and lust had haunted him. Now their synthesis lay between the palms of his hands, and he drew strength from it.

She sensed this. Her eyes rounded. For the first time Stanley thought he saw something like fear in them. Marginal and mitigated by contempt, but it was fear nonetheless.

"Tape it there," he said to the eyes.

"What?" said Jaime, startled.

"What?" said Djell, looking over his shoulder.

"You heard me, Jaime. Tape the gun to her head, and tape my wrist to the gun. Stay where you are, Djell, or your wife's brains will be all over your back."

Stanley shot a glance at Jaime. "Well? You deaf? Like that neighbor?"

"Wh-who m-me? Deaf? N-not at all. I…"

"Quit fucking around and get on with it then."

"See here," said Djell, with a clatter of instruments and a panic in his voice.

"At ease, Djell. Finish your job. Jaime?"

Jaime retrieved the roll of gray duct tape and peeled off a length.

"Longer," said Stanley.

Jaime made it longer.

"Good."

Jaime tore it off. Then he made little ineffectual gestures, as if to put the tape one place, as if to put it another, as if he just weren't sure of anything at all.

"Start with the middle of it, on the nape of her neck, below my hand," advised Stanley. "Cross it under her chin, and complete the loop over my thumb, above the pistol grip." As Jaime followed his instructions Stanley removed his hand from the back of Sibyl's head. "Now my wrist — not the slide! That's right. A figure eight, see? Good. Wrap the slack around the wrist. Now around the other side. Good. Leave the thumb. Back to Sibyl, except you want to go along the cheek. Good boy…"

In just a couple of minutes, Jaime had expertly secured the business end of a cocked .45 automatic to the kisser of the most beautiful woman Stanley had ever been close to.

And to think it was Stanley's .45.

"Now," Stanley said huskily. "This isn't half bad, is it?"

Sibyl made a little sound in her throat.

"You should be able to breathe through it," he said paternally, "like a straw. Might taste of gun oil and burnt powder. But it's not air-tight until it's discharged and the cartridge expands, after which it won't matter. Try it."

She tried it.

"It works, doesn't it?"

She frowned.

"Okay, Jaime. Now take one last wrap around my lower three fingers and the grip, there. Careful now, this thing has a hair trigger. Be delicate."

Jaime pulled another length of tape off the roll and held it to the work.

Stanley and Sibyl could see how Jaime's hands were shaking.

Sibyl made a noise in her throat.

Stanley smiled. "Maybe this calls for the hands of a surgeon?"

Djell could see, from ten feet away, how badly Jaime's hands were shaking. "Wait!" he said.

"How about the patient?" Stanley said.

"She'll be fine," Djell said irritably.

"We'll wait," Stanley said.

Djell peeled off his mask and hustled over, from one crime scene to another. He started to take the roll of tape and the end of the strip Jaime had peeled off it but still had his surgical gloves on, which were streaked with gore. He swore an oath to Wotan and quickly shucked them off, muttering, "Wait, wait…," as he threw them to the floor and relieved Jaime of the tape.

"Gently," Stanley reminded him. "Gently…"

Djell carefully laid the tape's adhesive side against the pedestal of Stanley's thumb, gingerly touching it into place. He wound the length of it around the knuckles of Stanley's pinky, ring and middle fingers, below the trigger guard, and thence over the back of the hand until the tape lapped its beginning, below Stanley's thumb and the pistol's hammer.

They could all hear each other breathing. It was louder than the regular breathing of the anesthetized Iris, louder than the unseen compressor motor or the unseen drip, louder than the dead air coming through the speakers of the silent boom-box.

Djell cautiously touched the tape here and there, until its entire surface adhered to whatever was beneath it.

"Real craftsmanship," Stanley said.

Balls of sweat were rolling over Djell's forehead into his eyes, and coursing below his temples. The surgical mask clenched between his chin and collar was dark with sweat. Jaime made inadvertent little squeaks, like a cage full of restive finches. Sibyl waited silently, never taking her eyes off Stanley.

"That looks very good," Stanley said. He picked up the cocaine scalpel with his free hand. "Now here's the deal."

They all looked at him.

"First, two good, fat lines of cocaine, so I stay awake. Put them on something I can snort off while standing up. Your hand shaking too much for that, Jaime?"

Jaime looked one way, and another. Then he hurried across the room and returned with a CD box. He held it up for Stanley's approval. The glossy square of plastic quivered in Jaime's shaking hand. A shard of light played off it onto the ceiling.

"Perfect, Jaime. Ingenious. Your hands always shake like that?"

Jaime looked at his hands and nodded. "Washed me out of surgical college. But one thing they're good for...." He indicated the scalpel. Stanley shook his head. "Get another one."

Jaime quickly did so, and fell to dicing lines of cocaine.

"You got the picture, Doc?" said Stanley.

Green Eyes, unable to look directly at her husband, raised her eyebrows interrogatively.

"I see a man taking unfair advantage of my wife," Djell muttered sententiously, a tremor in his upper lip.

"I believe you do," Stanley said. "You love her, of course."

Djell nodded impatiently.

"Which makes this a perfect setup."

Djell stopped nodding. "Why?"

"Because, as of now, I don't care what happens," Stanley said. "After Iris, what I've done to Iris, I got nothing more to lose. Whatever I had going when I came in here has changed forever. It's gone. You, Doctor, on the other hand," he indicated Green Eyes and the gun, "as of now, you have everything at stake."

Using his gun hand, he pulled Sibyl's head towards him, and pushed it away; towards him and away, towards him and away; a rocking motion. She moved with it like a good dance partner.

Djell went as pale as his wife's skirt. "Stop that."

"Do you, Djell? Have a lot to lose, I mean?"

"Please," Djell managed to say. "Yes..."

"Please?"

"Don't do that."

"Don't do what?" Stanley said, stopping. He looked at Sibyl, looked at Djell, then started to rock her head with the gun arm again. "You mean this?"

"No!" Djell hissed. "Please..."

"Okay." Stanley stopped. "Back up a couple of feet."

Djell did so.

"First, make a bed for Iris. Out of the way, but close enough so Jaime can monitor her condition. Then, put this gurney —" He brought his knee up against the underside of the gurney, still parked between himself and everyone else. The gurney jumped with a loud bang. Everyone else jumped, too. "Whoa. Don't be jumping around like that, Sibyl. You damn near pulled the trigger on yourself."

"Please!" Djell begged. "Please...."

"Shut up, and roll this gurney to the far side of the operating table, parallel to it. Maybe clean the dope off it first."

Djell nodded stupidly.

"Now, Jaime, you're going to have to keep a close eye on Iris over there, you hear? She's made a tremendous sacrifice and we don't want anything else to happen to her, do we?"

"Y-y-y..."

"Do we?"

"N-n-n..."

"I'll take that as an affirmative, Jaime. Can I take that as an affirmative?"

"Y-y-y..."

"You through chopping on that stuff?"

Jaime dropped the scalpel as if it were red hot and held the CD aloft.

"Okay. A couple more steps back, Doc. Don't want any accidents. Arm's length please, Jaime. Pretend you're lighting a firecracker with a short fuse. That's the stuff."

Jaime placed the straw parallel to the scalpel in Stanley's free hand, and backed away as far as he could, holding the CD box under Stanley's nose at arm's length. Stanley inhaled two arctic caterpillars of cocaine, one in each nostril. Within seconds he began to feel the first intimations of a powerful jolt to his metabolism, and seconds after that, the throbbing in his right eye socket began to diminish, like the bass beat in a passing automobile.

"Damn, Doc," he said. He dropped the straw onto the gurney and scrubbed his face with his free hand. "You're going to have to give me your connection's phone number when this is all over." He grinned stupidly. "I'm not going to pass out for a while, now, am I?"

The truth was, Stanley was now stoned enough to think he felt fine about every wonderful little thing.

Djell stood stock still, as rigid as a statue to Hippocrates in a burning hospital.

Stanley cocked his good eye and called Jaime. Jaime nodded his head like a wind-driven yard widget.

"After you move Iris and make her real comfortable, you prepare whatever you need to administer a local anesthetic to my T-6 vertebrae. My current reading informs me that a local to the T-6 will probably do the trick. Like I'm having a baby and the labor's gone on too long. Do you agree?"

The lure of territory at last familiar to Jaime damped the nodding of his head, until it almost stopped.

"I might experience a little discomfort. But the trick is, see," Stanley explained patiently, "the trick is, I've got to stay conscious the whole time. Understand? Because if I pass out or fall asleep or lose consciousness, well…" He jerked his bandaged eye at Sibyl.

A drop of his blood fell on the gurney between them.

Sibyl's eyes got large and rolled toward Jaime.

"Well. It's very damn reasonable to conclude that if I lose consciousness — or even my concentration — this cannon will go off in Sibyl's mouth. Highly probable. It's practically as certain as a law of physics. Got that Jaime? Sibyl? Doc? Everybody agreed on that?"

Nobody said a word.

"Just breathe through the barrel, honey," said Stanley. "And everything's going to be all right. You don't mind if I call you honey? Answer me."

Sibyl hummed into the gun barrel.

"That's the stuff. Okay. Now. Everybody understand what's going on? If I lose consciousness, Sibyl gets killed. It'll be a mess, too, for Dr. Djell most of all. It's true your personal life will be negatively impacted, Dr. Djell: but think of your business. Where would you and Jaime be without Sibyl? It's going to be hard enough to pick up the pieces without good old Vince and good old what's his name, Sturgeon, there." Stanley moved his chin toward the carnage beyond the foot of the operating table. "But Sibyl's irreplaceable."

Djell regarded his wife sadly. Jaime sighed loudly.

"So we're agreed on that? Sibyl's irreplaceable? Jaime?"

Jaime nodded.

"Can't hear you, Jaime."

"Sibyl's... irreplaceable."

"Doc?"

Djell nodded.

"Can't hear you, Dr. Djell."

"My wife is —."

"My wife Sibyl."

"My wife, Sibyl, is irreplaceable."

As Djell spoke Jaime moved his lips, like a furtive Catholic trying to blend into an Episcopal antiphon.

Stanley sighed loudly. "We have a consensus. That's a load off my mind. If not, we'd have to take a whole different approach to this situation."

Nobody spoke.

"Sibyl lies on the gurney, parallel to the operating table, with this gun grafted to her mouth. A little tricky to set up, but I'm confident we'll get through it. I receive my local anesthetic, and plenty of blow to keep me awake. That's straightforward. And while all this is going on..." Stanley cocked his good eye at Djell. Jaime and Sibyl looked at him, too.

"...when everything's in place," Stanley continued calmly, "Doctor Djell installs my brand new kidney..."

"Shit," breathed Jaime.

"...the one kindly donated by Iris, over there..."

Djell blinked rapidly, then squeezed his eyes shut and violently reopened them, as if he had seen a mirage.

"...right back in the slot you took my old one out of."

Sibyl's eyes, so penetrating before, so alert, so bold, now dimmed and went introspective, focusing on some point between the tip of her nose and the hammer on the .45—infinity, perhaps?

"In exchange," Stanley concluded, "for a job well done — that is to say, a job performed with absolutely no fuckups — you three will be free to walk out of here. I promise you a head start and, so, that much of a chance to disappear forever. Which you would be well-advised to do, because, as it stands, no matter what happens, there's no way the cops aren't going to find out about this place."

Stanley tried to smile, but the right side of his face was numb. The smile came out looking like half a knocked-down figure eight; half of infinity.

"You're mad," Djell whispered. "Completely mad."

"Yep," Stanley agreed. "I'm pissed, too."

Chapter 29

Djell and Jaime parked the gurney parallel to the operating table and then, at long last, Sibyl and Stanley lay down together.

Sibyl lay on her right side, on her gurney, and Stanley on his left side, on his operating table. They faced each other like lovers who'd pushed their twin beds together in a cheap motel room.

Djell and Jaime passed long strips of tape over Sibyl's ankles, her feet, her thighs, the trunk of her body, each beneath the gurney and back again. Stanley, too, was taped into place, with a couple of plastic sandbags braced against him to prevent his weight shifting during the operation. Two sandbags were carefully stacked under the elbow of his gun arm, to relieve the joint of its weight.

Stanley was still naked. He had been naked for some time, and might have caught the sniffles by now if it weren't for the large amount of narcotics he'd ingested, which made the blood hum beneath his skin like a dynamo pulsing electricity through the hull of a sinking ocean liner. Once Stanley was affixed to the table, Jaime thoughtfully covered his legs with a doubled clean sheet. Djell turned a crank below the table to elevate Stanley's right hip. Raised by the upholstered support, Stanley's nephrectomy scar, still not entirely healed, was plainly visible.

Jaime recommended a small intramuscular dose of Valium to both Stanley and Sibyl, to allow them to relax a little. Stanley permitted Sibyl to receive one, but balked at one for himself.

Having already silently promised to reserve Wednesday and Sunday mornings to attend Mass fingering his dead mother's rosary forever if the good Lord got him out of this one, Jaime smiled coyly.

"Aw," he said. "Trust me."

Stanley snarled.

Jaime wagged an admonishing finger. "Valium is a trade name for a generic tranquilizer called diazepam. C-16, H-13, C-1, I-1, N-2, O-1, give or take a little petroleum. It's often used as a sedative, but also in anticipation of the anxiety and tension contiguous with surgery. Not to mention, this was your idea." He held up a hand. "Bear with me, please. Valium is also a muscle relaxant and anticonvulsant. You hear what I'm saying? You have any idea what muscle convulsions might do to, say, the gonadal artery at the wrong moment, not to mention your trigger finger?" He shook his head, made little clucking noises, and clasped his palms together. "It's really tight in the abdominal cavity. God's own menudo, each and every ingredient in its appointed place. Very purposeful. Very ergonomic. Nothing is wasted. Manny is a good doctor, and I'm no slouch either. But you need to be slightly tranquilized." He upended the palms of his hands, "Try to help us out every chance you get."

"I'm not here to help," said Stanley. "I'm here to motivate."

"An interesting distinction, and I take your point. Still," Jaime cajoled, "have a dose. It can't hurt. It's not a sedative." He indicated Sibyl, whom he'd already injected. "You see how she's reacted."

Green eyes, wide open and staring at him.

Jaime held up the serum bottle and syringe. "Same supply hers came from, plus a clean needle. What service, huh?" The needle penetrated the pink rubber top of the jar with a squeak. He held the syringe to the light and watched the fluid descend its gradations. "Observe: about twice Sibyl's dose. A little Valium never put anybody asleep. With all that coke in you, you'll never know the difference. You probably already hear elevator music, and, sorry to disappoint you, but that's about it for special effects. Your surgeon here however will notice benedictions in your body. No spasms in delicate locations, for instance. I am your anesthesiologist. Trust me."

Did he really say that? Again?

Jaime sighed. "A shame to waste it." By way of a smile he showed some teeth. "Well?"

Stanley rolled his eyes toward Djell. "Let's leave it up to the guy with the vested interest."

Djell was breathing heavily. Mastermind and surgeon, never had control so thoroughly eluded him. Whereas he would have liked to disassemble Stanley organ by organ without benefit of anesthetic, the gun taped in his wife's mouth tempered Djell's enthusiasm for vengeance. Just barely.

"Fifteen milligrams will do," said Djell. "As Jaime says, Mr. — Mr. —."

"Ahearn. You guys never remember your patients, do you?"

"Just the ones who don't pay their bills. As Jaime points out, it's a mild dose. Even so, it will relax you. Muscular and vascular spasm will be minimized, making my job easier. You might have noticed as we operated on — on…" Djell cleared his throat.

They all looked at Iris.

"I never got her name, either," Djell admitted.

She was lying peacefully against the wall on a pile of quilted mover's blankets, as if asleep. The blankets happened to be cornflower blue, Iris' favorite color. Tubes connected her to two bags of fluids tacked to the wall. Her jet black hair covered half her face. Her shoulder rose and fell steadily with her anesthetized breathing. A huge wad of gauze soaked in rust-colored betadyne was taped above her upturned hip.

"Considine," said Stanley. "Iris Considine."

"She gave her all," observed Jaime.

"Yes," said Stanley. "She'll want to be discussing that." He leveled his eyes at Jaime. "Let's not disappoint her."

Djell got on with it. "You might have noticed that we occasionally paused the earlier procedure in order to allow spasms to pass. These spasms are caused by trauma to vital mechanisms. Drugs, including Valium, can alleviate only some of this trauma. We also administer anti-immune agents as well as antibiotics and a half-liter or so of blood."

Jaime smirked. "Type O-Negative, I believe?"

Stanley scowled. Jaime glanced away.

Djell spoke automatically. If it was a speech he had given a thousand times Stanley couldn't imagine when or to whom, but he had a list of at least ten people Djell hadn't bothered to lecture on the finer points of nephrectomy.

"You've got at least as much at stake as I do, Djell."

Djell nodded grimly.

"So let's do it your way."

"Excellent," said Jaime. He dabbed an alcohol swab at the inside of the elbow on Stanley's gun arm.

"Lopez!" said Djell sharply. "Don't act crazy. Not now."

"Who, me?" said Jaime, looking up.

Djell closed his eyes. "I think," he said quietly, "you can find a better site for the injection."

Jaime looked at the inside of Stanley's elbow, where he was swabbing. Then his eye followed the forearm to his bracelet of tape, the checkered butt of the pistol, the two little powder burns that fanned away from the back corners of the breech, the serial number filed off the slide, the blistered bluing of the barrel where it entered Sibyl's mouth, the yoke of duct tape, her wide open green eyes above.

Even the cool Sibyl, now, had begun to sweat. A fine dew of perspiration spread evenly over her forehead like condensation on an untouched glass of beer.

Sure Sibyl was sweating, thought Stanley. It was unavoidable. It would be one thing to watch Jaime and Djell cut up lonesome drunks. But now her two clowns were about to effectively, if vicariously, cut on her. Whatever happened to Stanley in this surgery would be, as it were, automatically transferred to Sibyl.

What Djell had done to Ahearn and nearly a dozen others, he was more or less about to do to his own wife. She and Stanley had something besides mere larceny in common at last.

Along with the gun. They had the gun in common.

Intimately connected. At last.

They shared a third thing, too.

Sibyl and Stanley were going to live separately, or die together.

This was way beyond mere sex.

And yet, Stanley thought, lying there facing her, it was a lot like sex.

Her sinuses packed by cocaine, Sibyl sighed raggedly through the gun barrel—the straw connecting her lungs to the outside world—and closed her eyes.

Sleep, partner, Stanley caught himself thinking. Sleep while I keep watch over you, and maybe catch a late flick on TV…

Jaime found a vein behind Stanley's knee and injected the Valium. Then he touched a place on Stanley's back. "First," he squeaked, "a local anesthetic. Subcutaneous. Little pinch."

Stanley felt a little pinch, as the needle slid under his skin.

"Couple minutes to let that take effect." Jaime withdrew the needle and swabbed the site.

Djell studied the dials on the portable perfusion machine, which was

labeled as a Nephrolander FX. He and Jaime exchanged some techni-
cal information concerning temperature, procaine and heparin ratios,
effluent clarity, titration, potassium radicals and so on, and made a few
adjustments. Once satisfied, Djell went to the wall-mounted sink and
began to scrub.

Stanley said nothing, but sweat was pouring through the pores of his
gun hand like water through a saturated earthen dam. Sibyl had
opened her eyes and begun to study him. He studied her, too. For the
first time he noticed that her eyebrows were plucked. The right one, the
downside one, concealed a small mole. His eye darted to her hairline.
Sure enough, about a quarter inch behind her hairline another mole
was visible, a fraction larger than the one in her eyebrow, but still quite
small. Both were a flat umber, raised almost imperceptibly above the
skin. He'd often noticed that moles and other beauty marks would
favor one side of the body over the other. He thought of it as one of
the odd characteristics that went along with the dichotomy between
symmetry and asymmetry in the human body. Whereas lungs, kidneys,
ovaries, not to mention ears, legs and eyes, occurred in symmetric pairs
in the human animal, other parts, like the heart and appendix,
occurred asymmetrically. He imagined that moles might occur on
Sibyl's right side only; on the hollow between the Achilles tendon and
the ankle, in the hollow behind the knee, in the hollow at the top of the
inside of her thigh, hard by the perineum. One, perhaps, would occur
on the small of her back, alongside the base of the spine.

He wondered if Djell had kissed them all, if that were a routine of
their conjugal act. Or, if not Djell, then some attentive lover, present or
past. He wondered if, by some mistake, Vince and Sturgeon had ever
missed their rendezvous with Sibyl— or if, say, the chloral hydrate had-
n't taken effect soon enough, or not at all, or if, perhaps, the intended victim had been more aggressive than most—whether she'd been forced to
follow through with the sexual charade, to go all the way with her victim,
and whether, in the course of this mistake, the drunken, lucky, doomed
fool might have managed to brush with his lips or touch with the tip of
his tongue so much as a single one of these delicate birthmarks.

It seemed to Stanley that he was witnessing in Sibyl's eyes a little
struggle between her distaste for him and her instinct for survival.
Something there was, no doubt, about the psychology of victimhood
that attracted Sibyl to her prey as surely as the smell of mice attracts a
cat.

It was a *natural* thing, as natural as yellow jackets using cement slurry to build a bullet-proof nest.

Stanley could see it in her eyes. Even now, completely at his mercy, she projected her need upon him like a picture upon a screen.

It wasn't a need for him, specifically. It was her need to survive—for which the first synonym, in her thesaurus, would be to *win*.

If sex was involved in the winning, well...

Sex was just a tool, like a row of tanks.

Surprise?

What did Stanley think sex was? Communication? *Special?*

He could feel the pull of her. Worse, he began to feel something inside himself, some force he'd never realized or even acknowledged, as it stirred, rummaging among the empty cells of Stanley's monastery, looking for something.

Something to *give* to Sibyl.

A token of his... dedication.

This realization horrified him. Something somewhere inside him not only had learned absolutely nothing, but did not care. Something inside him yearned to yield to this woman, to this force in the guise of a woman, to hand over whatever it was she wanted. It didn't even care what she wanted. It just wanted to give it to her.

It was a sensation almost like... trust. Blind trust.

The realization filled him with loathing and revulsion and hatred—for himself at least as much as for Sibyl—and brought him as close as he'd yet come to pulling the trigger. He even pressed it sideways a little. If it went off, well....

And then another layer of reality peeled away. It was like a wind lifting the tin roof off a house in silence, leaving the contents exposed within. Then the upper story is blown away, exposing the first floor. And finally the first floor too is gone, leaving the single resident in the roofless basement, cowering behind the water heater, barefoot. Naked. All protection, possession, comfort, concealment—gone.

But Stanley had another creature left in his basement.

Stanley wanted to live.

So this, finally, was what he and Sibyl had in common.

And, likewise, this is what made them irrevocably, mutually exclusive.

For in order for one to live, the other would have to die.

He heard the whisper of the sheets drawn aside. "I'm inserting a catheter, Mr. Ahearn," said Jaime soothingly, at work behind him, "in the back of your knee. You didn't even feel the Valium injection — did you? This will be your first IV, which you will hardly feel either. It will administer antibiotics and anti-immune products. Soon after I will administer amethocaine, the local anesthetic, a distant cousin to the one you now have in your maxillary sinuses, at the T-6 vertebra, just above your tailbone, also by stationary catheter. This will anesthetize most nerves within the trunk of your body from your knees, more or less, to your heart. Kind of like you're having a baby."

"I must caution you, sir," added Djell, who had appeared behind his wife, "that while you will be conscious during the installation of your new organ, the least movement could be disastrous."

Stanley watched the green eyes.

Djell gingerly put a hand on his wife's shoulder. "*Coraggio*, my sweet."

"Mustn't get touchy so early in the game," said Jaime. "Or, *finito es el partido*, as we say at the country club."

"Endgame?" Djell sighed raggedly. "It must be five o'clock in the morning."

Jaime shrugged and held up a latex glove. "So? We going somewhere?"

"No," Djell lamented, pushing his hand into the glove. "I'd just like to get some rest. I'd like to go home. I'd like to get my wife back. I'd like to be *normal* again."

"Come off it," said Jaime, holding up the second glove. "Take a look at the floor."

"Vince." Djell filled the second glove. "I'm going to miss that guy."

"You and me both," said Jaime. "Nobody in this outfit had his experience."

"Not to mention his failure rate."

"We're closing fast," said Jaime darkly.

"Fucking don't talk like that," shouted Djell suddenly. "You talk like you're trying to jinx us."

"Who?" said Jaime, professing amazement. He clasped his hands to his chest. "Me? Jinx this operation? What you want me to do, burn chicken feathers or something? You think I don't think there's enough dead people laying around here tonight?"

"Reminds me," said Djell, thoughtfully eying the two corpses piled along the wall, their feet at the head of the peacefully dozing Iris. "We oughta harvest them puppies."

Jaime closed his eyes and sighed loudly. "I'm gonna start a union."

"Can you think of something *better* to—."

"First things first," said Stanley drowsily. "Get on with it. Which reminds me, how long until Iris wakes up?"

Jaime shot a cuff and checked his watch. "An hour or two, I'd say."

"Can you local her like you did me?"

"It's called a regional. I already did."

"Good," said Stanley. Incredibly, he was thinking he might need Iris to help him out. If she could get beyond a simple thing like her thirst for revenge, that is. Either way, she still might see the logic of the situation, which was that she might help Stanley anyway, as opposed to placing herself at the dubious disposal of Jaime, Djell, and Sibyl.

Maybe Stanley could talk her into it.

And if things didn't go smoothly?

Who would be left to care?

Certainly not Sibyl. Nor Stanley.

That would leave Djell, Jaime and Iris.

They could sort things out for themselves.

Maybe get couple of lawyers on it. Expensive. Enough body parts to fund a platoon of lawyers.

Get it straight in a couple of years.

Everybody healed by then. Everybody friends. Adjacent condos.

Come out and sit by Stanley's grave in Oakland. Hold hands and tell his tombstone all about the settlement.

The inscription on his tombstone? Easy: *Lived, drank, died.*

Maybe they'd bury him with Green Eyes. Mix their ashes.

Stanley and Sibyl: gone to hell together.

He looked at Sibyl.

Sibyl, with her wonderful eyes, was watching him.

He liked that mole in her plucked eyebrow.

Made her seem almost human.

Those moles sprinkled up along some meridian of her metabolism, like stars in a constellation. Little ones, bigger ones, round ones, odd-shaped ones. They might occur in pairs, too, like Castor and Pollux, the twin stars of Gemini, all of them asymmetric to her right side, all-girl stars strewn along the arm of some estrogen galaxy...

Could Djell even suspect this romanticizing? Isn't that part of being married to a beautiful woman? To know that other men fantasize over her?

"Hey," he said. "What's your sign?"

Her eyes just perceptibly widened.

If a gun barrel hadn't been taped to her pursed lips she certainly might have laughed. As it was she said into the barrel, "You're a fucking idiot."

Genuine contempt. Some mountains, Stanley reflected, are never conquered.

Again he experienced the impulse to pull the trigger and get it over with. To commit suicide and murder. He'd already killed tonight. His first murder. He hadn't felt a thing. Was that what it meant to be an idiot?

He heard a rumbling noise. It sounded like a dog chewing on a bone. He realized his teeth were grinding. The hand taped around the grip of the pistol had begun to shake. His hand was frozen, cramped, clenched, cast in iron, boned by pain. The bladed sight at the far end of the gun must be quivering against the backs of her front teeth or her palate. He could see in her eyes that he was — what? — some sub-atomic measurement away from pulling the trigger *by convulsion*. One Angstrom? A billionth of a meter? The radius of a hydrogen atom? But what about Time?

How long would it take him to pull the trigger on this cannon, even if the distance required for the travel of the spontaneously enraged trigger-finger were a billionth of a meter? How was time measured, at such a distance? Did *instantaneous* cover the subject?

Faster'n a greased string through a guru.

Catbird!

C'est moi, pardner.

Where the hell you been? I got, like, existential dilemmas wanting consideration.

Do tell.

Sure I —. What the hell you mean, do tell? Can't you see what's going on? Don't you know I've got this gun taped into this woman's face, here, and this guy out back installing my new kidney?

Yeah, I can see that. But I ain't sticking around to enjoy it.

What? What are you talking about?

It appears as how you're doing stellar by your own lights.

But I'm asking you for help. I need, like, a consultation.

I just came back to get my stuff.

Stuff? What stuff?

Oh, you know. Tool box. Pair of gumboots. Couple Louis L'Amour novels I can convince myself I haven't read yet. No big deal. Stuff.

What's up?

For the first time in our coexistence, I don't know what to say.

So? Say nothing. Have a drink. I'm buying.

The little voice didn't speak.

Hey.

You let them cut on that girl.

What girl?

What girl, he says.

Stanley listened to his circulatory system moving his blood around. Goose flesh arose on all his exposed parts. The overhead light dimmed. The grinding suddenly stopped.

Rage replaced everything.

I didn't *let* them do it. I *made* them cut on her.

Good enough. I'm not arguin with you.

Since when?

Since I'm leaving.

What do you mean you're leaving? You've been gone all night. Just when a man gets used to having somebody to talk to when he talks to himself—.

My sentiment exactly.

I don't get this.

Bullshit you don't get it.

All I get is I get into these useless arguments with you and you start disappearing.

Yeah, well, that's not going to be a problem much longer.

What's that?

Nothing. I don't mean nothing. I just mean you're not going to have to worry about pissing away your life with me sittin and watchin from the prime vantage point of your inner barroom. That's all.

But I *like* my inner barroom.

Well, it's closed. Empty. Deserted. It's dark in there and it smells weird. You got it all to yourself. It don't agree with my aesthetic.

Aesthetic? What aesthetic?

You shouldn't have done it to her. Simple as that. But it's done and I'm movin' on to greener inner barrooms. Maybe head out West.

We *are* out West.

Further west, then. Where West becomes East. The Sunset District. Maybe Australia.

I don't fucking *believe* this. Except she's a goddamn scar-licking pervert, Iris is fine. She's going to wake up with a scar all to herself. She'll spend her days happily, filling out insurance forms with a Get-Well Bear in her lap.

Silence.

Wait and see. We're gonna wind up *living* together.

You lost me there, Pard. That's totally over my head. But I guess now you joined this club, you can handle it all by yourself.

WHAT FUCKING CLUB

The club that pulls the trigger to get what it wants. That fucking club.

The sensoria flooded back in. The light brightened to a curious ochre, as if he were looking at the world through pricey Porsche sunglasses. Somewhere something dripped. His nose made little *snerks* when he tried to breathe through it.

Hey, he abruptly thought. You don't think I'm going to pull this trigger now, do you?

Well? Aren't you?

Now? Why?

The question is not why, it's why not?

Hey.

You got nothing to lose.

Yeah.

You lost already.

Sure.

You been trying to kill yourself for three years. Why not now?

Yeah. Why not?

Stanley laughed.

He pulled the trigger.

Chapter 30

Do you hear anything?

No.

I pulled the trigger.

Bullshit.

No. No, I did. Nothing happened.

Have a look.

No, you have a look.

Me? I'm incorporeal.

We're all going to be incorporeal if somebody doesn't have a look.

Plus, I'm leaving. I'm already gone. You're talking to yourself.

So?

So have a look for yourself.

Stanley opened his eyes.

Two green eyes stared at him.

She's still there.

What? There should be little pieces of meat hanging off that duct tape.

I know.

Shoot her again.

Okay.

He pulled the trigger.

Well?

It didn't go off.

Try pulling the trigger.

I pulled the goddamn trigger! Twice. I pulled it...
Somewhere something rattled.
I better get my stuff.
Hey. YOU CAN'T LEAVE ME LIKE THIS.
Says you. What do you know about moral imperatives?
The WHAT? First it's aesthetics, now it's moral imperatives. Make
up your mind.
It's made up. I'm gettin my stuff.
No, no. Make up your mind about...
Whispering. Outer whispering.
Shh! Outer shushing.
Well? Outer voice.
Well what? Another outer voice.
What do you think?
I don't think. This is strictly empirical.
SO? Djell.
Shh! So keep cutting. Lopez.
For Christ's sakes, I'm almost through.
In a pig's eye.
Silence.
He's not moving.
So? That's good. If he moves he blows Sibyl's head off.
But I don't think...
I thought you said this was empirical.
True. I did say that.
So don't think. Is he out, or is he not out?
No. He's not out. But the arm might be.
Now you've said it! There's only one way now for any *of us to find out!*
You said this was empirical...
Silence.
A moan.
What's that?
That nurse. Don't worry about her.
I got so much sweat in my eyes I can't see.
Here's a sponge.
Check the machine.
Christ, I have to do everything...
Silence. A squeak of casters.
It's okay. You ready for it?

I don't know. My hands are shaking.
Want some blow?
Did he give it back?
I took it.
You're kidding.
Guy had his mind on other things. The scalpel, too.
You're amazing.
I know.
That trick with the heroin…
It almost worked.
It almost got us killed.
Silence. Rustle of plastic. Metal dicing on metal.
I can't hold the straw.
Manny, Manny, Manny. Are you worried about sepsis? You? Of all people.
No. But I bet he is. Hold the straw.
Sounds of snorting.
Whew. Shit.
The other one.
Ack…
Now me.
Snorting. Silence. More snorting.
You know, who are we kidding? He can hear us. If he was worried he'd have
done something by now.
Ask him.
You ask him.
Ask him what?
I don't know, I'm in surgery! Ask him how he feels.
Ahem. Ahearn.
What.
Ahearn?
What?
What's his Christian name?
Which one is that?
The first one.
The nurse called him Stanley.
Right.
Try it.
Yo. Stanley.
What, goddammit.

Stanley?
What?
Hey. Hey Manny. I think he can't respond.
You think?
It worked, Manny. It worked. He can hear us but he can't respond.
How can you tell?
Look at his eye. Hey, Ahearn! See? His eye knows his name.
What's that prove?
Hey, Ahearn. Fuck you, Ahearn!
Cut it out!
He can't do anything! Don't you see? Hey, Ahearn. Pull the trigger, motherfucker.
I did pull the trigger. I am pulling the trigger.
You'd shoot if you could, wouldn't you Ahearn? Huh? Wouldn't you?
Don't touch him!
What's the big deal? He's paralyzed!
He's still got a gun in his hand, goddammit. It could still go off.
Oh. True.
Silence.
So now what?
Silence.
Catbird…?
Silence.
Hello?
Silence.
Casters on tile. Instruments on cloth.
Whispering.
Louder, assholes. No secrets. No secrets or I blow the dame's head off. Got me? Got me?
Okay.
He could hear the perfusion machine. It sounded like boiling porridge. A moan.
Can't you do anything about her?
You mean other than steal one of her kidneys?
Yeah.
Well. She's kinda cute. If I weren't so thoroughly queer…
Jaime, try to take the situation seriously.
Hey, Manny. See this syringe?
Sure.
Where is it?

Well-ll… It looks like it's firmly embedded between the T-5 and the T-6.
Oh yeah. Right. He's—.
He's frozen. Paralyzed. And I'm staying here to see that he stays that way. You
want something done about that nurse, do it yourself.
Can he see?
Barely…
They fucked me. Now would be a good time to pull the trigger. Now.
Right about right about now now now. He pulled the trigger. Now now.
He pulled the trigger. Now.
Iced or not, we still have to get that gun out of his hand.
I have an idea about that.
Did you say something?
No, I—.
Let me show you what I think.
Silence.
Laughter. Quiet at first, a quiet laughter. Then the laughter became
louder. Mentally disturbed laughter.
You laugh like you just escaped to Costa Rica only to find a letter from the IRS.
I always *pay my taxes.*
Yeah. This isn't funny. Hold it like this. No.
Oh. Sure. Of course it's not funny. Don't twist it…
Silence.
We're completely screwed, here, aren't we?
Silence.
AREN'T WE—
Someone slammed a big metal door to an underground parking
garage.
What metal door?
What parking garage?
I could certainly use a conversation with myself right about now,
Stanley thought. Maybe if I take a little rest…

"Well," said a gravelly voice. "What have we here? Ain't we met
before?
Stanley said eagerly, "You're back — you're back!"
"I'm back?" The voice was suspicious. "I never left. *You're* back."
"Oh. It's you. I was expecting — a friend of mine. Catbird. You seen
him?"

"Don't know no Catbird. I don't see nothing but a purple sleeping bag. And—."

"What."

"Is that blood?"

"Where?"

"What do you mean, where? You're swimming in it."

Stanley laughed.

"What's so funny?"

"Drowning," laughed Stanley. "You swim, you drown. What a relief. Drowning's about the easiest way of dying I've heard about lately. Drowning, did you say?"

"Swimming."

"Drowning." He chuckled. "It sounds downright civilized. I hope it works this time."

"Suit yourself."

"Say—."

"Yes?"

"Is your name Jasper?"

"Right in one, mister."

"Have we met before?"

"I was wondering the same thing. You eat at St. Anthony's?"

"Where they serve meals to the homeless? No. No, I... I was almost homeless, once. But say, where is this?"

"St. Anthony's?"

"No, this. Here. Now. Where are we?"

"Why, mister, this here is the Panhandle of the Golden Gate Park in fabulous Californ-eye-yea, U.S. of A, World, Solar System, only four and a half light-years from Alpha Centauri, as the stoned crow aviates."

"Jasper..."

"As for the Now of it..."

"Yes...?"

Laughter. Slow at first, and deep. That is to say, profound laughter. Increasing tempo, getting louder, lowering in pitch to a belly-combusted cackle.

"Jasper...? Jasper..."

Throw it over there.
Buddy, that's cold.

You don't know the meaning of the word.
That voice… A woman's voice…
My Christ, said Djell. *What next…*

Pain is next. Why don't they ask me? Stanley could hear irrigation sprinklers. He could smell juniper and eucalyptus and diesel fumes. For that matter, he could smell Jasper.

"Got to get you out of here. Say, haven't we met before?"

"I think I was here once already. Couple months ago."

"Say, that's nothin'. I sleep here most nights. Ever since word got out about a guy I found in a sleeping bag… kinda like the one you're in now… nobody wants to camp here anymore. Plenty of room."

What's that smell?

Blood.
I think—.
Don't. Just do it.
Dragging me around a tremendous exploding fire door.

"—know you from—"

Just the majority of it.

"No, no. Can't say as I remember."

Leave just enough to aim with.

A tremendous exploding fire door won't stay closed.

A resonant boom in an underground parking garage, onto which the metal door closed. The echoes fade into the ragged buzz of a single fluorescent tube.

Somewhere something dripped. Something whined. Caster clatter. After tremendous concentration he realized the colors he was seeing were somehow tuned to the music he was hearing. Oh, yes, there was music. Plaintive trumpet. He couldn't tell where it was coming from. An irrigation sprinkler rotated by, a jet of water shot through the juniper. In the grass just beyond the skirt of water two seagulls stood watching him. They were interested in his eyes. Eye. Jasper was telling him a story about the bus system, while Stanley wished Jasper was… what? Who? Although *vice versa* would do. Someone To Talk To. Women don't count. Do I think that? Stupid. Stuck on stupid. Dumb as a box of rocks. Laughter sounds like a Chihuahua locked in a closet. Acts like. Sounds like. Walks like. Quacks like. Must be laughter. Or a Chihuahua. Scar tickles, of course. Pink tip of wet tongue on purple ridge of scar, glistening radioactive under hand-held black-light. Smoldering incense smells like guano, two-and-a-half units. Tree roots exposed and peeled. Gravel and burnt matches. Empty cellophane bag labeled RED HOT. Taste of acetone. Somewhere something hit a floor with a sickening thud, a watermelon dropped from a great height. No more slamming doors? A conversation, then, while we wait. A little one-on-oneself. The beep of a video game. Must score. Oh yeah? Explain the game. Well, I hate to tell you this, but it's called The Moral Imperative. Beep. The what? "They got that at St. Anthony's, too." Deconstruction. "They gave it away." *We Can Build You.* Damn. Philip K. Dick had to get in here somewhere. If they can build you they can take you apart. "Come on let's get us a coupla transfers and— say." Say? "That's blood." Mine. Whose. Theirs? Whose? Mine and theirs. Hers, too. Iris. The girl gave her all. Talk her into it. Just ask her. *We Can Build You Something To Live On.* It's only the spare. Her spare. Afford it. Over the top *vis-à-vis* methods of self-preservation. Ditto, pre-spousal altruism. Bartendress! A drink for every concept! Ice in a glass. Purling *uisge beatha.* Somewhere something screams. Maybe car alarm, maybe robot, maybe neighbor's television. If things made sense at this point, they might not make sense later. Let's see you get out of that one. Oh my god, it's Gray Eyes. She brought the kids! Come on in, honey. Join the party. What do you say to a kid? Ahm, this is Dr. and Mrs. Djell, and that there with the blood all over him is Jaime. My surgical team. I'm going to be okay, aren't I fellas. That's Iris. Oh, she's going to be okay, too. Just napping. I just know it. And Jasper. He—. What do you mean, this all looks *familiar*? If that's so, why don't you explain it to us? Typical? Typical? I'll show you typical—. Mary? (her name) Mary. Let's don't fight. Please God, after all these— let's don't…. Her name aloud in years. Silence heard me. Not until *pock…* I didn't know Lieutenant Uhura made it with—*Pock-pock… To go where no man has— pock*—. Is this Thursday? Night? *Pock…* You got a lime? *Pock-pock-pock:* Oh for the wand of non-awareness. *Pock…* How genuine a night is the night when all life's aspirations become glandular, announcer holds up envelope, and the Secret of Life, which is *pock* fill 'em up, on me *pock No, no* let me get this round, four rounds left, no ammo and enemy activity just beyond the bridge, sir, if they're from Berkeley, throw cig-arettes at em, you can see the whole East Bay from up here… How much is the complete *Flammenwerfer* Surround System anyway? *Not so much as a single kidney.* Installed? The Big Head shakes No, the Big Hand slams dice on the bar — Bam! *Still in the box* comes the *pock* mortal coil, good for heating coffee, *my coil and them Louis L'Amours,* craps again. *Inner voices travel light.* But Shane, *Shane*… Face it, boy. Should have married that girl when you had the chance, Lt. Corrigan, still in police school. What chance did a man have? No bankroll, big Catholic wedding. She always ran after the wild ones, the mutts, the no-goodniks. — *Additional dialogue by the man who brought you* Absalom, Absalom — *Oh yeah?* voice, falling off a building: *Who's thaaaatt*… Skip to random select. How much of real life do movies make up, anyway? *This much, buster: pow-pow, pow!*

"And now, *The Edge of Night*…"

Exactly…

Chapter 31

His right arm was gone. That was the first thing he noticed. He reached for the TV remote and there was nothing to reach with. It was that simple.

There was a smell of disinfectant, too. And IV lines attached to the remaining arm. A tube climbed the side of the bed like a Virginia creeper and disappeared beneath the sheets, waist-high.

Except for the television the room was dark. But that didn't make any difference. A man can tell when one of his arms is missing. For one thing there's a shallow depression under the sheet. If there had been a tattoo it would be gone, too. You can always feel it, a tattoo missing. Like it was stippled on water. There would be the necessity of carrying around safety pins, to pin up the empty sleeve. And compassionate women would light cigarettes for you in bars for up to two years after the fact. Just as soon as you take up smoking.

"Damian," said a woman on the television. Beneath her voice a synthesizer pulsed insistently.

Damian is propped up on a couple of pillows in a hospital bed. Plastic tubes probably should have been spilling out of his nose like petrified mucus, but that would have spoiled his looks, which are considerable. He lies in enough light to bleach a whorehouse bed sheet but he says, "Berkeley. Is that you, Berkeley?"

Reverse angle, close-up on her face, where glycerine tears agglutinate. "Yes, Damian," she sobs. "It's me."

"Wh-where are we?"

"St. Vincent's, Damian. On 6th Avenue. The Village?"

"Wh-why? Wh-what happened?"

Berkeley is not a day over twenty and has cheekbones like Carrara has marble. A tear launches off her cheek and out of the shot. "Oh, Damian. I— You…."

"Berkeley." As methane rises to the surface of a tar pit, so Damian is coming to his senses. "Is something the matter?"

The tempo of the music has quickened. The point of view trades three times, three each for her face, unable to bring herself to answer his question, and three each for his face, unable to ask it again.

"Oh Damian," she finally manages, "They— they've stolen your kidney!"

Her perfect hair drops out of the shot, allowing the camera to slowly close on Damian as Realization steals over his face, towards the commercial, slow as time-lapsed film of thawing tundra. The music crescendos in turgidity until his head dissolves into a bottle of fabric softener.

The lack of one arm presents logistical difficulties, at least in the beginning. After a futile struggle to reach the call button, the cord of which someone had draped over his right shoulder in percipient thoughtfulness, Stanley discovered the TV remote control lying on the covers to his left, next to his remaining hand.

But he couldn't see to his right, and it was then that he remembered his missing eye.

How quickly, he mused, one adapts to adversity.

He couldn't find the power switch on the remote. In the dark he unintentionally increased the volume, then hit the channel selector, and he found himself on a very loud public access channel, featuring a guy wearing a propeller beanie and playing a dulcimer while reciting poetry atop a surf-blasted rock.

> …*I'd rather be a pagan, suckled by a policy outworn*
> *so that I, smitten by this pleasant condominium,*
> *might hear old Trinitron blow some other theme*
> *than the one currently depresses me.*
> —*O, Prozackia*…

As Stanley left-handed the remote toward the television, throwing like a girl, he suddenly remembered Green Eyes throwing something to him — what?

Unexpectedly, the remote hit the screen's glass just so, and fissured it, before clattering to the floor. The tube issued a prolonged, insidious hiss before it imploded with a sound like a stepped-on flash bulb, and the room plunged into darkness and silence.

Stanley wiggled the fingers of his left hand. Not bad.

To his right, phantom digits wiggled sympathetically.

The door opened a few inches, showing a wedge of light.

"Ahearn?"

Stanley closed his eye and said nothing.

The door closed. He opened his eye. There stood Sean Corrigan, and Dr. Sims.

Sims switched on a light. He appeared the same: stethoscope, spectacles, clipboard; lines of blue and black ink on the breast pocket of his white smock.

Corrigan didn't look like he'd even changed his clothes lately, let alone his personality.

The detective and the doctor stood at the foot of the bed, considering Stanley as if he were a special rock in a carefully groomed meditation garden.

When his eye had adjusted to the light Stanley said, "Dare I ask?"

Corrigan scratched a couple days' growth of whiskers on the side of his face with a folded copy of the *Examiner*.

Dr. Sims said, "Welcome back, and congratulations on surviving another assault on your infrastructure, Mr. Ahearn. Quite extraordinary. Miraculous, really."

"Did you find me in the park again? I saw Jasper — I mean, I heard his voice. He recognized me. I think. So I figured—."

Dr. Sims raised his eyebrows.

Inspector Corrigan said, "The park? No, we didn't find you in the park, Ahearn. We found you in the basement of a funeral home in Oakland, bleeding from several wounds."

This got Stanley's hopes up. "They did it, then? They did it?"

Corrigan and Sims exchanged a glance.

Corrigan said, "Did what, Ahearn?"

"Installed my new kidney? The kidney that—" He stopped.

Corrigan and Sims waited.

Stanley closed his eye. If being a criminal depended on keeping his mouth shut, he was going to have a short, lousy career.

Corrigan cleared his throat mildly. "You were saying?"

Stanley bit his lip.

After a while Corrigan said quietly, "I told you not to mess around with this case anymore. First that kid MacIntosh got himself killed on account of you. Then it turns out they killed his computer-programming buddy, too. Harvested all his organs and sent him up the stack."

Stanley said nothing.

"His name was Tommy Quinn. We found his teeth."

Stanley opened the eye.

"You never met the guy."

Stanley closed the eye again and shook his head, once.

"Well Ahearn, we could easily make you for accessory to murder in both cases. Fit you like your birthday suit. And then there's burglary, possession of a loaded and unregistered handgun, assault with a deadly weapon, two or three counts of manslaughter… There's even possession of cocaine and heroin with intent to sell."

This elicited a single, soundless laugh from Stanley.

"Take your pick. Kick in special circumstances on account you got these guys killed while you were committing other crimes — it's the gas chamber. Or lethal injection, if this goddamn state ever gets it together."

Stanley wasn't listening. Behind his closed eye he was seeing a *guiro* atop a folded *rebozo* in the sunlit dust adrift above the closed lid of Giles' mother's grand piano.

"Life plus twenty-five, at least," added Corrigan.

Stanley opened his eye and turned his head with its out-of-focus barrier to his monocular vision—his nose—until he could see the shallow depression in the bedclothes on his right side. The call button was lying there. The overhead light was bright and cruel and specific.

"And while you fiddled around withholding evidence, they harvested yet another guy. Same M.O. — a boozy chump like yourself, a sheetrocking schlub who got himself chatted up by a brunette with green eyes. He went home with her, she slipped him a mickey, and he woke up minus a kidney."

"Ted Nichols is alive, then?" Stanley asked suddenly.

Sims had fixed his eyes on something no one else could see. His right hand moved to retrieve a ballpoint pen from his breast pocket but stopped with one finger on it, then dropped purposeless to his side.

Corrigan regarded Stanley closely. "Septicemia — blood poisoning to you — killed him two days ago. He died miserably, I might add."

Sims blinked back his thousand-yard stare and refocused on Stanley.

Stanley groaned.

Corrigan summoned an expression of extreme revulsion, but it was plain he was wracked by uncertainty and guilt. He looked like a man who'd just found a diamond ring on a human finger in the stomach of the trout he was cleaning for dinner. "The place was a crime scene, for God's sakes.... We had no idea Nichols was rolled up in that carpet in the back of that truck."

I didn't either, Stanley wanted to wail.

But it wasn't true.

"I don't recall mentioning his name," Corrigan added quietly.

Stanley didn't either.

Corrigan bored in. "You know the sheetrocker's name."

"I do?"

"You just said it."

"I must have heard it on the TV. I was watching just a few minutes ago…"

Stanley instantly regretted saying this. But the remark was so callous that even Corrigan was taken aback.

The detective heaved a sigh great enough to carry the force of a curse and said, "To hell with it. The guy is dead. But what if I told you that after Fong heard what happened to Nichols he sang like a cheap tea kettle?"

Stanley rocked his head onto the useless shoulder. "So put the cuffs on me, Corrigan," he spat loudly. "Or should I say, put the *cuff* on me?" He held up the left hand.

Corrigan looked disgusted.

Sims nodded vaguely. "We did what we could for his pain."

"But it was pretty painful anyway," Corrigan snapped, his eyes centered on Stanley's good one. "As a bad way to go, it's up there with getting *amanita phalloides* in your omelette."

"Poor guy," said Sims. "We figure it was the dirt on the aster. Or maybe in the carpet. The dehydration didn't help either."

"The basement of that funeral home looked like a slaughterhouse," Corrigan said grimly. "We didn't even think to break into that van until twelve hours after we got there."

"Iris," said Stanley.

"And you," said Corrigan, "survived. Of all people."

"Iris didn't make it?" blurted Stanley, suddenly panicked.

Sims glanced at Corrigan.

"Well?" Stanley shouted. "Did she?"

Corrigan was trying to get a grip on his smile. It was nice to have gotten a genuine reaction out of Ahearn at last, and he wanted to savor it. Finally he said, "Iris made it. No thanks to you."

Stanley made a slit of his good eye. "She was there," he said lamely, hastily. "It's all a—."

"Oh," Corrigan interrupted warmly. "It's all a blur, is it? Are you sure it isn't a *jumble?*"

"I remember a lot of yelling. There were guns around, too. One of them went off. But I was out of it. They had me all doped up, see…"

"They had you all doped up, see…"

"Yeah," said Stanley. "I thought I was a goner. And Iris… Tell me, Inspector Corrigan…"

"Yes? *Mister* Ahearn."

"That woman with the green eyes. Her name was Sibyl. She may have been married to that insane surgeon. They seemed close…."

Corrigan produced his little palm-top computer and started it. "Dr. Djell." He tilted the little screen toward the light. "Cashiered out of the medical fraternity eight years ago—."

"Yes, I'm sure he must have been," said Stanley hurriedly. "But, tell me. Did his wife…?"

"Sibyl Djell," Corrigan read. "Born Sibyl Carmegian, in Modesto. Registered Nurse, attended medical school but never got to her residency, dropped out when she married her husband. Drove a Mercedes, her taste in clothes ran to the expensive, worked out regularly at—"

"Yes," interrupted Stanley impatiently, "that's the woman. The last time I saw her she was in a… a tough spot. Did she—."

The door banged opened a few inches, pushed awkwardly from the outside.

Sims pulled the door all the way open.

Iris rolled her wheelchair into the room.

She paused to look the scene over. Corrigan, Sims… and, at last, the violet eyes fell on Stanley.

She pivoted expertly and glided to the side of his bed.

"Darling," she said.

Stanley blinked.

Everybody watched him.

"Iris...," he blustered. "You... I..."

Her terrycloth robe was cornflower blue. Two blue plastic clips shaped like little birds with tiny loquacious orange beaks and heaven-lifted eyes held her hair away from her face, which was bloodless and pale. Still pretty, she looked older. Dark circles traced her eyes, which were reddened as if from weeping. Her feet were swaddled in blue mohair mules. A Get-Well Bear tilted in her lap, orangish-brown against the blue terrycloth. Except for its rigid arms and shirt-button eyes, it looked like something you'd need to buff car wax.

Iris set the brake on the chair and folded her hands protectively over the bear.

Corrigan said, "Not only did Iris make it, Ahearn; but because of her, you made it, too."

The obvious exhaustion and pain in Iris' face resolved into the open-mouthed, fixed smile of the house-sized devil who swallows the train tracks at the beginning of the Tunnel of Love.

"Really...?" Stanley breathed uncertainly.

"Someone's finally done you a turn like the one you did Hop Toy's kid," Corrigan went on, affecting a neutral tone. "Kind of like, you might say, life has provided a new hero to rescue the old one. To kind of even things out."

If Iris added nothing to this, her expression revealed less. But Stanley detected in her eye a gleam indicative of — what? Hate? Disgust? Triumph? Rage?

Desire?

"You have Iris to thank for your life, Ahearn."

"Well," mumbled Stanley. "Well I..."

If his hospital bed were flying through the dense atmosphere of an unfamiliar planet his bearings could have been no more awry. He managed to utter a thank-you. And he sent a phantom impulse to his gone right arm, telling it to extend its hand and to spread its fingers to cover one of Iris' hands, as well as the brainless head of the Get-Well Bear, in order to deliver a tactile cue as he thanked her, to make a familiar, reassuring gesture. Nothing happened, of course. He twisted his chin over his right shoulder to get his nose out of the way, so his remaining eye could look again at the shallow depression in the sheets where the arm should have been. There would have to be a new order of tactile cues. But was he expected to learn them today? Right now? The audience watched him struggle. What did they think? That an arm gone missing was a ploy for sympathy?

Affecting an uncertain dignity without taking his eye off the bedding he said, "For whatever you did back there, Iris, thanks. That was... a pretty hairy spot I got myself — us — into. I wasn't expecting you... or any... help...."

It sounded more like a plea than a declaration.

A long silence ensued.

"I thought it was... all over for me," he finally managed to croak. "I mean us. All over for us."

Corrigan cleared his throat. "Indeed it might have been curtains, Ahearn. If Iris hadn't showed up those maniacs would have done you for certain. Thanks to Iris you're lucky to have come out of it with only what injuries you—" He stopped. Corrigan looked from Dr. Sims to Iris and back to Stanley.

An apologetic smile flickered over Corrigan's mouth.

Stanley didn't understand it, but the smile was unconvincing.

Stanley covered the void at his right shoulder with the palm of his left hand. For the first time, he felt the stump. It protruded about four inches from the joint.

Right under the call button.

Pocketing his computer Corrigan shook out the copy of the *Examiner* and showed the headline.

SEAL ROCK HERO THWARTS RENAL BANDITS

"Here," he said. "Let me read it to you."

San Francisco Police Department Chief Investigator Sean Corrigan announced today that, in cooperation with members of the Oakland Police Department, the gang of organ pirates that has been terrorizing the singles bars of San Francisco for over a year has been "literally destroyed."

Five bodies were recovered late this morning from a makeshift operating theater located in the basement of the Chippendale O'Hare Columbarium and Mortuary building at 34 Avenida Del Fumador in Oakland. None of the identities of the victims has been released. All five died as the result of gunshot wounds. Three additional victims survived the shootout, all of them in critical condition.

"The revised score is now six to two," Corrigan interjected.

Police believe an argument among the gang members as to division of spoils from their illicit pillaging of body parts degenerated into a shootout.

Still trying to sort out victims from perpetrators in the case, an anonymous source from the Oakland coroner's office described the scene as "something out of a splatter movie". Investigators from both the Oakland and San Francisco District Attorney's Offices declined to release further details of their ongoing investigation.

Highly placed sources, however, who spoke on condition of anonymity, have informed the *Examiner* that the successful resolution of the case involves "a brave little lady" who is said to be employed as a nurse at S.F. Children's Hospital, as well as a man named Stanley Ahearn. *Examiner* files show Stanley Ahearn to be the same man who saved nine-year-old Tseng Toy when she was swept into the surf at Seal Rock, over three years ago. Two months ago, Mr. Ahearn became the ninth victim of the gang, losing a kidney to their predations.

Investigators withheld further details pending the continuing collection of evidence at the scene, notification of next of kin, and a coroner's report....

Corrigan folded the paper and threw it onto the bed.

"For your scrapbook, Ahearn," he said, in a voice that would digest bones. "They got some of it wrong, of course. They always do. But, famous as you are, you're probably used to that."

Stanley opened his mouth, but no sound came out.

"Close your mouth," said Corrigan, obviously enjoying Stanley's discomfort. "And be satisfied you've still got one eye, one arm, one kidney, and both cheeks of your ass."

Stanley's head involuntarily jerked his good eye toward Iris.

She watched him like she was watching an ant farm.

So, thought Stanley, her kidney didn't make it into my back.

Where is it, then?

How long do I have to live?

He sagged against the angled pillows as if the air had been let out of them, and looked straight ahead at the dead television, relegating Iris to the world occluded by the out-of-focus bulk of his nose.

Corrigan shot his cuff and looked at his watch. "The short version. Iris' mother has tickets to the ballet." He sighed determinedly, running a finger around the inside of his flexible watchband. "Iris talked me into this. I resisted at first" — he shrugged — "then I said okay." He clasped his hands in front of him. "Since *most* of the scum in this case are dead now, and since you have paid a heavy price in bringing the bulk of said scum to justice, *via*, I might add, their just desserts; and despite certain facts — that you withheld evidence and lied to investigators; that you caused two or three people to buy the farm a little sooner than they might have otherwise — and since I can't prove you ever knew anything in advance about the Ted Nichols guy because, you'll be glad to know, Fong told us nothing. He refused to drop a dime on you. So you got one friend, at least." Corrigan squinted. "You owe him money or something?" He raised the palm of one hand. "Don't bother to lie to that. I know it's because you saved his cousin Tseng's life. Anyhow," he clasped his hands, "on account of all these extenuating circumstances, and because Iris here was so persuasive and then got her mother in on it…"

Stanley was taking all this in, but hardly dared to hope that everything seemed about to be swept into the past.

"…On account of all this and I'm worn out and heartily sick of you, and because most of us think you already more or less got what was coming to you…" Corrigan's smile appeared, showed some brown teeth, then went away again. "…I'm not going to prefer any charges against you, if the D.A. lets me get away with it, which he probably will."

Stanley blinked.

"The story in the paper stands as is." Corrigan pointed at the *Examiner.* "It just doesn't look good, to be prosecuting a guy who's a hero twice over."

Stanley blinked some more.

"Ain't that just ducky?" Corrigan added, watching him.

The room was as still as a photograph. Beyond the door and down the hall an elevator arrived with a ping.

"I hope I never see you again," said Corrigan. But…" He rolled his eyes toward Iris and sighed heavily. "I probably will."

Stanley steadily maintained his out-of-focus nose between his good eye and Iris.

"I guess that's it for criminal nephrectomies, Sims. For the time being, at least. Always a pleasure, and thanks for your help."

Sims and Corrigan shook hands.

"Good night, Iris," said Corrigan, leaning over her shoulder to plant a kiss on her cheek. "You have a ride home?"

She must have nodded yes.

"I'm outta here, then. I always get in a nice nap at the ballet." Corrigan patted her shoulder and he straightened up.

"So long, hotshot," he said to Stanley, and left the room.

Dr. Sims watched him go. "Well," he said, as the door closed. He retrieved his pen and turned a few pages on the clipboard. "Let's see, here…." He whistled three tuneless descending notes as he scanned a page from top to bottom. "Okay. You going to stay a while, Iris?"

She must have nodded yes.

"Hmmm." Sims checked his watch and made a few notes on the clipboard. "Shananne will be by with the night drill in about half an hour. She can get all she needs off this. Well, Mr. Ahearn." He drew a few lines under his breast pocket. "Miraculously, you're doing fine. Quite a constitution you've got there. We'll have to make a study of it before you run it into the ground. Maybe we can get a grant. Defer some of these pesky bills you keep piling up." Sims made a toothy grin, then erased it. "Some excellent help you've got here, too. To have so fierce an advocate as Nurse Considine —" he indicated Iris with the clipboard, as he hung it at the foot of the bed "— you're a lucky man."

Still Stanley kept his nose between his good eye and Iris.

Sims opened the door. "I'll be by in the morning. Want me to dim the light a little?"

Neither Iris nor Stanley responded.

Sims dimmed the light anyway. "There. Like a cozy banquet for two at Ernie's."

The door quietly closed itself behind him.

"Oh, yes." The door opened again. "That catheter can come out tonight, too." The door closed again.

Startled, Stanley turned his head towards the disappearing Sims. This brought Iris into view.

Chapter 32

The door swung silently closed, and Sims was gone.

Stanley kept his head tilted. The focus of his eye oscillated nervously between the plane of his nose and Iris' face and the closed door and the dark television and back.

A thin grim smile crept over her mouth. The whites of her eyes were webbed with fine red veins, like suet.

She let him wait.

Something rolled heavily past the closed door, toward the elevator lobby at the end of the hall.

A phantom thumb counted phantom fingers in space. One, two, three, four. One, two, three. One, two. One....

"When I came to," Iris began, "they had nearly severed your arm. They used a Stryker saw — you've probably never seen one. Cuts bone without tearing flesh? I was surprised they had it."

She reflected. "Djell and Lopez. What a pair. Once they had the arm severed they took a break. Did some cocaine. While they were chopping it up they argued about the best way to get the gun out of that woman's mouth without blowing her head off."

Her laugh was a mirthless puff of air inching a dead leaf along a sidewalk.

"Finally they began by cutting the tape that held her head to the gurney. Then they tried to roll her over so the arm would be straight up over her mouth. They figured this would at least take the dead weight of your finger off the trigger. The two of them, trying to be real careful, both of them holding onto the arm, turning the woman — they were not at all sure what they were doing. They bickered. It being so hot under the light, the tape got even stickier. Blood had run down your arm and all over the tape, too. Everybody was sweating prodigiously. It was difficult for them to find loose ends of the tape, and when they did it was dicey to peel away. That was good duct tape.

"So they slit the tape down the back of her head, along the nape of her neck. But tape stuck to her hair and face, and it still held the gun in her mouth. The dead hand was taped to the gun. The dead finger still curled around the trigger. They were afraid to touch it. There was so much blood on the gun they were afraid to try to uncock it. While they were arguing, it became obvious that neither one of them knew the least thing about guns. The safety, for example, wasn't even mentioned. Guns had been the department of the two dead guys.

"All they knew was it had already killed twice and now it was cocked and loaded and stuck in that woman's mouth. After a lot of talking and some yelling they went ahead with the decision to rotate the arm straight up over her. I don't know why. They told her to turn her head with it. But the rest of her was still taped to the gurney. Her eyes got big and started to blink. She tried to say something but you couldn't understand her. And at some point enough torque developed...."

Stanley winced.

"You liked her, didn't you?"

Stanley half opened his mouth to say nothing. Just perceptibly, he nodded.

"Yes. You liked her. She seduced your mind or something. Anyway, that cannon blew the back of her head right through the gurney. And all over the floor. It sounded like somebody hit the gurney with a sledge-hammer."

Somebody slammed a metal door...

Stanley realized that his breath was whistling in and out of his half-open mouth.

"They went nuts, as you might expect, and they weren't paying any attention to me at all. The surgeon went hysterical — straight into hyperspace. He'd just killed his own wife, after all. The anesthesiologist immediately started crying. He cursed over and over again, in Spanish. I'm not sure what it meant.

"The doctor ran out of gas first. He gulped air like he'd surfaced from a deep dive, and when he'd caught enough air he started wailing and screaming all over again.

"Eventually they stopped and just stood there, in shock, silently weeping.

"And there was you, of course. You...."

Stanley blinked the single eye. *Me.*

"Blood was everywhere. From your arm and your eye and from the woman. All over everything. Before the anesthetic took effect on your arm Djell had actually initiated your transplant incision, so you wouldn't get suspicious, and that was bleeding too. As soon as they realized your arm was dead they quit on the nephrectomy and went right into the amputation. He was pretty good, that guy Djell. I mean, think about it. Your gosh-darned hand is taped to a loaded .45 in Djell's wife's mouth. Your finger is on the trigger. The hammer is cocked. And this guy amputated the darned arm without setting the gun off. Darn, I said to myself, that's a darned good surgeon."

"Yeah," Stanley said softly, locking his lone eye on one of hers. "How's your nephrectomy scar?"

Her smile faded momentarily, then quivered back into life. She kept her gaze, however, directly on Stanley.

Loathing, he realized. Her loathing bathes me. Me, the despicable.

Yet there was an aura around the hatred, a backlight. Emanating from what?

Oh, Stanley realized suddenly. Look at that.

Desire pooled the hatred in her eyes like an oil slick around a wreck.

Now, he thought, we're getting the proper perspective. Until now he'd seen or heard nothing that made sense.

But now he could see that Iris hated and wanted him — both. Hated him and wanted him completely, passionately, and absolutely. Instead of fissioning her into a hopeless case, the twin emotions had fused her into a guided missile. No compromise would be possible.

To Stanley, this dual compulsion made sense.

Don't do it, babe, he wanted to tell her, *it's not worth it.* But he was the wrong person to be explaining to Iris the futile cocktail of loathing and desire — he was, after all, a mutilated expert. But while he had plenty of expertise he had no credibility. Trust was not a tent under which he might seek shelter from the gale of her volition. Forever gone was the hour when she might have listened to him.

He wondered if Sibyl had ever detected in his eyes — when he still had two of them — the drive he now saw in Iris'.

Would Iris notice the condescension he now felt? No. She wasn't looking for it in Stanley any more than he had been looking for it in Sibyl.

Her mouth was perfectly caught between a smile and a snarl. The smile made the snarl look triumphant. The snarl made the smile look... carnivorous.

"My scar's fine," Iris said simply. "How's yours?"

"I don't know. Do I have one?"

"Yes."

"Is there... Is there a kidney... under it?" He laughed. It was the briefest, most false laugh he'd ever heard himself laugh. "Is there... an aster there? Too?"

She smiled. "No, Stanley. There is no aster sewn to your back."

His single eye began to water. "Where is it, then? My... Your — I mean... That kidney...?"

She dropped one hand and patted the side of her wheelchair, just over her right hip.

Stanley raised the eyebrow over the good eye.

"Right where it belongs," she said.

"You *got it back?*"

She nodded.

"How?"

"Sims, of course. Djell might have been okay, but Sims is the best in town."

Stanley nodded sadly.

She abruptly leaned forward and Stanley involuntarily started. "Listen up, now," she said, lowering her voice. "We're not finished." She sat back in the wheelchair and resumed her conversational tone. "It's hard to explain, but they finally *got over it.*"

"Who?"

"Djell and Jaime."

"Got over what?"

"His wife's death."

"They *got over it?*"

She smiled.

"They got over it," Stanley repeated, more or less to himself.

She waited.

After a minute he said, almost inaudibly, "I don't understand anything."

"True. We'll fix that in a minute. But it wasn't long before they were doing a lot better than you would have been doing, under the circumstances. If it had been your wife, I mean."

She smiled with relish.

He struggled to avoid imagining what it must have looked like.

Iris opened her hands. "Amazing resilience — the kind that gets people through medical school. Always the first step in dealing with grief, they talked for a long time. And what they decided was, this was the end. The game was over. They were finished. Without Sibyl they were washed up, true. But also, they were never going to be able to get rid of so many bodies. Somebody was going to notice something. There were too many loose ends. Vince and Sturgeon, for example, had families."

"God almighty."

Iris nodded. "Just regular guys. So they came up with a solution and called it their Big Casino."

He saw dozens of playing cards, blowing along a street.

She nodded. "The Big Casino. Based on a quick calculation, and counting the organs of a guy I didn't even know was there...."

"Ted?"

She looked at him, disingenuously interrogative. "Was that his name?"

He said "Ted Nichols" before he realized that of course she knew the name. She just wanted to hear Stanley say it.

"Counting Nichols, the dead wife, you, the two guys, they figured they had close to a million dollars worth of organs. The money was practically at their fingertips. All they had to do was harvest, deliver, get paid — and get the hell out of the country, straight into retirement."

"That's incredible," Stanley whispered. "Impossible. I can't believe they thought they—"

Iris flicked a hand. "Struck me as pretty bold, actually. After all, it was either go for it or roll over and die. So, anyway, they got your arm disentangled from that... well, that *mess*, really."

Stanley was feeling a little faint. He inhaled deeply.

"Breathe from the diaphragm and you might not puke."

Though it did him no good whatsoever, Stanley tried to yawn. He often yawned, right before he vomited.

"Try to take it easy," Iris said. "Lie back. Convulsions won't do that catheter any good at all. But finally they got the gun separated from what was left of her head. The arm comes with it and they've this weird appendage all wrapped in a towel cause by now there's *a lot* of gore. They covered the woman with a sheet. Now. What do you think these two clowns did next?"

Stanley could only shake his head and yawn involuntarily.

"No, really," she said, tenting her fingers beneath her chin and watching him. "You knew them better than anybody alive, probably. After they got the gun detached from this pulp on the gurney, what do you think is the first thing the one guy says to the other, the very first?"

"I don't know…," moaned Stanley. "I don't know!"

"*We got a lot of work in front of us. Put that thing with the others.* He was referring to your arm and the gun taped to it."

For a second Stanley didn't get it.

Iris nodded. "So Jaime lays the arm — your arm, Stanley, your *thing* — all wrapped up in a bloody towel and still taped to the gun, on top of the black guy you killed, who is stacked on top of the white guy I killed, who are both laying on the floor — *right next to me.*"

Now he got it.

"I'm playing possum, of course. Which wasn't too hard. I am hurting pretty bad by then, I can tell you. But there's no accounting for what shock and adrenaline can enable a body to put up with." She burped.

"Excuse me," she said, daintily patting her mouth. "Some of these darn drugs…

"Jaime goes back to the gurney, and the both of them stare at the woman's sheeted cadaver for a bit. The husband, Djell, says, *God knows I loved you Sibyl. And I know that you would have wanted us to get on with our business according to our best lights, and mourn you in our own good time.*

"*In Cabo San Lucas, for instance,* said Jaime.

"*Better it should be Rio. She would want all these organs* — and here he sweeps the room with his hand — *put to best use.*

"Now Stanley," said Iris, "this is very serious. This sweep of his hand — along with the two cadavers and you and the wife and the guy I didn't even know was there yet, the guy in the van — this sweep of his hand included *me.* You understand? This sweep of his hand included *my* organs going to *best use.* Got that?"

Stanley nodded dumbly.

"*So let's get on with it,* Djell says. And the Jaime guy says, *Not much anesthesiology going on here.* And Djell says, *Good. You can assist me. Shaky hands don't differentiate shit from chocolate to a cadaver donor. Not to mention warm ischemia.* And Jaime says *Who's first?* and Djell says, *We might as well continue with this one. He's all wired up.* And Jaime says *You want I should bring him out of it? Let him watch? After all, he—* and he points to the dead wife.

"*No,* Djell says then. *It won't bring Sibyl back. And besides, it'll slow us down.* Are you with me, Stanley?"

Stanley blinked.

"Good. I want you to know exactly how it went, Stanley. I am just thinking it was pretty extraordinary of this guy Djell to let bygones be bygones like that, in the name of efficiency, when he says to Jaime, *It's a lot of work. We're going to be at it for the rest of the day, at least.* True enough, Jaime agrees, and he starts pointing at you and counting his fingers. He points at the dead woman and counts some more. He doubles his figures for the white guy and the black guy and adds more for the guy upstairs, which I didn't understand at the time but finally he throws a few of his nasty fingers at me. *Wow,* Jaime says. *This is twelve kidneys — Ten,* corrects Djell, pointing at you. *Amyloidosis. Oh yes,* says Jaime. *But twelve lungs.* Yes, Djell confirms sadly. *And twelve corneas,* continues Jaime, *and six livers as well as spleens and pituitary glands and whatever else you think we can handle. —Oh my god!* he slaps his forehead *Tickers — there's six tickers! We're never going to have to work again!*

"*If and when we get out of this pickle,* stipulates Djell, *we'll never be able to work again, either. Okay. Onward. Let's fortify with some blow…*

"And the next thing you know these guys have sniffed up about fifteen grains of cocaine apiece, they've rolled you over, Stanley, and are about to initiate a cruciate abdominal incision. I believe you saw some photographs of one recently. Otherwise known as the Big Zipper."

Iris paused. "Stanley? You following me? You look a little gray."

Stanley felt a little gray.

"Anyway, there isn't that much more to tell. I had to do something or I was dead meat. You too, of course. And it was easy. The gun was right there. Before they knew what had happened I had the drop on them. You know, it was a funny thing, that arm of yours being still attached to the gun." She smiled. "It was just like a stock. You know those old pistols they used to make, where you could attach a stock to them and kind of turn them into a short-barreled rifle?" She raised an eyebrow.

Stanley's mouth was filling with bitter saliva.

"No?" she asked, a little severely.

He abruptly nodded.

"I thought so." She smiled again. "Well, I'm here to tell you, that add-on stock is a good idea. It makes for very straight shooting. Just one shot each, was all it took. Which was a good thing, because that was all the slugs left in the clip."

For the first time she looked as if she were looking at something more interesting than a specimen of loserhood. "That .45 automatic…" she shook her head, "that's a lot of pistol."

Stanley shivered.

"Anyway, darling, here we are, together at last. And I'm going to take real good care of you. After a while, who knows? Maybe you'll learn to take care of me."

Stanley didn't say a word.

The door swung open and a cart entered, followed by a young woman in a nurse's uniform.

"Hi, Shananne," Iris chirped, not turning around.

"Oh, hi, Iris. I didn't know you were still in here. I can come back—"

Stay, stay, oh please stay… Stanley thought loudly.

"Oh, no, no," said Iris pleasantly. "Just visiting our local hero, here."

Shananne showed the tired smile endemic to the night shift. "Guess you two got a lot to talk about."

Iris actually blushed. "I guess so," she said. A little silence passed among them like a handful of water until it was gone, and Iris said, "So. How's tricks?"

"Busy," Shananne said. "These cutbacks got me hopping all over the place tonight. I got three floors to cover. Three floors! Time I get through the first round it's time to start back on the next one. Can't even weasel time for a coffee, with all this work."

"That Floyd," Iris smiled. "He likes his coffee."

Now it was Shananne's turn to blush.

Her eyes watching Stanley, Iris said, "Want me to handle this one?"

Stanley went cold. It was as if a platen of dry ice had been applied to his heart. He whimpered internally.

"Oh," said Shananne, "would you?"

"I'd be delighted," said Iris over her shoulder. She looked back at Stanley. "Anyway, it looks like I'm going to be taking care of Stanley here for a good long time."

It was plain to both Shananne and Stanley that Iris was enjoying herself. "Can you manage from your chair?"

"If you'll hand me Doctor's most recent commandments," Iris said,

"I'll be fine."

Shananne retrieved the clipboard from the foot of the bed and handed it to Iris.

"Thank you," Iris said, and set it on the bed without looking at it.

From her cart Shananne extracted a tray containing a covered beaker full of cotton swabs, a bottle of alcohol, capped and loaded syringes, and a paper cup with three or four variously sized and colored pills in it. She placed the tray on the bed next to the clipboard.

"Thank you so much, Shananne," Iris cooed.

"Thank *you*, Iris," Shananne replied, backing out of the door.

"Give my best to Floyd."

"Before the hour strikes."

"He's on five, is he?"

"Two pings up."

The two women laughed gaily, conspiratorially.

The closer hissed the door shut.

Iris released the brake and rolled her chair as close to the head of the bed as it would go.

Like a rooster that needs to turn sideways to see the ax, Stanley jerked his head to watch her.

Resetting the brake, Iris selected a syringe from the tray and sat back in the wheelchair. She propped her elbows on the armrests and tapped the capped syringe thoughtfully into the palm of her opposite hand, like a teacher with a ruler.

"Look, Iris...," Stanley began huskily.

"Relax, Stanley," she interrupted brusquely. "You know the routine." She leaned forward and plucked away the blanket covering his right shoulder.

For the first time Stanley saw the stump. Close to the shoulder, it was white and withered. Toward the stump it was discolored, a purplish black bruise eliding into a graying yellow, the terminus crusted with congealed blood and a rust-stained gauze dressing.

The stump jerked twice, as if to lift something.

Stanley wanted to look away, to put his nose back between his good eye and the stump, but he couldn't bring himself to do it.

Iris steadied the stump and expertly swabbed it at the shoulder. "First the antibiotic." She injected the serum. Practically before he realized it was happening, she had discarded the empty syringe.

"Now your favorite," she said, picking up a second hypodermic.

"Morphine." She smoothly injected him again, right next to the first puncture, then swabbed the two sites as one.

"Nothing to it. Right, Stanley?" She dropped the second empty syringe next to the first. "In a moment or two you should be feeling decidedly groovier than you feel now."

Cocking his head this way and that Stanley searched her face in vain for some clue, some iota of betrayal, accusation, guilt, or even forgiveness. "Iris," he croaked.

"Not a word, my hero. Don't bother. There's nothing you can say. We're going to take care of each other, Stanley. You and I. Now," she smiled, "you've got all the scars a scar-loving woman could want. Plenty to work with. It'll take me months just to memorize them. Might never — ever ever — get bored with them. What do you think of that?"

I think that's the shittiest thing I ever heard, Stanley thought.

"We're going to get a little bungalow out in the avenues," she continued. "I know you're fond of the apartment I already rent. And I am too. But you know what? It doesn't have a fireplace, and I want a fireplace. You know why?"

Stanley jerked his head stupidly, meaninglessly, uncomprehendingly.

"I'll tell you why. I want a fireplace with a mantle, so I have a place to mount that dead arm of yours with that empty gun taped to it. Kind of like the musket we won the war with, you know? What do you think of this idea? Isn't it neat?"

Shitty, thought Stanley. *Shitty idea.*

"I've already arranged it with Corrigan. He's going to speak to the Oakland coroner who, Sean happens to know, moonlights as a taxidermist. Corrigan set you up, you know," she added parenthetically. "When he saw you weren't going to come across for him he let you run. You should have told him what you knew." She patted the blanket over his knee and his whole body jumped. "As it was, you got a couple hours' jump on him." He was terrified by her touch. "You didn't get a new kidney, Stanley, but with tender-loving dialysis you might last another year. We'll get you a rocking chair. You can spend your final days planted in front of a nice warm fire, right where you can contemplate your souvenir from the organs wars, mounted on the flagstones above the mantle."

Stanley's skull had begun to vibrate atop his spine.

But she wasn't finished. "I'd like to say we could take your truck out on the freeway once in a while. You know, for a little..." she nearly blushed, "you know. Your favorite thing…?"

He couldn't believe what he was hearing. This was no olive branch. It was a mauling from a Get-Well Bear.

"But, gosh, you can learn to settle for reciprocal scarlingus, …can't you?"

He narrowed his one eye at the little brown stuffed bear in her lap. *If I had two hands*, he thought, beaming hatred, *I'd tear that fucking thing's head off.*

"Stanley," she chided. "Are you listening to me?"

He leveled his eye at her.

"Because," she said coyly, "there's more."

"That's okay, Iris," he whispered. "I've heard enough for one—."

"No you haven't." She made a tight smile with her mouth. "It's not that I begrudge you your favorite thing, Stanley. …Not exactly."

No, he thought. *I'm sure it isn't.*

"I mean, I just don't feel right… but it's not —"

"No rush," Stanley said quietly. "We needn't rush… recovery…"

She nodded thoughtfully.

Then she abruptly pinched his leg, hard. "Feeling the morphine?"

Indeed, he had begun to feel… simple? Numb? Simply numb? Her pinch was vague and far away.

He nodded.

"Shananne is a good girl," Iris said. "Always gives a hundred and ten per cent, especially to a hero. She had me flying like a kite a couple days ago." She placed a hand on the edge of the coverlet. "Let's get that catheter out of the way."

Stanley thought to clutch the coverlet to his chin. One hand, the left one, physically reacted to this thought. The other couldn't. His left hand did fine, clutching at the blankets, and the IV pole attached to its arm rattled. The morphine was good, but it didn't prevent him from despairing of the impulse that went from his brain to a hand that no longer existed. Five non-existent fingers gripped the sheets. Ineffectually.

Iris gathered the cloth where the phantom fingers failed, and tugged.

"Now Stanley," she grimaced, condensing sheet and fingers into her fist. "Be a good boy."

With superior strength she pulled the coverlet until the fingers of his real hand peeled away from it, one by one. "Be a good boy," she whispered maternally.

She swept the coverlet aside.

He didn't understand what he saw. A tube was there just like the last time. A short rigid plastic tube stuck up and connected to another, flexible tube, which led away to a waste vessel hidden beneath the bed. There was a clamp on the flexible tube, but it wasn't closed.

And like the last time, the sight embarrassed him.

"Oh yes," Iris said dreamily, "one more detail. Do you remember the night you called Fong from my apartment?"

Stanley couldn't remember anything anymore.

"You asked him to search a newspaper database for cashiered surgeons or doctors — people who had lost their licenses to practice?"

Stanley's lower jaw quivered.

"Well," she continued, "you had something there. Fong eventually turned up one Dr. Manfred E. Djell. I say eventually because, while you had asked Fong to search back a couple of years, it was just last week that it occurred to him to extend the range of the search as far back as the database would go, which is just over ten years. And there your boy was. The very same unpleasant Dr. Djell who so recently perished in the Chippendale O'Hare Mortuary massacre. He lost his license about eight years ago. There were multiple minor infractions — such as writing illegal prescriptions — and an interesting felony for which he wasn't prosecuted because nobody would testify. You had quite a good hunch, there. But do you know what his specialty was?"

Stanley's teeth had begun to chatter.

"Of course not. Well, he practiced SRS," she said. "Even his legitimate specialty was shady."

SRS? What the hell did that mean? Stupid, Reliable, and Sober? Was Djell a detox specialist? *Probably not.* Stanley kind of wanted to know. He kind of didn't, too. But a certain monocular data-trickle from the badly-lit room was distracting his mind.

Iris told him. "It stands for Sex-Reassignment Surgery."

Stanley built a very dumb look on his face. Despite the morphine he was getting a headache.

"Fong told me to be sure to tell you as soon as I caught up with you, at the funeral home. But what with one thing and another, I forgot. No sooner than I got the gun in my hand and regained my composure, however, I remembered. So I had the good Dr. Djell do a little work," she finished cheerfully, "before I shot him."

They both considered his pelvis.

There were bandages there, along with the catheter.

His head began, ever so perceptibly, to wave back and forth on its stalk like a plastic ball with a painted face atop a steel spring glued to the back shelf of an automobile that's just come to a gentle halt. He made a noise, too, in his throat. It sounded like a tree frog caught between wet asphalt and a gumboot.

"You want a little more light?" Iris asked him tenderly.

Stanley moved his head slightly to one side, then to the other, leaving it in each position for no more than a few seconds. His teeth clacked audibly.

"Yes," she said complacently. "I had them do a little more work."

A tear welled out of the duct of the one eye that remained in Stanley's head.

"They tried to defend you." She laughed. "They called it an outrage. Men…. They called it a waste of time and talent, too. They were sure you wouldn't appreciate it." She shook her head. "You're all alike. Indefensible. Some men, of course," she added, raising a pinky toward the gauze and tape at the base of his abdomen, "are more alike than others."

The tree frog in Stanley's throat made a feeble, final protest.

"This is only Phase One. The complete deal can proceed only in stages, separated by time. This fact actually helped Jaime and Djell kid themselves into thinking I might let them live long enough to finish the job, once they got started. Wrong." She shook her head. "You don't have that kind of time."

She placed both her hands down there and gradually worked the tube loose. To Stanley it felt as if someone somewhere were boning a fish. A fish that may once have been a real good friend of his.

The catheter removed and dropped into the rubber disposal bin, she made no effort to cover him up. Nor did he. They sat for a while, quietly sharing his abjection.

"Trim," Iris said thoughtfully. "That's what Jaime called it."

Stanley cocked his head as if to see her, but could not take his eye off the compelling object of its contemplation — or, truthfully and worse — the non-object. If he had looked at Iris he might have seen that, in the dark air of the little room, her two violet eyes had narrowed into the twin punctures of a snakebite.

"He called it trim."

She rounded one hand in the air a few inches over the wound as if she were smoothing the hair over the forehead of a dog.

"Slang for the female genitalia, in some parts of Chicago."

"Oh," Stanley said after a while. But it sounded merely like a parting of his dry lips.

"Evocative term, isn't it?"

But his lips weren't dry. Bile leaked from their corners and trickled over his chin.

"Leave him enough to aim with, I told them. But I think they cut it a tad close. What do you think?"

It was late at night. With all the cutbacks, the hospital was only able to maintain a skeleton staff. Shananne wasn't even on the third floor at the time. She and Floyd were having coffee in the dispensary, two stories above. Everybody else was asleep. Or half dead.

Only Iris heard Stanley scream.